CAST N

By Nancy Leonard

ISBN: 978-1-949872-75-0

Cosmo Publishing
UNITED STATES OF AMERICA

November 2022

“PNWA finalist award for mainstream fiction, Sept, 2022”

Acknowledgment

Thanks to my primary editor, Elizabeth Thorpe, for her many levels of editing and support.

Thanks to my Blackfeet editor, Margie Yellow-Kidney, for providing Native authenticity, points-of-view, and friendship.

Thanks to singer-songwriter, Sam Bradley, who inspired me in the world of music, leading directly to themes and inspiration for this novel.

And finally. It is impossible to adequately thank Terry Persun, my mentor and educator. This book would not have seen the light of day without his help and friendship.

To Peter, my hero.

CAST NO SHADOW

It's tempting to circle and circle like a hawk in the sky. At some point, you must break into a dive and risk colliding with the rocks below—if you don't, you'll starve to death in the rarified atmosphere. But if you do crash, there's still a possibility your ashes can be reconstituted, and you can fly again.

Bruce Weingarten

CHAPTER 1

BRUCE

IT'S BEEN MANY YEARS since I knew what my mother was thinking, when Father's domination was just beginning to be felt, and before she began to disappear as a parent. When Father was unnecessarily hurtful to me, or increasingly caustic to my mother, she used to whisper in my ear, "Let's go pack our suitcase and run away." It was a game we played back then.

It's obvious why I remember those old words. I've been summoned to Father's study, which is well known to me. I've been called in here since I was a nine-year-old child for *attitude adjustments* and discipline.

Now, almost twenty years later, the mahogany walls seem to have darkened over the years, or maybe it's my point of view. There are no bright colors here, only heavy wood furniture and low-level lighting. No soft cushions or fanciful pictures on the walls lessen the intimidation.

This must be something important. Alec, my foster brother, is slouched in a wing chair, giving me an impassively measured look. We are almost never together. Our father, Frederick Weingarten, has kept our lives separate. He's made certain we don't like each other. If I'd been more perceptive when it started, if I'd understood, maybe I could have fought it off. Maybe Alec and I could have been real brothers. Now it's too late. The animosity is ingrained and mutual. There is no trust. He could hurt me.

It's not that we aren't bright. We both could have gone places on our own, especially Alec. He went by Chris Chambers during one early period of his life. That's what his Stanford law degree says. Now I think of him as Alec Cummings.

I'm not sure whether he has a legal name, or any legitimate papers. He's gone underground. Father's interests have paid him well, more than enough to disappear. I know, vaguely, about his Swiss bank account. That's what I don't understand. Alec could get entirely out if he wanted. He's got the legal savvy to develop a new identity — do it right. Escape.

In contrast, I have the same identity I was born with. Father doesn't use me the way he uses Alec. I'm the visible pawn in his plan to develop an international empire. Someday, I'd like to sit him down and ask who he's building it for. I wonder whether he thinks about it late at night after the evil of the day is done.

My shoulders slump as I realize the impossibility of challenging father in any way, then glance at Alec to see if he noticed my weakness. The old man has done his best to make me think I'm not worthy, but that Alec might be. And possibly Alec does want all this. It's a question I never could ask either of them. I don't want the answer — not if I'm to be cut out. It's an answer which could free me but could kill me too. Unsatisfied pursuit has defined me.

It's late in the evening. I hear Alec sigh for the umpteenth time. We've been waiting over an hour, attempting to control our impatience. We'd both rather be doing anything else. But it's the time of day he likes to see us, reminding us of our subservient place, our utter dependence.

I turn to him. "What's up in your world, Alec?"

He gives me a half smile. "Hanging out with my climbing buddies. Planning an ascent in South America. Unless your father has other plans. You?"

"Toeing the corporate line. American Oil is forming partnerships with both the Russians and Ukrainians, playing one against the other. It's at a critical point — part of the old man's master plan to engineer my promotion to regional vice-president."

He grimaces at me in sympathy.

"I've been skulking around behind the scenes, negotiating, influence-peddling, making myself known as a viable candidate." I swallow, feeling a twinge of nausea. "The old man will come unhinged if I don't pull this off."

Alec is possibly the only one on this earth who understands.

Glancing around, he lowers his voice to a whisper. "It's bad enough I owe the bastard so much I can't ever say no." He pauses, then adds, "And it's my fuckin' birthday. A lot of things I'd rather be doing."

"Sorry," I offer contritely. "Happy Birthday."

He smiles thinly. "Thanks."

It's as near as we come to being close — when we both acknowledge being trapped.

We could pass for brothers, tall with blond hair and the same blue-gray eyes. But our haircuts are different. My three-hundred-dollar corporate haircut differs from Alec's longish hair, haphazardly hanging below his chin, in keeping with his climber appearance. In addition, he has impressive shoulders from hauling himself up mountains.

He leans forward in his chair and lowers his voice. "I'm considering...." He lowers it even more. "We could get out of this. Have you thought about it?"

Before I can answer, the door opens, and I straighten automatically as Father enters the room. His slicked-backed dark hair has remained unchanged for as long as I can remember, as has his expression — rigid and cold. We stand up to formally greet him as he expects.

After an unsettling silence, he begins. "We have a situation." He pauses again to let us guess who might be at fault this time, then turns his gaze on me. "My impotent son has been unable to get his lady-friend to *extract* herself (smirking at his play on words) from oil and gas negotiations ongoing in Montana."

My fear reaches another level. I don't want Ellie connected to Father's ambition in any way.

"My informants at American have let me know her participation has jeopardized Bruce's promotion." His voice hardens even more. "I can't afford to risk any more time on thls."

I drop my eyes, swallow, then force myself to meet his stare. It's hard. My hands start to shake, and I fight off the impulse to gnaw on my fingernails.

"I've waited long enough. I'm turning this over to you, Alec. This is a little outside of your typical responsibility, but I want this kept within the family."

Alec nods, guardedly.

Clammy nausea develops as it always does when I've failed Father. He always makes me pay. Against my will, I remember the last time I let him down — a promotion I didn't get as quickly as he expected.

I'd been called into this same study, him letting me stand in front of his desk for a full five minutes before he even raised his eyes to me. “It’s not as though I didn’t expect this,” he’d muttered. “I’ve given you all the advantages, legal and otherwise. Still, you fucked it up. Fine. I’ll pay more money, bribes, to get you your promotion.” He dropped his eyes again. “I don’t even want to look at you. Now get out of here.”

Ellie’s name jerks me back to the present, forcing me to blink my eyes and refocus.

“I’m following Eleanor’s whereabouts,” father continues, “and have people listening in to her phone conversations. She’s in Seattle now, planning on driving to Browning next Thursday or Friday.” He scowls at me, affording himself the pleasure of one last reproach. “You fly out of Kennedy tomorrow morning so you probably can’t resolve this. But damn it all to hell! Get on the phone tonight and see whether you can get her to withdraw immediately.”

I nod weakly as the nausea increases.

“Alec, if he fails, I want some muscle. She doesn’t know you or even recognize you. I’m positive she hasn’t even seen a recent picture.” He stares at Alec for several seconds, waiting until he finally gets a nod in confirmation.

I was proud of Alec. He made him wait.

“Get a short haircut, drive to Coeur d’Alene and intercept her.”

Despite my own anxiety, I see Alec draw a quick breath. “Intercept her?”

Allowing himself a self-satisfied stare, he continues. “Put on shades and a suit. Rent the most expensive car you can under an assumed name. Pay cash. I’ll let you know exactly where she is. After she crosses the Idaho border, follow her.” He leans toward Alec. “When you find an opportunity alone, I want you to threaten her. She has family in Cleveland. Mention them. Tell her the sister will be hurt if she doesn’t cooperate. I’ve got details to make it convincing.”

Alec and I stand there speechless. Corporate deceit aside, terrifying someone is horrible. And Ellie…? My God. I haven’t let myself get deeply, emotionally involved. But to allow my Magirlfriend to be scared to death? It’s a line I can’t cross. Can I? One more escalation of those defining lines I’ve allowed myself to step over again and again. I’ve agonized whether to break free of this multi-billionaire trap, but it would shatter the empty facade I’ve become. It would involve running and hiding, maybe for decades.

I know his vindictiveness and shudder, feeling another piece of my infrastructure crumble.

Father has done his best to turn us both into crap, but I know Alec desperately doesn't want to do this. He holds his breath.

"Father," I say, gathering up the last molecules of my courage. "This is insanity. We can't go there — frightening women. Not Ellie.... Don't you think...?"

"Bruce," he says, his voice reduced to a hostile whisper as his eyes study mine. "Are you going to fight me on this? Are you?"

My eyes shift back and forth between him and Alec.

Father gives me a wry smile, a revoltingly confident appraisal. "Is that going to happen, Bruce? Do you have it in you?"

"I.... I'll talk to her tonight."

Father checked his watch. "You have 'til midnight. If Alec doesn't hear from you by then.... Midnight, got it?" He gives me his icy smile. "You can leave. Close the door on your way out."

I've been dismissed.

With as much dignity as I can muster, I exit, collapsing on the striped settee outside his office, staring at my hands. *Fucking-assed coward*, I think to myself. Minutes pass. I'm suddenly overwhelmed with a memory. I'm standing outside this same study many years ago, one of the last times I stood up to Father's displeasure.

* * *

Every morning I ran into the school building to see my best and only friend. Only nine years old, Chris Carpenter already stood out, brilliant among a group of smart, privileged kids. My personal life was fast becoming a wasteland, but I was still too young to perceive it. My mother was evolving into a shadow person, but it was happening so gradually, I hadn't noticed. Not really.

Chris and I spent many late afternoons at our house, him often staying for dinner. Father was always nice to him, went out of his way to be pleasant, which was unusual. I knew Chris had trouble at home. He never wanted to leave our house. I loved it because we could spend so much time together. We were pretty much ignored, which was fine by us. If we were hungry, we'd ask the servants. I never went over to Chris's to play. We both knew his house was off-limits for me without ever talking about it. Father employed Chris's dad, one of a pack of vice-presidents, as a liaison with Wall Street. Both his parents were polite the few times I met them. They were two-dimensional.

One evening after school I got a call on the landline in my room. Cell phones were just coming in.

"It's Chris." He was whispering, choking.

"What? Are you okay?"

"Bruce, help me. Help me. My dad hurt me. I'm bleeding."

"What? What? Where's your mom?"

"I don't know. She left." Another frantic plea, "Help me! Can your dad send someone?"

I never wanted to disturb Father, but I knew I'd try. I didn't know it then, but it was a decision which would shape the rest of our lives. "Yes. I'll run. I'll call you back."

"Don't call. Just come. There's blood all over." His voice was weak, "I'm scared."

I gathered up my courage to go interrupt Father. I stood outside his study door trembling and took a deep breath.

"Father? Father?"

"Go away, Bruce, I'm busy." His voice was irritable as it always was with me.

"Please, Father. There's been an accident."

I could hear his exasperated sigh through the door. "Then get in here and tell me."

I fumbled with the doorknob and slipped inside.

"Be quick. What do you want?"

"Chris is hurt. There's a lot of blood."

"Well, have him tell his mother."

"He can't. She left. He doesn't know where she is."

"Where's his fucking father?"

"I don't know. There's a lot of blood." I pleaded again. "He was scared."

Father deliberated for some time as I stood before his huge desk in silence, fidgeting with acute anxiety.

"Call him. See whether he's better."

"He said 'Don't call — just come'." I wanted to jump up and down, but of course I couldn't.

After drumming his fingers on his desk for several more moments, he picked up the phone and spoke to one of his assistants, then turned to me. "Jackson will be here in a minute. Go with him and check on Chris. Jackson will call me. A lesson, Bruce."

He leaned forward over his desk for emphasis. "It can be profitable to have someone owe you. Big time."

"Yes, Father. Thank you, Father."

"This better be worth it, Bruce."

"Yes, sir," I said, frightened I'd pay if it weren't.

Jackson knew the way. He'd often taken Chris home. We went together to the front door. It was nearly dark outside, but no lights were on inside. We knocked loudly several times, but no one came, so we tried the door. It was unlocked. I didn't know the house well. We started yelling, walking around the first floor, turning on lights as we went. Then I heard someone calling from the rear of the house. We hurried toward the voice. Jackson flipped on the kitchen overhead light and we both gasped. I'd never seen so much blood in my life, not even on TV. Chris was lying in a pool, half the size of his body. We could see where he dragged himself to the phone to call me. His body was covered with blood. He seemed confused.

"Stay here," Jackson said to me.

I stood at the door. Even from that distance it appeared Chris's hand had been half cut off. Jackson wrapped it in a dishtowel and called 9-1-1. Then he called Father.

Chris was so white it scared me. "Is he going to be okay?" I asked, as Jackson tied something around his upper arm.

"Later, Bruce," Jackson replied impatiently. "Later."

In minutes we heard the siren. Medics ran into the room. While they were working, Jackson was constantly talking to Chris. "Don't be afraid. I'll take Bruce home and come to the hospital. We'll get you help. Stay awake. Stay awake." I remember Jackson accompanying Chris to the ambulance, constantly talking to him, reassuring him. They were already starting IVs. The siren came on and the emergency vehicle disappeared into the night. After the ambulance left, I was told to wait in our car. Jackson entered the house, not reappearing for some time.

For several days I asked many questions, but each time Father forcefully told me to forget I was involved. He didn't want me to have nightmares, he'd said. He let me know I was never to mention it to anyone. I did as I was asked, never talking about it to anyone outside the family. I only saw Jackson a few times after that. He disappeared from my life.

Chris wouldn't be in a regular classroom for over a year, and by then he had a new last name, Chambers, which he kept through law school. We were told to forget his old one, which Chris appeared willing to do. I remembered it though, and I know he did, but we never spoke of it. As it turned out, we were sent away to school together following his many surgeries.

In the weeks immediately following, I was relieved the event turned out to be so important. Father appeared grateful I had bothered him. I was informed Chris would eventually come to live with us. It appeared my life would be fabulous with my best friend becoming a permanent part of my life.

I couldn't have been more wrong.

* * *

The memory comes to an abrupt ending as I find myself still sitting on the striped settee, having barely moved a muscle, waiting. The image of a child wanting to escape returns violently. But escape is not the ending I want. I want to be a man left standing.

The antique wooden clock on the wall counts off the seconds loudly, the sound echoing through the deserted foyer. After ten long minutes Alec emerges, sickly pale, slowly shaking his head. We both understand we've caved. Nothing left to decide. I hear Mother's footsteps coming down the hall. She walks past us, pausing briefly to glance at our anguished faces. No suitcase in her hand I think morosely, as I try my best to smile at her. It's a total flop. Her shoulders droop as she continues on into the study, followed by the terminal sound of the heavy door closing.

Alec continues past me through the front vestibule, not making eye contact. "Give it your best shot, for God's sake," he pleads, his head turned away from me. Another heavy door opens and closes with finality.

Crap. If I can't talk Ellie out of this, I will have let Alec down, too.

I'm motionless. I can't seem to make myself move off this damn chair with its slippery green and tan material, preventing myself sliding off with my heels digging into the floor. Mother finally comes out, pauses, then gives me a desolate stare — disappointment, fear, defeat — until I turn away from her. I wonder whether she knows what I'm about to attempt, or what will happen if I fail. I dig in my heels again, thinking back once more, putting off calling Ellie just a few more minutes.... Thinking back.

* * *

From our first drink, I knew I'd pursue Ellie O'Connell. I was twenty-seven and abruptly interested. I'd never had a serious relationship and was feeling unusually alone. She'd just broken off with some guy and I realized she wouldn't be available for long — too beautiful, too intelligent without rubbing it in your face, and too desirable. I was blown away.

Making her even more desirable in the weeks and months to follow, she wasn't alluding to any commitment or uncomfortably probing my private life. I spent money on her, lots of money, and we both enjoyed it. For two years, she had seemed perfect for a non-inquisitive corporate wife. Recently though, she'd begun pressing me, inquiring into what I believed, who I was beneath the surface, what I wanted in life. How could I tell her? I didn't know the answers. I'd never been allowed to think about what I wanted.

* * *

I finally pull out my cell. I can't put this off any longer. Glancing at the damn hall clock, I punch in her number.

"Hi, Ellie."

"You all packed?"

"Yeah. I'm only going for a week. I'll be in the air on route to Turkey for most of the day each way. At least it's premier class, so I can stretch out." I clear my throat, gathering my courage. "I.... I'm hoping you've given up on Montana."

"No way. I'll be driving to Montana on Friday. I just got word. Everyone was so impressed with my preliminary presentation they want me to be lead negotiator." She pauses, then her voice escalates. "Come on. You must be proud of me."

"Ellie, listen. Listen," I say, trying to avoid pleading. "Can't you bag this? It's not worth sticking it out in no man's land for three months. You'll be living in squalor for God's sake."

"Are you serious?" Her voice carries a note of astonishment. "This is important work. It's what I'm trained to do. I like the people there. I've met...."

"Ellie, please," I interrupt. "How about if I really make it worth your while? You could join me after the Turkish conferences. I'll meet you in Paris for a week on my way back. We could spend some quality time together." I play my big card. "I want to talk about our future. It's time."

"I've been wanting that, too. But I have to do this first. Then I'll take a week. Anywhere you say."

"Could you...? Would you just do this for me? Just because I ask you?" My voice is becoming plaintive. "There are things I can't tell you. I've never asked you to do something important for me. Not like this. Please, Ellie."

"It would be huge for me to give up on this. You'll have to tell me the whole truth before I could decide. Tell me everything. If you can convince me? If it's that critical?"

I can't. "You'll just have to trust me."

Silence for a long moment. "Then I'm sorry. You go to Turkey. I'll go to Browning and get the negotiations set up. We can get together right after your trip and we'll talk it out. I promise I'll listen. Okay?"

It's not okay. This will never be okay. Tick-tock, tick-tock.

"Bruce?" She waits. "Bruce?"

"Fine, Ellie," my voice now emotionless. "I'll call."

"Bruce, I'm sorry. I can tell this is important to you."

It's come down to this. Can I confess to her, tell her the truth about the pressure, the obscene choices I'm forced to make? Do I trust her enough to explain it all? Or could I run and hide with her? Try to start over with her somewhere? Would she understand? Hang in with me? Support me? Maybe she could save me.

If she let me down, I'd have nothing.

"Bruce? Are you there, Bruce?"

"Goodbye, Ellie," I say dispassionately. Slowly I put the phone in my pocket.

I drift. I feel hollow. I picture myself helpless, flowing down an endless waterslide out of control, arms flailing but irreversibly down. I wonder whether Alec feels the same way. The second hand continues to move. I hold my breath.

It's a second after midnight.

CHAPTER 2

ALEC

I'M ON THE WAY to hurt a young woman. I have to. I'm a rabbit in a snare. I'm trying not to think at all past this point.

Even in my dreams I'm tormented, but I've made the decision to go ahead. My foster father has commanded it after giving me everything I have: an intact body, the best education money could buy, including a Stanford Law degree, and something resembling a family. He has groomed me, maneuver by maneuver, bringing me to this point. And he could destroy my future — forever.

I shudder but retain a glimmer of self-respect. Underlying everything else, there's a possibility she could die by another's hand if I don't do this thing. Nothing concrete brings me to that conclusion — possibly my own rationalization.

Frederick has demanded my services before, making use of my excellent education, to do things outside the law. I have willingly complied. This particular atrocity is supposedly being done for Bruce's career. But we all know it's for the Weingarten Empire. And winning is everything.

Bruce and I don't love each other. We don't hate each other. We co-exist — twin planets in one solar system, with Frederick Weingarten the brilliant sun around which we orbit. I wonder whether he questions how this all ends. Does his universe expand endlessly, or collapse in on itself? Years of planning and plotting, and the only thing standing in the way of his mapped-out triumph is this insignificant girl.

* * *

Sometimes the black irony amuses me. Two years ago, Bruce fell for this blonde, chose her potentially as the perfect corporate wife. I've only seen her across a crowded room soon after they started dating. I haven't been allowed to meet her. Bruce never discusses me with her. It's part of the plan. Or maybe I'm the non-entity who could be conveniently disposed of when my usefulness is over. Yes. That thought has crossed my mind.

I've been carefully divorced from the family history, expunged from the Internet — also part of my job. My only personal space in this world is a modest apartment in a low-rent district of Seattle. I now exist under another assumed name, my professional climbing name, Alec Cummings. Two years ago, the former Chris Chambers gave up his private law practice and disappeared. Frederick made it worth my while. Actually, much more worth my while than even he knows. I have over twenty million dollars stashed in Swiss bank accounts.

I'm twenty-nine years old and climb recreationally with a high level of competence, both on bare rock and ice, and at very high altitude all over the world: The Alps, Himalayas, South America, and Mt. McKinley in the states. Whenever I have time, I go to far-off places and scale mountains. It helps reduce the claustrophobia of my other life.

My friends are in the climbing world, but they hardly know me. Mostly we talk about future climbs and women. We drink a lot. No one asks much about backgrounds. It usually works well enough, but sometimes I feel like a ghost.

Now all my debts are coming due. After what I'm about to do, he'll completely own me. No more allusions of transitioning to an independent life, which usually begin with my favorite fantasy, slipping poison into his martini. He never drinks around us. I wonder whether he considers poison a possibility. I wonder whether Bruce has the same thought. We don't trust each other enough to ask.

Bruce is being considered for an influential Vice-Presidency in a multi-national energy conglomerate. This would allow Frederick to control and allocate vast oil and gas assets in the Middle East and skim off the top. The entire sordid deal now hedges, according to the puppeteer, on whether I can scare Ellie off the Montana project. Her stubbornness supposedly makes Bruce appear weak. Unacceptable. In addition, she's working on a compromise that would allow local drilling by small independent contractors, bypassing big moneyed interests. I'd laugh at the irony were it not painfully consequential for an innocent young woman.

Bruce has tried everything: sex, persuasion, subtle bribery, pleading, unsubtle bribery — all to no avail. It seems Ellie O'Connell is determined to do the right thing. In the immortal words of the Knight in the Temple of Doom — "He chose poorly" — or perhaps Bruce chose too well. She has integrity. It's another reason it turns my stomach to do this. She has principles.

I was informed of her movement along Interstate 90 and lay-in-wait just outside of Ritzville in eastern Washington State. I'm currently following her just west of Missoula, Montana. If I don't get an opportunity soon, I'll probably get a chance along the more isolated road north to Browning.

It's been pleasant to follow her these last four hours. Her sapphire-blue convertible maneuvers in and around other traffic, her blonde ponytail fluttering joyously in the wind of the lowered top. She's naturally attractive, wearing large sunglasses under a ball cap, and happily oblivious in the warm sun of the mid-September afternoon.

Please don't stop, I think helplessly. What I'm about to do is so ugly.

I'm wearing the required mirror sunglasses and a suit. My hair is very short. Even that disgusts me — cutting my hair for the old man, giving him one more piece of myself. Will there be any image left the next time I glance in the mirror? I sigh, and sigh again.

My plan is to return the car, change into casual clothes, and disappear completely — one more of my skills. As my hair grows out, I'll reappear in my climbing world. I don't think anyone will connect the dots. I've carefully nurtured my other identity, kept my living arrangements secret. Even the old man and Bruce can only get me by cell. I don't think Frederick has bothered to trace me. He doesn't know he should worry about me. Not yet.

Suddenly she swerves down a long exit ramp leading into a deserted rest area. Stepping out of her car as I pull in beside her, she gives me a casual smile, then walks up the grassy incline to the restrooms. I avoid eye contact, wait a few seconds, then follow her to the block building, continually watching the parking lot. If anyone else pulls in this won't be possible. Her fate rests with the off-ramp.

I hear her steps inside the building headed toward me. Emerging, she again gives me a friendly smile, twisting the knife I feel in my gut. I can't put this off any longer. Stepping close, I grab her left arm and drag her behind the building. She hardly struggles. She's too surprised.

"What...?"

I shove her hard against the concrete wall, grit my teeth and slap her twice. "I need to get your attention, Ellie," I say, as her eyes fill with tears. "You need to bail on this job. Leave it now. If you don't, people are going to get hurt — your family in Ohio. I'll start with your blonde bombshell of a sister. Lizzie, isn't she? Begin by cutting off her honey-blonde hair. It all depends on you. Get it?"

She's appears more confused than frightened.

"And to let you know I mean it, I'm going to hurt you." I hold her eyes with mine, pull back my right arm, make a careful fist, and punch a rib.

"The first of three," I say.

She stares with horror at my balled right fist. I hit a second one. She hasn't made a sound. She studies my hand, waiting. My hand shakes as I make a fist for the last time, gazing into her eyes through the mirror lenses.

She stares defiantly. "Then do it," she seems to say. I punch forward. She still hasn't uttered a sound. I'm proud of her, whether that makes even the slightest bit of sense. I wish I were done. I desperately want to be done. My soul is crying. I pull out an iron bar. It's shaking in my hand, making slow wobbly circles in the air.

Now terrified, she tries to pull away from me in a last frantic attempt. She can't escape. I raise the bar and start to bring it down against her left upper arm. In the last half-second I try to stop the bar, shaking, fighting against myself, but can only partially slow it. I think I hear a crack. And I hear more. She screams, primal, tortured. She finally cannot help it, starting to shake from the shock of it all, as am I. Her face is pasty white and sweaty. I carefully lower her to the ground, leaning her against the wall as gently as I can.

"I'm sorry. I'm sorry," I mutter. Vomit rises in my throat. I spit it out as I leave her, walking as normally as I can down the gentle slope toward my car. Another vehicle, a black BMW coup, pulls in. Turning away from the driver as he emerges, I slide into the seat of my Audi SUV. Go. Go. Go. But I want to stop. Run back up the hill. Help her. "God damn it all to hell," I mutter over and over as I drive off, pounding the steering wheel. Maybe the guy in the BMW will help her. Speeding down the road, I only realize I'm screaming when I hear the sound.

I have no idea of time. Escaping should be my first priority. Missoula is only ten miles away, twelve miles tops. Almost immediately, though, I approach a dirt road curving away from the highway off to the right. Without conscious thought, I turn down it, disappearing around a curve, out of sight from the highway, and pull over.

I make a quick decision to wait until I hear sirens. I feel sick, very sick. Stepping out of my car, I kneel on the ground in my fancy suit and vomit again and again until there's nothing left but dry heaves. I keep seeing her eyes as she dares me to follow through with my threat. She was so brave. I was a monster — a dark monster.

When I can, I jog to the curve in the road with a view of the highway. Five, then ten minutes pass. Nothing. Finally, I see the BMW drive slowly past me on the main highway. I can't see if anyone is inside other than the driver. I'm hoping he's going slowly because he has an injured girl in the car. But what if she passed out and couldn't call for help? What if the guy never got near the restrooms? What if she's not found? It's starting to get chilly as the sun drops suddenly behind the high Rocky Mountains behind me. What if I hit her too hard and she's bleeding internally? Oh, God. Oh, God. She could be dying at this very minute.

I feel nausea returning and shiver violently. What if the guy knows my car? What if the police are already searching for me? I should have driven down the road as fast and as far as I could when I had the chance.

But I know I've made another decision. I'm going back.

I can't drive this car. It might be recognized. I rip off my suit coat and replace it with a gray hoodie, frantically struggling with a pair of jeans, and exchange my wingtips for running shoes, fumbling with the laces. I put a knit cap on my head and check whether my cell is in my pocket. I'll call for help if I need to. I'm decided.

I start running through an uneven field, the stubble of mowed hay crunching under my running shoes. It takes five minutes to reach the rest area. As I approach, I see her car is still parked in the lot. Holding my breath, I peer around the concrete structure. She's gone. The man must have found her.

A huge lump forms in my throat. I don't want to be a slime of a rat, dealing with sickening guilt. I want to be the hero rescuing the hurt girl.

I slide down on the ground next to where she sat, put my hands behind my head, and cry — deep wracking sobs. If the police show up now, it doesn't matter. I never in my life wanted to hurt anyone, not even when my biological father mutilated me. He was drunk. I never knew him. My new father took me in. I thought I was saved.

Now I really am an orphan. I've been one all along and couldn't accept it. What family murders the soul of another family member? Why didn't I face it before I hurt the poor girl?

I'll do anything to make it up to her, make it my purpose in life to protect her from any further harm. I need to think about this in detail, but for now I need to make sure she'll be okay — before I can continue to live with myself.

Any past debts to the family will be paid by my silence. I won't bring them down — not yet anyway. I'm mesmerized and horrified by the spot where Ellie sat, trembling in pain and fear. For now, I'll release myself from this fucking bondage the only way I know how.

Impulsively I wrench the damn ring, the family shackles, off my finger and throw it away into the tall grass. Water wells up in my mouth and for the second time I fall to my knees and vomit. When I can stand, I look for the ring, but it's lost in the long grass.

Why I wore it as long as I did, I'll never know. Habit I guess, or some faint hope it really did represent something of a family that I could hold on to. Bruce never wore his ring after the ceremony, all those many years ago. Old Weingarten rarely wore his. Only when we were alone in his study did he slip it on — when he was asking us to do things. As I stumble across the rutted field to my car, I think back to that night when the trap was set.

* * *

Fifteen years ago, Bruce and I entered the high school phase of our education at our exclusive boarding school. We were vaguely aware we were rivals in some bizarre competition for family honor and success.

The evening in question we stood before his massive desk, silently, for an excruciatingly long time. Finally, he began. Old man Weingarten let us know in no uncertain terms we were being measured, but only against each other. There would be one winner, and not only for treasure — for whatever passed between us as love.

He shifted his gaze from one to the other before beginning. "I've amassed this corporation and built it into a mega-conglomerate, almost a kingdom. One of you will lead us into the future. I don't believe in shared control.

"Fortunately for you, there are no other contenders. We are a family, bound by blood — genetic blood and the blood on your kitchen floor, Chris. So now I have two sons." His eyes narrowed ominously. "I want you to understand the rules so there will be no misunderstanding. You are special. You both are intellectually capable. Only one of you has the courage, the discipline, and the ruthlessness to win the prize." He opened a desk drawer, withdrawing several small objects. "In the meantime," he continued, "these rings were created for you, establishing you as a viable candidate. Wear them proudly and do not take them lightly. If you choose not to wear them, put them somewhere secure."

He then presented the three boxes and opened the lids. They contained three identical gold rings with large ruby center stones. Weingarten took out one ring and slipped it on his own finger. I put mine on. Bruce kept his cradled in a tight fist. Then old man Weingarten walked out of the room.

I remember feeling special, chosen, proud I was to be treated equally with his biological son. I was too young to identify with how Bruce must have felt. I remember his surprising face after the meeting. In contrast to me, he looked sick. Maybe he was brighter than I was all along. Maybe that was when he knew he was trapped.

* * *

The area around Missoula is familiar now. I've been researching the area for several days and know this is the only large medical facility in the area. The black BMW is parked near the Emergency Room entrance. Now closing in on the equinox, the sun hangs low in the sky at 6:00 in the evening. Pulling into an indoor parking garage, I drive down to the lowest basement level, park behind a large wall, and look around. No security guards or people running in my direction. Muted voices echo from somewhere up above.

Pulling up the hood of my sweatshirt, I jog up several flights of narrow cement stairs, follow signs to the ER, and finally locate the antiseptic waiting room. There's almost no one here. Only a man I assume to be the guy from the BMW is apparently waiting for news. Avoiding eye contact, I hunker down behind a pillar. My heart is beating so strongly I can take my pulse by the pounding in my fingertips. It gradually returns to normal, but it's another fifteen minutes before my hands warm up.

After an hour or so, a doctor appears. He speaks quietly, but I can make out the gist of their conversation. My victim appears to have no serious injuries, thank God. Not yet, anyway. Frederick will learn I accomplished my mission. Maybe it will work. Maybe she'll quit. I would. Someone else can do her job and get Bruce off the hook.

I need to reason this through. If she doesn't quit, the old man will quickly arrange another beating or worse. I consider my adopted brother. Bruce could have stopped this plan dead in its tracks. He knew I was considering breaking away. He caved. Frederick kicked him out of the room for the final instructions, thought he couldn't handle it. Well, I managed. I valiantly agreed to beat up a defenseless girl. Waves of self-loathing threaten to overwhelm me.

When I get a grip on myself, I try to think. I don't know to what lengths the bastard will go, but I believe I can better protect this girl if they think I'm willing to play along. Okay, Ellie. You don't know it, but you've just inherited a guardian angel. If I'm going to disappear, I'll try to make amends before I vanish for good.

* * *

I wait until she leaves the hospital with the guy from the BMW. A nurse takes her out to his car in a wheelchair. I guess he's decided to help her, stick with her. I watch as they drive the short distance to the motel next door. Obviously, my car could be recognized, so I walk across the adjoining parking lot and check in. It's ridiculously dangerous. The only reason I can come up with is it keeps the problem in focus. I'm so shattered I can hardly think. And I want to be near her for support, which makes even less sense.

I don't know what I'd have done had they driven off. Hailed one of the cabs outside the hospital? Follow that car. My thoughts are spinning. I fantasize walking to their room, admitting to them I did it, then offer to help by ordering take-out. Maybe I could go to the pharmacy and pick up pain pills. Augh! She's still vulnerable and probably doesn't realize it yet. I wonder whether the threat has sunk in, and what she'll decide when she has a chance to think things through.

My stomach has finally calmed down enough to eat a cup of yogurt and sip bitter coffee from a two-cup coffee maker in the room. I'm currently stretched out on a shiny floral green bedspread in the room next to theirs and have some time to reflect. I feel totally lost and alone. Did I ever really have a chance — after the night so long ago?

* * *

I was nine years old and had been in Lindgren Academy for six months. There was a social hierarchy based on how rich and influential our parents were. Don't ask me how we knew our place, but we all did. I was comfortably in the middle, but Bruce, my best friend, was at the top.

We bonded because we were similarly unhappy. Back then, I believed I alone had serious problems. My father, Daniel, was a mean drunk who abused my mother, and was increasingly coming after me. He was Weingarten's underling, succeeded in holding himself together at work, but when he got home he'd head straight for the bottle, and by age nine I was adept at disappearing. My mother was not always so lucky.

After one last trip to the emergency room with a black eye, she abruptly left several days later, telling me nothing beforehand. She arranged to have me spend the night at Bruce's, got me off to school, and disappeared from my life. Why she hadn't taken me with her, I could never understand. When I came home from school the following evening, my father was alone in the house. As I crept by the door, I caught a glimpse of him, sitting sullenly in the darkened living room. Several empty whiskey bottles littered the floor with the heavy drapes closed against the half-light of early winter. Stale cigarette smoke hung from the ceiling further reducing visibility.

The only light came from a cable news channel on the TV with the sound turned off, but it was enough. As I tried to slip past the door, he saw me, hoisted me up, and carried me like a sack of potatoes into the kitchen. He started yelling, pounding me with a handy wooden spoon, blaming me for Mother leaving. I fought him kicking and screaming until he grabbed a knife from a rack, held me down with his other arm, and cut across the entire top of my hand, severing all the extensor tendons before he fled. I remember crawling to call my best friend. The rest is a blur.

Now all I have is an obvious scar extending the entire top of my right hand and the memories. I even remember when I loved Bruce. He had saved me.

I don't know when I became aware that I was being groomed to join the family business, and debts would have to be paid. Likewise, Bruce's dislike and mine came on gradually, steadily increasing over the years. We had been molded into rivals, both used and manipulated by a beast.

I never saw either of my biological parents again nor wanted to. I assumed my mother deserted me. Now I wonder whether they're both dead. Maybe the monster killed them.

CHAPTER 3

BRUCE

MY PLANE TOUCHES DOWN at JFK International at 8:30 p.m. New York time, after my return flight from Ankara. The airport is still abuzz with peak-hour arrivals, dodging each other in the outflow area. Switching on my cell, I see two messages from Ellie. I swallow and check the calendar on my phone. It's over by now.

I have a two-hour layover, so I walk aimlessly around to stretch my legs, eventually finding my way to the familiar VIP lounge and collapse into a leather armchair.

I put off calling Ellie, trying to focus on my failed business trip for some relief, but that's almost as grim.

The Middle East is a mess and getting worse daily. Assad is holding on, God knows how. Russian oligarchs are as frustrated as we are, believing they can't make a move until this Syrian debacle is settled one way or the other. Washington is trying to negotiate with Putin under the radar, wanting him to do something to help resolve things, but it's not going well for a variety of reasons. A lot of our money and final contracts have been frozen in sanctions. Father is fuming over this, but for once he's not blaming me. Neither of us can control world politics. Still, everything I touch currently seems to be blackening.

My anxiety resurfaces. I've been able to subdue my concern for Ellie, being so far removed, but now I'm going to have to confront it. The two stiff glasses of scotch on the plane didn't numb me — not enough anyway. I talked briefly with Father. He didn't mention Ellie or Alec. He's careful on the phone. I should have stopped in Connecticut to see him, but I couldn't stomach it. He's made his point, anyway — I damn well better get the VP position, or else. I wonder vaguely what the or-else would be.

I sigh deeply several more times, when my phone rings. It's Ellie. Swallowing quickly, I answer, "Just landed. How are you?"

"Bruce. Try not to get upset, but something happened."

"What? What happened?"

"I was driving to Browning and — and some thug followed me to a rest area and he.... Well, he pushed me around and threatened me and my family." She pauses. "Do you think this could have anything to do with why were you were trying to get me to quit? Did you suspect I was in danger?"

"Of course not. If I was that worried, don't you think I would have...?" My God, Ellie. Pushed you? Are you hurt?" My hands are suddenly icy.

"I'm good now. Some guy who found me has been kind enough to take me to his home. His entire family is taking care of me."

"Why? Taking care of you?" I collapse into a chair. "Listen. My flight to Missoula is boarding in less than an hour."

"Come on. I knew it would take you time to get here."

"You don't even know these people. What if...?"

"For God's sake, Bruce," she interrupts impatiently. "I'm not an idiot. These are nice people. I'm a good judge of character. Besides, if I were going to be assaulted, he would have done it last night in the motel room."

"What! What motel room?" Now I'm on my feet and pacing around the VIP lounge. People are starting to stare.

"I only told you, so you'd know I'm not keeping any secrets. I was in some pain and couldn't drive. He wasn't about to try anything. He's a college professor. Oh, for crap's sake."

Completely terrified, I shove one trembling hand in a pants-pocket as I collapse again into a chair. Struggling to hold the phone steady with both hands, my voice becomes a horrified whisper. "Couldn't drive? Ellie, what happened?"

"I'll tell you when you get here. I was scared to be alone."

"For God's sake, Ellie. You need to get out of this whole mess. You are, aren't you? Let someone else take risks."

"Bruce, no one's scaring me away. I'm furious! My company is sending a team to support me on Friday. I'm fine. I'm certainly not going to bail on this until I talk to them at least. And, how dare he? How dare they, whoever they are?"

I feel my face flushing. "God damn it! Where the hell are you, anyway?"

"I'm at a cabin near East Glacier."

"East Glacier? Where the hell is that?"

"Calm down. It's just outside the park, fifteen miles from

Browning."

"What? Why?"

"The guy who found me — he and his family let me stay overnight, to help me. He'll drive me to Browning tomorrow."

"Why in the hell do you need help? You said you were okay. Are you okay?" I'm almost in tears.

"Bruce. Jeez."

"Why do you need someone to take care of you? Tell me the truth."

She sighs. "Because the guy broke three ribs and my arm."

"Whaaaaaat!"

"I knew you'd go ballistic. I'm perfectly capable of taking care of myself. Really, I haven't made any mistakes. Would you like to talk to Paul?"

"Ellie. Ellie, my God!"

"Please, let me get him. He'll tell you I'm okay."

From inside a fog, I hear her call this guy's name. My conflicting emotions have thrown me into a state of quiet hysteria. Why? Why? I don't understand, unless dear old Dad had further instructions. That must have been why Alec was so pale, coming out of father's study after I'd been dismissed. My hands continue to shake. I'd start pacing again and groaning if I wasn't in a public place. The entire lounge is dead silent. Everyone is looking at me. A few people start whispering to each other.

"Bruce." I hear on the phone. "Wait. Here's Paul Thomas."

A man comes on the line. I try to pull myself together. He sounds like a professor, subdued, serious. I'm having difficulty focusing on what he's telling me, how he couldn't leave her alone because of her injuries. I'm furious. I've been yelling at Ellie, but it's me I'm mad at.

I'm confused and sick. I've known all along what Father is capable of. I chose to bail and let it happen. It's no wonder everyone despises me. Join the club, I think morosely. The professor is winding down on the phone. He'll drive her up to Browning himself tomorrow. I agree to meet her mid-morning.

Ellie comes back on the line. "I know you're upset. But I'll be fine."

"I'll change my flight and go straight into to Great Falls. I'll rent a car and meet you at your apartment, okay? Early tomorrow?"

"Good. I'll need you. See you then."

I sit and stare out the darkened windows of the airport, both hands now balled into fists. She needed me a week ago. Now it's too late.

* * *

I'm able to change my flight and have an additional hour before boarding. Finding an isolate spot, I call Alec. He usually doesn't answer immediately but returns the call on a disposable if he thinks it's going to be a sensitive conversation.

He calls back immediately. "Hello," he says in a terribly emotionless voice. He doesn't use my name. I suppose it also makes him sick.

"What the fuck happened? You — you monster. I just talked to Ellie. Why?"

"You know why. Your dad ordered it. We don't cross him, either of us."

"But...?"

"After you left, he ordered me specifically, blow by blow, to do what I did. I had a lesson from some thug Frederick employs on how hard to hit her to dislodge ribs — not shatter them so they wouldn't puncture her lungs. I practiced with him on a punching bag in a gym until the guy was satisfied."

"No." I moan into the phone.

"Having her die would've caused — complications. He admitted as much."

"I can't believe you...."

"Don't give me that," he replies with instant hostility. "You knew, or you should have known." He takes a deep breath. "He threatened me, threatened everyone, starting with your mother. He can blackmail either of us now. I've done things, illegal things. And now violence."

"But?"

"What if this doesn't work? He might up the ante next time. He's got us by the balls. If I quit, he'll put me in prison — or worse." A pause. "I've got money hoarded in Swiss bank accounts. Do you?"

"No. He's never needed to bribe me. I've been the heir-designate, or so I thought. Maybe it's you. Has he dangled it over your head, too?"

"Of course," I hear a sigh of disgust. "What's funny, even ironic, is I don't think he was ever going to choose. He kept us in line with it. He wanted the girl involved to help control you. Don't you see? If you cared so much you didn't want her hurt, he could control you by threatening her — and if you let it happen he could threaten to let her know that, too."

The truth almost breaks me. Why hadn't I faced this?

Alec continues. "He always sets us up, so we have no choices and no chance. But now this girl got away from his trap. She was too strong to be controlled. It gives me a little satisfaction, even if had I to...."

I'm fighting back tears. "Alec, we have no choice. We have to keep doing what he wants."

"We live in a cage, Bruce. We can stop this. I'll share the money. We'll set up new identities. Please." I can hear his desperation. "Let's bag it all. I won't hurt anyone like that again, ever. Ever. It was horrible. You should have seen her face."

"I don't want to hear it." I put my hands over my ears, somehow managing while holding onto the cell phone.

"You need to hear this." He's almost screaming. "I pulled out a metal bar and broke her left arm. I could hear it crack. She screamed then."

"Stop, for God's sake, Alec," I moan. "Stop."

"No, I want you to know. Please. Let's get out of this hell now. What if your dad orders me to kill Ellie next time? Would you go along?"

"No. Of course not." But we both know I took a little too long to say it. I had to think a second, a glimpse into hell. I gasp in horror.

We sit in silence for a minute or two.

Finally, he murmurs, "Goodbye, Bruce. Call me if you decide to disappear."

We hold the phones silently connected for another few seconds, somehow wanting to prolong the connection — the chance. Neither of us knows what's going on in the other's head. I wonder whether I'll ever hear his voice again.

I know one thing. If I could summon up the courage to face down Father, he'd destroy me mentally, possibly physically. He'd let Ellie know I had allowed this. He'd destroy us. She would hate me.

I'm a lost soul. His will is so much stronger than mine.

I'm doomed. It's a good word, doomed. I'm doomed. It rolls around in my head like a melody you can't stop hearing. *Stop it,* I think. *For God's sake, stop*. Doomed. Doomed. Doomed.

* * *

Leaning against a front bumper of my Lexis SUV, I cross and recross my legs, trying to appear relaxed. I'm currently parked in front of Ellie's apartment on the Blackfeet Indian Reservation. The wind is blowing a steady thirty miles per hour, making me jittery. All the way here dust tornados swerved across the road, flattening the grasses alongside, before skidding away to the east, adding to my feeling of isolation and hostility. I'm a foreigner here.

A native man glances coldly at me. Neither of us sustains eye contact as he moves quickly away. I wait.

It's late morning when a black BMW coupe pulls in the parking area. I can make out Ellie in the passenger seat. A tall, fit man swiftly emerges, much younger than I expected. I walk over to meet them.

"Hello. I'm the college professor, Paul Thomas," he begins, holding out his hand.

"I'm Bruce Weingarten," I say, staking my claim. "I'm grateful for all you've done. From what I understand, you've been taking care of Ellie for two days."

"My brother's family and myself," he explains. "There was no way I could leave her on her own."

I walk around to Ellie's side of the car and gasp. It's one thing being told about something. Alec did this? I can't wrap my head around it. In truth, I had no inkling this would happen. I'm shocked into silence, abruptly understanding I'm standing precariously on some kind of continental divide — one foot on either side. All I have to do is shift one way or the other and the rest of my life will be defined. Surprisingly, I also think of Alec and feel his anguish but the feeling pales as I focus on Ellie.

Her face is somewhat swollen with a cut lip which is only partially healed. She needs time to recover after I turn her in the seat. I want to wrap my arms around her and say all the things I haven't allowed myself to say — the truth. Thomas's presence stops me.

I feel his eyes on her, on us. I don't trust his motives. And, as much as he's trying to cover it up, he wishes I weren't here, either. I'm wondering what went on these last two days. Ellie is trying very hard not to glance at him. I size him up as a rival.

After he brings in Ellie's bags, I walk him out to his car. We share a disingenuous handshake. He gives me a cool, appraising stare before driving off. Frozen in the middle of the road, I watch until his car disappears, trying to understand my emotions. I want him gone. And I want him to stay gone.

After adjusting to this, I hurry up the narrow sidewalk. I want Ellie out of here, for both our sakes. I go to her, carefully putting my arms around her. I want her to collapse into my arms, but I feel distance between us.

"Let's lie down for a while," she says. "I need to sleep. I keep waking up in pain and taking more pills. Then I have to wait until they kick in. I'm exhausted."

I'm exhausted, too, with jet lag and tension. Ellie drops immediately into a deep sleep, while my mind spins with unresolved issues. If a miracle happens and I get this vice-presidency, maybe I can break out and find some peace. I've worked so hard, given everything in me, to get this promotion. I intend to shift my loyalty to the firm. Father will make me suffer, of course, but maybe I can find the strength to outlast him with Ellie at my side. But then I think about the beating. Father would let her know I was involved. That image is so unbearable that the cycle begins again.

Hours later I'm still awake. I wonder what it would feel like to be truly good, worthy of being trusted by another good human being. Suddenly I want that warm image so much that I hold my breath. But abruptly the fleeting emotion eludes me, skidding away, like the dust devils on the highway. As hard as I try to retrieve it, it's gone.

* * *

We had greasy tacos for dinner, adding to my feeling of discontent. I'd panicked, tried desperately to persuade Ellie to leave. If her new friend, Professor Paul, believed she was in danger, he might also insist. I got his number off her phone and called him. It was a disaster. I embellished the beating and Ellie got hysterical — said I was doing it to torture Paul. Torture Paul? Are you kidding?

What if the asshole did get upset? All it accomplished was putting more distance between us. I'm feeling icy cold from her. She's disconnecting; doesn't want me to touch her.

* * *

I've retrieved Ellie's car after meeting with her corporate friends. I did my best to make her work sound hazardous. I've apologized to Ellie, over and over, for involving the asshole yesterday. I'm hitting a brick wall.

Parking in front of Ellie's apartment, I walk up the path. She's nowhere to be found. Where the hell is she? I'm wondering whether her interlude with Paul was as innocent as they're portraying. She's been over-the-top upset over the phone call. I wonder whether he snuck up here. Damn them both if he did. I feel my anger upping a notch and start pacing around the room.

Finally, after ten minutes or so, she pulls in with an Indian who's a stranger. I glare at the guy.

"Bruce, this is my friend, Win Sanders. He stopped by and asked whether I needed anything. Ice cream sounded good."

"Hello," the guy says. "Ellie's been telling me what happened. Unbelievable."

"Yes. Unbelievable," I say dismissively. I'll be damned if I want to spend time talking to a reservation loser.

"Win runs the entire reservation volunteer fire organization. He's responsible for many lives."

"Good for you. Someone's got to be in charge."

"Bruce, what in heaven's name is the matter with you?"

"It's okay," Win says, watching me carefully. "Gotta go. See you later."

"I'm sorry." I hear her say as she walks him to the door.

She returns and stares at me.

"Suddenly everything I say is wrong," I almost yell. "What the hell do I care about this guy, Ellie? It's you I care about. You're getting sucked into this place." I'm unexpectedly terrified for both of us. "You're in danger. Why can't you see it? I don't express it well, but I'm really worried."

She softens. "Okay, Bruce. Calm down. I'll be fine."

No, you won't, I think.

* * *

It's Sunday. Ellie and I are falling apart. I got a call from Father who's furious she's still here. He hardly ever loses it, but he was close to yelling at me on the phone. He's never done that in my life. Caustic degradation is his weapon. I'm almost trembling. He's capable of anything. I wonder whether he really would kill me if he thought it would help. It's unbelievable I don't know the answer to that question. He didn't say on the phone what he wanted done, but I knew. He wants Ellie gone or dead. How can I get her out of this? I've thought of leveling with her, but it's obvious she'd tell her people, they'd give her a lot of protection, and bring my family down. They should.

I don't know which way to turn. I'm scared and furious and I can't see a way forward. Ellie's gone again with several girlfriends. I was strongly encouraged not to join them. Another guy, a tall muscular man, had come along to pick up Ellie. I sensed his immediate hostility.

"Bruce, this is Willie. He's a close friend of Win Sanders and Paul."

Neither of us held out our hand. We stood staring at each other some distance apart.

"So, Bruce," the Willie-guy said. "Are you staying long?"

I had to fight glaring. This was ill-concealed disdain. The guy was no fool, maybe a worthy adversary. His tone of voice was subtle and understated. I don't think Ellie noticed us squaring off.

"No, not long. Enough time to accomplished what I need to." I stared at him coldly. "So, what exactly do you do? Ellie mentioned something about "Long's Adventures?" Intriguing. What kind of adventures do you have?"

"More than you might imagine. People usually have a good time with us if they choose to. Sometimes people make wrong choices. Then they can get into difficulty."

"I bet they're glad to have a big, strong guy like you to get them out of trouble."

"You'd be surprised. Sometimes brute strength does come in handy."

We stood, staring coldly at each other, seeing who would blink.

Finally, Willie addressed Ellie. "I'll leave you with the girls," he said with a smile, then started down the sidewalk. At the last moment he stopped, yelling back at her over his shoulder. "Call me, Ellie, if you need help. Any help at all."

He paused, staring meaningfully at me. A last parting shot across the stern.

I'd like to do him harm. He'd like to do me harm. I watched, seething, as he jogged purposefully toward the Big Chief Mercantile.

I tried trailing the girls when they took off in the truck, but I was afraid they knew they were being followed. I ended up at the liquor store, bought a large bottle, and gulped a few swallows in the car — more than a few. Bringing the bottle inside, I continued swigging more Scotch, cooling my heels.

She's been gone almost two hours. *Where the hell is she?* I hate them all. Finally, I hear the truck pull in. The women, Susan and Cora, walk her to the door, give her a hug, and wave before driving off.

I've been brooding alone, helpless, while my world falls apart. Ellie seems to be beyond any reasoning. I've lost her. It's becoming apparent how much I've depended on her to provide a normal place to rest, away from the chaos of my family and professional life. We've hardly said a word since she arrived ten minutes ago. Something has changed irrevocably. I take another long swig. I haven't been this drunk in a decade.

Finally, I can stand it no longer.

"Ellie, what in the friggin' hell are you doing here?"

"You know what I'm doing. Trying to get the oil and gas contracts distributed fairly with environmental protections."

"Let me level with you, Sweetie. Surprise! Someone's going to steal it all in the end. Who cares?"

"I care, Bruce. It's what I do. I care about the people here."

"Well, you stoopid, naive fluff," I slur, exploding. "That's what Dad calls you — lower class fluff. Don't you have a clue?" I'm screaming now. "You're going to blow all the effort I've put in for two years — Two fucking years — Father's plans. And if you think he's going to take it lying down ...."

"What does your father have to do with this?"

"Don't you goddamn get it? He's the guy pulling all the strings." I take one last swig that empties the bottle. "I was going to break loose and tell Father to fuck off. Now I'm buried." My voice rises another notch, "Choose. Last chance. The job or me."

She stands staring at me.

I try to throw the empty bottle into a nearby wastebasket, miss, and collapse onto the couch, watching the bottle roll effeminately across the floor. In desperation I plead, "Don't you have any feelings for me at all? Don't you know what you're doing?"

"I don't understand." There's fear in her voice now. "People are counting on me. I can't quit."

I leap unsteadily to my feet almost falling. My head is spinning. Rage overcomes me. "You — traitor." Grabbing her arm, I slap her ineffectively with my right hand. She loses her balance, trips over a footstool, and crumples onto the end table. A book and a desk lamp go flying as she sits hard on the floor.

I stand over her screaming and crying, "Hypocrite. You never cared. You fucking used me, too. Don't you know? You've killed me. I'm dead."

Suddenly the door flies open. The Indian I met yesterday, Win, and another Indian come barreling in.

I feel myself flying through the air, manhandled out the door, and thrown on the ground.

I'm picked up and held, my arms pulled behind me.

Another truck pulls into the parking lot.

Win hauls back and hits me in the mouth, hard. I feel a tooth rattle loose in my mouth and spit it out.

I'm raging, struggling and lunging.

Two more guys run up. One is fucking-ass Willie, the other man is Paul, who turned Ellie against me. I'm going to get beaten up, killed maybe. I don't care. Just end me. Nothing matters anymore. Everything died with her betrayal.

I expect a lot of pain but stop thrashing, exhausted. Too many of them.

Instead of them all ganging up on me, Willie starts holding Paul off. Now he's the one screaming and lunging against Willie's arms. Paul's entire body is contorted in the effort to get loose. The brawl goes on for some time.

Finally, Win goes over and slugs Paul in the mouth.

I'm drunk, dazed and confused. Why did he hit his friend instead of me? Win keeps saying Ellie's name over and over.

Willie finally lets Paul go and he sprints to Ellie's apartment.

I start struggling again, kicking and screaming obscenities.

The three remaining guys drag me to my car, the two biggest guys holding my arms.

Win gets in my face. "You asshole. If you show your face on the res again, I'm going to stick a big knife in your gut and twist it for ten minutes before I kill you. Get it?"

I spit at him.

He grins, makes a fist and slugs me in the mouth again. Another tooth gone. One more punch to my gut.

"Gotta say," he says. "You're one brave son of a bitch."

I'm thrown headfirst into the car, my body swirling in pain and fury. I eventually manage to find the keys and am barely able to fight off the impulse to try to mow them down with my SUV before I escape.

Stopping at the first motel in Great Falls I could find, I answered the inevitable question about my face with a stony glare, and now sit on the bed with ice in a pillowcase pressed against my jaw. It was a bad drive down. I probably drove onto the berm a dozen times what with the alcohol and pain. I need to call Alec, but I need to calm down first and sober up. I'm a lost soul. But the vice-presidency hasn't been lost yet. Maybe I can salvage it.

I'm sobering up fast, too fast. Oh, dear God. What I did. What I said. I'm so sorry. All that was possible with Ellie, all the dreams I had, are gone. I need to apologize — do something to make this better. Not perfect. Just better.

The only good feeling I've had recently was spitting at Win. It was the first courageous thing I've done in a decade, even if I was drunk. Father was spot-on. I'm a worthless pile of shit.

I walk around Europe and the Middle East in my expensive suits — a phantom, circling real people, people who have lives, people who care about each other. My mother and I have conversations about the weather. Father filets me with verbal knives.

I find myself groaning over and over. Ellie won't forgive me. It's pointless to call her. I'd settle for less disgust. A plan. I need a plan. I'll call the company and sound positive, pretend I'm on top of my game, name achievements. Maybe I can make something a success. Maybe the other guys in the running for the grand position will screw up or have an accident. Maybe I could arrange accidents.

Suddenly I stop in horror. This has to stop. I'm becoming my father. Making that suggestion would finally make me his heir. He'd love it if I offered murder as an option. He'd absolutely love it. He'd love me, or whatever passes for love in our family. No. No. I can't let him turn me completely. I've got to fight it.

I think about Ellie. I'm already a monster. How did it happen? Father.

I slowly pick up the phone to call him. Water wells up in my mouth, disgusting me.

"Yes?"

"Father," I garble, speaking slowly to make myself understood with the swollen jaw. "Ellie is swarming with protection. Her team is up from Tennessee and her friends from the EPA. She refuses to quit. She's…. We're not together now."

Silence.

"Father?"

"Shut up. I'm thinking."

Minutes pass. I move the ice pack. My mouth is killing me. It's Sunday. No dentist is open. Should I go to the local emergency room for drugs? I'd have to come up with some explanation.

"Father?"

"All right. This is what we're going to do. We'll need Alec's services again."

I tense up. Alec wants out.

"We need to cover our tracks. Everyone will be watching her, maybe her family, too. We won't target them directly. Maybe our sweet Eleanor would quit if one of her friends were seriously hurt. Pick somebody. Someone she cares about."

I swallow some blood. "Okay. There's a big guy who has me figured out. He knows what's going on, not exactly, but enough. He hates me. I hate him. His name is Willie Long."

"We don't go after him directly. Ask around. Find a family member he loves. Then contact Alec. He'll tail 'em. We'll go from there. Call me when you have it arranged. You have twenty-four hours."

"Yes, Father."

"Fucking shame we couldn't move Ellie. Next time find a hot body with no scruples, or so weak you can control her. Maybe you'll learn. Women are nothing but problems."

"Goodbye, Father," I say wearily before I realize he's already hung up. I keep going down the water slide.

I wonder which of those women my mother was.

* * *

"Hello."

"The old man has a job for you."

No response except a deep sigh.

I've done my research and explain the situation. "Willie Long is the guy we're using to persuade Ellie to leave. He has a kid sister. Her name is Natasha Long. She's called Tashi. She goes to school in California, UC San Diego. The old man wants her followed. He hasn't decided what to do next, but he wants you to get right on this."

Silence.

"Alec?"

"Yes. Yes, I'm here. What do you think he's going to have me to do when I find her?"

"He's going to use her as a threat, a warning, like Ellie."

"I wish you'd stop saying 'he' Bruce. You're going along with this."

"I'd hate to have you think I'm a hypocrite," I mumble bitterly.

"Have you thought about my offer to split the money and get out?"

"Every day. Every hour. I can't. Not yet. First, I want to see whether I can get the Vice Presidency. It's all I have in the world that's mine."

"What if I refused this?"

"I'm reasonably sure he'd try to kill you to silence you, then find someone else to do the job. You're not even family, whatever the hell that means."

He sighs. "Where is she now?"

"Back at college, I assume."

Indistinguishable muttering. Then, "Fine."

"Enjoy the warm weather." I hear his phone click off. My flippant statement fell flat. His acquiescence was discouragingly frightening in a convoluted way. I thought I'd have to work harder to convince him. After you beat up one girl, the next one must be easier.

* * *

It's fall now, and the academic year is well underway. Alec has been trailing Tashi for weeks. He says she's a wild lady and he's been having a ball going to hangouts she frequents. He says he's trying his best to keep this impersonal. She's hot.

Father wants her to have an accident, something suspicious, something comparable to Ellie's incident, making it probable the events are related. He implied something much worse would happen unless Ellie quits. Alec is searching for an opportunity. He says he has several ideas, but it's difficult. She's never alone and doesn't have a car.

Father continues to monitor Ellie's cell, keeping me informed as though he's doing me a favor. She communicates frequently with Paul. Sometimes Father gives me transcripts with personal details, letting me know I've been replaced in gory detail. He wants me to hate her. He's not successful, though. She's a good person. This mess is all about me. I've tried to call her, but she won't pick up. My personal life is a wasteland.

My phone rings. Alec on my cell.

It seems Win Sanders, the Blackfeet who knocked out my teeth, had a girlfriend who was just killed in a plane crash. Tashi is going home for the funeral and there may be an opportunity. Father called him with the good news and ordered Alec to fly to Montana. I sense gloom in Alec's voice. When I asked him what he intends to do, he eluded my question. I guess he doesn't want to think about specifics either. I remember Alec telling me he'd never do anything like this again, but here we are.

I'm horribly depressed. I detest the girl's brother and wish he were the target, not this innocent girl. Now that I've calmed down, I'm not even sure whether I want the big asshole beaten up. I want to let it rest, but I'm not in charge. Plus, I'm on my way to Moscow for almost two weeks. When I return, maybe this will be resolved for all our sakes.

CHAPTER 4

ALEC

IT'S LATE OCTOBER. I'm getting out of this cesspool as soon as Bruce's vice-presidency is resolved. Even Chairman of the Board, Weingarten, must realize it's all unraveling. People can't be closely managed — not indefinitely. Bruce and I could have split the hidden money, brought the whole house of cards down, but he hasn't managed to cut the cord yet. Maybe it's the whole *blood is thicker* thing.

To protect my new target, I've been trailing her around southern California, pretending to find an opportunity to hurt her so Weingarten senior won't hire someone else to do the job. But now my life has taken another strange turn. Of all the strange places on earth, tonight I find myself leaning against an unadorned wooden wall in the rear of a community center on an Indian Reservation in Browning, Montana. Tashi's here for a funeral along with hundreds of friends and relatives. Most of the people here are of Blackfeet blood, but there are many white friends and mixed-race people, so I don't stand out.

As I've followed Tashi, I've been charmed by her. I've never known anyone like her — not that I know her, but I've been close, very close. She hasn't noticed me. I've been careful with hoodies, sunglasses, sitting with my back to her, watching in near darkness. It's been fun. I mean her no harm, in fact the opposite, so I don't feel guilty. She's young, wild, and consistently high-spirited. I have lively female climbing friends, but there's something about this girl. I'd like to hold her hand and run through a downpour with her. I laugh at my romantic fantasies, very unlike me. The energy in a room goes up several notches when she enters it. I've been tempted to set up an encounter tonight, but I won't. It would be dangerous on so many levels.

The main reason I can't approach her is that Ellie is here. I'm possibly still recognizable, my hair not grown out enough in the past six weeks, but more important, she still has her arm in a sling, for God's sake. The guilt almost paralyzes me. She's accompanied — I should say protected — by the same man who took her to the ER after the beating. He obviously doesn't want her out of his sight. Neither would I if some son-of-a-bitch stranger beat her up. I shudder in self-loathing and double my resolve to protect her and Tashi. At least I know whom old man Weingarten is targeting. Ellie is currently off his radar.

Minutes ago, I was standing at a counter getting coffee when someone bumped into me. I turned, smiling, to let them off the hook when I recognized Ellie. "Oh, sorry," she said. "I get a little off-balance with this sling."

"No problem," I muttered, and hurried away. Jesus H. Christ. If I'd been recognized, the entire Blackfeet Nation would likely have peeled off my skin. I moved to the other side of the hall, resting my eyes on Tashi, then letting out a long sigh of relief.

Last weekend in San Diego, I was doing my usual slinking around at an outdoor college party when I was sorely tempted. Several fraternities had merged resources and erected a massive lawn tent on an expansive grassy area overlooking the Pacific at dusk. There were hundreds of people there, no one knew everyone, and no one was carding us or checking student ID. I made up a story and joined the group. They had a good band, wine and beer were flowing, so I was able to keep an eye on Tashi, interspersed with dancing, and drinking my share. This has not been painful duty.

That night, It appeared Tashi didn't have a guy acting possessively. She wore a lime green summer dress to set off her exotic attractiveness. She was animated, knew half the people there, and was cruising around laughing, dancing, and being hugged by guys who wanted the hugs to linger. I was entranced. I spent the entire evening talking myself out of approaching her.

This gathering, on the other hand, is a sad occasion but somehow filled with warmth. Tashi has been circulating, reconnecting with friends, talking to senior tribal members, and returning frequently to her brother who puts his arm around her shoulders.

It's only a matter of time before I give in. I want to wrap my hands in her long black hair. I'd like her to want to touch me. My fantasies are getting more detailed. She has half the room wanting her, at least that's my perception. Maybe, when all this is over, I can find a way to meet her. For now, let it lie. Be her protector. I notice a guy in her group start watching me, pointing me out to another guy. I glance away. When he's distracted, I'm gone.

CHAPTER 5

BRUCE

I'VE BEEN BACK IN THE STATES for twenty-four hours and talked to Alec. He hasn't pulled this off. Father is livid. He believes Alec is playing for time. It's what I also believe. It's too late to find another enforcer, the VP position decision is looming. Father told me he'll deal with Alec. I didn't ask what he meant. The one hopeful thing is perhaps the old man will get so apoplectic he'll have a stroke.

Alec would agree. Father's all but ruined our lives. I texted Alec to prepare to be shot in the back. I have some loyalty.

He texted back he wants to meet but won't set a date and time for obvious reasons. I'm sure he wonders where my red line is. I wonder that myself.

Ellie and I just endured the long-awaited phone call. She finally picked up. I surprised myself by admitting the naked truth — spilled my guts to her, that I desperately needed her, admitted my emptiness, my isolation. I even alluded to Father's viciousness, but it was excruciatingly too late. I was so defeated that I degenerated into cold rage, unable to suppress threats. Maybe she has been playing me all along. I trust no one.

If she had expressed devotion long ago, maybe I could have broken free of this quagmire. But every time she attempted to talk to me about real feelings, I masterfully deflected her. Couldn't she see how close to the edge of madness I've been? Well, I'm over some tipping point now. Before she called me back, I'd been dialing her number, punching it in over and over, canceling it, doing it again — hoping, damn it, for something. Redemption, salvation? My thoughts are circling like random sparks, dying, then reappearing somewhere else.

What do I expect from her at this point — a formal separation declaration and a contract to sign? She wants nothing to do with me. The end. I have a hallucination of my head being cut off, bumping and rolling down the road. I fight to push that thought under using hate. I feel myself descending into blind rage. It feels slightly better than utter despair.

Sleep alludes me. Alcohol helps. The business in Russia went well, better than well. I have two oil pipeline deals ready to go if Syria and Turkey would only get their shit together.

The thing making me most furious is I've worked so hard and should have this V.P. thing on my own merit. Why the company would hold me hostage over this Ellie-situation is beyond me. I suspect they're simply sticking it to the old man. Everyone hates him. But I want this so badly. I'm sick unto death being Father's point man.

I'm currently waiting for Alec at the restaurant at the Park Lodge in East Glacier. He got hold of me an hour ago, probably not leaving enough time to arrange his assassination. I suspect he's requested this meeting as a formal ending. I've been made to understand he doesn't want a personal relationship with any of us. I finish my drink in one swallow.

"Hello, Bruce," he says quietly as he approaches the table.

"Alec."

It's always awkward. We never know exactly whom we're meeting. Our egos shift around a lot depending on how we feel about each other and ourselves at the moment.

"Tomorrow's the big day, I hear."

"You probably know more than I do. Dad has spies. But, yes. Tomorrow is supposed to be the announcement."

"Well, I hope you get it. Lord knows you've worked hard enough."

His unexpected support surprises me. "Generous thing to say. No one thinks I'm worth shit."

"I don't hate you. Your father's the Svengali."

"We're both smart guys. Why can't we get out?"

He gives me a half-smile with more than a tinge of sadness. "Well, that's why I wanted to see you. I'm going to do it."

I can only stare.

"There's a lot you don't know, and you may hate me for some of it, but you need the truth. I can't spend my life fending off requests to hurt or kill people. I've known it for a long time." I see him swallow. "It's why you may hate me. I waited 'til the last minute to tell you. I was afraid your dad, and maybe you, would have found another enforcer to hurt Tashi." He takes a deep breath. "After I beat up Ellie O'Connell, I swore I would protect other victims from your father's mania for power."

A faint roar starts behind my ears. "I may lose the promotion because of what you've done."

"I know that."

I turn away from him, my stomach is falling out from under me. It's several moments before I can mutter, "My career is all I have. No friends, no family in any real sense of the word. I'm trapped, squirming under Father's thumb. If I don't get this . . . I'll be ground into dust."

"Bruce?"

I avoid his eyes.

He lowers his voice, but I can hear the urgency. "Bruce, look at me."

Reluctantly, I force myself to look up.

"I'll help you if you don't get it. I've told you. I'll share the money."

"I have enough money. Don't you see? This position is all that I am. I've spent all my life trying to prove my worth to Father . . . and myself." I pause then say slowly, "It's all come down to this." My calmness chills me.

"It won't kill you to stop."

"You're sure? You're sure?" I say with rising fury. I feel my fists clench.

He notices, staring at my hands.

"I'm up against my last wall here."

Alec pauses, then says, "If you want to kill me, you'll have to find me."

The joke fell flat. We sit and stare at each other. Neither of us knows what the other is capable of.

"I've lost my appetite," I say finally. "Do you want a drink?"

"Doubles," he says without a smile.

* * *

I'm sitting alone. It's almost midnight. Alex and I had numerous drinks and choked down dinner. It was a tense meal. Even the alcohol didn't dull my dread. I'm sitting on my bed, twirling my ancient brass room key over and over in my fingers. I've been waiting for months, years, my entire life, for the call tomorrow. It's all come down to this. Maybe I could be a separate being — not live in an echo chamber of someone else's megalomania. With a very good lawyer, I should be able to extricate myself from....

The phone rings. It's Father again. Third time today. I almost don't answer, but that would anger him further. He'd put it on speed-redial until hell freezes over. I could smash the phone, but I need it tomorrow. My lifeline. "Trapped again." I almost laugh manically.

"Father."

"Well, Bruce. It's all come down to this."

"Yes."

"It's nice in a way, clear and definitive. We'll find out what you're made of."

"Yes." I say with some confusion. "I guess."

"The girl is still there. Nowhere to hide from the truth. If you don't get this, it will be because you didn't have enough balls to get rid of her, one way or another."

I sigh. "I've hoped it would be on merit."

"You're a sucker, Bruce." He laughs contemptuously. "You didn't play the game well enough to win. You never did get it. It's got nothing to do with effort. Oh, fuck. Why do I even try to explain it?"

"Father," I say with bottomless fatigue, "I've done my best. Let it play out."

He laughs again, the disgusted hostile laugh which has become part of my DNA. "Well, that's the truth. It's why she dumped you. Your best was transparently lacking."

When I don't respond he adds, "Maybe you'll luck out somehow. Your mother is hoping for luck. She's given up on your ability. She told me last night you'd be happier with a small life. Maybe you can surprise her for once."

I feel nausea as I always do when talking to Father. I imagine I can feel the stomach acid dripping.

"Oh, by the way. I've continued to monitor Ellie's calls. You remember Paul, don't you? I find their expressions of love very entertaining. It's my new diversion. She's leaving from Browning at nine-o-clock tomorrow morning to pick him up at the airport, trying to beat a blizzard coming out of Northern Canada. If you by some chance get the promotion, you might let her know it was no thanks to her. And if you don't.... I'd sure as hell make her pay."

I don't say anything.

The phone clicks off. He never says goodbye.

Exactly why he shared the news about Ellie I'm not certain — probably to jerk my chain for fun. And Mother's disappointment.... That hurts the most. "New boyfriend — you loser." I hear it as surely as though he said it aloud. "Loser." My stomach continues to churn.

* * *

We sit together in stony silence. Alec called minutes before eight, offering to wait for the call with me. We have nothing left to say. I have no idea why I agreed, but I sense he didn't come to gloat. In the past fifteen minutes I don't think I've moved a muscle except my eyes, which circle the room, searching for a pleasant place to rest — anything to divert me from the call to come. The wilderness pictures on the wall partially distract me. Despite redecorating, the rooms reflect the lodge's age — over 100 years old — darkening wood like Father's study. I resume twirling the old-fashioned room key in my hand.

There's a two-hour time difference. They said the announcement would be out after 10:00 East Coast time. My hands are ice. We wait. A few minutes after 8:30 the phone rings. Please God, I think.

"Hello. Bruce Weingarten here."

I can tell, the first second, the first half of a second. It's the tone of voice. "They're sorry. It was extremely close, maybe the next opening, so sorry." I can almost hear them saying, "Loser." I hang up.

Alec can tell. The blood drains from his face. I'm sure my color matches his. Rage boils up, but it's cold, super-cooled oxygen. A dull roar begins, a sound unlike anything I can remember — and building.

I turn to Alec. Much to my surprise, I can talk slowly. "Ellie killed me. I want her punished. She's on her way to the airport in Great Falls. Will you do it?"

"No, Bruce." He stands, reaching for my arm.

"You owe me," I say in a dead voice. "You could have prevented this. Will you run her off the road?"

"You can't do this. A blizzard's coming. You could murder Ellie. I won't let you...."

The coldness explodes into heat and rage. He did this to me, too. I know karate — I took lessons as a kid. Out of nowhere, I leap up, twirl around, and flatten him with my foot, a direct hit. His head hits the dresser as he goes down, not out cold but almost. I see blood under his left ear starting to stream down his face as he struggles ineffectively to get up, then collapses motionless on the floor.

I race from the room, down the corridor, down the stairs and outside, then notice, vaguely, it's arctic outside and I didn't grab a coat. Wearing only my sport coat, I'm frozen by the time I make it to my Lexus. Five thousand pounds ought to do the job. Flooring the gas pedal with the car in reverse, the tires spin in the frozen gravel, then catch. The steering wheel is ice. I'm barely aware enough to turn on the heat — too focused on the other thing. Shifting, I careen out of the parking lot and onto the main road.

Knowing the area well now, I gun the SUV out of East Glacier, through Browning, then south, down Highway 89, to a point just outside the border of the reservation. I pull over and wait, blinded by my rage, hoping she hasn't passed this spot yet.

My hands are fists, my neck corded in fury. The roar continues, escalates. I beat my hands on the steering wheel. Echoes of failure pulse in my head: "So sorry . . . Next time . . . Loser . . . Make her pay . . ." Moments later a small white car approaches from the north. As it passes me, I see the girl in the passenger seat turn to glance at me. Ellie. She recognizes me. I have no idea who the other girl is. Vaguely familiar, though. She's unlucky. Wrong place.

I yank the wheel to the left, pull onto the isolated highway, and follow them at a distance. Their car is probably less than half the size of mine. I pull closer. They speed up. They're frightened. Good. It's colder still, fifteen below zero on my car thermometer. In the past few minutes the temperature has fallen ten degrees, and it's starting to swirl snow flurries in ghostly patterns. The wind is starting to push my Lexus around. I can only imagine what it's doing to their tinker-toy car.

Let's do this. I gun my car and pull parallel to them on their left, swerving hard into them. It almost pushes them off the road. I've never done this before, but it's easy. The road is starting to get slippery. I pull out and hit them again, a jarring screech, metal on metal. I see the face of the other girl, who's driving hunched over the wheel, trying to dodge. She doesn't appear afraid but focused, slowing down then speeding up, trying to elude me. The unfolding drama and their faces frozen in the moment mesmerize me.

It's starting to snow harder. The wind grows more vicious. The sun, which was low in the east, is suddenly gone, enveloped by the approaching storm cloud. I'm having trouble seeing the side of the road as swirling snow whitens the blacktop. My car shudders as the wind sideswipes me as I approach for one more hit on their left side. Except here the land is flat. They might just skid off to the side and be okay. I need a place where they can roll and trash their car.

I pull back behind them to try to think. Almost immediately, I see a heavy guardrail ahead on the left-hand side, probably over a stream or protecting an embankment. Time only to react, I pull my Lexus onto the right-hand shoulder and run parallel to them, glancing at Ellie who's staring at me in horror. If I can get the timing right...? I slam into their car. The driver veers the car off to the left at the last second, barely missing the metal head of the guardrail. The car does what I envisioned — tumbling and rolling, over and over, down the steep embankment toward the frozen river.

Mesmerized as I watch it settle, I hear a prolonged screech as my car sideswipes the same left railing. Sparks explode in the gathering gloom. I hear a muffled explosion. Immediately I'm having trouble controlling my car. A tire is blown. There's nothing to do but keep driving. I can't see the bridge behind me, already lost in the blinding snow of my rear-view mirror. My car continues swaying in the wind, wobbling down the road, tilted onto the rim of the left front tire. I glance at the car thermometer — minus twenty. Jesus, it's cold. I can only make fifteen miles per hour with the blown tire. I dimly realize I'm going to need rescuing. At least the heater is working. I check the gas gauge. Half full. I'd better ration the heater. I wonder how long it might be before I'm found. I have no coat or emergency supplies. I suppose that should bother me, but all I can focus on is the icy road, stretching then disappearing into a whirling wall of snow twenty feet in front of me.

After a few hundred yards further down the road there's a new sound, a grinding noise. More sparks flash from the wheel well. My knuckles are white on the steering wheel. The car is tilting even more strongly. I realize the fender is rubbing against what remains of the tire and the rim. As hard as I push the accelerator, I can't control it. The car veers sharply to the left, sideswipes another guardrail, and whips around on the glare-ice to finally settle itself, heading the wrong way on the former right side of the road. I turn off the wipers. The snow encloses me in a capsule of isolation.

I exist.

As suddenly as it began, the mania dissipates. I rest motionless in the seat, no longer a sentient being — rather a human form made up of individual cells. Staring directly ahead into the whiteness, I automatically turn the car off. There is no sound but the brutal wind and the feel of the pulsing gusts shaking the car.

I begin to become aware of the intense cold. I'm not sure I've ever felt cold like this, terrifying, menacing. The wind howls for fifteen or more seconds at a time, tipping the car sideways, then righting itself. The noise is unnatural. I'm alarmed my car might be rolled completely on its side. Beginning to think, I finally decide I'll wait before I turn the heater on again. I'm frightened. It could be hours or days before help arrives. I have no food or water. Could anyone get out here? Gradually, my thinking moves beyond myself. Something very bad has happened.

A gut-wrenching sensation suddenly grips me — the girls — the girls in the car are dead. If they aren't dead, they're dying in the cold. I did that. *I DID THAT!* Is there an emotion worse than horrorstruck? I scream.

Nothing makes sense. I don't want them dead. I can't remember wanting them dead, or even punished. I shake my head. I've probably killed someone. Alec said it — *murderer*. I'm sure of it. I've killed Ellie and another helpless girl. Am I the first murderer who wants it back? I want it back. Dear God in heaven, I want it back. I grab my stomach in pain. Is there anyone who could get here to help them?

No one will believe me. I groan aloud, in pain and horror. Ultimately, I start the car, thinking I'll try to drive back to put them in this car to keep them warm. I manage a few feet in reverse then try to pull forward, turning the wheel frantically from side to side. The car won't move.

The wind shrieks endlessly. I put my hands over my ears to mute the sound. I can't imagine fighting my way through the storm on foot to help them, but I try anyway. Stumbling two hundred feet against the wind, it blasts me to my knees. I don't have a coat or a hat. I try crawling. The wind flattens me violently on the frozen ground. Somehow, I get to my feet and fight my way back to my car. *You impotent shadow of a man.* Think of something.

Does anyone know where we are? Alec knows, but maybe I've killed him, too. I start gulping air. *Murderer. Murderer.* I'm close to bashing my head against the steering wheel.

What can I do? It's swirling whiteness outside. I'm guessing the wind is gusting at seventy miles per hour. I try my phone. Maybe someone can get out here. I don't care about myself. Those dying girls.... Please God. I push the button on the phone. It's dead. I sit immobile in my cold, ruined car. Tears stream down my face. I can't remember when I cried last. Sobs wrack my chest, intermingled with my intermittent screams.

CHAPTER 6

ALEC

MY HEAD IS ENVELOPED in a blast of light and I fall hard, fighting to stay conscious. Blackness.

* * *

Blinking my eyes, I stare at my watch. It's several seconds before my vision clears enough to see the hands. I've been unconscious for almost an hour and struggle ineffectively to get up. There's blood on the floor and the dresser corner. When I finally manage to get to my feet, I stumble to the bed and collapse. Bruce is long gone. I'm seeing two of everything and my head is splitting. The room is spinning wildly, round and round.

Dear Lord, what can I do? Who in God's name would believe this story? I'm not sure where Ellie is — probably somewhere in a car headed toward Great Falls. I think that's what Bruce said. I flip through my contact numbers, punching in the number I have. Nothing. After I think a minute with no new ideas, I call 9-1-1.

"9-1-1 Glacier County. Where is your emergency?"

"For God's sake, listen. Someone is trying to kill Ellie O'Connell, run her off the road in the freezing cold. Someone's got to help."

"What? Who is this?"

"It doesn't matter. Do you know how to get hold of her?"

"Hell, no. Dave Miller might, the police chief. He's her friend."

"Can you patch me to him? It's life or death."

"Maybe. Hold on. Just hold on.

Several minutes pass. I'm moaning in frustration. A cop comes on the line. He sounds troubled, agitated.

Trying not to sound like a raving lunatic, I explain the barebones of the story. He seems to comprehend more than I would have expected, asking several questions to validate my story. I tell him it's been over an hour since Bruce left.

Apparently, moments ago, he got a call from a woman who was with Ellie in the car. They'd been run off the road and were trying to stay alive. Their connection went dead before he could determine a location. We're both horrified. The worst blizzard in two decades is bearing down on the girls who may be badly hurt. The officer tries with me to estimate where they might be, then hangs up to start making phone calls.

When I get on my feet, I'm so dizzy I can hardly keep standing and have barely enough sense to grab my coat. As I wobble down the hall, I stop several times to lean against the wall. Several people give me horrified stares, asking whether I need help, but I keep going. Eventually I manage to wobble to my car and glance in the rearview mirror. Blood is caked on the side of my face and my left eye is almost swollen shut. I have a deep crease of torn tissue under my left ear. Goddamn him for that, I think. I tried to help the bastard. I hope he rots in hell.

Snow swirls through the Lodge parking lot, beginning to bank against tires. The cold is unbelievable, well below zero. What should I do? I have no friends within six hundred miles. In desperation, I call 9-1-1 again, and ask directions for the nearest health clinic. I can't request an aide car. What could I tell them? Starting the car, I wait, shivering as it slowly warms. It's many more minutes before I'm able to drive. I hope I don't pass out on the way.

CHAPTER 7

BRUCE

IT'S BEEN HOURS. The snow is drifting against the side of the car, almost up to the windows. I turn the car heater on for ten minutes, then off for as long as I can stand it. When severe shivering starts, I switch it on again. I'm wretched and grief-stricken. Ellie was bright, happy, hardworking. I realize in horror I'm thinking about her in the past tense. If I could trade her life for mine, I'd do it in an instant. My life is over. I'll admit the whole thing. I wonder whether I'll be executed. It doesn't matter. The only other thing I care about is being warm before I die.

Unbelievably, out of the gloom, a man materializes on horseback. The girls could still be alive hunkered down inside their car. Maybe he can find them. The man jerks open my door, holding it ajar. "You're letting in the cold air," I say automatically.

Confusing conversation ensues. Suddenly, I recognize him, Paul Thomas. He pulls a knife from his boot and holds it to my throat. *Okay, kill me*, I think. *Just let me tell you where the girls are first*. I try. "Listen. Listen. Listen," I stammer. He can't hear me, insanely out of control. His eyes are madness.

He pushes the knife deeper. I feel the blood starting to drain down my neck. If they are dead, I'll join them. Father has surely killed me, too. The death spiral into hell is almost complete, but my urge to live is still there. I try frantically to push the knife away, but he's so strong in his rage. The knife digs deeper....

Another man appears out of the blizzard on horseback. Leaping off his horse, he tries to stop Paul from killing me, straining to pull the knife away from my neck. Paul turns on the second man, who I now recognize as Win Sanders. A scuffle begins. Paul grips his friend around his neck, attempting to strangle him. Suddenly, two more men appear out of the gloom, racing toward us on snow covered horses. Bounding from his saddle, one manages to pry Paul's hands away from Win's neck, pleading with him, talking him down.

I don't understand any of this, except I'm still alive for the moment. The knife had slipped to the ground. I make a sudden move for it, managing to grab the handle. The man, who I now recognize as Willie Long, whips around, knocking the knife out of my hand. All is chaos.

Gradually, Paul is brought under control. When things seem stable, Willie turns to me.

"Where are the girls?" he asks, his hands grabbing both lapels of my sport coat and shaking me hard.

I'm able to tell him, gasping between words. "A thousand feet or two north. Off the road. Down an embankment."

A stranger climbs in my SUV with instructions to turn me out in the blizzard if the girls are found dead. My hands are tied securely in front of me. They all despise me, glaring at me, talking about cutting off body parts. I don't care. If I still had the knife, I would stick it in my own heart. I descend back into wretchedness.

Only one thing makes breathing worthwhile. I want them to find Ellie and the other girl. I want to know if they're alive. Several hours ago, I would have been happy to cause Willie pain. But now.... "Go," I scream as the wind rattles the car. I batter one of the men with my tied hands. "For God's sake, go. Find them." One man strikes me back, a hard blow. I don't care. I don't want to be a murderer more than I want life. "Find them," I scream.

They glare at me with bloodshot, angry eyes before turning away. Three men on horseback disappear immediately into a white wall of snow.

I'm left alone with a man who stares at me with silent loathing. I'm freezing. He has down clothing and I know he's warm. After a while, I ask him whether he'll put the heat on. He stares at me coldly and slowly shakes his head. No. I try to deal with the cold. It's horrible. Finally, when I'm shivering so hard the car shakes, he turns on the heat. I pathetically huddle as close to the heater as I can.

He mutters, "Just enough to keep you alive in case we need you."

He detests me. We sit in silence, listening to the gusts of wind shake the vehicle. He's turned on the heater twice when I shiver enough. I thought about faking shivering, but I don't have it in me. I want him to know I desperately want the girls found alive. If I die, I want someone to know. Finally, I work up the courage to say something.

"I want you to know..." I say, shuddering in the cold, "...th-th-th-that I'm so sorry. I want the girls to live. Can you possibly believe...?"

He punches me hard on the jaw. "Shut your lying, fucking mouth."

I don't blame him.

Another hour passes. We are both despairing. He gets tears in his eyes several times. I blink back tears, too. The girls must be frozen solid by this time. I cringe at the image, trying unsuccessfully to stifle a groan.

Suddenly the radio comes to life. Someone is screaming, "Sam? Sam, can you hear me? Which side of the road?"

"I'll find out," he yells, grabbing me again by my jacket lapels. "Which side of the road, east or west? Which side did you push them off the road?"

"The east s-s-s-side," I chatter. "I — I got on the b-b-b-berm and pushed them across the road. They just missed a guardrail. Went down a slope to the east. I assumed...."

Sam goes out in the storm to check the left side of my car to confirm what I said. The terrible cold flows in through the open door. I shake harder.

"Yes, yes," he screams into the radio. "There's a lot of damage on the left side, too. We didn't see it because the car was turned around. The east side. He thought we knew. Find a guardrail."

Twenty minutes pass. Sam never switches on the heater. I'm shivering hard. I don't think he cares now whether I die. I put my bound hands up in front of my face, trying to keep them from freezing, blowing on my balled fists. The finger tips are turning blue. It's killing cold. Sam's hatred is colder still.

Finally, the radio crackles to life. I steel myself.

I hear someone's voice yelling, "We found them! Ellie's unconscious, but stable. Susan seems okay, maybe a leg fracture. They were in a friggin' sleeping bag."

Sam starts joyfully screaming.

"We're trying to keep them warm. We're hopeful. Keep an eye open for a dozer coming your way."

I put my tied hands over my eyes. I don't hear any more. I'm silently speaking under my breath. "Thank God. Thank God.

Thank God." Tears start rolling down my face and freeze almost immediately.

I glance at Sam. He has tears streaming down his face, too. He seems like a good man. I wish things had been different. I turn my face away from him. I don't want him to see me crying. He might sock me again, but finally I turn to him, "You can hit me again. Kill me. I'm so thankful."

I see him ball his fist in my face, a wordless threat.

I had to say it.

Sam has finally turned on the heater but I'm still shaking uncontrollably. I want to say thank you, but I keep quiet. In about ten minutes, we make out headlights approaching from the south out of the snowy darkness. Sam puts our headlights and the flashers on. The dozer stops. Sam keeps my hands tied but grabs my coat, manhandling me out of my car into the blowing snow. We stumble to the cab and are wedged inside.

It's so warm. I'm still shivering so violently it shakes the seat. When I let myself relax because of the warmth, I'm close to sobbing again. Panting, I try to take in as many breaths of the heated air as possible.

Behind us trail two emergency vehicles. We keep heading north in the darkness. The snow is deep now and drifted. The only things keeping us on the road are the reflective tips of metal posts mounted along the berms. We crawl from post to post, sometimes stopping to get our bearings. Finally, through the front windshield, I see a faint glow of light. Our headlights illuminate a small tent. Men from the ambulances pile out and run toward it.

In a few minutes the men, who must be Paul, Willie, and Win, emerge and head toward the emergency vehicles. Sam pulls me out of the cab of the dozer and we head for the second ambulance. I've been made to understand the dozer will go on to Browning and the ambulances will head back to Great Falls. Paul comes up to us. Sam pauses, opens the door, and gets in the ambulance alone, leaving Paul and me alone in the blizzard. If Paul leaves me alone out here, I'll die in minutes. He won't have to do a thing. But I've seen his rage before.

I wonder numbly how badly he'll beat me first. Maybe he'll beat me senseless before I freeze to death, the only thing I can hope for. My hands are tied. I'm helpless.

I square my shoulders, bracing against the wind. Just do it, I think. Resigned, I wait for the blows.

A minute passes. Then another. And another. I have to lean hard against the wind to remain on my feet. I can see his eyes, the craziness. Finally, he yells, "Just get in the fucking, goddamn truck, Bruce."

He's going to let me live. Before I step into the cab, I turn. "If she dies," I say in a flat monotone, "you can kill me later."

He nods in cold agreement.

I crawl into the cab, into the warmth. Who are these rescuers, I wonder? Heroes, I think for the first time. I hardly know any brave people, except Alec, and I may have killed him. No one wants to look at me, touch me. I've been told Willie's girlfriend isn't in danger. *Please, Ellie*, I think. *Try to stay alive.*

The rear door of the aide-car opens. Two men quickly pass the stretcher inside with unconscious Ellie. She hardly appears to be breathing. Her face is porcelain-white under the oxygen mask. A surge of tenderness and anguish overwhelms me. What in the universe did she ever do to deserve this? I know there is nowhere lower I can or will ever go. Stillness settles over me. I would trade my life for her life in an instant. I'd give every drop of my warming blood to warm hers.

Paul leaves for several minutes, then returns, settling down to hold Ellie's hand. He doesn't accuse me. His concern is only for her. I've ceased to exist — for both of us.

* * *

I'm sitting in my cell. I'm warm. They even gave me several sandwiches and lots of hot coffee. I'm alive and I'm warm. The EMTs did a quick evaluation and decided I'd warm up on my own, so I was brought directly here. I've asked several times whether there's any word on the girls. It's almost midnight when an officer approaches my cell. "Mr. Weingarten, I'm sure you'll be glad to know both ladies are going to recover."

"I'm so glad," I mumble. I'm sure he thinks it's my neck I'm worried about. After giving me an ambiguous stare, he leaves me alone. I collapse on my bunk, wrapping my arms around my head, and curl up in a fetal position. I'm as grateful as I will ever be in my life. Ellie will live and be okay. For the second time today, I burst into uncontrollable sobs.

* * *

I've been here five days and it's now five days before Christmas. My lawyers have told me I'll be spending the holidays here, then be sent home to Connecticut under house arrest until the trial. They tell me as though I should be pleased, months locked up with my parents in our palatial home. If they'd asked me, I would have chosen to stay right here. Father may kill me, psychologically, at least.

I've had a lot of time to think. I have absolutely no idea where my life may go next. The lawyers are all a flurry, running around, lawyering, gathering evidence, taking depositions, and planning strategies. They can't understand why I'm not more engaged. They don't understand. I've basically given up on my life.

I have some money from my grandmother squirreled away. I could live a quiet life somewhere, someday. If I ever get out of prison, I'd like to find an out-of-the-way place, hide out, do a little bit of good, if for no other reason than to push my self-loathing farther underground.

They have Christmas music on an intercom. I'm enjoying the simple melodies in an unexpected way. I like the old traditional carols most of all. The echoes of childhood pleasure give me some peace. I'm not sure whether I ever really listened to the words before. And the jailers have been decent to me. It's more than I deserve. I can't seem to focus on anything. After engineering billion-dollar international business deals, I can't seem to decide whether I should take a nap before dinner or not. Sometimes at night as I try to go to sleep, I find myself on my knees by the side of my bunk, whispering to myself over and over, *Thank God no one died. Thank God no one died.*

CHAPTER 8

ALEC

I'VE PERMANENTLY ADOPTED my identity as Alec Cummings, having severed all ties with the Weingarten quagmire. I'm living below the radar, hardly denting the interest on my investments, in a small attic apartment full of climbing gear and high-altitude clothing.

It's been almost three weeks since my head injury, courtesy of Bruce. I had a serious concussion and, after an overnight in the local hospital, was instructed to spend several weeks on near bed rest. I found the best hotel in Great Falls with room service and holed up, paying cash, and planned my disappearance. After ten days, when I was doing well enough with Tylenol to control the headaches, I flew home to Seattle.

It's the Christmas holiday season and I'm hoisting a few with my climbing friends at the Tractor Tavern in Ballard, a neighborhood bar just north and west of downtown Seattle. There are no pretensions here. Local fishermen mingle easily with imported tourists and college students, Ballard being a bedroom community for the University of Washington several miles to the east.

The rustic brick building was constructed in 1902, now a renowned music venue supported by a modern sound stage and great acoustics. A sizable longhorn sheep skeleton head provides the backdrop for bands crowding onto the stage. Alternative rock music provides the nightly entertainment and is of high quality. The Tractor is small enough that the entire physical space vibrates along with the music. Pitchers from the bar are hoisted overhead, full of cold beer being transported through the jammed-together crowd, to long tables wedged against side walls. Tonight, several hundred music enthusiasts cram the available space with outside lines stretching around the corner.

I sigh in happy contentment tonight. I've never needed the perks of the upper-crust business world. And single malt scotch would stand out. I bought myself a bottle for Christmas but keep it under wraps. Beer is the drink of choice of my crowd.

Seattle is a fine place during the holiday season. The clubs are packed with local rock bands and larger international bands come home for the holidays. Here was the incubator of Nirvana, Pearl Jam, and Foo Fighters, and the new bands of alternative rock: Fleet Foxes, Death Cab, Band of Horses, The Head and the Heart. It's one of the most innovative music environments in the world.

It's also home to some of the world's best climbers — people like Ed Viesturs, in a class by himself, Scott Fisher, who tragically died on Everest on 1996, and two mountaineer founding fathers, the Whittaker brothers, Jim and Lou. People come from all over the country, the world, actually, to connect and form climbing teams. It's been a great place to forget problems. I smile blissfully to myself, ordering one last beer. I've had my arms around a wide variety of local women, while enjoying my share of microbrews — probably more than my share of both.

I'm off on a climbing trip to South America in three days, trying to increase separation from the world I'm trying to leave. I haven't heard any rumors of the senior Weingarten's frame of mind, him dealing with the crushing humiliation of Bruce's failures and downfall. I don't want to be on the same continent for a while. Before leaving the country, I'll destroy the last remnants of my previous business dealings and deepen my obscurity.

Now, late in the evening as the last band winds down, I swallow the remains of my beer and become pensive. I've followed Bruce's incarceration from a distance. Possibly, he can put this catastrophe behind him. He's the luckiest bastard on the planet those girls survived without serious injuries. I imagine he was shaken to his core. But I hate him now. That I barely managed to pull back from the same brink doesn't change my feelings. He set out to hurt the same girl I assaulted. I'm dealing with horrible guilt. Maybe I should allow him more compassion, but he came close to killing me, too. I think of him now with disgust. He'll go to prison unless a miracle happens.

Old man Weingarten is keeping a very low profile. As far as I know, he has made no attempt to contact me. Things have gone seriously wrong for the old man and he knows it. I could bring them both down. Had anything happened to those girls, I would have, the hell with the consequences.

I intend to climb in the southern Andes, drink a lot of South American beer, and try to completely become Alec Cummings. And when I return, I may track down a certain young Blackfeet lady.

CHAPTER 9

BRUCE

THE TRIAL IS APPROACHING IN A MONTH. I'm surviving my time in Connecticut better than I would have thought possible. Mother and Father have been in Europe for most of the time and will remain there until after the trial. I sense father was threatened in a way he never envisioned and wants to keep his distance. I rattle around in the manor house alone except for several servants.

Father made it obvious before they left that he can't stand the sight of me. It's only one step removed from how we've always related. One surprising thing is he can't hurt me anymore. I expect nothing from him. For the first time in my life, I just don't care. It's incredibly freeing. His contempt runs off my back. I give him an amused smile following his insults and it drives him ballistic. He's had me by the balls my whole life. He could shoot me, I suppose. Other than that, he can't touch me. But far worse, I have to live with myself.

I spend most of the time coming to terms with what I did. My appalling attempt at punishing Ellie for my abysmal failure is a part of every waking moment. I've composed messages to both Ellie and Susan — expressing that sorrow and guilt will be a part of me until I die, explaining over and over my thankfulness that they've recovered. I never sent them. On paper they seemed like deceitful lies.

My foster brother survived my farewell gesture — incidental information obtained from the medical clinic in Browning after his *unexplained accident.* Alec disappeared completely after he was discharged. The old man was furious, kept asking me whether I knew anything. I could honestly say I didn't, withholding the information that I nearly killed him. I simply informed Father that Alec hates me.

I'd give anything for the opportunity to apologize, to attempt to make amends for the grievous injury, but he's done what he said

— dropped out and gone far underground. Good for him. He had more courage than I did. Maybe he can make a fresh start in a new life. It's impossible for me to hope for that, but I'd be gratified if he could. I'm abysmally ashamed. Just one more injury at the hands of a Weingarten.

At some point I'd like to have a candid discussion with Mother to see whether anything remains of the person I loved as a child. I tried during the brief period before they left for Europe but could never catch her alone. Father seemed always to be with her. Maybe it was her choice. After what I did, I probably disgust her.

I wonder how long I'll be in prison. The lawyers want me to engage, develop a defense — lie. I can't. I won't. I've told them I want to admit everything, take whatever punishment I'm given. It seems to me the only way I can atone. I want to start over in the future without lies, even if it's after many years. I believe the suits only want to prove how smart they are by getting me off. It's not what I want.

I'm ready for the trial to start. Going to prison is only changing the scenery. I can't get away from my mind, so it doesn't matter. The only thing I want is for someone, somewhere, to believe I'm truly sorry. It means everything to me. But I know words are empty.

CHAPTER 10

ALEC

I'M BACK IN THE STATES after three months climbing in Chili and Peru and partying in Rio. I've grown my hair long after cutting it last September and have lost a little weight, which is surprising considering the extent of my recreational drinking.

I've started to manufacture a history for myself, creating a past that incorporates as much truth as possible. The reason is obvious.... I'd like a friend who knows me.

At this moment, I'm back in Browning, Montana, pretending to watch a basketball game. I'm actually watching Tashi. I couldn't forget her the whole time I was in South America. She's home on the Blackfeet reservation during spring break from college. I checked the school schedule, took a chance, and here she is. She's as intriguing as I remember, catching me watching her several time and smiling. Once or twice I smiled back. I'm trying to decide how to approach her. I'll get an opening. I'm focused if nothing else.

It's been a decade since I've been to a local high school game, but the crowd background noise, the creaking of bleachers, even the gym smell of floor wax, are universal. Unique here are the native drums, foot stomping, and chants which echo around the walls. Basketball must be the winter highpoint for this small town.

One of Tashi's younger friends is the local star, a tall, good-looking kid who plays center-forward and has charisma to burn. Tommy Black River is his name, according to the roster. He's about six-two and has long black hair in braids. He and Tashi have been yelling gentle jibes back and forth throughout the game. Now, just afterwards, I'm watching him joking with at least a half-dozen girls, who follow him adoringly around the gym.

People are standing around talking, laughing, and yelling to friends, obviously in no hurry to leave, when suddenly I glance down. Tashi is smiling impishly up at me.

"Hi," she says. "Do you know me?"

"Don't think so."

"You been looking like you'd like to, so I thought I'd make it easy on you. I'm Tashi Long."

I give her a one-sided grin. "Fair enough. I'm Alec Cummings."

"So. Are you from around here?"

I've been thinking up excuses for being here during most of the game. "No, just passing through on the way to L.A. My aunt used to live near here and I loved it. I took a side trip."

"It's pretty grim here in the winter," she says playfully. "We have to make our own heat."

"Is that so," I say, smiling pleasantly at her implication.

"Yes. We're all going to the Dead Moose Tavern in East Glacier for my last night. I'd let you buy me a beer."

I grin back at her with raised eyebrows. "A little forward, aren't you?"

"I'd call it in a hurry. I'm leaving for the airport in eleven hours."

"Okay, lady. It's a date. I'll see you at the Moose."

"Hmm? That's what we call it."

* * *

I'm holding her close in my arms for a slow dance. She's a little tipsy and I'm taking advantage of it. We've hit it off, to put it mildly. I've been getting unfriendly glances from several of the locals who have elbowed in for few dances, but we've kept reconnecting. The bar's about to close and I'm considering how to extend the evening. What I really want to do is invite her back to my room at the lodge, but one hot evening is not what I want. I've decided I want a lot more. She feels warm and affectionate in my arms and keeps studying me, obviously trying to figure me out.

"Can I give you a lift anywhere?" I ask.

"I'm staying with my brother and he's big and mean," she teases. "Do you have any better ideas?"

I search her face. "Are you propositioning me, Tashi?"

She gives a big sigh. "I'm not sure," she says, suddenly serious. "To be honest, I don't want to say goodbye."

"Listen to me. I have a room at the Lodge. If I take you there, I have a pretty good idea of what could happen. You're very beautiful and I like you a lot."

"Amazingly direct."

"I've had a few and so have you. And as long as I'm being truthful, I'd like to contact you in California. I don't want just a hot night. What do you think about that?"

She gazes away for a moment then looks back directly. "I'd like to chance it anyway."

We don't say much during the short drive to the Lodge. Walking up the long wooden staircase, I find my room key, then unlock the door. Helping her out of her coat, I pull her to me. She has no idea I've been fantasizing about this for months. Her lips are sweet, her hair so silky. I've wondered for so long what it would feel like in my hands. This is going to be more difficult than I thought.

I'm trying hard to keep this casual. It's what I want — at least I think I do. It feels like she's being careful, too. But this is very nice.

"This is going to sound bizarre, but I don't want to offer you a drink. I'm sort of trying to keep my head on here."

"Why?" she asks. It's a serious question.

I'm going to try honesty again. "Tashi, I've seen you before. I was here, coincidentally, during the funeral last October. It's a long story why I happened to be there, but I saw you then. I was interested." I see her amazed look and laugh. "I've been in South America for the past three months and thought about you. I came out here to see whether you might be around."

Now she's studying me. "It was dumb luck I was here. School break."

"Maybe it's fate." I respond. There's a limit to my honesty.

"It's flattering, to tell you the truth."

I reach out and touch her hair.

"Why were you in South America?"

"I'm a climber. I climb all over the world. It's an — avocation."

"Are you rich? How can you afford the lifestyle?"

"I had a very rich grandfather. I have a trust fund. It won't support me forever, but now I'm enjoying the benefits."

"Then what?"

"I honestly don't know." And that's the god's truth.

She shakes her head. "Are you good at it?"

"Not world class," I answer honestly, "but a cut below. I'm comfortable almost anywhere."

"Any 8,000-meter peaks?"

Impressive question. Only a small percentage of the population knows there are only fourteen mountains on the planet over 8,000 meters. An Italian, Reinhold Messner, was the first to climb all fourteen by 1986.

I smile. "Two. I'd love to try K2 but it's probably beyond me. Annapurna was the most difficult I've tried, by far. I was fortunate to get past 24,000 feet." I pause, remembering a recent near-catastrophe. "And you can get into a lot of trouble on Denali. I did. I'm impressed you know about 8,000-meter peaks."

She gives me an enigmatic smile. "I'm curious about many things, Alec."

It takes me a moment to sort out my response. "You — um — surprise me. Away from my climbing community, I don't talk mountaineering much."

"I live near the park. And I'm Blackfeet. The mountains are a part of me. Even though we have poor climbing rock, I grew up hiking with friends. And, of course, we have the glaciers."

"That's how I got in trouble at Denali. I was glacier hiking alone and fell through the snow covering a crevasse. I got wedged in the bottom and it took me six hours to rescue myself. It was close." I shudder, remembering. "I was cold and shaken when I made it out. I don't go on glaciers alone."

Her eyes change. I'm done talking, too. I take her over to the bed and start caressing her. Strangely, I feel like I've known this girl for a long time. I feel at home with her. I feel a lot more. Her hair is so primitive. I want to see her breasts with her hair falling in the peaks and valleys. I want to take my time with this girl. I hadn't noticed before — she has greenish-gray eyes. So beautiful. So exotic.

"Tashi," I murmur. "I'm bewitched."

She smiles seductively and kisses my palms. My hands are rough from the rock climbing. Her lips slide over the rough places, the calluses.

"I love the roughness," she whispers softly. "I like a man who uses his hands. Use them on me."

I move my hands up and down her arms, the sides of her neck, up to her mouth and use my thumb to lightly touch her lips. She reacts to the lightest pressure by gasping and jerking back, then laughs. "More, please."

We both laugh together.

She moves to lean forward over me and her long black hair cascades over my chest. Even with all her clothes on she's the most beautiful girl I ever saw.

We hold each other hesitantly. I know what I want. I want her.

"Alec," she says haltingly, "let's save something for another time."

"Let me hold you," I murmur. "It's perfect."

She lies next to me. I gaze into her eyes, smiling to myself with the secret I'm withholding from her. That I've waited a very long time for this.

Finally, I close my eyes and feel her heat.

* * *

She flew back to school and I drove — fast. As soon as I got to Southern California, I called her. I had waited all of two minutes after I made it to the small apartment my climbing buddy keeps near LA. It took me those several minutes to decide how to approach her. She didn't pick up and I was incredibly disappointed. I had to laugh at myself.

I'm going to see her as much as I can while trying to maintain some cool. I don't want her to think I'm as eager as I am. I'm going to have to develop some cover story of what I do with my life. I'm guessing a boyfriend who's a climber and never climbs could be suspicious. I can get Devon and John to do infrequent excursions if I foot the bill. They're less financially secure than I am. *Leaches* comes to mind, but they're good guys and dependable in a pinch on the mountain. I pick up the phone again to call her. It's been ten minutes.

* * *

I've been down to San Diego three of the last four weekends. I'm not the only guy in her life. She fits me in. When I left for South America, there was no one special. Now I have competition. Did I think I could stroll into her life, pluck her off the vine?

My competition is a good-looking jerk with potential — a medical student who's finishing his third year. He has an obvious career path compared to me. But they aren't an official couple —

not yet. I've met him. He was dropping Tashi off and I was early picking her up for a night out. Tashi obviously was enjoying herself.

Giorgio is dark haired with a decent build. I was encouraged to call him Gio. I'd rather puke. I was tempted to have him call me Your Highness but fought down the impulse. He sized me up as an under-educated, climber dude — did everything he could to rub my nose in it. Little did he know. We were alone for several minutes outside Tashi's apartment when I saw my chance. I blasted him with such a convoluted verbal assault that I could see him replaying it in his mind, trying to decide whether he should take offence, or how much. It was all I could do not to laugh at him. He backed off.

Tashi doesn't have any idea of my past. She's beginning to push for more information. I want to spend the summer near her if I can finagle it so I'm making an extra effort to expand my back-story. She's graduating in June with a degree in social work, hoping to get a master's degree in business administration. Her goal is to expand tribal business opportunities. Her summer is locked in with a job at the community college in Browning, living with friends to save money for grad school. And her adored brother, Willie, is local.

I could fund her degree in a heartbeat, but of course I couldn't approach her now with such an offer. Maybe someday?

More than anything, I want to share with her who I am. If this becomes a serious relationship, I owe it to her. Who am I kidding? This already seems serious to me. And Bruce's trial will be next week, starting Wednesday to be exact. I won't be there for a variety of reasons. Tashi mentions it from time to time, wishing she could be there to shoot daggers at Bruce. I pretend ignorance. If she only knew, I could be called to testify and break out in a cold sweat just thinking about it.

CHAPTER 11

BRUCE

DESPITE MY INDIFFERENCE, there's been a plea bargain which seems rational — a prison sentence of two years. I'm being escorted to the courtroom for the final hearing. It's a formality, a chance for those injured and their families to hate me in person. I understand. I've asked whether I could speak to Ellie and Susan in private and apologize, but it hasn't been allowed. I've been told they don't want to talk to me. One of my lawyers told me privately Ellie is too frightened of me. More than anything else, that makes me terribly sad.

The hallway outside the courtroom is thick with people. The background noise is unnaturally loud, reverberating off twenty-four-foot-high, metallic, ceiling tiles in the hundred-year-old building. Two armed guards are attempting to clear a pathway through the crowd to get me inside the courtroom. One of the guards is forced to grab my arm to prevent me from being thrown against a wall. The crowd noise grows increasingly loud with an angry undercurrent, even a few pointed threats. I'm not used to being jostled and I'm handcuffed, or I'd put my hands over my ears.

It's not a huge courtroom but packed — people standing shoulder-to-shoulder in the rear. I'm led to the defense table where my team of lawyers sits. My body is stone-rigid in an act of self-preservation. If I let myself think, I start trembling in anguish, but suddenly, catching a glimpse of the girls sitting alive and well at the prosecutor's table, I'm overwhelmed with gratitude. It's a secret I have, but it makes me feel a little better. Still, it's hard not to wither with all these people despising me. Walling myself off again, I sit quietly and stare straight ahead.

There's a heightened buzz throughout the courtroom as families and close friends enter and settle in the two rows reserved directly behind the women. I easily recognize all the rescuers. I've realized for some time now how much I owe them — possibly my life.

Montana is a capital punishment state, but in addition I might someday have a chance to have some semblance of a normal existence. I'd like to smile at them, but it would appear ridiculous. No one comes to sit in the empty rows behind me, increasing my sense of isolation.

Ellie is so beautiful. I'm overcome with what might have been as she exchanges meaningful looks with Paul. He sits just behind her, keeping his hand constantly on her shoulder, frequently leaning forward, whispering to her. It's obvious she loves him. It's excruciatingly painful.

I glance at Ellie's parents, whom I knew well, but I can't stand it for long. They're decent people, even quality, but I never gave them or myself a reasonable chance to connect. Her father glares at me with barely controlled contempt, her mother staring with apparent satisfaction. If things had been different, I could have been accepted into a loving family.

The procedure is over in minutes. I formally confess, agreeing with the plea bargain. I'm asked if I want to make a statement.

"Yes, your honor, I do," I begin, taking a breath then choking. It takes several more moments to control my voice. "Ellie and Susan.... From the bottom of my heart, I am sorry. I did a despicable thing. I'll be living with shame and guilt every moment of my life" I pause and take a breath. "As I deserve." I don't embellish it. What else could I say. I search their faces and feel their quiet hostility. The disgust and hatred from the audience is palpable. I'm immediately led away to a small room off the main hall to wait for the van to take me to prison.

I stand alone in my handcuffs. The room where I stand is perfectly square, as tall as it is wide or deep. Back when this building was built, dramatic high ceilings were probably common. The architecture distracts me from my despair. For some reason, everyone is speaking in lowered tones, as if my depression and emptiness are shared. Even my lawyers and the police are standing across the room as though they don't want to be near me. I don't want to be near me either, but there's nothing I can do about it.

The door opens and Robert Swanson, one of my lawyers, comes in. "Bruce," he says, "there's a young woman outside who wants to speak to you. I told her I would ask."

I sigh.

"She says she's Eleanor's sister. She says she doesn't want to yell at you but has something she wants to say. Of course, you're under no obligation...."

I hold up my hands, shackled together. I need a minute to think. Regardless of not yelling, she must want to gut me. Lizzie mistrusted me when I was with her sister. Do I want to put myself through this? I've gotten used to my numbness. It's my hiding place now. Still, I'll have a long time to hide and this will be interesting at least. I want to apologize to someone, but she's not the one. She'd probably physically attack me.

"All right," I say grudgingly. "What the hell."

Robert goes out and returns with Lizzie, walking her up to me. I ready myself for the psychological onslaught and give her a flat stare. She appears confused how to begin, licking her lips. I turn to Robert and say, "I'd like a little privacy, Bob, if you please."

"Of course, Bruce," he replies, and goes to sit on the other side of the room, keeping his eyes riveted on us.

She appears nervous. "Bruce, I never was a big fan."

"I do know that." I say, squaring my shoulders, readying myself for the onslaught.

"I wanted to say — to say I wish things had turned out differently."

I continue to stare at her on my guard, convinced she'll attack me.

"I did see through you, always. I knew how guarded you were. I never believed you loved Ellie. But there were a few times, when you thought no one was watching, I felt you almost — almost allowed yourself to feel something and care. And I wanted to say...." She pauses. "You can be better, have a better life, if you sincerely try."

It takes a few seconds to stop fearing an assault. I stand there.

"That's all, Bruce. That's all I wanted to say."

I feel a crush of emotion I try to hide. No one has said one word of encouragement, not one. But now, a person who should hate me, makes an effort. I stare at her, shocked into silence. She turns and walks to the door. At the last second, I call out, "Lizzie."

She stops.

"Thank you," I manage to say.

She nods to me and walks out the door.

Well, that was something. Unsettling. Of all the people in the world I might have predicted would show a little compassion, I would never have picked Lizzie. Everyone thinks I'm filth — the entire planet it seems. Mother and Father never showed up. I let the old man down big-time. If he could physically harm me and get away with it, I believe he would.

I thought Mother might have at least called. Her one and only child, her 30 year old baby, is going to prison for at least two years. I wonder whether the word has gotten out yet in the social hierarchy — not any old club. 'The Club.'

I'm sure it has. It's hard to plug all the holes and dad's lawyers, even though they drink from the trough, love nothing more than sticking it to the old man behind his back. It's the only way they can get back at him. He pays them well, but they have to put up with his disdain. I should know. Distain has kept me in line my whole life. There's nothing like a waft of failure and degradation swirling around to keep you in line. From one who never came close to making the grade, I know.

I've been thinking about this. I'm not sure when I gave up the honest fight, quit trying to win approval, but somewhere along the line I tried the darker way — a little cheating here, a little bribery there, moving on to fully using people. Ultimately permitting violence. Ellie had become father's most recent tool.

He had demanded of me, "Get her to toe the line, Bruce, or I will. I expected after all this time you could control the bitch. Are your bedroom skills that lacking?"

He knew how to draw blood. I didn't even complain when he called her that. I was too much of a coward. By then Father could have disowned me, ruined me. He knew too many of my failures and illegal solutions. He would have let me go down. Well, I'm going down anyway. Way down.

I would have liked to hear from Mother, though, and try not to let it bother me. I suppose she's under Father's boot to the neck like the rest of us. I wonder what he does to control her — or did. I'm struck with the idea he doesn't have to any more. She's given up. She's a shell.

A long time ago, I loved her. Now I look through her. She's ornamental. I could never tell whether she was happy. Once, many years ago, when Father suddenly turned his face away from a conversation with her, I watched her mannequin smile dissolve, disgust instantly replacing it. It always stuck in my mind. I wish I'd found a way to ask her about it. I can't remember a real conversation between my parents, just politeness in public, or mother's scripted social responses to orders issued.

I'm numb. It's helpful. Feeling is the opponent. I'm almost comfortable here, standing in handcuffs. What do they think I'm going to do — vault out a window?

Robert, the only lawyer I can bear to talk to, is handling everything. My remaining responsibility is to stand here and do what I'm told. I'll be doing so for a very long time — two years at least.

I'm afraid of prison. Bad things happen to people in prison, but it's not the worst thing I'm afraid of. I'm afraid I will cease to exist. You have to have a reason to live. I can't think of a thing. I wonder whether there will come a point in prison when even breathing becomes too much?

I'm depressed. Is there a word for world-class depression? Is it *suicidal*? But you have to make some effort to even do that.

I keep revisiting the encounter with Lizzie, though I'm trying not to because it makes me feel something. Those two years, when I was seducing her sister with expensive crap and trips, she always saw through me. Ellie was a striking blond charmer, twenty-one, when she and I started dating. I even fancied we were kindred spirits of a sort. She was shrewd and self-centered, but she handled her self-interest in a way which made you like her anyway. It's why she surprised me. I know she loves her sister. I would have thought she'd try to slip me poison.

She went out of her way to give me a bit of hope, a tiny glimpse of blue sky. I'm abruptly humbled. The rescuers gave me some small hope for a future. For the same reason, I'm grateful to Lizzie. The emotion is so foreign I have difficulty absorbing it and stare down at my handcuffs.

I turn toward a new sound, movement in the hall. The policemen indicate we're leaving the room, moving to the van which will take me to prison. Apparently, they aren't putting on leg cuffs. They're so demeaning, hobbling along, the ultimate disgrace. I glance at Robert. He gives me a sad nod. He's nearly my age and trapped by my old man, too, so he understands. Ordinarily I'd hate the pity, but isolation overwhelms everything else. Just before I step inside the van, I catch myself searching for Lizzie. But she's gone. There is no one.

* * *

Bars and heavy metal screens partially obscure the windows of the security van. I sense nothing except occasional jostling. I'm trading one kind of hell for another. The best period in my recent past was the few weeks I spent in the jail cell in Great Falls. The guards were — charitable.

The men chatter incessantly in the front seat, occasionally glancing back to see whether I've managed to remove my handcuffs or whether I'm trying to kill myself. Neither is true nor likely. I don't care enough to try either form of escape.

I wonder whether I'll be raped? I have no idea whether the movies about such things are exaggerated or true. I wonder whether it would hurt? How much? Would I scream? Should I ask the guards? Would they laugh?

For the first time, I'm grateful to my lawyers I'll only be in prison for two years. Another despicable thing I did — I didn't try to help the lawyers who were trying to help me. I could have spent decades in prison. I never even said "Thank you."

The van rumbles on and on, approaching the place I can hardly bear to think about. Out of the emptiness, I recognize a profound longing. I want to feel and be able to give love. It's unbearable it's so far out of my reach. I picture myself a charcoal drawing of a man dressed in rags, gray, skeletal, reaching for something — a distant light. I liked to draw as a child. Maybe I'll try to recreate the wretched thought then tear it up. I twist so the guard can't see my face.

We travel through rolling prairie, the endless wind of the Northern Plains blowing last year's dried grass flat against the ground. Plowed fields are left fallow. It's unusually cold with gusts pushing the van sideways from time to time. I wish it were a sunny day with blue sky, but today it's thickly overcast. Colors are washed out of the landscape. This will be my last view for a long time. It bothers me. Like everything else, I took beauty for granted.

On the right as we approach the prison is a large mound with 'Montana State Prison' spelled in white stones on its flank, similar to Montana town's names placed high on adjoining high hills.

We pull up to the security gate with adjacent forty-foot-high, chain-link walls, rolled razor wire on top, and guards posted in tower positions with guns. I haven't allowed myself to think about the physical reality of prison. Now I'm overwhelmed with horror.

About a half-mile away across fallow fields, but within a barbed wired area, I glimpse an ordinary farm with a red barn near a modest house. I gather up my courage and ask, "What are the buildings down there?"

"It's for low-risk prisoners who work the farm," the burliest guard responds. "You won't be there. You've been classified a violent offender."

He smirks at me as though he's enjoying himself. I sink even lower. One minute at a time, I tell myself. Follow instructions. Walk where they say. Do exactly what they tell you to do.

* * *

I've made it through all the procedures and the degradation. I missed dinner but was handed two dry cheese sandwiches and two lukewarm cartons of milk. My cell door finally slams shut with a metallic clang so loud I jump. I'm finally alone. The cell is tiny, dimly lit, and obscene. A gray wool blanket, a flat foam pillow, and a rough sheet lie on the thin slab of mattress. It's entirely colorless. I'd give anything for something red or blue. I become aware of constant noise, a low undercurrent of rumblings of voices, occasional shouts, cursing. I wonder whether it will be dark at night. There are bulbs intermittently dotting the ceiling down the long corridor. I need darkness to sleep. I always took blackness and quiet for granted.

I make my little bed and lie on its hard surface, waiting to see whether the lights will go off. They took away my watch, but I'm guessing it's around nine when the lights dim in the corridor. The background noise fades gradually except for an occasional cough or muted muttering from time to time. Just when I begin drifting off there's a loud scream and angry voices erupting with guards yelling responses. Endless noise was something I hadn't thought to dread.

I guess this is as dark as it gets. It's a very long time before I feel myself drifting off. I want my mother to pack her suitcase and take me away. I feel completely abandoned. I wonder whether anyone, anywhere, has one good thought about me tonight. I feel my heart pounding. Several times a guard walks by and looks in. "Leave me alone," I think, turning my face into the hard pillow.

Once a guard stops, shining his flashlight directly into my eyes, making me wince. "Weingarten. Are you all right in there?"

"Fine," I mutter, rolling quickly onto my side in a fetal position. "Don't worry about me."

I'm as far from all right as it's possible to be and still be alive. I feel like I'm continually shrinking. Soon I'll be so small I won't even cast a shadow.

CHAPTER 12

BRUCE

I MANAGE TO GET to my feet after being jolted awake by a loud buzzer. I've probably had two hours sleep but start stumbling through the day, trying to follow instructions. The constantly escalating noise continues to upset me: guards yelling orders, prisoners arguing, expletives which never seem to end, and worst of all, cell doors slamming, causing me to jump each time. I'm so distressed I can't focus on what anyone is telling me. Things have to be repeated.

The guards are irritable, wanting to ignore me like everyone else. I've tried hard to do what I was instructed to do, but eventually I made a mistake.

It was after lunch and I was supposed to go to the outside yard for exercise. Instead, I took a wrong turn and then another and was suddenly in a dim musty hallway smelling of chlorine and wet laundry. As soon as I realized I was alone, I started to go back. Three men were walking my way.

"Well, lookie here," the biggest one taunted.

I recognized them from the lunchroom. I didn't want to have anything to do with these guys. The one who spoke had been sitting with several menacing buddies. No other prisoners sat anywhere near them. There was a barrier, several empty seats deep, separating them from the rest of the inmates. The leader was huge with the biggest tattooed arms I'd ever seen off a pro-football team. His shoulders reminded me of a bull I saw at a rodeo, but it was his eyes that frightened me, flat and dangerous.

I tried to move to the far side of the empty hallway, hoping to get around the first corner about fifty feet away, even giving them a half-defeated smile before gazing down. I knew something about pecking orders. The leader took a quick side step and slammed me against the cold concrete wall, my face rammed sideways and held there with one meaty hand.

"Ain't you the pretty boy?" he said. "Damn — Designer hairdo. How much that 'do cost ya?"

I didn't say a word.

"How much time ya figure we have, Steel?" he said, starting to untie my pants.

"Ten minutes 'til the bell," a man with chin-length dirty blond hair answered. "You goin' first, Charto?"

"More than enough time," he muttered.

I felt myself being swung around facing the wall, my arms held painfully above my head and out to the sides. I felt several hands on my pants and I tensed myself for what I knew was coming. *Dear God,* was my last thought. I closed my eyes and tried to ready myself....

I heard a voice from way down the hall. "Let 'im loose, Charto."

I felt the hands pause and a gruff voice say, "Jus' turn yourself around, Wes. This ain't none of your business."

I opened my eyes. My face slammed into the wall happened to be turned in the direction of the voice. A black man was speaking. He and three other men stood at the end of the hall.

"You already in big trouble, man," he said. "Just step away. You don't fuckin' need any mo' solitary."

I felt the hesitation in the hands holding me. They finally started to loosen.

"Sure thing, Wes," he muttered. "You owe me one. Maybe one day I'll find you alone."

The black guy said nothing else. I straightened my pants and hurried toward the men at the end of the hall. I started to try to thank him when he interrupted me. "Get the fuck outa here," he urged. "You ain' out of the woods yet."

I hurried around the corner and finally took the correct door to the exercise yard. I had forty-five minutes to walk in circles in the enclosure and try to get my head on straight. I only had to stop to throw up once.

* * *

Carrying my lunch tray, I search for a safe spot at the metal-topped tables when I recognize the black man who protected me yesterday. Approaching him, I swallow. "I want — I want...."

The man turns toward me. I see for the first time how young he is, probably younger than my 30 years.

I try again. "I wanted to thank you. My name is Bruce Weingarten."

"Look here, dude. You gotta pay attention. You were almost ruined, if you know what I mean."

"Yeah," I admit sheepishly. "I got lost."

He sighs. "See here, white boy. I don't wanna be your new bes' friend, but if you want to eat over here, it's okay. And don' you make a move alone. Shit. Everyone knows 'bout that."

I gratefully slide my tray down at his table. "You're right," I mutter. "I've gotta wake up."

"Tha's a fact, white boy," he says, and I see him roll his eyes at his friends. "I'm Wes."

"Nice to meet you," I mumble.

* * *

It's been four days. I'm staring at eternity behind these walls, like a drop of water, trying to fill an empty bucket. It seems to me the bottom will never be wet, let alone enough water to leave this desolate place. I've started my countdown. I have seven hundred and twenty-six more days to go. They let me go to the prison library for the first time and I asked the inmate-librarian when leap year was. He smiled sadly and replied, "You're lucky. It was last February so you won't have to wait an extra day."

He knew immediately why I asked. I was amazed he made the leap. People here surprise you. The librarian's name is Walter. He's a smart guy but made a lot of bad choices, and here he sits. He'll be out in ten months unless he blows it. He had to sit through the leap year day last year — that's how he knew.

He might be worth getting to know. But then I stop myself. Exactly how much am I worth? Maybe I'm the one not worthy of his time.

It's bad being in the cell, but worse outside. I might feel safe eventually, but after what happened before I'm terrified I'll mess up again. It's hard to pay attention to details. My mind is scattered as I try to settle into some safe routine.

The cell is better. I feel safe here, allowing me to consider past choices. I need to understand exactly how this all happened, how I descended into the rat hole. The closest thing to a normal life was with Ellie, who didn't look beneath the surface. Not that I blame her. My façade was always present. I was a master of deception.

I never fully comprehended I had a choice. If I had, I honestly think I might have been able to pull myself together — get help, get out, run away far and fast. Unexpectedly, I sit up on the edge of my bunk and wrap my arms around my chest, leaning forward, rocking and moaning. Stupid! Stupid!

I'd been hanging on by my fingertips. Was I so devoid of imagination I couldn't see any alternative? I always blamed Father, but at some point, you have to square your shoulders and break out. Alec did. Damn it. Alec did. He offered to help me until I smashed in his face in gratitude.

I rock back and forth some more. I hear steps in the hall, one of the eternal guards. With great effort, I stop moaning and rocking until he passes. Then I start again. Is this what hitting bottom feels like? I thought I already had. I start sobbing, muffling my sounds with my pillow.

When I'm calmer, I take several very deep breaths and try to remember what love felt like. I've only been close to two human beings in my life, my mother when I was small, and Alec before Father made us enemies. It's another thing I need to deal with. How could you do that to a little kid? Take away a friend when it was all he had. I shudder at the evil. The poor little kid, I think, and then realize it's me I'm thinking about.

I return to my mother's memory. I'm thinking of the lost real mother, the vague shadow of a loving mother, who roams outside my memory. I can almost remember her arms around me, holding me. I'm not sure.

I do remember trying, when I was ten or eleven, to try to get her alone, to ask her whether she wanted me near her. It seemed to me we were never together, she always seemed to be leaving — leaving the room, leaving the conversation, not seeing me. Now I begin to understand the feelings I had then. I wanted to shout "I'm here. Look at me." I freeze in shock. It's as if someone just hit me on the head. Maybe it wasn't all me — maybe it had something to do with her.

There's so much to think about. How can I receive love or try to give it if I can't remember what it feels like? Can you learn it? And what if you can't? Now I'm really frightened. What if it's too late?

* * *

I've existed here for four weeks, eating all my meals close to Wesley and his friends, keeping just enough space to not intrude. I've said almost nothing to any of them, but I feel safe there. In this place, it's worth a lot. They've pretty much ignored me, and I haven't wanted to push the contact. They're probably barely tolerating me as it is, and I don't want to lose the little bit of security I have.

I spend my days in the common room with its cracked linoleum floor and metal utility tables pushed to one side between meals. Aluminum chairs dot the open area. I talk to no one. Sounds echo constantly in the vacated courtyard. Furniture is scraped along the floor. Mutterings and shouts of the men produce an uneasy undercurrent. I see Charto and his thugs many times daily. It takes my constant attention to maneuver out of their way.

For several weeks, I was the target of catcalls, thinly disguised threats, almost all with sexual content. The situation never quite rose to the point when I needed an intervention by the guards. It finally seemed to peter away as they went on to harass another poor schmuck.

Then yesterday Charto and his gang split up, herding me into a corner, laughing loudly, and sharply bumping into me as they passed. I was terrified, dropped my empty tray, then managed to hustle over toward Wes's table. It was several minutes before my hands stopped shaking. I caught Wes's eye and shook my head.

Today I'm calmer, mostly because I'm sitting behind Wes with a wall at my back. Charto and his boys are occupied on the far side of the area.

"Hey man," Wes says finally. "You gonna sit like a wart on a frog forever?"

I grimace self-consciously. "I didn't want to bother you."

"You ain' botherin' me. I can't figure you out, though. What's a rich po-lite white boy doin' in a place like this hellhole? This ain't exactly a country club."

"Yeah, well. I'm not rich, not anymore. You could say I've got nothing."

"Well, we're even then," he acknowledges. "I've got nothing, too."

"No," I argue. "You've got a lot more than I do. You know your way around and you have friends."

"You don' got friends on the outside?" he asks.

I shake my head. "Nope. I've got no one."

"Damn it, man. Whatcha been doin' out there?"

"I fucked my life away," I mutter morosely.

He nods in agreement. "I know 'bout that."

We're quiet for a while, then I ask, "How long you been here?"

"Seven years."

"Seven years?" I exclaim. "What in the hell did you do?"

"Robbery — stealing car parts. I was 17 and a dumb shit-head and got caught."

"17? And they put you in for seven years?"

"Twelve. I got five more to go. I'll be way over 30 when I get out."

That sets me on my heels. Two years seems like the end of the world, but twelve? A lifetime. "What will you do when you get out? Do you have friends on the outside? Family?"

He stares at me in disbelief. "No friends," he finally admits. "Jus' like you. And my family.... They used my money to buy drugs."

I swivel in my chair to study him. "Any plans when...."

"Nah. But you know...." He leans forward to emphasize what he's about to say. "I wanna beat the odds. I'm gonna get out of here and never come back. Somehow. It's as far as I got in my thinkin'."

I nod again as we sit together, silently considering.

Finally, he asks, "What did you do to get in here?"

I grimace. "I tried to kill two women."

I see him lean away from me, just an inch or two, but I could see it. He asks the question with his eyes. "I was a monster, Wes. I only have one dream. It's not to be a monster anymore. If I can't figure out a way to do it, then I'm dead, one way or the other."

"No shit, man," he says quietly.

I turn away and hide inside myself. Again, I consider whether I deserve to exist. Bizarrely, I glance to look at the wall behind me and am surprised this hollow man can produce a shadow. Once I even lift an arm to see if the phantom responds. It does. I smile grimly to myself — another low point.

But now a new thought intrudes. Maybe the shadow follows me to remind myself of the loathsome things I did in my past life. But maybe I could move ahead. Shadows can form in front of me, too — lead the way forward.

CHAPTER 13

ALEC

IT'S BEAUTIFUL SAN DIEGO weather, sunny in the low eighties and I've picked up Tashi for an afternoon at the beach. We put the picnic basket and some chilled champagne in the trunk of my black Audi and head out. I'm a happy guy. We're headed to an isolated beach she knows about where there shouldn't be many people to bother us.

A steep path leads down from the level of the highway and parking area through high rock walls leading into the bottom of the bowl. We settle down on a worn Blackfeet blanket placed on the rust-colored sugar-like sand. The small beach is surrounded on three sides by sheer rock walls, making it a tall amphitheater that concentrates the sound of the waves. There's almost no wind in this sheltered cove except for the movement of the air when the big swells come in. There must be a major storm offshore because the breakers are spectacular. We laugh because we have to speak between the crashes of the waves on the steep beach. It's amazing what you can communicate in fourteen-second intervals.

She's stunning in a white bikini, which contrasts with her tan skin and long black hair. The surf is too threatening to allow swimming, but we've waded along the shore as I occasionally pick her up in my arms, threatening to throw her in. She's been laughing and kissing me, spurred on by a shared a bottle of champagne along with strawberries, cream cheese and raisin bagels.

I'm currently lying on my back while she tickles my chest with her hair. We manage to do a lot of kissing in fourteen-second gaps, too, and we're laughing about that when I hear a scream.

Sitting up, I immediately locate a small boy who's fallen from the top of the cliff onto a tiny ledge, part way down a sheer wall. His mother is trying to reach him but slips almost immediately, hugging the rock outcropping for dear life.

Leaping to my feet, I yell to the mother, "Stop. You'll fall. I'll get him." I have to shout several times over the sound of the surf to calm her. Finally, she nods and crawls on her stomach to a safer place, all the while watching her son and yelling encouragement.

It takes a few seconds to size up the situation. If he panics, even a little, he could fall off the ledge. I decide I can't wait for help while calling continually to the boy, "Don't move. I'll get you. I promise. Don't move."

I take a minute to plan a route. The boy lies on a foot-wide shelf, down about fifty feet from the top. Directly below him there's a hundred-foot drop. He's barely hanging on to a tiny rocky bulge with his eyes squeezed shut. Sandstone isn't the best rock for climbing, but this section of wall has good handholds and cracks. It's steep, though. Almost perpendicular. Slipping on my running shoes, I grab my t-shirt. "Call 9-1-1," I shout to Tashi.

Slowly, methodically, I make my way up to the boy. I have to angle far to the right to get a good pitch, but it goes easily. I keep reassuring the boy whose name is Diego. "You're doing great, Diego," I yell. "You're helping by being so still. Good boy. Good boy. I'm coming."

It doesn't take long. In five minutes, I'm approaching the boy from his right side as he faces the rock wall. He's crying. I keep maneuvering closer and closer until I'm only ten feet from the boy. "Hello," I say in a normal tone of voice. "You're very brave. My name is Alec and I'm going to help you up the hill. I'm going to use my body like a safety fence around you the whole way up."

He nods tearfully.

"Just do exactly what I say." He nods with his eyes still shut. "You have two feet and two hands. Only move one part at a time. If you move one foot, keep both hands and the other foot on the rock. I'll show you where to put each foot and hand."

Appearing to understand, he nods again while squinting open his eyes.

We start out, working back around to the right where it's a little less steep and the handholds are better. But eventually he has to move off the ledge. He doesn't want to. It takes me several minutes to convince him. Finally, he starts out. He moves, then I move. I keep my arms around him like a cage. In a few minutes, I hear a siren coming our way.

We're over halfway up when I see several rescuers peering over the ridge top. We're only twenty-odd feet from the top, but there's a very steep climb remaining.

"Looks good," one of them affirms. "Do you want a rope lowered down?"

"Yeah. I don't want to chance it if I don't have to."

They lower down a rope end and I'm able to wrap it around Diego's waist and tie a knot with one hand. I heave a sigh of relief and glance up. Three guys are grinning down at me. They could lift him up the last twenty feet with the rope, but it would be good for the kid to finish this. He's safe now.

"Let's let him climb the last pitch," I say.

They understand and smile.

We make it up the last face, foot-by-foot, handhold by handhold. As we get close to the top, he's grinning ear to ear. We haul ourselves up over the last bit of rim rock and stand up. He manages to give me a huge hug before his mother grabs him. Finally, approaching me, she collapses into my arms.

"It's okay," I say, awkwardly patting her on the back. "You've got a great kid there."

Diego is smiling shyly at me. I extend my hand for a man-to-man handshake. "You're the man," I say to him. "You were cool and climbed like a champion. Maybe you'll grow up to climb the biggest mountains in the world." I realize I'm wearing a t-shirt with the Matterhorn on it. Taking it off, I give it to Diego. "I'm going to give you this because you were so brave."

I turn to see Tashi studying me with the weirdest expression. "Come on," I yell to her. "Let's get out of here before they put me on the six-o'clock news." I hurriedly climb down to her level on the sand, and we start grabbing our stuff. I pull her upward toward the parking lot, completing a quick escape. I wasn't kidding. The last thing I need is to be recognized.

I shake my head in surprise and satisfaction. The climbing was a piece of cake for me, but the little boy could have panicked any second and fallen. "Wow!" I exclaim in a flush of success. "Man, I'm stoked. Wasn't that kid great? Jeez. I'm so proud of him. Man-oh-man!" I can hardly temper my excitement, barely able to sit still after climbing into my truck.

I notice she hasn't said a word. "Tashi?"

"You were — incredible."

"It's what I do. The climbing was nothing. The boy not panicking — THAT was what was so awesome. Unbelievable."

"You don't get it, do you? It was you. I knew you could climb, but how you were with the boy. He trusted you. You enabled him to be so brave. I've never seen anything like it. I was very proud of you."

"Good. Being a superhero to my girl feels fine, too." More good news.

"Let's go get something to eat, and then I want to show you how lucky you are to have me as your girl."

It's gotten a little serious. "Are you my girl, Tashi?"

"I give up, all right? I've tried to fight it, but I give up. I'm your girl, Alec. Anyone else is a total waste of my time."

* * *

It's later, and I'm taking her in my arms. I'm still bare-chested. We never made it to a restaurant. We barely made it back to her apartment. She kept touching my arm, my leg, and my chest until I told her to stop before I ran off the road. I drove the rest of the way trying to keep my eyes off her hands, balled in fists in her lap.

This is going to be different. We both know it. We've waited, but the waiting is over.

I watch her lift her cotton top over her head, her bikini top underneath. I remove her breasts from her top, mesmerized by her beauty. She reaches behind her back and lets the top fall to the floor.

Her nipples are light brown. I can hardly keep my eyes from them. She runs her hands through my hair, kneading her hands down my shoulders. "Tashi," I say, over and over. This is not going to be a drawn-out affair. Not this time.

I pull her beneath me. She's pleading with me to hurry, to have her.

It's been almost six months since I first started trailing her. I feel like I understand her well. I also have a lot of pent-up desire. Beautiful, beautiful, Tashi. If you only knew. I feel like I've been waiting my whole life for this. I'm overcome by her wildness. I'm wild. I stretch her arms out to the side, holding her hands as I move into her. Mine. She finally is mine. She moans, lifting her body up to meet mine. I gasp my release.

I want to stand in front of her and protect her. The image makes me smile. It's the truth. And I've been doing it already.

"What are you smiling about?" she asks me.

"How completely happy I am," I respond.

Someday soon I'll have to tell her.

* * *

We're eating cross-legged on her bed, eating Chinese takeout, and watching the late-night news. It's been a big day in a lot of ways. They're interviewing Diego's mother and a grinning Diego, who's wearing my over-sized t-shirt. They're calling me the *Lone Ranger*, climbing in to save the child in danger, and then disappearing in a cloud of dust.

"It's what I'm calling you from now on," she says." And I'll be Tonto."

"I like it. Maybe they'll make a movie, 'The Lone Ranger and Tashi'."

She rolls onto her stomach on the bed and props herself on her elbows. "When are you going to tell me where you came from? What life's been like? You've been very evasive."

"I'll get to it," I say. "But right now, I have other things on my mind." She smiles, giving up, and holds her arms out for me. I've been successful distracting her one more time.

* * *

We've lived a movie script the last few weeks. I come down on weekends, park my car, and literally run for her door. She screams, throws herself into my arms, and we end up in giggles. The term besotted comes to mind. I'm spending some energy trying to keep a lid on my dreams.

She's finished up her last term paper, has a final tomorrow and another on Monday. Then we're off to Montana. In between schoolwork, mutual passion, and eating, we're having fun throwing out stuff: wall posters, notebooks, dried flowers in an old mayonnaise jar, and various mementos. Her old junky furniture, including a scarred desk and chair and a variety of lamps, and a painted aqua chest-of-drawers, sits on the curb with a cardboard for-free sign. We've already given away her bed. Tashi's room is reasonably well emptied, but we laugh over several things left I'll haul to Montana, a stuffed green orangutan and the James Franco commemorative bulletin board complete with his faded pictures. The burned-out lava lamp she also considered keeping for sentimental value. In the end it was also tossed. I didn't ask.

We've separated boxes of keepers, including books and photos, from more boxes targeted for Goodwill, continually adding to the pile of garbage bags to toss in the dumpster.

I've gotten a snapshot of Tashi. She's been going to school on a shoestring. No money spent on clothes, shoes, purses, or technology. Everything is hard-used and wearing out. I get the idea it's been a hard pull, managing pennies. There isn't much to donate. Her tiny closet wasn't half full. It's apparent we can put most of her saved stuff into the small trunk of my car. At my insistence, I'm paying for several large boxes of keepers to be shipped to Montana.

She's done. We've had several pleasant nights with her close friends. Most are graduating, moving to locations far away, so it's been mixed happiness and sadness. It will take all of fifteen minutes to load my car tomorrow morning and we'll hit the road, taking three days to get back to Tashi's world. I made it in two going the other way, but I was in a hurry.

We survey her empty room for the last time after delivering the boxes to be shipped and cleaning the emptied space. The few things to go in the trunk are sitting in a pile in the middle of the floor and hanging on a few hangers in the closet. As a graduation present, I'm taking her to a San Diego upscale restaurant, including tonight in an exclusive hotel. She left her cobalt blue silk dress hanging in the bathroom, and when she comes out for dinner, she blows me away. She is simply lovely.

I hand her a small box. "Just one more present." Opening it she sees a gold chain, dangling a gold feather with three decent sized diamonds. "For my wild Blackfeet lady," I say.

Her eyes tear up. "I may give you some of that wildness back later," she says.

* * *

Cruising up Highway 15, we've pushed hard the second day, aiming for Idaho Falls for the final night on the road. By the next evening, we'll be in Browning. It's been a lovely drive up through the relatively unoccupied, central western U.S., sometimes driving for fifteen minutes without seeing another vehicle. We've talked and talked. She told me she's a generalist, interested in almost everything. I'm impressed with her depth of knowledge and curiosity.

It's been a challenge. We approach topics which force me to deflect and equivocate. I dread telling her my entire sordid story, but I have some redeeming things, too. I can't go on like this much longer but keep putting it off. It could put a dampener on the trip if she decides to kill me.

After pulling into a modest motel, we walk to a family restaurant across the street for dinner, order burgers and fries to go, then head to our room. The overhanging pall of the truth is looming.

We make slow gentle love. An inner voice reminds me this may be the last time. My combination of love, sadness, and desperation colors everything. Passion begins to overtake me as I bring her along, once more stifling my damning voice.

We're lying in the afterglow. "Alec," she says softly, "it will be okay. Tell me."

I hold her expectant eyes for a long time. "Tashi," I say finally, "how much do you trust me?"

Lord knows I didn't tell it all in the beginning. I've talked around the edges. I haven't told her there's a lot more to tell. She sensed I was editing. It's such an ugly story. But she's right to push. If she's going to really be my girl, she needs to understand who I am, what I've been capable of, and to be personally brutal, what I might be capable of in the future. I believe I've changed, but is it an illusion? Maybe I've merely covered up my most inhumane side by removing the pressure. At one point, in the not very distant past, I was persuaded to assault an innocent girl.

Tashi's lying in my arms half asleep with a mellow smile on her face. For the first time, it hits me — if Tashi and I have a real relationship, I'm going to have to interact with Ellie. I wonder whether she could possibly recognize me. We were inches apart. I looked into her eyes as I broke her arm. Can I share that? Ever?

I'm amazed I never thought of it until this moment. The pursuit of Tashi has overshadowed everything. I've never fallen for anyone like this in my life. Can she love me if she knows the whole truth? I sigh deeply. You either trust or you don't.

She rolls onto her side with her head on her hand and bites her lip. "I can tell you need to tell me more, something you believe you did wrong. But you did a wonderful thing at the beach. It has to count."

"I hope so," I mutter. "I really hope so."

She's not letting me off the hook this time. "All right," I continue. "This may be the last time you feel about me the way you do now. You need to know the truth if we are going to go on. I owe it to you." I steal one last gaze of her still-trusting eyes then shift mine away. "When I was very young, my drunken father tormented my mother until she escaped, leaving me alone with him. I've asked myself a million times why she didn't take me. Probably I'll never know. The night after my mother left he blamed me, cutting me horribly with a knife. I almost bled to death. My friend's father rescued me. Paid to have my hand repaired. It took five surgeries over a year's time. He also paid for an excellent, private education, including law school. I have a law degree from Stanford."

"You're a lawyer? Stanford Law?"

"Yes."

"But — my God."

"I know. I know. Let me get this out, okay?" I feel my chin trembling so much I have to clench my teeth momentarily to stop it. "My adopted father has a massive empire. I owed him my life. He asked me to do things as payback. I felt I had to. He started out asking business favors. They got progressively more illegal, more dangerous." I glance at her and find her eyes open like saucers. "I closed my private consulting practice and worked only for my adopted father. I changed my name, went underground, and the illegal demands escalated."

I pause, wishing I could stop. Run away. But, instead, I force myself to continue. "My foster father is the devil himself — a powerful psychopath. He stops at nothing. He steals people's souls — he stole mine. He asked me to beat up a girl, as a threat." I take a final deep breath. "You, Tashi. I was ordered to hurt you." I pause. "Don't you see? I couldn't do it, ever. I was terrified he'd hire someone else, maybe he'd have you killed, unless I appeared to be playing along. I pretended to be stalking you for months, in California. I was actually protecting you."

She gives me a baffled stare. I know this is incomprehensible.

"Think, Tashi," I manage. "Who else was beaten in the past?" I watch her face change from dread to horror.

"Ellie?" She gapes at me. "You?" she whispers.

I nod, my heart pounding.

It takes several seconds. "No!" she screams, pushing me away.

The sound slices me apart. I reach for her and she jerks her arm away from me, twisting violently to sit up on the side of the bed.

I manage to speak. "I couldn't keep the lie going. It's been strangling me. I'm so sorry. I'm so sorry."

She's sobbing now. Slowly I put my arms loosely around her. Any second now she'll push away for good. She'll leave me. Just a minute longer. Let me have another minute....

Seconds pass. She pushes herself out of my arms, but her sobbing lessens. Finally, she's silent. I wait. I can barely make myself breathe.

"You aren't bad," she murmurs. "Maybe you were, but not now. I don't believe it. You can't make me believe it."

A glimmer of hope.

"Do you mean you could possibly forgive me?"

"The man who saved the little boy on the ledge is a good man. I can't let you go." Tears start flowing down her cheeks. "I dream about you at night. You're always the good guy in my dreams."

We're silent together. Still together.

"You were protecting me? Even though I never knew?"

"For months. Making up excuses so they wouldn't find someone else to hurt you or Ellie until the whole Blackfeet Nation became her bodyguard. Then I only watched over you." My voice trembles. "You or Ellie might be dead if I'd refused." I turn to her. "But it's no excuse. I could have brought him down instead."

She shakes her head, but she hasn't pulled completely away. She's quiet for a long time, finally whispering, "Do you think Ellie can recognize you?"

"I disguised my voice. My hair was cut short. I was wearing sunglasses." I bow my head. "My appearance is totally different now."

The silence lengthens. "You're.... You're not going to tell them?"

I ask her.

"Can you tell me who it would help?"

"No, but...?"

She sighs, still turned away from me. "I'm counting on you being the wonderful person I know. It seems to me to be the best thing for everybody. At least now."

I'm stuck in suspended animation while my heart pounds in my chest.

"What about you? What about us?"

"I need some time. We should slow way down."

"Anything, Tashi. Anything so you won't completely shut me out of your life."

She finally turns to me. "But how? Why? Why did this horrible man target us, Ellie and me? What's the connection?"

"The man is Frederick Weingarten, Bruce's father."

She gasps, standing up by the side of the bed, and stepping determinedly away.

I understand.

More time passes before she speaks, "You'll see Ellie. Maybe tomorrow."

"Yes. I'm terrified." I feel my hands start to tremble.

"I'll be there, Alec," she says softly.

As I gaze into her troubled eyes, I recognize real love for the first time in my life. And I know her love hangs by a thread.

CHAPTER 14

ALEC

WE HAD AN EARLY DINNER, after which I dropped Tashi off at her brother's apartment where she'll spend the night. Willie is working, but I'll meet him briefly this evening. A large get-together is planned for tomorrow, Saturday afternoon and evening, at a friend's cabin. I'll be meeting a crowd of new people, close friends, one of whom is Ellie.

I've checked into a local motel while I decide what to do. The meeting with Tashi's friends and family had better go well if I'm going to stay in the community. Dread is an understatement. I'd rather face a bivouac on Everest's summit in a blizzard.

Tashi is currently reconnecting with a girlfriend with whom she may share an apartment. I'll meet her in two hours at her brother's. Returning to my room, I lie on the bed, staring fixedly at the ceiling. I need some time to think through my disclosures. Tashi is handling the truth astoundingly well. Her strength and loyalty overwhelm me. I feel privileged to be allowed to share space with her.

I wake abruptly, realizing I'd drifted off to sleep, and now have only a half-hour to shower and drive to her brother's apartment.

Arriving, I see a blue pick-up parked outside. I remember her protective brother from the funeral, the half-brother without any native blood. Tashi and I have discussed what to tell people about my past, deciding I'll be a climber with some general college experience — no degree for now. I hate eliminating my past, but I can't exactly start with the truth. *Hi. I'm Alec. I beat up Ellie last year, but I'm really sorry and I've given up being an enforcer.*

Yeah, that would go over well. I roll my eyes to myself and knock on the door.

Tashi greets me, smiling.

I hear a man's deep voice. "Hello there. Come on in."

Willie and I meet in the middle of his living room and shake hands. Luckily my hands aren't sweating.

"So," he says. "I understand you're a dedicated climber."

"I'll need a serious job sometime soon, but climbing is addictive."

"I've known some professional climbers. Some of them are dead," Willie says, not mincing words.

"Some of the best quit only when the mountain ends it for them. So far, I haven't been involved in any catastrophes." I grimace to myself. "All right, a couple of near-misses." When he doesn't respond, I continue, "You think it can't happen to you — probably a lack of imagination."

"It's hard on the families at home," he adds, watching me carefully.

"It's one thing to risk your own neck. I don't have close family who worry. But now," I glance at Tashi, "maybe high-altitude climbing involves too much risk? I hear you."

The brother is even bigger than I remembered, six-three or so, with a climber's big shoulders. Tomorrow's gauntlet looms large. I'd prefer to keep him on my side.

"What about you?" I ask. "Sounds like you've been able to put together an outdoor lifestyle and combine it with a career."

"Yeah, it's a good balance for me. And I love the independence."

"It's incredibly beautiful here," I say, smiling at Tashi. "I know Tashi's missed it."

"And I've missed my big brother."

"The best big brother," Willie says.

"Biggest, strongest, handsomest. Best cooker of French toast and marshmallows."

"All true," he says, turning to me. "You've been all over the world, I understand. I saw a good cross-section while I was in the navy, but this area stands alone. And I have great friends here. I'm a fortunate man."

I study Willie. He's quality. I'd value him greatly as a friend. I wonder whether it would ever be possible. Real friendship demands honesty. And I couldn't fool him, not for a second. He's watching me closely, apparently sensing some undercurrent he doesn't understand. I'm sizing him up, too. It's not hostile, but we're not relaxed, either.

"I'm looking forward to meeting Susan. Tashi's told me about her."

That brings a real smile. "She's small and fierce. One of the bravest people I've ever known. You'll get your chance tomorrow."

I smile back with as much enthusiasm as I can muster.

"Well, nice to meet you, Alec. I'm headed back to the warehouse to go over equipment lists. Our tourist season is starting, and I don't want any problems with supplies." He nods. "Till tomorrow."

We shake hands before he hurries out the door.

I take a deep breath and exhale slowly. Tashi smiles wryly. "One down, a zillion to go."

* * *

The family of friends has gathered. I've been introduced around and had pleasant, superficial conversations with everyone. Dave Miller, the policeman I talked to during the blizzard, is here with his wife, Linda. I'm hoping my voice doesn't sound familiar. Brothers Sam and Paul Thomas were part of the rescue crew and their blizzard exploits are brought up frequently as well as their satisfaction that 'damnable' Bruce has been put away. I watch Paul for any sign he's connecting Ellie with my manufactured history and am especially guarded around him. Win Sanders and Lew Black River are Blackfeet men who grew up as brothers from birth. Both Ellie and Susan have been especially friendly, attempting to welcome Tashi's new friend.

Everyone has been interested, trying to get to know me, so I've had low-level stomach pain that is finally diminishing as the afternoon lengthens without catastrophe. Tashi encouraged me to share my mountaineering exploits so I shared some funny incidents and near catastrophes. My rescuing Diego and our movie idea of *The Lone Ranger and Tashi* was a big hit.

The evening is progressing uneventfully as I attempt to stay in the background, sorting people out. I keep brushing into Ellie, making up a trivial excuse, and running away. She once laughingly accused me of hiding from her. It's obvious she has no inkling of who I am. I keep remembering our horrible afternoon nine months ago. I notice Tashi watching us, her body as tense as my own.

Paul seems like a quality guy, despite Bruce's blow-by-blow stories of Paul's explosive rage-control problem. He seems normal and relaxed to me.

Tashi has shared some of Sam and Paul's history, ultimately

intertwining with Bruce's and my own. I know much more of their background than these people are aware of and am constantly on guard not to give myself away. I spent an hour with Paul many months ago, although he's not aware of it, in the Missoula emergency room after I hurt Ellie. My life would be enormously less complicated if I hadn't gotten involved with Tashi, but every time I consider giving her up, I push the thought under. Lack of bravery is not my problem, but possibly insanity is.

As the evening lengthens, I'm getting fewer probing questions. My arm is loosely draped around Tashi's shoulders, sipping only my second cold beer in an effort to stay completely sober, and feeling satisfied with how things have gone. People are starting to bring out food. Several of the men have built up the campfire and resupplied the tub with drinks and more ice. A wooden table is set up across the clearing.

Ellie approaches carrying a heavy cast iron bean pot. Just as she walks in front of me she trips, stumbling toward the fire. I leap up to steady her as she almost drops the pot. Catching it in the last second, I slide one hand underneath and with the other I grab the heavy wire handle, handing it to her. She reaches out for the handle when her hand stops in midair.

A horrified expression distorts her face as I follow her eyes down to my fist holding the wire handle with the scar blazoned across the top.

She stands motionless, her hand suspended in air, reaching out. She gasps. Everyone notices. It becomes dead silent around the campfire. After many seconds, I slowly lower the pot to the ground. We stand there frozen, her eyes locked on mine in horror. I swallow hard.

Out of the corner of my eye, I see a figure barreling toward me. Paul. He crashes into me as his momentum pushes both of us against Willie. "Hold him, Willie," he growls.

Almost automatically, Willie's huge arms encircle me. I hear Tashi screaming and see her struggling violently across the campfire, caught in Win's arms. Chaos ensues. Most people are frozen in place. Paul punches forward, hitting my rib cage, once, twice, three times, each successively harder. I hear bones crack. The pain is excruciating. All the air has been rammed out of me as I start gasping for breath. People start screaming. I hear Willie start yelling as he swings my body away from Paul, partially putting his own between us. It all becomes a blur. Noise is becoming fainter.

I see Paul pick up a large log with a sharp edge, his voice frigidly calm. "Hold up your arm."

He's going to break it. Justice. I slowly raise my left arm. His eyes are crazed. Screaming from several directions increases. Willie raises his own arm in front of me. I glance at Tashi just as she brings her right leg forward and kicks back, catching Win sharply in the shin. It's enough so he loses his grip, letting her escape. She's fast, leaping over the fire to stand in front of me, then holds up her arm. "Break mine, Paul, if you have to."

Everyone is stunned. Paul finally screams, "He's the one, Tashi. He's the one."

"I know it," she screams back.

Paul stands motionless for several long seconds, the log still raised, wobbling in the air. Finally, he slowly lowers it.

I'm choking and discover my mouth is full of blood. I'm drowning. I sink to my knees out of Willie's arms, vomiting a huge amount of blood. Someone shouts, "He's going to bleed out. Call 9-1-1" as I pitch forward in the dirt.

Blackness.

CHAPTER 15

ALEC

I OPEN MY EYES A SLIT, then close them again. My eyelids are too heavy. I'm somewhat awake, but it's impossible to open my eyes again. I hear a voice talking to me. "Alec? Mr. Cummings? Can you hear me?" There's a weird rhythmical whooshing sound.

I try to answer, but nothing comes out.

"Try to move the fingers in your right hand."

It takes me a long time to process. Left? Right? Move. With a lot of effort, I move my fingers on what I think is my right hand, then give up and let the blackness overwhelm me again.

* * *

Sometime later I hear a voice. "Alec? Please try. Can you hear me?"

It sounds familiar, a nice voice. I want to hear more of it, so I really try. I open my eyes and discover I can keep them open a slit if I try hard.

I see her. "Tashi," I whisper. No words come out.

"Alec, I'm here." The sound of her crying seems a long way off.

Oblivion.

* * *

I hear a man's voice. "Try to breathe, Alec. We're going to take you off the ventilator for a few minutes. Try to breathe deeply.

I try several breaths then fade away. I hear a far-away voice say, "We'll wait eight hours and try again."

* * *

When I open my eyes next, it's late at night. I know because the curtains are open, and everything is black outside except for an orange-yellow glow from a nearby area light. I force my head up a few inches from the pillow to gaze around. Two people are asleep in my room. One is a big guy curled up on a cot, and the other I believe is Tashi, sleeping in a recliner with a blanket pulled over her head. I can see her long black hair.

A nurse arrives in a few minutes, takes my pulse and blood pressure, and checks several other monitors. She's very quiet so the two people don't wake up, but she sees my open eyes and whispers, "Welcome back."

I stay awake for a while, breathing through an oxygen nasal cannula. I feel somewhat out of breath. After a while I let my eyelids close and drift asleep.

* * *

When the nurse reappears, it's daylight. While she's taking my blood pressure, she asks me a few questions, name, the President, month of the year. I mumble the answers and I think I got them right. She smiles and tells me they're going to try letting me swallow some clear liquids in a bit, then leaves. I notice Tashi smiling unsteadily at me. The other person is Willie. He also smiles a bit.

She comes over and takes my hand.

"What happened?" I manage. "Where am I?"

"You're in Missoula at University Hospital, in Intensive Care. You've been unconscious for six days, more or less."

"Am I...?"

"Your lungs were full of blood. You have tubes everywhere. They – They didn't think you were going to make it." She bites her lip.

Willie has come to stand behind her with his hand on her shoulder. "We were very worried. They think you'll be okay, now, in some time."

I'm still somewhat confused. "You don't hate me?" I glance back and forth between them.

"Tashi told us everything. How you kept our girls safe for months.... After the first time. Just get well. We'll hash it out."

I nod and whisper, "Thank you." Just that small effort exhausts me.

"I'm going to get some breakfast," Willie says. "I'll bring you something, honey." He leaves us alone.

I close my eyes but reach out my hand. She picks it up and holds it to her cheek, which is wet. "Tashi," I murmur, "I thought you'd abandon me." I hear the anguish in my voice.

"I fought for you. Don't you remember?"

"Yes," I whisper. "I remember."

* * *

I've had yummy red Jell-O and chicken broth. I was exhausted after six bites.

A doctor appears around nine, holding a chart. "Hello, Mr. Cummings. You're one lucky guy."

"I know nothing," I mumble. "What happened?"

"We're not exactly sure. You had three broken ribs. Two splintered and punctured both lungs. They both collapsed, but you had just enough of one lung still inflated to keep you alive. We've had a machine assisting your breathing for the past six days, and tubes are still draining fluid out. I think we're ahead of the game, though."

I try to process everything.

"You'll have to tell us what happened. No one has given us any reasonable explanation."

"I was trampled by elephants," I say. "Leave it at that."

"Fine," he says with only a hint of disbelief. "I'll alert the local zoo they might be missing some pachyderms. You're probably going to have to handle some questions from law enforcement, but we can put them off until you're better." He checks his chart again. "We'll be doing x-rays in an hour or so. Make sure we're still winning." He listens to my breathing, asks me to cough, then smiles and leaves.

We're quiet for a while.

"How are you feeling?" Tashi asks.

"Not very good. Did I almost die?"

"Yes, it's been terrible." Her face crumples again.

"How are Ellie and Paul?"

She sighs. "Everyone trooped to the E.R. in Browning. They stabilized you there, but it was two hours before you could be brought here by helicopter. Dave kept giving us updates. I had plenty of time to tell everyone all you told me. They know how hard you tried to make up for everything, keeping us safe for months. These are wonderful people, Alec. They're trying to understand."

"Ellie and Paul?" I ask again.

"She needs some time. She's scared of you and has hated you for so long it's part of who she is. She's very loving, Alec."

My eyes ask the question.

"Paul's the basket case. He's getting more psychiatric help. To tell you the truth, it's progress he didn't kill you those first few seconds. He managed to plan out what he wanted to do. It's just he didn't know how to massively injure you and not kill you."

"Yeah. He might want to work on that," I say, closing my eyes.

"You didn't even try to defend yourself. He could have bashed in your skull. The old Paul probably would have. As it was, he came close. It's why he's messed up. Especially now he knows you tried to protect us both. He wants to come and see you."

"Not yet," I whisper.

"No, not yet," she agrees.

I pause to gather my courage, then ask, "Tashi, have you forgiven me?"

"I don't quite know."

"How...?"

She shrugs, then leans over to kiss my chapped lips.

* * *

Tashi is down in the cafeteria getting some dinner, and Willie is reading a Time magazine in the recliner, when a uniformed police officer walks in.

"Mr. Cummings."

"Yes?" I say, opening my eyes.

"I'm Officer Miller, Dave Miller. You met me at Sam's the other night."

"Dave, sorry. Of course. I remember you now."

"I'm here on official business to take your statement about the incident — about how you got hurt." He pauses. "On the record."

"O-kay," I say slowly.

"Do you want to talk off the record? We can consider how you might want to say what you want to say?" he glances at Willie who's thrown away the magazine.

"O-kay?" I say again slowly.

"Well, for starters.... Have you thought about whether you want to press charges?"

"For what?" I ask.

Dave begins a small smile. "Like, maybe.... I heard about the elephants. Or if someone hit you?"

"You don't remember? I tripped over a log. Been drinking. Fell off a ledge to the riverbank on top of a big rock. Hurt like hell. I was spitting up blood. Stupid."

"Actually, I don't remember. I was indisposed at the time of the incident, reading a magazine in the cabin bathroom. *Playboy*, if I remember correctly. I was gone awhile."

We smile at each other.

"Okay," Dave says. "On the record. You're saying this was just a horrible accident. You tripped and fell from a ledge on top of a rock?"

"Big sharp rock."

"Okay. You fell down the river bank on top of a big sharp rock."

"Yep."

"That's it?"

"Pretty much."

He scribbles a couple of things on a form. "Anything else? Why didn't anyone there remember what happened?"

"Um.... I went off on my own to visit the river. After more than a few beers."

"Sounds reasonable."

"It does?"

He smiles again. "Good enough. Anything else?"

"Yeah. I want to thank everyone. For getting me help so fast."

"So noted," he says, folding his notebook and stashing it in a back pocket. "I like simple explanations. Hard to dispute. You'd think you had some training in the law profession."

I smile innocently.

"Off the record again." He sits in a nearby chair, scooting it close to me, then asks in a lowered voice "What danger remains...? From old man Weingarten, I mean?"

When I look at him in surprise, Dave responds, "Tashi filled us in."

"Well then," I clear my throat. "I've thought a lot about it. Either Bruce or I could bring everything crashing down. His father should be grateful enough to let us alone." I sigh deeply. "Unless he attempts to shut us up, permanently. I don't think grateful is in his vocabulary."

"I see."

"Maybe he's preoccupied with salvaging his empire. It wouldn't do him any good to lash out vindictively." I grimace. "But I can't count it out."

A glance passes between Dave and Willie and I see Willie nod.

"One more thing." My eyes glance at the outer door. "You need to know. I've disappeared. Until this."

"I understand," he says, seriously. "They have 'crucial/confidential' on all of your medical records, and the staff has been briefed." Then he adds with a small smile, "Well. Glad you lived. Harder for friends to explain deaths. Untidier." He stands, starting toward the door then turns. "Oh, and I'll tell the zoo they're off the hook for lawsuits. Those damn elephants."

They're trying to discharge me. I owe money. The bill is seven pages long. I've given no history. No health insurance. I was brought in unconscious, covered in blood. The people who accompanied me to the hospital stated they just met me and hardly know anything about me except that I like to climb mountains. They weren't even sure of my name. I've asked to speak, with the hospital administrator, one-on-one, hinting I can work something out. I grin in anticipation — the fellow is galloping over.

"Mr. Cummings?"

I smile.

"I'm Carl Watson, the hospital director. I understand you'd like to discuss your bill."

"I'm hoping we can come to a compromise. I have a bill before me for three hundred and sixty-five thousand dollars. You saved my life and I'm grateful, but I'm just an itinerant climber." I pause for dramatic effect. "I'm wondering if I offered an immediate payment of two hundred thousand, you'd call it square? I slide a cashier's check across the over-bed table.

I can envision the wheels going around. *Who is this guy? Should I hold out for more? I might get nothing. It could take years. This guy is no fool. We always overbill hoping to get as much as we can.*

Two hundred thousand in hand now?

Some minutes pass. I sit quietly and wait.

"Mr. Cummings, this is very irregular. I should run this by the board. But I'll get the ball rolling on my own initiative." He smiles at me. "I don't suppose you'd let me know a little about yourself?"

I smile mysteriously and shake my head.

"I'll have our house lawyer draw something up," he says, folding the check and putting it in his jacket pocket. He gives me a grin. "Well, it's been interesting. I'm very glad you lived."

"Funny," I say. "A lot of people have been telling me that." We shake hands gently and I walk gingerly to the restroom to pack my toothbrush.

CHAPTER 16

ALEC

I'M ENJOYING THE LATE afternoon sun in my new home. No mowed yard here, just wind-swept grassland. For once, if I'm still, no body part hurts so I'm relaxed, recuperating with a friend of Tashi's, Sally Winslow, who's tied down with a sick husband. Sally is a seventy-five-year-old Blackfeet lady who can use the money and is a great cook. She's eternally cheerful, and constantly bustling around, doing endless chores. Her hardscrabble ranch rests on the prairie plateau, abutting the road to Heart Butte. The small apartment was available, forty feet from the main house, sitting empty since her mother died several years ago.

Home-cooking is helping me regain my lost fifteen pounds, plus this arrangement takes the pressure off Tashi's and my evolving relationship. Best of all, everything is now out in the open. Her friends endure me, even knowing what I did. I exist here with an authentic past life and I can discuss it.

With some time and distance, I've come to believe Weingarten is a monster of limitless proportions. His lust for dominance and power feeds on itself. Winning is everything and never enough. If he finds me, retribution could be appalling, and I've left a trail a professional could follow. I don't sleep well.

Should I bring the Weingarten house of cards down? I'm going to talk it through first with Willie. He seems to be incredibly fair and pragmatic.

Bruce is now two and a half months into a two-year sentence. I dwell on his past choices. I don't know his inner core. I should hold out an olive branch, but I can't seem to do it. I can't help visualizing him racing off to kill those girls before I passed out. And he could have killed me. He's a damn lucky bastard. Someday he'll have a chance to live an honorable life. It's all I want for myself now. A chance to be a decent human being.

One thing. Tashi has no idea how much money I have squirreled away. I'll need help deciding what to do with it. The two hundred thousand was a drop in the bucket.

My phone rings. It's Tashi.

"Hello," she says with a mischievous undercurrent. "What's your courage level?"

This doesn't sound encouraging.

"What would you think about talking to Paul and Ellie?"

I groan out loud. "When are you talking about?"

"We're on our way over. Unless you'd rather hide."

Shit.

"All right. Come ahead," I mutter with an obvious lack of enthusiasm.

I hear her laughing as I click off the phone.

Ten minutes later they pull in the driveway with Ellie driving her own car and Tashi driving mine. I'm resignedly slouching in one of Sally's lawn chairs, the kind with the woven green webbing you replace every three years when you start falling through the seat.

Getting out of their cars, they walk over to me. No one shakes hands. Paul settles on the porch steps, I move gingerly to the grass, while Ellie and Tashi sit awkwardly on chairs.

How can I say it? Finally, I blurt out, "I'm so guilt-ridden, Ellie, and wretched."

"I believe you," she says quietly. "If I didn't, I wouldn't be here."

"I'll try to explain."

She nods.

"I've wanted to…." I begin helplessly, then can only shake my head as my throat closes up.

Ellie begins. "I know about Bruce's father, and how you watched over us."

I have to forcibly move my eyes to hers. "After I hurt you, I intended to escape, get far away. I couldn't. I drove off on a side road to wait for sirens, to make sure someone was coming to help you."

No one says a word.

"I waited and waited. I was on my knees, throwing up, I was so distraught."

A wave of nausea reminds me this is not all in my past, and I swallow several times. "I kept hoping the guy in the BMW would find you. Help you. There were no sirens. His car drove by, but I couldn't see inside." I glance again at Paul who's staring fixedly at the ground.

"I returned through the fields on foot to the rest area to make sure you'd been found, terrified that you could be dying. I was going to call for help, but you were already gone."

Paul shakes his head, his face dark and foreboding. His scowl frightens me, reminding me of our last encounter.

I pause to collect my thoughts. "I — I was pretty sure you were taken to the hospital in Missoula. I went there disguised, sitting with Paul across the waiting room, waiting until I was reassured you'd recover."

Finally, Ellie murmurs, "I'm glad you came back to help me."

My hands are icy. *Yeah. A real hero*, I think in disgust.

"Paul was much more worried. I just remember the pain," she adds.

"I'll never forget how brave you were. Your fear still haunts me." I put a hand up to cover my eyes. "For a long time, I cried myself to sleep. You've never done anything despicable of course, but it was the blackest hole. I considered suicide constantly. The realization I could try to protect you and Tashi probably saved my life." Now I study her face. "To this day, I believe if I'd refused outright, Bruce's father would have sent another enforcer to harm you. Or worse."

"Is he completely crazy?" she asks.

"If lust for absolute domination is crazy, then yes. He'll probably try to have me killed when he knows I betrayed him." I shudder. "But I couldn't let him kill you or Tashi."

"It means something you risked yourself to protect us."

"I've just been trying to keep us all alive." I take a long breath. "What did you think when you got my note?"

"What note?" she asks.

"The block-lettered one which said *I'm sorry*."

She shakes her head. "I thought it was from Bruce, apologizing for hitting me."

"He hit you? When?"

"Two days after you.... He was furious I wouldn't quit the job."

"Oh, dear God," I say, putting my head in my hands again. "Paul why don't you just shoot both of us?"

"Don't think I haven't thought about it," he mutters grimly.

I stare at his dark face, part of my penance, finally turning back to Ellie. "When I stood at the rest area, gaping at the empty spot on the concrete, I vowed I would spend my life trying to make amends. I threw away the ring — the last link to the Weingartens. Since that exact moment, I've tried to do the honorable thing."

We sit in silence.

At some point Paul sighs, then says, "I could easily have killed you. At the river. It was as close as it comes. You were moments away from death. I was out of control. You don't know about my — difficulty. You might as well hear this. Maybe it will help me." He studies me with his penetrating stare. "After all this time, I keep seeing Ellie when I came around the corner of the restroom. She was shaking from head to foot, white with pain and moaning."

Tears start filling my eyes, but I also see Paul's body tense, his jaw muscles become rigid, his fingers slowly form two fists. For several seconds, again I fear for my life. I'm defenseless here. Prey cornered.

He takes several long breaths, picks up a stone by his feet, and starts rolling it over and over in his fingers as if to distract himself, then glances at Ellie. He seems to be able to let it go.

He continues with a flat voice. "I couldn't believe anyone on earth could do something so horrible to someone like her. It keeps circling round and round in my head. I'm getting help dealing with it. I did manage to think about how it would hurt Ellie and my friends if I killed you. I was able to temper what I did, just a little. I'm trying to get better, but I lost it. It would have ruined my life and Ellie's if you'd died."

I hear the pain in his voice.

"Paul, there's so much guilt. You, me, Bruce. Forgiveness is not something you say. It's something you feel."

"I agree."

"I'd settle for you tolerating me. I'll keep trying. Maybe down the line you can feel it more. I'm trying to forgive Bruce. But I can't."

"That sounds right." His voice is returning to normal. "I can't pretend to feel what I don't. At least we can start with honesty." He studies me with resignation, finally throwing the stone away. "Tashi has drawn a line in the sand with me and with Willie. She told us if we don't give you a chance, she'll leave here. She told us to fake it until it's true." He gives me a wry smile. "I'm not sure that's honesty, but Willie and I get the point. Willie has been looking forward to her coming home for years. It would hurt him deeply if she left. He's motivated to make it work. I'd do anything for Willie and Tashi, so I'll try, too."

Tashi is smiling smugly at me.

"What did I ever do to deserve you?"

"It's what you're going to do for me in the future. I figure you owe me."

"I figure I do."

Both Ellie and Paul appear more relaxed, even smiling at Tashi. It feels like I've moved past the crouching tiger. "Paul, I need to suggest if you're going to beat me up again, short of killing me, you take lessons first. Weingarten Sr. got a thug to teach me how to break ribs, so I wouldn't cause internal bleeding."

Everyone's staring at me aghast.

"We went to a gym and practiced on a punching bag."

"It must have been hell growing up in that family," Paul admits.

It was better for me than Bruce, but it was bad enough. I can only imagine what it was like for him. I need to keep it in mind when I hate him. His father forced us to detest each other — let it be known we were in a winner-take-all competition. He was always taunting us the other guy was better. We knew he was doing it, but it still effective. And the asshole was Bruce's biological father. Nothing he did was ever good enough, but he couldn't give up trying."

"Is Bruce malicious?" Ellie asks.

"When we were young boys at school, Bruce was a caring person. He saved my life, standing up to his old man that one time, pleading to get me help. I hold up my scared hand, then quickly hide it again as Ellie recoils. "His father offered me sanctuary when I had no one. But his charity was an illusion. He molded us to become his puppets. We had no one to confide in, no one to help us understand what was happening.

"He sounds inhuman," Ellie says, shaking her head. "I never suspected."

"Pure unadulterated evil. I think about trying to bring him down, but mostly I want to be across the planet from him."

"What about Bruce's mother? Didn't she ever help him or you?"

"Weingarten convinced Bruce his mother despised him for his weakness."

"Who was she? You were in the house."

"To this day I don't understand it. Either she didn't care enough, or she was terrified of the old man. She was always playing a part, a mannequin. She had beautiful clothes, styled hair, the same pleasant smile when I interacted with her. But if there were any disagreements or discord, she disappeared."

"Did she love Bruce?"

"Early on, when I first came to live at the Weingarten's, Bruce and I would talk about our mothers. Mine deserted me, leaving me alone with a violent drunk." I glance at both of them and shrug my shoulders. "Later on, I saw Bruce look to his mother to stand up for him when his father would eviscerate him over some failure. She wouldn't or couldn't. He was progressively alone. Over the years, she detached from both of us. To this day, I don't know which mother was worse. We were both abandoned."

We all sit quietly, thinking. The shadows lengthen across the prairie. Some of these thoughts are new to me, too.

"Do you still have the BMW?" I finally ask Paul.

"Yes, why?"

"Don't sell it, okay? Promise me. Unless you sell it to me. It means Ellie is safe, cared for. I love that friggin' car."

I see an emotion cross Paul's face, astonishment and even a bit of confusion.

"It's possible I might be able to stomach you someday," he says.

I lean forward on the grass, wince a little, but hold out my hand to shake on the deal. He pauses a few seconds and gets to his feet. I smile at his hesitation. He finally takes my hand and shakes it.

"Weakest handshake I've ever felt," I say.

"Yeah, well, it's the best I can do," he says, but there's a ghost of a smile to take the edge off.

"Ellie?" I say, turning to her. "Is there anything I can do to help? To make you more comfortable when I'm around?"

She considers her answer for a while. "Try not to be alone with me. Anxiety is a gut reaction, but I'm no longer afraid." She smiles. "I won't avoid you, either. We can both stop slinking around."

I'm exhausted after spending another day outside on my lawn chair, interspersed with three daily strolls. I've been at Sally's for four weeks and it's going on two months since I was hurt. The doctor says it's normal to be so tired, but I feel like an old man.

There's still gunk in my lungs and torn tissue, and when I take a deep breath, I gurgle.

The doctor doesn't know how I'll do at extremely high altitude. My dream of climbing K2, the world's second most deadly 8,000-meter peak, is probably ended for me. To my surprise, I discover mountaineering at death's precipice no longer excites me. Possibly, those experiences were a distraction from the hideousness of my personal downward spiral. Now that death has become more of a reality, I'd rather enjoy living. Preferably with Tashi.

I've climbed on Annapurna, enough of a personal accomplishment. An even higher percentage of climbers die there than K2 even though it's two thousand feet lower. I was lucky to get within two thousand feet of the top. Two of our team managed to summit in perfect conditions. *The mountain favored us* is the way the locals put it. I was with three world-class climbers. They're all alive to this day, which says something. As am I.

I struggle to walk a mile, during which I have to stop several times to catch my breath. I used to run numerous five-minute miles. Now it's one step at a time.

I'm just returning from my last stroll when a pale-green dinosaur of a car pulls into Sally's driveway. A Pontiac from the early seventies, I think, as I walk up to the driver's side to say hello. A gray-haired woman pushes the door open.

"Hello," she says. "I'm Vinnie Long, Willie and Tashi's grandmother."

Oh God. I've heard of her. She's a one-person judge and jury. "Hello," I manage. "Are you here to see Sally?"

"Don't you wish," she says, grinning at me. "I'm actually here to see you."

Oh God, I think again, trying to not let her see me wince.

She laughs. "Uh, oh. I can see my reputation got here ahead of me."

I smile lamely.

"Come on over here," she says, pointing at the two chairs. "I ran into Sally in town and I thought I'd drive out here so we could have a talk without an audience. Seat yourself down, Alec. I brought you some cookies."

It's a beautiful late afternoon so we settle ourselves on the chairs in the sun.

"Yes, Mrs. Long, I've...."

"Vinnie," she interrupts. "Everyone calls me Vinnie, and I know all about you. You're the main topic of conversation among my young friends. My kitchen has been overloaded with people trying to figure you out. I decided I'd come out here and meet you for myself." She appears to be enjoying this. "So — you're the reformed enforcer."

"You don't mince words, do you?"

"Nope, too old. Just a waste of time. I have to say, this is a first. Your story is very entertaining. Now tell me the truth. Are you sure you're rehabilitated?"

"What?"

She smiles at me deviously. "You heard me."

It takes a few seconds to articulate my answer. "I never hurt anyone, or anything until...." I stop for breath and start coughing compulsively.

She leans in, interrupting my coughing jag. "What makes you think you won't get 'inspired' to do something like that again?"

When I manage to stop coughing, I show her the top of my hand. "I imagine you've heard my sordid story. I believed I owed Frederick Weingarten. The chains were tightening. Then Ellie.... There's no possible excuse. Nothing."

"You understand my beloved granddaughter is involved, very involved. You're not exactly what I have in mind for her."

For the first time my eyes cloud up and I look away. "I'm not the man I have in mind for her, either."

I sit silently for a while, feeling the warm sun on my tense shoulders and stretch my neck.

Finally, she asks, "What about Bruce? What's his excuse?"

"When I first met him, he'd talk about how much he worshipped his father. Mine was a disgusting drunk. We were little kids. His father was very successful, mansion, lavish parties, vacation homes, cars, private jets, the works. Very soon the happy fantasy started breaking down. He played us against each other, more and more as time went on. I remember once in elementary school, sixth grade maybe, Bruce became editor of our school paper. His father asked him why he didn't do something worthwhile like becoming the captain of our lacrosse club like I did. 'It was something which got noticed,' he said. 'Not writing stupid baby stories.'" I fumble for words. "I remember Bruce crying in front of me in his father's office. I don't think we were ever friends after that."

I lurch out of my chair, starting to pace back and forth.

"Alec, what's going on?"

I halt, turning to face her. "I've been holding onto my hatred for Bruce. Forget all the rationalization, he tried to kill people. He deserves to be hated, doesn't he? But, are we so different? It's all degree, isn't it? And if it is, why should I hope for forgiveness, or deserve it?"

"You're right," she says seriously. "You should go out and kill yourself."

I gasp.

"No. That's the deal. You've already figured it out. Either you kill yourself, or you put it behind you and try to live the best life you can — one or the other. No compromise. Choose one."

I'm finding it difficult to breathe and it's not my lungs.

She smiles merrily. "You shouldn't kill yourself. I'd take the other choice if I were you. I've decided I like you. I'd suggest you jump off a cliff, if I didn't. And I'll tell Willie and everyone else to give you a chance. Then I'll let Tashi out of the trunk I have her chained in."

I look horrified.

"Just joshing," she says. "Goodness, you're a serious young man. I have to go. Enjoy the cookies. Only half of them are poisoned."

I watch her walk to her car, settle inside, wave her hand, and inch slowly out of the driveway. I wince as she misses the mail box by less than an inch. I sit there in stunned silence and pick up a cookie, carefully inspecting both sides.

Finally, I take a bite.

As Vinnie disappears slowly down the road, I see my Audi pass her going the other way. Tashi pulls in the driveway and runs over to me. "How's the invalid?" she asks.

"Shaky. I just survived a grilling by Vinnie."

"I saw her in town. She said she was bringing you some poisoned cookies." She gives me a horrified look. "Oh my God. You haven't eaten any, have you?"

It's a second before I realize she's kidding. "Shit, Tashi," I say.

"Well. How'd it go?"

"She said something about letting you out of a trunk."

"I know she was worried. Grandma doesn't usually get worried.

You don't know her of course, but she was almost killed three months ago. She probably shouldn't be driving," she muses, shaking her head. "But Dave checked her out and told her to keep it under thirty. Grandma promised on her word of honor. And I think she's trying and...."

"Tashi...?"

"Oh. Sorry. Seriously.... Do you think she really liked you?"

"She said she did. She also said if she hadn't she would have told me to kill myself. I don't exactly think she was kidding. It was a strange conversation."

"No, she probably meant it. Grandma doesn't say things she doesn't mean. Good. You're doing well. Ellie, Paul, Willie and now Grandma. I'd say we've done it."

"Done what?"

"If any of those people had a real problem tolerating you, this would be much harder. As long as you don't go raging crazy, we can co-exist, even socialize with everyone." She smiles to herself smugly. "Then it's only a matter of time until they see how wonderful you are."

I swallow hard. "Tashi, do you really think we could work?"

She nods with a smile.

"I'm so happy — for you AND myself," I say. "I know how important this is. These people are trying so hard."

"It's everything, Alec. You'll see. Besides, you need a loving family."

"I do," I whisper.

"Let's go inside," she says. "You look exhausted."

I can barely walk inside without getting seriously light-headed, lying down on the bed with a sigh.

"Just rest," she says. "I'm going to show you how much I love you."

"You've never said you loved me before."

"I wanted to be sure. With everything I've learned about you, I needed time to get it all in perspective. When you were hurt, I shook the whole time. I don't know what I would have done without Willie. He's the best brother in the whole world. He stayed with me the entire time, even with what he knew about you. I hope someday you can know how wonderful he is."

"If he's so good to you, Tashi, how can I not love him?"

She leans over, kissing my lips softly.

"Clear something up for me. Win alluded to an event involving Willie. Something violent happened in the past showing how much you meant to him. Do you know what it was?"

She gives me a pained expression. "Willie's mother died when he was small. Several years later, my father married my mother, a full-blooded Blackfeet woman. "I'm seven years younger than Willie and always his baby sister. He still considers me his personal responsibility. I don't remember a time when he wasn't watching over me."

"Not much has changed."

She nods in agreement. "After his senior year in high school, I had just turned thirteen. I was a handful and boys were interested."

"I can imagine."

"Yes, well, there was this older guy who started following me around. I didn't pay much attention, but one day he showed up at my door. He talked his way in. No one was there but me. I was so naïve, I didn't have a clue what was going on. He started talking provocatively. Made all sorts of suggestions of things we could try. I didn't understand any of it. He grabbed me and kissed me. I finally understood and started to fight him. He had his hand under my shirt and started fondling me. I screamed. That's when Willie got home." She grimaces. "You can imagine. Willie was big and strong. He started beating the guy to a pulp — blood everywhere. I thought he was going to kill the guy. I ran out in the street and stopped a passing car. They came in and managed to pull Willie off."

I start to ask the obvious question, but she holds up her hand.

"The guy was a mess. Willie had almost killed him. He was in the hospital for several weeks. Even though there was cause, the judge told Willie he had to choose between some jail time and joining the service. That's why Willie joined the navy."

I try my question again. "Is the guy still around?"

"As you can imagine, he and Willie avoided each other for years. He lit out, stayed away from the res for long periods, but always returned. He was terrified of Willie. Got into a lot of serious trouble, dragging people down with him."

"What happened to him?"

"He was killed several months ago in a forest fire, the same one that almost killed Lizzie. His name was Red Clearwater."

I knew the story. "The guy who set the fire on purpose."

She nods slowly. She pauses. "I'm glad he's dead for a lot of reasons. Most of all I didn't want Win to go to prison for scalping him."

I search her face. She doesn't appear to be kidding.

Her lips press on mine then start moving down my neck to my chest. She starts to unbutton my shirt. Her lips follow there. "I love you," I whisper.

"Alec. I do love you. What would I have done, had anything happened to you?"

Dear God. Please don't let anything happen to Tashi. I'll do anything, anything.

Her lips move lower. "Just lie there. You're recovering. I'm going to see whether I can get you out of breath moaning."

"Lie with me," I say. "I can at least roll on my side."

"No," she says. "Lie on your back. I want to play. Close your eyes."

I start to speak but she puts two fingers across my lips. "Hush, darling," she whispers. "I'm free all day."

I lie there with my eyes closed, a big grin on my face. It promises to be a great afternoon.

CHAPTER 17

BRUCE

I'VE BEEN IN PRISON for four months — no letters, no phone calls — not one. Nor have I called or written anyone. Several people inside have tried to connect with me, including the prison chaplain, George. He's small, round-shouldered, and thin as a rail. I haven't opened up to him. Why would I? I don't have any formalized faith in God or in man for that matter. Strange, though — I appreciate the way he swings by to say hello every week or so. He always gives me a smile. He's persistent and I like that. I'm starting to think I might let him in, just a little.

Then there's Wesley. I've wormed my way into his gang. His other friends ignored me at first, but I have a strange kind of gallows humor which broke the ice. They started laughing at me, mostly when I explained in great glorious detail how I'd messed up my life. We have a lot in common after all. They watch my back and for that I'm extremely grateful.

The last person is Walter, an inmate who acts as the librarian. He's as close to an adult friend as I've ever had. He's in for robbery. He lost his job, then his house and wife, and was living out of his car. But he had to move it often and the battery died. He couldn't replace it, so he robbed a house to get some money for a new battery and got caught. He said he was the world's worst thief, one more failure. He'd been a mortgage broker before the big recession. He's smart and has a black sense of humor. We get along.

Charto is only one of the many terrifying individuals here, all dangerous in unique ways. I've learned how to survive but it takes constant watchfulness as I struggle anxiously through the endless days.

Listening to other men's stories helps me fight off debilitating depression. They've led failed lives like mine — coping with dysfunctional or malicious families which led to absurd decisions. The nights torment me endlessly with frustrating dreams and nightmares.

I'm beginning to allow myself to think about when I get out of here. I have over two million dollars stashed in low-interest bonds, mostly CDs, left to me by my maternal grandmother. Even Dad can't get at them. Alec knows vaguely. I haven't told anyone else. Most of my prison companions will have to live off the streets. No one here knows of my past life. In my prison jump suit, I'm just like everyone else. I talk differently now, use fewer big words, even keep my opinions simple. I blend in. Only Walter has some idea of the world I came from.

He and I are currently sitting in the tiny space behind the reference books by the ancient wooden card file discussing second chances.

"You can do this," I point out again. "You're a good person. Your son wants you in his life."

He gives me an unconvinced glance. "I'd humiliate him. I let him down."

"Was he always perfect? He must have made some bad choices?"

Walter stops filing old index cards. "He was perfect. I can't remember he ever let me down."

I feel a sudden rush of anger. I can't remember once when I didn't let Frederick down.

"Walter, I read his last letter. Greg wants you to come to Idaho. Wrote about helping you get a fresh start. He doesn't sound humiliated."

"You really think so?" He looks up at me, apparently holding his breath.

"Even your ex-wife encouraged you to go. She wouldn't have if she thought you'd harm Greg."

"I'm scared stiff," he admits, lowering his voice to a whisper. "My release date is in less than two months."

"I know. But you have someone who wants you. And besides," I say, grimacing, "you have to do this for both of us."

He gives me an affectionate pat on the arm before ambling off to get a cart of newly-delivered donated books.

Last week I was trying to encourage him, so I told him my horrendous past. I was surprised he didn't draw away from me in revulsion, but he didn't. At times I let myself think how completely and utterly alone I am.

I wish I had a sibling. Maybe he would contact me. Alec probably won't be inclined to connect since I splattered his blood on the walls of the hotel room. Even some of the biggest losers here have people who come occasionally on visiting day. Every once in a while, I think about Lizzie. I wish I could tell her she gave me hope. Maybe she regrets what she said. Maybe she hates me. I was talking to the chaplain last week for a few minutes. He suggested I write to people I wronged, not to get a response, but to make myself feel better. Maybe I might. Maybe I'll write to Lizzie.

Dear Lizzie,

I'm trying to apologize to people I hurt. I thought I would start with you.

I've been here for four months and am trying to comprehend what happened to my life. I'm not close to understanding it, but I wanted you to know I deeply regret all the anguish and pain I caused everyone.

You probably can't believe me, but I thank the universal powers constantly and humbly that no one was profoundly injured.

I also wanted you to know I think often about the small kindness you showed me in the courthouse. No one else cared. Thank you from the bottom of my heart.

Bruce Weingarten

* * *

I've now been here over six months. I never expected to hear from Lizzie or from Ellie or Susan. None of them responded, but I felt better. I've been thinking about the men who risked their lives, Paul, Sam, Willie, and Win. I've written them all apologies. I used to hate them. I might have killed any one of them when I was enraged. I admitted it all. It takes all I have to force myself to think about it. Maybe I should die for wanting them all dead. I can't decide.

At least I don't hate anymore. I don't want anyone dead, not even Father who hasn't allowed my mother to contact me. Or worse, maybe she doesn't care enough to bother. I've started talking to George and discover he's become a friend. He has a very caring nature. In my old life, I would have mocked a person like him.

Now he helps keep me sane. I'm glad to see him coming down the hall.

The mail just came and miraculously there's something for me. It's a letter from Lizzie. I haven't opened it yet. I find I'm so excited I want to put it off. I'm also afraid. It might not be encouraging. If I don't open it, I can pretend it's from a friend with kind words.

It's after dinner and I'm back in my cell. It's lights out in a half hour. I still haven't opened the letter. I take a deep breath. Okay. Here goes...

Dear Bruce,

I'm sorry I took so long to write back. I've had some difficult things in my life, but they have worked out and I'm back with Win. His family ranch is the place I'm planning to spend the rest of my life if he'll let me. We're going to be married at Thanksgiving.

I've thought about you often and hoped you were finding some peace. As time passes, all of us involved in the blizzard are going on with our lives. I hardly think about it. Life pushes us forward. It didn't end in a tragedy, so we have all have moved on.

My life is full of good teaching experiences, love of Win, our friends, and happy times in Browning and East Glacier.

I am learning to ride a horse rather well and spend time with Win's sister, Alice, training young horses here at the ranch. Write again, if you'd like. I'll share our correspondences with Win.

Lizzie

I'm lying in my bunk, thinking about what Lizzie wrote. I wonder what happened in her life which caused her pain, but happy she and Win are together if it's what she wants. I remember him punching me in the mouth and knocking out teeth. My shift in perspective astounds me. I now recognize the blizzard rescuers as heroes. I want to apologize in person to atone, but it's probably impossible they would tolerate me in any way.

It was a wonderful letter, a gift I didn't deserve. As smart as I thought I was in the old dark days, I was an asshole of monumental proportions, somehow believing myself deserving of three-hundred-dollar bottles of wine, trips to Europe in corporate jets, $10,000 weekends in Paris or London, and rows of suits hanging in even spaces in huge closets. I sigh deeply. And what good did it all ever do me? Today, after six months in prison, I would trade it all for a letter from a friend — if I can call Lizzie my friend. The longer I'm here, the less I want. A sudden feeling of warmth rushes over me. I realize I'm happy lying here, on my thread-bare mattress, making pictures in my head of a ranch near Browning, Montana, and young horses learning to be handled. Maybe Lizzie would send me a few pictures. I'm going to make myself wait a month or so before I answer the letter. I don't want to risk being a pest.

Eight weeks ago, I was assigned a job working in the prison business office paying bills. They don't let me directly handle any money, of course, but I help organize things, run errands, and clean up. Everyone was formal and aloof at the start, careful with emotional interactions and personal details, but after several weeks it appeared it became more trouble than it was worth to keep the distance. I believe they came to like me.

I've started providing information from my old financial days on how they should invest their retirement accounts. No one provides adequate support for employees untrained in money management. Arnold, the department curmudgeon, continued to glower at me for several more weeks, but finally came around one afternoon last week, admitting he needed help to reason out a life-insurance decision. He grudgingly muttered his thanks, and I moved him over into the win column.

As time goes on, I've been given more responsibility. The office staff shares some of their everyday problems and joys. I'm starting to care about them. I'm happy when their kids win a basketball game or are in a school play. I watched a video of Cliff's seven-year-old daughter who was a fairy and waved a wand with enormous enthusiasm. He was extremely proud.

My favorite cashier, Charlotte, even asks me for ideas on how to handle her challenging 14 year old son — like I'm the one to ask. *Just don't send him out to kill anyone*.

I'm using my lunch hour to write to Lizzie. I've dutifully waited the four weeks, but think I can do it now without appearing so needy, which of course I am.

Dear Lizzie,

I don't want to make a pest of myself but thank you sincerely for your last letter. It's hard to admit yours was the first letter I received since I arrived here. It made me happy. I'm discovering the joy a simple thing like a letter or a smile from a co-worker can bring.

Yes, I do have a regular job here. I'm the world's best prison assistant-assistant accounts payable person. I get to help pay for such important stuff as toilet paper, printer ink cartridges and socks. Seriously, it's probably the most important work I've done in my life. I used to move money around.

I'm glad you are so happy with Win and you have many positive things in your life now. I think about training young horses. If I could do that, I would be the happiest man on earth. I'd love to do something in the free fresh air in vast open spaces when I get out. I'd like to never put on a suit again.

Bruce

P.S. Do you think you could send a picture or two of the horses and the ranch?

CHAPTER 18

ALEC

IT'S AN UNUSUALLY WARM saturday afternoon in late November, two days after Thanksgiving. Many friends have spent days preparing for Lizzie and Win's wedding, filling the ranch house with dried grasses, white plumes of local bear grass, orange and gold flowers, and red berries. That I was invited at all overwhelms me with humble gratitude. I've been slowly accepted into the group, mostly due to love directed at Tashi.

Win and Lizzie's ceremony combined Catholic rites provided by a local priest representing Lizzie's upbringing, and a Blackfeet shaman incorporating traditional elements. I was deeply moved. The shaman's words more closely represented my personal views of oneness with the earth and the universe and harmony with all.

The event itself was held in Win's mother's living room of the family home on the ancestral six hundred-acre Sanders ranch, land which has been in the family since the late 1800's. The house is pale gray green, a classic two-story farmhouse style, set out on a high plateau overlooking Two Medicine River. The land itself comprises almost a square mile of hayed-off grassland, alternating with fields of spent wildflowers. The house and barn are reached by a two-track road extending all the way from the main highway. The boundary of the ranch accommodates to the varied topography, plunging down a steep hillside, cut through by deep ravines, and ultimately descending to the northern banks of the river. The water below is brilliant silver in the reflective light. I take deep breath after deep breath for the simple joy of taking in some of the freshest air on earth. Golden afternoon sunlight slants from the descending sun as it approaches the mountain peaks to the west.

People start spilling out to join me on Sarah's long front porch for more pictures. Everyone is glowing with happiness as we watch the main wedding party now stepping outside. Win, an elegant and classic native man, has his long black hair tied back in the traditional

Blackfeet style, which is surprisingly perfect, overlaying a tailored black tux. Lizzie is a world-class beauty, a plain and simple fact, dressed in the simplest of unadorned, strapless, cream satin. They both appear exquisitely happy, but in my entire life I've never seen a man so deeply moved by this turn of fortune than Win. His love for Lizzie is worn externally.

There were only two attendants: Paul in a tux as best man, and Ellie as maid-of-honor in a dress of deeper cream satin. I settle myself happily in a far corner of the porch, watching the picture taking. It gives me peaceful time to consider this interconnected group.

Several people catch my eye. Lizzie's parents appear extraordinarily pleased. I had a moment earlier to talk to Sean O'Connell, Lizzie and Ellie's father. I forced the issue. I'm not sure why. I know her father would rather have kept his distance from me, even though both Lizzie and Win have been working on him.

"Win is an incredible man," I began.

"He's unique," he replied, not completely meeting my eyes. "A rare combination of warrior and intellectual. And it doesn't hurt he's besotted with my daughter. I believe they'll be deeply in love their whole lives."

"And Paul?"

He gives me a complicated smile with some irony, possibly because Paul punished me in a way he would have endorsed.

I understand his antipathy. Returning his wry smile, I respond by saying, "I respect Paul, but we've had a complicated history."

I'm of the opinion that Sean is enjoying my discomfort. Finally, he continues, "He and Win are so much alike, both battlers. It's no wonder — the closeness they feel for each other. And he makes Ellie feel treasured."

I cleared my throat, working up my courage. "I wanted to say.... I know you've heard my story by now. I hope for your forgiveness someday."

He turned then, now studying me seriously. "I believe in redemption. You tried to protect Tashi and Ellie. She and I have talked about it. But give me and Jeanne some time."

I nodded, agreeing with him.

Tashi comes and goes, giving me frequent hugs before flying away to spend time with her family and friends. I've let her know

I'm in a happy place, generally accepted by people who know the real me, even acknowledged by Ellie and Paul. I've had a mask on for decades.

There's no wind today, which is unusual for this time of year, the last rays of the southwest afternoon sun warm the porch setting. The picture taking goes on endlessly with seemingly thousands of combinations. Several were taken with me grinning down at Tashi, my head turned to avoid a full-faced picture. I want to continue to not exist. Vinnie has been central in many, but finally comes to join me at the end of the deck.

"Phew," she says. "I have this one smile, and I've been plastering it on my face for half an hour. My jaw hurts."

"Tough life," I manage, coughing a bit after taking a conspiratorial breath. Even after five months, I can still feel the roughness when I inhale deeply.

She studies me with a droll expression. "You've settled in well, haven't you?"

"I'm accepted here," I smile back at her. "It's a gift beyond measure."

She nods seriously. "I often wonder how Bruce is getting along."

"I have trouble caring after he broke my face." I admit. "I should, I suppose. He had the same misery I had, doubled. I got a letter from him, trying to apologize, saying how sorry he was."

"I've heard several people did. I wonder whether he meant it."

"I imagine he meant it. I'm sure he's sorry, but I don't know whether he's mostly sorry for himself."

"What are you two talking about?" Lizzie interrupts as she and Ellie come over, arm in arm.

I feel like I've been caught doing something wrong. "Bruce," I admit.

"I was wondering whether he feels real regret?" Vinnie asks. "I know he's tried to say he was sorry."

"I got an apology," Ellie reveals. "I threw it away. I wanted to read other people's letters to see whether they were Xerox copies." Then she smiles grudgingly. "I'm not ready to forgive. Mostly, I like him where he is."

"I answered mine," Lizzie says.

"What?" Both Ellie and I say together.

"Yes.... I.... His letter was so sad, so modest. I wanted to give him a little encouragement."

"He tried to kill me," Ellie says.

"I know. But thank God...."

"Enough," Ellie declares. "Okay? Just don't invite him over for brunch."

"No. I won't. I promise. But...." Then she gives it up.

They get ready to move on when Vinnie says to Lizzie. "You are a beautiful woman, Lizzie, in every way. Give an old lady a kiss."

Lizzie walks over and gives Vinnie a long hug and kiss before the two girls move off arm-in-arm. I stand silently with Vinnie, considering what I just saw.

"What do you think of that?" she asks eventually.

"I feel like I've just been taught a lesson, but I'm not sure what it is."

"You have, my boy, you have. You can give me a kiss, too. I'm collecting them today."

"It's a privilege, Vinnie. It makes this wedding day perfect."

CHAPTER 19

BRUCE

I'VE BEEN HERE almost eight months now and am surprisingly content. How anyone can be happy in prison is a mystery, and probably says a lot about how my life was before. I don't have any stress, now that I've learned how to stay out of trouble, and I've made some friends. The bad guys have given up on me and moved on to more vulnerable targets. Walter from the library got his release and wrote me a letter. He also e-mails me on the special monitored prison system, but I made such a fuss over Lizzie's letter, he figured he'd write me one, too. He's in Idaho and has found a job in a sub shop, which is a start — plus he's near his son. It gives me great satisfaction.

Chaplain George considers me one of his greatest success stories — not that he's converted me to anything, but I started out as such a tormented mess and have improved so much.

My co-workers bring me special treats from home. Christmas is coming up in a week and I got roped into helping with the inmate Christmas show. I have absolutely no talent, but they needed someone to do the spotlights, so I volunteered. The rehearsals are hilarious, mostly because most of the star attractions have absolutely no talent either. Wes is the one exception. He plays beautiful bass guitar. He's even encouraged me to ask permission to get a cheap instrument so he could give me lessons. I did it. He doesn't know, but it's the most valuable gift anyone has ever given me — a gift of their time.

Day after tomorrow is the last visiting day before Christmas and several of my friends are having relatives coming from out of the area. I'm trying not to feel down, but the holidays have always been hard for me, even when I was small. I always knew there was something missing.

Wonderful news. I just received a Christmas card from Lizzie. As usual I wait until I'm back in my cell to open it. Just having it in my pocket has made it a special day. I also got a card from my mother, postmarked in Saltsburg, Austria, over a week ago. Inside was a long form letter sent out to the thousand or so people they wanted to impress.

There was a note, scrawled quickly on the bottom in my mother's handwriting, almost as an afterthought, saying she missed me, especially during the holidays, and hoped I was well. She said she 'desperately' wished I could be there with her. Strangely, the letter had been opened and resealed, not the traditional slit they do here to monitor mail. Maybe Mother felt obligated to say something personal. After all this time, I doubt the sincerity of anything she writes. It seemed to me it was like the obligatory Christmas Eve church visit, but I tried not to feel bitter. It was the first communication I've received from Mother since I've been here. I didn't get mentioned at all in the form letter to the thousand friends. I guess having your son secure a job in the prison accounting department didn't make the cut.

I can't wait any longer, so I open my card from Lizzie. It's a Charlie Brown Christmas card with Snoopy lying on his decorated doghouse roof with all his bird friends visiting for Christmas.

Dear Bruce,

We are gathering for Christmas at Sam and Cora's cabin. Since you are not too far from here, you know we've had a lot of snow, but the roads are passible. Enclosed are some of the pictures you requested of the Sanders family ranch. His sister and I are working with some of her young horse students. Win is taking the pictures and making faces at us, which is why we both look like idiots.

He and I were married at Thanksgiving and I'm completely content. The beautiful longhaired woman is Alice, my new sister-in-law. Her life revolves around the horses and I'm lucky enough to get to work with her. She is magic with young colts and fillies, so much patience. The rest of the pictures are of the family ranch. Of course, it's his mom's now. Win and I hope to build a house not far from where these pictures were taken.

Are you ready for a surprise? Win and I are coming down on visiting day to see you with a few small Christmas gifts. See you then.

Lizzie

I'm going to have Christmas visitors bringing presents! I scramble to think of anything I could give Lizzie. I doubt she'd like a laced wallet they make in arts and crafts. I'll think about it. I'm amazed Win is coming, too. It's the first time I've seen any of the rescuers in person. I wanted to say something specifically to him in the letters to Lizzie, but it always seems like pandering or worse. He probably wants to make sure I'm not going to jump over some barrier and attack her, but it's still nice. I decide I'll think good thoughts, not muck it up. Still, I'm nervous.

* * *

It's one o'clock and I'm allowed to go into the visitor's area. I've never been here before and don't exactly know how to act. There are ten metal utility tables and chairs, and as I come in Win and Lizzie stand and she smiles. It's awkward. It's not as though these are old friends. Lizzie is even more beautiful than I remember, her cheeks flushed with anticipation. Win is understandably reticent. Still, I feel an aura of curiosity and tolerance from him rather than hostility.

"Hello, Bruce. How are you?" Lizzie asks.

"Self-conscious," I manage. "It's easier in a letter."

"Just relax," Win says. "We don't know how to act, either."

"It means a lot you came." I hesitate, trying to express my thoughts.

"It's going on a year," Lizzie offers. "Have you thought about what you'll do when you get out?"

"It seems a long way off to me. Still, this isn't so bad. Everyone here is similarly stuck. I think of soldiers in Afghanistan, and this feels pretty comfortable. No one's shooting at me, I get three meals a day and I'm warm." I groan inwardly, wishing I hadn't brought up the reminder of the blizzard catastrophe.

"An understandable perspective," Win adds with raised eyebrows.

I understand immediately he recognized my specific discomfort. It's several moments before I can continue. "You're changed in a place like this. Torn apart, then put back together. But, no, I have no plans. Not yet. My parents aren't going to welcome me home."

We're quiet for a few uncomfortable moments when Lizzie

changes the subject. "Did you like the pictures?"

"The setting is breathtaking," I say, suddenly overwhelmed with emotion. "Incredible, but more than that...." I struggle to find the exact words. "They are the essence of a real home. I study them often, especially before I go to sleep, imagining what living there would be like." I clear my throat. "I need to express.... Your letters and encouragement have meant a lot, Lizzie. I don't understand how you can do it. Especially," I smile wryly, "since you always hated me."

"That's too strong. I'd have called it cautious disgust."

I choke and laugh. "Then why?"

"I guess it's because I always go for the underdog. And you were the under-ist-dog I ever saw in the courtroom."

I nod my head in resignation. "And you, Win? Why are you here?"

"Several reasons. First, I don't know you at all and don't trust you."

I smile at his honesty, gradually getting to know a very complex man.

"I didn't know if you could cause Lizzie psychological pain. And second," he smiles wryly, "I was damn curious. You've always been an interesting dude."

"Yes," I concede with a smile. "Interesting I am. It's nice to see you when we're not trying to kill each other. We had a shaky beginning."

"Good way to describe it," he adds, obviously enjoying the memory.

"Just coming through security today must have been unpleasant. I'm grateful you came with Lizzie. I would never want to hurt her in any way." I risk a fervent glance at her. "She has a generosity of spirit that leaves me in awe."

Win turns to study her with such affection that it embarrasses me.

"Her kindness is a boundless gift," he says carefully.

"It's been everything," I say quietly. "Just to be given a little hope. I've come from a very, very low place. Now my only wish is to do some good someday."

Win scrutinizes me with an intensity that makes me squirm in my seat.

"And.... And I want to tell you how happy I am for you both. I understand you just got married."

"Yes," Win says. "I'm a very fortunate man."

"Yes," I agree. "You are."

"You seem good, Bruce," Lizzie says. "I'm surprised. I thought prison would — I don't know — hollow you out. But you seem stronger somehow."

"I feel stronger. I don't want to go into it, but my life before had been constant mental earthquakes."

"Alec has told us...." Lizzie says, then apparently regrets giving out that information.

"I didn't know he was up there," I blurt out.

Win interrupts, "He doesn't want it known. By anyone — especially your father."

"No. No, of course not. You can tell him. If my life depended on it."

We all sit silently staring at each other.

I sigh deeply, then continue. "Alec had a lot of reasons to hate and rose above it. At one point, I despised him for his lack of loyalty. But he was heroic, the courageous one. I know that now. If you get a chance, you might tell him. I wrote him, but.... Well, anyway...." I glance down at my hands.

Changing the mood, Lizzie lifts a shopping bag onto the tabletop and smiles. "Bruce, look. We brought presents."

"Before you do, I have a small gift for you. Can I do mine first?"

"Of course."

I glance at the guard who nods. I had to get special permission to hand her this gift. I pull out the pen and ink drawing I completed in the library yesterday. It's a copy of Lizzie's photo of one of the foals with Win's sister bent over hugging him. "I used to love to draw as a kid. It turned out better than I expected."

They study the picture closely. "It's incredible," Win says. "You captured Alice perfectly."

"I'm going to have it framed to match your small Russell pen and ink drawing," Lizzie says.

She lifts out of a paper bag a tiny Christmas tree decorated with Hershey's kisses and two other wrapped packages. They obviously have been unwrapped by security and rewrapped.

"Go on. Open them," she smiles.

The first one is a small photo album. "It's for your pictures. I'll send more."

I open the cover and see more pictures of the ranch in deep new snow, horses playing in it, and the ranch house appearing like a Christmas card with a wreath on the front door.

"It's paradise, Lizzie."

She smiles warmly in agreement. "The second one is from Win."

The smallest package is a beaded Blackfeet bracelet of blue and white beads with leather fasteners. I put it on.

"I need to tell you...." I can't continue.

"I have one more gift," Win says. "I wasn't sure how this would go. I needed to feel your spirit first. I now believe you are trying your best. When you get out, Lizzie and I want you to come up to see the ranch. Something for you to look forward to."

I have to wait until the lump in my throat resolves before I'm able to say, "No one in my entire life has given me a greater gift."

They stand, we shake hands, and they're gone.

I somehow make it back to my cell and crash on my bunk, unable to move as I think this all through. Tears form. In different circumstances, I wonder what kind of life I might have had.

For some reason, I wake up in the middle of the night. There's dim light from the outer hall, enough to see my little tree. As I come to consciousness, I realize I have the photo album on my chest. I feel the bracelet on my wrist. It's already a better Christmas than any I can remember.

CHAPTER 20

ALEC

THE SPRING AND SUMMER MONTHS have flown by without problems surfacing related to my past. Occasionally, I wonder if the old man has discovered my whereabouts, but even those thoughts are rare. Apparently, he can't afford the connection a retribution might bring. And Bruce could choose to bring any foul-play out into the open. He has little to lose now.

The summer tourist season is coming to a glorious end. The aspen trees are deep yellow now with the sky turning cobalt blue above them as evening approaches. I've developed an enduring love for the Northern Great Plains and the Park. Willie's Uncle Nick wants at least two more seasons, then plans to sell out to Willie. I've been allowed to guest guide for Willie's Glacier Park tour business. It went so seamlessly that Willie is considering having me employed in the business permanently. This turn of events and would be the answer to my life's dream of working outdoors in the mountains. I owe my good fortune completely to Willie's generous spirit. We recently discussed him giving me this opportunity, knowing my past. He smiled and replied, "I'm Vinnie's grandson. She's big on second chances." Bless them both.

The pay is meaningless. No one here knows that, not even Tashi. They would all be aghast at the huge fortune I have squirreled away, plus there's nothing like money to cause problems between friends. It's not that I don't trust Tashi, but it's a burden I have yet to resolve.

I could talk it over with Bruce when he gets out, but I'm not sure I can stomach being in the same room with him. I don't understand my feelings myself, but he's part of a life I'm doing my best to forget. Most of the time I hope he moves to another continent, but then I remember he's the only one on this planet who truly understands how I got to be who I am, experiencing the same dark journey

If Daddy Weingarten found out about my squirreled away

assets, he could still decide to do me and those I care about, a lot of harm. Deadly harm. I'm positive he's capable of it. Bruce knows I'm here, but I'm almost certain he hasn't told his father. Even with all the pain and dislike between us, there's still some loyalty. The old adage 'the enemy of my enemy . . .' I furrow my forehead trying to get the idea in focus. Lizzie and Win have discussed whether I could forgive Bruce. It's not only the terrible blow to my head. He purposefully tried to do deadly harm to women I now care deeply about. I recoil at the thought.

Win and Lizzie have seen him three times and are planning on going again. I can't understand Lizzie. Personally, I'd want to kill him if I were her. Maybe it's because she knew him before he turned into a monster. She asked me straight out what I'd do if I confronted him, and I had to tell her I'd probably cross the street to avoid him. But later, when I thought more about it, I decided second chances should be allowed. And I thought about Willie.

I know Bruce has some good in him. He probably saved my life when I was a child, lying bleeding on my kitchen floor alone. Oh hell, yes. I'd try if only for that, stretch myself, talk to him, and see what he's like now — out of curiosity if nothing else. Win said he's beginning to understand him, believes he's raw and vulnerable and trying so hard. I went back and told Lizzie 'Okay'. She smiled that beautiful smile of hers. I know why Win is helpless around her.

I've talked to Susan about it several times, giving her some background of what drove Bruce that terrible afternoon in the blizzard. She doesn't seem to have any fear of him at all. She says she believes he was tormented and wants to talk to him about it face to face. Susan is amazing that way, she likes to understand people almost as if they're scientific specimens. Well, she's going to get her chance. Lizzie told me she and Win have invited him up here when he gets out. Blew me out of the water again. Said she just told Ellie the same thing, just to warn her if she wants to avoid him. It's six months away so Ellie and Paul can take a cruise to Timbuktu if they want to.

I see Ellie walking in my direction. I have an idea what she wants to discuss.

"Hi, kid," I say.

"Did you hear the good news?" she asks flatly.

"Good news?" I say with one eyebrow raised.

She grimaces. "You know we try to be honest with each other? About the past, I mean? And our feelings?"

I feel a twinge of the old guilt. "I haven't asked you for a while. Is it still hard?"

She looks me directly in the eye and smiles. Even that open smile took a while. And to this day I don't touch Ellie. I'm always afraid it would put her in a difficult place. But we're friends now.

"I can honestly say it's not hard. Not anymore." And as if to prove it, she goes up on her tiptoes to lightly kiss my cheek.

I feel a rush of surprise and pleasure. "That means a lot, Ellie. You know I'd do anything for you now."

"I know, Alec, and I'll tell you a secret. There are times when I get a kick out of my previously evil friend and our violent past. And now you know I'm really nuts."

"Not so nuts. I've killed myself trying to be your best friend. I've even mostly convinced Paul."

"But it's not the same with Bruce." She violently swipes the air with her hand. "I can't comprehend Lizzie. I truly can't. I know she loves me. I don't understand how she can be a friend to him. It's such a betrayal." She gives me a bitter smile. "Can you explain it?"

"See the little dent right below my left ear? He almost killed me, Ellie. It was almost a deathblow. I find this hard to understand, myself."

"So.... What are you thinking?"

"I'd hate him completely too, had I not seen the other side of him murdered long ago. He was tortured. There's no other way to put it. You can't imagine the anguish. Bruce and I often stood in his study, in front of the old man's desk, trembling in our boots — we "big, grown men." Weingarten tormented us with lies and manipulation. I heard him tell Bruce many times his mother was disgusted with him, didn't ever want to see his face. He said it so convincingly I believed it. To this day, I'm not sure whether she wasn't a monster, too."

We both stand quietly thinking. "But, Alec, that doesn't explain Lizzie. She must know I never want to be in the same state with him. I'm angry, furious she seems to have chosen to hurt me."

"Do you really believe that's what she wants?"

"Lizzie was a self-centered, oblivious young person. She's not that way now. No. I don't believe she's doing this intentionally to hurt me, but it does. Deeply. I've let her know that. She says she has to follow her conscience." She shakes her head. "Why is this so important?"

"She sees something in him. It's all I can figure. Something worth the anger and fear she's causing you." I sigh. "It's hard for me too. She said she'd warn us when he's coming, so we can avoid him, but I told her I'd give it a shot. And maybe the line between us is pretty thin." I fight glancing away. "You know that, too," I say softly.

"Remember when you came back to help me. You said you were throwing up you were so guilty and upset. Maybe if I believed he had serious regret. He said he did in the courtroom, but who could believe him? I won't get close enough to talk to him."

"That's fair, more than fair." I allow myself to take her hand. "Do what makes you feel happy and safe. It's all I want."

"We've come a long way. I feel better about Lizzie, too."

"We'll get there, Ellie. I thank my lucky stars every time you smile at me."

CHAPTER 21

BRUCE

EIGHT MONTHS THROUGH my second year in prison, I'm starting to anticipate freedom. I exercise regularly, although, unlike many of the inmates, I'm not focused on putting on enormous muscles. I've lost weight, but what's left is lean and mean. The diet is limited, but I try to eat as much protein, fruits, and vegetables as I can. My business office friends bring in fresh fruit to snack on. Still, I'd kill for a greasy cheeseburger and fries. I wouldn't kill, honestly. I scare myself when I even think that phrase.

My coworkers have gradually become real friends. I have offers to visit after I get out, and incredibly even job possibilities. Most inmates would give anything for a steady job when they're released. I've alluded to the fact I won't be starving and can afford to set myself up in a small business. As my discharge approaches, they have nothing but good wishes.

I'm fortunate to have other friends now. My lawyer, Bob Swanson, and I communicate using regular mail, avoiding any possibility of being hacked by Father. His idea. Plus, he has successfully left the company, escaping the cesspool. He admitted that protecting himself was the most challenging thing he's ever done. I can only imagine. He and my employee-friends have been able to provide me with modest things to improve my world. It's like life, best to not outshine the average guy. Friends are worth more than stuff.

You need permission to be allowed anything out of the ordinary. I ask for modest things and am polite. I've learned a lot about human nature, both good and bad. People are predictable and a lot alike, whether they fly in corporate jets or live in the next cell. I try to cultivate kind people and let them know I appreciate them.

I've been allowed to accumulate some decent paints — oil and watercolors, plus some good canvas and paper. I work on projects as much as I can, surprising myself with what I can accomplish. I paint from my imagination and ideas from magazines, anticipating having real scenery for inspiration. Coworkers have my paintings, and several inmate friends proudly have them propped up in their cells. Several have brought me meaningful photos from their old life and I've painted them — a family home, a beach where they played, even their mothers. They're unbelievably grateful. I have a waiting list.

I acquired an old guitar plus a couple of instruction books and am slowly, with Wes's help, learning to play. It gives me peace. The guitar is a cheap Chinese knock-off Bob found in a pawnshop — something that wouldn't inspire envy. He went out of his way to find a Red-label Yamaha with incredible sound. I never have enough time to play it.

Before I go to sleep, I think about women. Besides the obvious fantasies, I long for someone to care about. I had Ellie within my grasp. The memory causes stomach pains unless I turn it off. Here was this lovely person who wanted intimacy, for God's sake, and I was too busy, or distracted, or in too much personal pain. I should have kissed my lucky stars, cashed in my chips, and trusted her with the truth. It wouldn't have killed me no matter what she decided. More important, I should have imagined that I could end up completely alone. I wonder whether I'll ever have the chance to love someone like her again.

I'd have to be dead not to appreciate Lizzie. I've encountered a variety of comparably beautiful women around the world, but she's beautiful inside. Win knows how I feel about her. I love her. We even talked about it once when Lizzie was out of the visiting area, talking to someone about my release. I told Win I hoped I would be allowed to remain her friend.

It was a daunting conversation. If he thought I was any kind of a threat, I'd never see her again. Besides, I couldn't hide what she means to me, he's too smart and intuitive. He responded that they both give me the gift of her friendship. It's all he had to say. Not that he controls her, but they are a couple in every sense. If I could wish for something for myself, it would be such a relationship. You can take all the perks of wealth and burn them.

I had my second Christmas inside these walls. Wesley and I performed at the prison Christmas concert. He played his bass guitar and I strummed, doing five traditional Christmas carols. We got applause like we were in Carnegie Hall. It was glorious. I was buzzed for a day afterwards.

Lizzie and Win came for a second Christmas visit. I presented them with a small oil painting of the family ranch house in the twilight from a picture Lizzie sent. It was an overdue wedding present. I had one of my friends make a simple frame for it in the prison woodshop. Lizzie cried. God help me, but I do love her.

They brought me a giant chocolate Santa, a Christmas tree, this time with mini-Tootsie Rolls, and two books on Montana. One, a novel Lizzie loves, and the other a history of the Blackfeet tribe and area from Win. The best gift was they encouraged me to stay at the ranch for several weeks. I can take my time planning what I want to do next, and I'll have them to bounce ideas off of.

I'll make it now — a little under four months to go.

CHAPTER 22

BRUCE

IN TWO DAYS, May first, I'll be a free man. Charlotte and Cliff in the business office have become almost family. If they had a prison brochure, they should say in capital letters, *COME TO PRISON – LEARN TO MAKE FRIENDS,* alongside a picture of carefully made cots in the cells with designer pillows and a rubber plant.

I have two convict friends with whom I'll stay in close touch. My librarian friend, Walter, is making it on the outside. He has a steady job now as a woodworker in a furniture factory in Boise and is rebuilding a life with his son. I'm very proud of him. I talk to him regularly using my allotted weekly phone call.

It took me a year to work up the courage to call Lizzie and Win. The first time I felt so guilty for bothering them, forcing them to be friendly, that I could hardly talk. The call lasted three minutes, but they encouraged me to call again.

My second attempt, I made a list of topics first and the call went better. I've been daydreaming about the drive up to the ranch for months. In my dreams, people are glad to see me. Ellie was always happy to see me. How could I not have realized it's a gift worth everything? But I try not to beat myself up over my previous stupidity. George, my chaplain-friend, tells me over and over, "Your life begins with today. Don't look back."

My other close friend, Wesley, hasn't had a break in his life. His mother was a fifteen-year-old druggie when he was born. He was passed around among relatives and strangers. It's amazing he's alive. He's been here for a good part of his life and isn't totally embittered. That's fortitude.

Wesley and I are equals now, both scared of the future and trying to hang onto hope. He's afraid of reentering the outside world and has three more years to go. He doesn't know it, but he's already helping me by giving my life purpose. I'm constantly encouraging him and have promised to help him get a real start when he's released. We talk about problems on the outside. The economy is floundering along, difficult for even ordinary people. I know from Walter what a struggle he's had as a felon, trying to start over. Wes is trying to encourage another prisoner, Tweets Wagoner. He's paying it forward.

Tweets has been here since he was seventeen, ten years, getting his name because of his love of birds. He's been called Tweets so long no one even knows his real name. He's very smart, at least that's what Wes says, and it makes it worse for him, knowing his life is draining away. Several months ago, he gave up, lost his head, and started screaming, throwing himself repeatedly against the chain-link fence. Even scared the guards. Wes talked to George, who talked to the warden, and together they got him some help and a job in the library.

Tweets trusts no one. He has no real friends here after all this time, but he's started opening up to Wes. He says all Tweets does is read and dream, a ghost here. It's heartbreaking to Wes, who has the softest heart. What a waste of a good human being. I'm planning how I can help him from the other side.

And, of course, there's Chaplain George who knows everything about me I have to tell. We talk about the world I came from and what I could have become, both worst and best. We talk about choices. I desperately want my life to mean something. I think about it constantly.

On Lizzie's last visit she came by herself. Win was called out on a fire at the last minute, and she didn't want to cancel on me, so she went through the whole unpleasant experience, including a three and a half drive, one way, alone, to encourage me. How do I ever pay that kind of a gift back?

We had a rare opportunity to talk about Ellie and Susan.

"Have you told them," I asked. "I can't bear to add more pain on top of everything else. Tell me the truth, Lizzie."

She surprised me by laughing. "I think Susan may try to engineer a meeting. She's fearless with a strange sense of humor. She told me she'd like to challenge you to an off-road duel with her in a bulldozer." She paused. "She even knows a guy who rents them out. A friend of Sam's. I was not entirely sure she was kidding."

"That's amazing." I responded. "I'll pass. But at least she doesn't seem frightened or intimidated."

When she didn't go on, I prodded, "And Ellie."

"It's been hard. She still has frequent nightmares."

I cringed when I heard that. It was hard to talk about because Ellie is her beloved older sister. I could see Lizzie pull away from me as she empathized with her sister's pain, lowering her eyes.

We sat in silence. I swallowed several times. "I'd give anything to erase the memories. Should I not come?"

Lizzie gave me a weak smile. "She said she'd be happy if she never lays eyes on you in her lifetime."

I bit my lip and closed my eyes.

"Listen to me," Lizzie said. "Do you think I haven't thought about this? A lot. Win and I both want you to have an opportunity to start over, a chance to make amends for some awful things. I know Ellie. She'll get over this, especially if she sees how hard you're trying." She lowers her voice and leans forward. "It's for her, too. Don't you see. Fear and hatred are hurting her."

We tried to lighten the visit after that exchange, but it was difficult. We talked about hopeful things until I felt somewhat better. After she left, I thought about friendship. How it's not always an easy gift. Which, of course, makes it all the more valuable.

I'll have a fresh start thanks to my maternal grandmother's legacy. With Bob Swanson's help, I've arranged a bank account with a debit card and applied for a credit card. During these correspondences we've shared horror stories involving Father. Bob's flying out to personally help with the discharge process, having purchased me a three-year-old dark blue Nissan sedan. I didn't want anything fancy to stand out. I don't feel the need to stand out again in my life. I hope to find a nice little shop somewhere and be a businessman.

Lizzie and Win's sister, Alice, whom I have yet to meet, have decorated my guest suite in early ranch style. I'm told it's in the back of the tack room with a very old couch and bunk beds. I can almost smell the leather and saddle soap. Lizzie and Win are living with Win's mother while their house is being built a quarter of a mile east along the bluff edge. They've sent more pictures and my little album is full.

Most of the rescuers and their friends think Win and Lizzie are crazy at best, or painfully disloyal, to have anything to do with me. I don't agree because I know my heart. I've stopped blaming other people for my problems. I've written an exploratory letter to my mother and received a note back. It was short and unemotional. Disappointing. Possibly she had to clear it with Father. One line intrigued me, though. She was referring to my lack of possessions now and said simply, “Even an empty suitcase is hopeful.” I’ve read it over and over, wondering if she remembers our ancient plan. It’s comforting to believe she might.

CHAPTER 23

BRUCE

ON MY LAST VISIT to the business office, the morning of release, I see balloons and a cake. Pink and yellow rolls of crepe paper are draped over my desk. All six of the office staff are clapping and cheering, even grumpy Arnold who has become my biggest fan. I'm speechless. The cake is homemade chocolate, a little lopsided, with candles. Charlotte said she knew it wasn't my birthday, but the candles made it seem more special. It didn't need the candles. I've never had a homemade cake in my life. I get officially released at noon and they received permission to walk out and take some pictures. George will be there, too. I inhale three pieces of cake, trying not to glance at the wall clock every few minutes.

After the obligatory paperwork, and many locked doors opened, I emerge, carrying a small canvas duffle containing the few personal items taken away when I checked in two years ago: my Gucci wallet with $500 in cash, my Rolex Yacht-Master, a pair of handcrafted Italian shoes, and the $5,000 suit I remember carefully folding as if it were yesterday. These things are not a part of my world and I hope never will be again. I don't put the watch on — it would feel ridiculous. I wonder absently whether the old credit card in my wallet is still activated. I don't know how hard it will be to get one as a convicted felon.

I walk through the last security gate with a giant grin I can't suppress. Bob is there to greet me, wearing a matching grin. My friends are lined up to say goodbye, dissolving into hugs and handshakes with Cliff pumping my hand endlessly. I think Charlotte is going to cry. Arnold looks like he lost his best friend, and George shakes my hand and whispers, "You were my greatest success. My friend." I have on a new pair of jeans, blue checked shirt, and a pair of black Converse shoes Bob brought along. The Ferragamo loafers will stay packed.

Bob hands me the wireless keys as we approach my car in the

parking area. "Do you want to drive?"

"If I can remember how."

I stumble through placing the ranch address off a crumpled scrap of paper into the car GPS. Task accomplished, I turn to Bob, giving him a thumbs-up.

"Congratulations," he says. "I'm proud how you've handled all this."

"You've been a big help and a lot of encouragement," I reply sincerely.

"Now tell me. I can't even guess how you feel. Are you in a good place?"

"I don't worry about being on the streets with nothing. I have a nice car and a place to land with friends. I'm at peace." I turn to look at him. "I'm beginning to trust."

He nods as if understanding my meaning. "I'm also surprised Lizzie and Win have been so generous. Why, do you think?"

"I don't know. I absolutely don't. When we sit down, it's one of the first things I want to ask."

"What about your parents and the family business?" He asks with the sardonic smile.

"I'm reasonably sure Father wishes I'd died in prison now that I'm not useful." I laugh grudgingly, not at all surprised that Bob doesn't disagree.

"And your mother?"

"Did you ever know her at all?"

"In the five years I worked for your father, I saw her only half a dozen times. We never had a real conversation."

I experience a vague hollowness. I wish I felt more, pain even, but I remember her the same way Bob does.

"I've made a few gestures to her," I admit finally. "I'll continue to try — to satisfy my curiosity if nothing else." Shaking it off, I ask, "How's your new life?"

"I'm free now, too. I lost almost everything getting out. But partly due to what happened to you, it seemed like the blackest sinkhole." He takes a moment, dramatizing his words. "My wife and I are reconciling." He gives me a delighted grin.

"I know you've been trying hard. Congratulations."

He nods in agreement. "I almost blew my marriage apart in the morass. I'm still on probation, but I think we'll make it."

"I'm very glad, Bob." I smile. "You look ten years younger. Weight of the world off?"

He nods happily. We're silent for a few moments absorbing the good news. It still surprises me, on occasion, that I can feel real joy at another's happiness. I'd kept emotional distance, even from Ellie.

"Are you driving up to the reservation now?" he asks, sliding into the passenger seat.

"As soon as I drop you off at the airport, get a hamburger, a beer, and a half gallon of mocha chip ice cream."

"Well, good luck to you. I sincerely wish you the best."

"I know you do. I'm deeply grateful. For the friendship most of all."

"Another one of life's mysterious turns. When I can help, let me know."

"Goes both ways."

I'm filled with nervous anticipation. Lizzie told me in her last phone call she's pregnant. She said everyone is laughing at her because she was supposed to be headed toward a high-society, self-indulgent lifestyle, and here she is a ranch wife and pregnant. She said sometimes it surprises her, too, but then she looks over at Win and what could she do?

The drive has been spectacular. The new grass shoots are an unnatural yellow green. All the colors are startling. I haven't been able to see much other than sky from the gravel exercise yard. The mountains are hazy gray blue in the distance, the river colored a deeper cobalt blue, contrasting with shimmering gold and silver glints from the sun's reflections. I want to try to paint it all. I've been able to get some excellent quality oil paints and have been working in my cell every evening. I'm improving continually. The colors are probably off due to the artificial light, but I'm amazed at what I've accomplished. I might like to have a small gallery or art supply store somewhere.

Following the GPS, I'm getting close, finally crossing a second beautiful river, flowing east from the Rocky Mountains. "Two Medicine River," the sign says. The road climbs steeply from the valley floor in several long switchbacks, leveling out on the top of the high bluff. Almost immediately there's my turn to the right. I'm fighting the impulse to bolt. After two years in a controlled environment, everything new seems overwhelming.

The narrow dirt road winds through rolling prairie, blanketed with unfolding pink wildflowers and emerging hay fields. An older farmhouse with a peaked gray roof, is poised in the distance. Beyond it, overlooking the entire panorama of the river valley, is the newly framed outline of Lizzie and Win's house. Grasslands below stretch to the eastern horizon with the river running through it all.

I've called ahead and can now see four people, waiting on the pouch.

As I get out of the car, Lizzie hurries to give me a hug. Win holds out his hand.

"It's so beautiful. I can't possibly tell you."

"One of the most wonderful places on earth," Lizzie agrees.

"Let me introduce my family," Win says, as two women approach me. "This is my mom, Sarah, and my sister, Alice."

"Hello, and thank you," I say.

A tall fit woman in her middle fifties with shoulder length, reddish-brown hair walks up to me, shaking my hand with surprising strength. She has arresting light gray eyes. I can see where Win got his looks. She's stunning.

"Welcome," she says. "We're pleased to have you."

She seems to mean it which is so amazing I can only nod vigorously.

"Anyway," she goes on with a smile, "Lizzie and Alice have been outfitting your room. I hope you don't mind we put you in the barn. We're full up in the house until the kids get their place done." She pauses, then says, "Besides, it's a very nice barn, much newer than the house."

Win literally pushes the other woman forward. "Say hello, Alice."

"Hello," she says.

I've already been warned Win's sister doesn't talk easily to people she doesn't know well, so I'm prepared. "Alice, it's good to finally meet you. I've heard wonderful things about your work with horses."

Alice smiles guardedly at me. Her deep-set hazel eyes show an appealing hesitancy, inspiring me to try to put her at ease as I smile back.

"Come on. We'll show you where to put your things," Lizzie

says, glancing into the car. "Do you have things?"

"Not much. I'll have to make a shopping list." I remember suddenly the hopeful empty suitcase. "I made a quick stop in Missoula and bought several pairs of jeans, a few t-shirts, a hoodie, and a toothbrush to hold me over."

The five of us walk three hundred feet to the new barn, still yellow with new wood. It has a long center aisle with six stalls on each side with good quality woodwork and heavy hardware on the doors. Four stalls are for family horses. Lizzie has her own horse now, a gray mare named Silk with a black mane and tail. The rest of the stalls are for boarders Alice trains with help from her mom.

"Do you have any old gentle ones?" I ask. "I might want to try riding sometime."

"Any of our family horses except Win's are so well-trained you could ride them," Sarah encourages. "Especially if you start out in the paddock to get the feel of them. We'll help you."

"Have you ridden before?" Win asks.

"It's been years — since I was a kid."

"Let's show you the apartment," Lizzie interrupts eagerly.

Walking down to the end of the corridor, we enter the tack room with bunk beds at one end and a tiny bathroom in what looks like a closet. A stuffed, somewhat sagging, maroon couch with rounded upholstered armrests from the 1930's sits next to a rough-cut wooden rocking chair. A standing lamp with fringe completes the depression era atmosphere.

"We emptied out Mom's attic," Alice manages as I smile back at her.

The furniture is separated from the saddles and other riding equipment by an oriental screen decorated with bamboo and butterflies. Eclectic. In the middle of everything stands a large square space heater, set well away from the walls.

"What do you think?" Lizzie grins.

"It's the most beautiful apartment I ever saw," I admit truthfully. "Especially considering where I just came from."

"You'll have to shower in the house," Sarah adds, "which means we'll see you more."

"It's...perfect."

We amble back, settling on the front veranda, warmed by the late afternoon sunshine. In the quiet, I can just make out the sound of water flowing over rocks in the river far below. The air is filled with the sweetness of new grass and wildflowers.

"We're having dinner at six, but how about some cookies and milk to hold you over?" Sarah asks.

I groan, then try to explain. "My friends in the business office — they had a huge chocolate cake. After I ate half of it, I celebrated freedom with a hamburger and way too much ice cream. But...? I pause, trying to phrase the question, which has dominated my thinking on the trip up. "I need to ask. I've been thinking about this for weeks. How can you do this for me?"

"Ask Lizzie," says Win. "She's the one who started this."

I turn to her. "Why, Lizzie? I didn't have the courage to ask."

"You remember before? In your past life when I tried to get to know you? Occasionally you'd let down a little," she replies seriously, "after a drink or two. You used to say we were alike somehow. I pressed you to tell me what your life was really like. I had suspicions of a hidden side." She pauses, then turns to confront me more directly. "You always backed off — especially when we'd talk about parents. Once, I mentioned something my father had encouraged me to try that helped me. You responded you had to depend on yourself because no one ever helped you. 'Made you strong,' was how you put it. But it was the way you said it. You seemed completely vulnerable for a moment. Then the wall went back up."

I nod slowly, remembering.

"I didn't think about it much back then, but when I saw you in the courtroom — no one coming to encourage you through it — I got mad. What kind of unfeeling bastards would let their kid go off to prison all alone? It bothered me. Then I got your letter. That bothered me, too." She grimaces. "Well, it seemed like I should hold out a hand. So, I did. We got to know each other by letters. I became more convinced you could change if you had a chance. Now I'm glad."

I feel frozen, unable to respond. No one else says anything.

"There's something else," she says. "I had a feeling — a premonition — that you weren't bad. Not deep down. I've met a few people who had cruelty as part of their DNA — wouldn't ever change. They might be able to cover it up well enough to fool most people. But instead...." She looks forcefully at me. "I decided you were covering up the good."

My chin trembles as I gaze across the river valley. We sit quietly for several minutes.

"We have two hours before dinner," Win says, finally breaking the silence. "What would you like to do? Take a tour of the area? Take a walk? Take a nap?"

I take a deep breath. "I've decided. I'd like to ride a wild horse. And I want to start at the top. None of these tame ones. I'd like to try yours, Win."

"Probably not a good idea, man. If Cloud thinks he can get the best of you, he'll take off."

"I'm not afraid." I look around at everyone, sitting in stunned silence. "Not anymore. I need to feel alive again... Risk something."

Win gives me a serious look, deliberating. "We might find you broken in a heap somewhere, or never hear from you again."

Even Alice speaks up, "You could get hurt. Seriously. I don't even ride Cloud."

"Nope, my mind is made up. I'll keep him to a trot — is that what you call it?"

"I'd hate to have you die your first day out, Bruce," Lizzie says, more seriously than I expected.

"At least ride him in the corral first," Sarah cautions. "See whether he's listening to you."

"Nah. I've been confined for so long. Afraid so long. I need to take chances. I'll just ride him around the barn a few times."

"Your funeral," Win agrees finally. "I'll saddle him."

"Win, I really don't think..."

"Lizzie. Sometimes a man gotta do what a man's gotta do. Besides, he'll probably live through it."

"Well, if you're sure."

Win walks off humming and grinning.

He's back in five minutes with Cloud and another saddled horse. "In case I have to go find him," he says.

"Can someone hold him while I get on?" I ask, approaching the horse cautiously from the rear. Cloud kicks out, barely missing my right shin.

Win, wearing a fixed, very broad smile, takes the bridle firmly.

"Nice horse," I say, patting his neck. I put one foot in the stirrup and hop around a few times on the other foot, unable to swing up as Cloud sidesteps around the yard. Looking over at a frowning Alice, I smile confidently.

"Whoa. Whoa. Spirited horse," I say.

I try unsuccessfully to get on, finally managing it on my fourth try. Cloud shimmies around, stomping his feet like he can hardly wait to get this fool in the dust.

"Okay, turn him loose," I declare. "Stand back."

I hear Win express what I'm sure everyone's thinking, "This is going to take about thirty seconds."

I bounce awkwardly in the saddle for fifty feet down the road then turn, giving them all a grin of success. Touching Cloud's flanks firmly with my heels, he's off like a bullet. I hear Win yell loudly, "Holy shit!"

We race an eighth of a mile, whirl and gallop partway back, stop on a dime, whirl in a tight circle, then race off again. In the distance, I back him up twenty feet, circle the other direction, then race up to the group, sliding to a full stop ten feet away.

"Polo," I say.

"What?" Win stammers, clearly stunned.

"Polo. I played polo."

"Oh, my God," Lizzie bursts out.

We all start laughing. Even Alice is choking, giggling so hard she can't catch her breath, hiding her face behind her hands.

Eventually, I trade horses with Win.

"Let me give you the quickie tour," he says, still shaking his head.

We approach the framed-in house with roof trusses in place, ready for plywood. "Nothing special," he says, giving me a self-satisfied look. "Two thousand square feet and room for kids, but it's going to have a view to blow you out of the water." He pauses. "I've wanted to build a house here all my life."

"It's going to be the best house on the planet," I say, meaning it.

We continue riding east toward the open plains. Win keeps chuckling from time to time, then laughs heartily.

"What?" I ask.

"I keep seeing Alice's face. She was sure you were going to die. Especially when it took you four times to get on this damn horse. And afterwards..." I don't think I've heard her laugh so hard in her entire life."

I turn in the saddle, grinning at Win.

He grins conspiratorially back at me.

We start down a steep trail, winding toward the river. Some distance down the bluff face and around a curve, is a flat area covered with a grove of trees. Spring water pours out of the sheer cliff, forming a pool about thirty feet across before it spills over high rocks, cascading down the lower side of the cliff all the way to the river below.

"It's cold water now," Win cautions. "But later in the summer we all come down here for a dip. It's courtesy to ring the bell on the trailhead. Sometimes we don't bring suits."

"Gotcha," I say.

We continue along obvious tire tracks, worn into the grass, which finally disappear into the eastern horizon.

"This trail goes along the bluff ridge for miles," Win explains. "Further than we usually go. It follows Two Medicine the whole way. Help yourself. There's usually no one up here but family."

"Win, you are the luckiest man on earth."

"I agree," he responds seriously, "now that I have Lizzie."

My legs dangle over the lip of the porch after dinner, while I watch the sun start to disappear behind the Rocky Mountains. The eastern slope of the Northern Rockies, known as The Rocky Mountain Front, and locally as The China Wall, is much steeper than the west side. Two Teutonic plates collided eons ago, one subducting under the other, causing a sharp two-thousand-foot uplifted fortress, extending all the way from the Canadian border to southern Montana. The immensity of the mountains helps put my challenges in perspective. The Sander's clan has welcomed me so warmly I've finally relaxed enough to count my blessings.

I don't have to line up for the security count before going into my cell for the night. The night sounds here are more likely crickets and hoot owls, not clanging doors and grumbled swearing. But best of all, I don't have to see Father's face, glowering at me over his foreboding desk. I sigh deeply, over and over. Lizzie and Win come out with a cup of coffee for me and sit down. In a few minutes, Sarah and Alice join us. Together we watch the shadows of the mountains, lengthening across the flat grasslands far below us, extending east as the sun descends. I can almost see the line of darkness move east.

We're sitting silently enjoying the view when Sarah chuckles,

Lizzie joins in, and when Win laughs out loud, I hear Alice start laughing.

"It was the funniest thing I ever saw," says Sarah. "You played us, Bruce. I keep remembering you starting off, bumping down the path on the trot."

"No, Mom," Alice says. "The funniest was when he couldn't get on Cloud. I wanted to go over and push his fanny up. I couldn't stand it."

We all look at Alice. Win has his mouth open. Even I know Alice never says anything. It was nice.

"I've never seen you be funny in all the time I've known you," Lizzie declares. "The closest you ever came was biting sarcasm. I still can't believe it."

"I can't believe it myself. It emerged in the billing office at the prison. They used to kid each other, and I realized making friends laugh is a gift you give them. I started looking for ways to make them laugh, too. I hardly know myself."

As real dark settles in, I rise unsteadily to my feet. "Whoa. I'm going to be stiff."

"You'll deserve it, cowboy," Win says. "Are you going to bed?"

"Yeah, I'll turn in. I've been alone in my cell in the evenings for so long it seems like part of my DNA. Besides, I need some time to get this day in perspective." I shake my head in disbelief. "Imagine where my day started and where it's ending."

"Just a second," Lizzie says. "I'll get some towels and an extra blanket and walk you over. It's supposed to get chilly tonight."

We stop at the door of the tack room. "Everyone likes you, Bruce. I wasn't worried, but your little stunt totally broke the ice, even with Alice."

"I'm hoping she'll let me help with the youngsters. I've thought about it for months. I'd love to handle young horses."

"I bet she'd appreciate it. Sarah doesn't want to do more than part-time help. And, oh, you'll hear Alice up early, banging around, starting to clean some of the stalls."

"I'm thrilled about the baby, Lizzie. You seem so contented."

"It's a boy. We just found out. Win can hardly contain himself. He says he keeps imagining a little warrior following him around."

"Win seems good with me here, Lizzie. He's a good man. Maybe he can deserve you."

Her smile lights up her face. "You have no idea. I feel honored to walk at his side. He risks his life all the time in his job for other people."

"How can he trust me?"

"We've talked about it. He's always believed he could see, feel other peoples' spirits. Even when you were at your worst, he thought he saw something else there. 'Complicated,' he always said. Now, he feels positive about you."

"God. I hope he's right. I want to become a good person. I probably want it more than anything on earth."

"He also said you were brave when he punched you. He liked that."

"Did he tell you I spit at him, after he knocked my teeth out? Willie and Lew were holding me."

"Yes, and he hit you again."

"I like him better when he's laughing at me."

"I'll tell him. There's an alarm clock by the bed. Breakfast at seven. Goodnight. Sleep well.

I'm sitting in the old rocking chair with a rag and saddle soap, polishing some of the bridles. It's a small mindless thing I can do while I'm thinking about my day — waking up in a cell and ending it in paradise. I'd like to live in this area. The problem with that idea is all the people here who hate me. I don't want to spend my life avoiding them. There are a thousand small communities where I wouldn't have any history. But now I have a few friends here.

I don't have to decide now. The electric heater pours out heat, soaking into my bones. It feels so good I keep working on the leather long into the night.

CHAPTER 24

BRUCE

IT'S JUST BEFORE 7:00 when I hurry over to the house. It did get cold last night. I can see my breath as I jog. The sun is up but heavy dew still coats the grass. Everyone is sitting around the kitchen table planning their day, except Lizzie, who got up extra early to drive to her school for her Friday classes. Win will be leaving soon for his twelve-hour shift at the fire department and Alice is discussing the training schedule with her mother.

"Morning, Bruce," Win says. "I've been wondering. Did you ever get your teeth fixed?"

"Glad you asked," I reply. "I've got a humongous bill around here somewhere."

"Damn. I was hoping they'd do it in prison for free." We sit grinning at each other as Sarah and Alice shake their heads.

"Any plans?" Win asks.

"It's a perfect day for a drive. I want to visit Browning and East Glacier, be a tourist, but I wanted to ask Alice whether I could watch her work with the horses, maybe lend a hand." I study her face. "Don't feel you have to, Alice, if it feels wrong."

"That would be fine."

"Good. I have things to do," Sarah says. "Yell, Alice, if you need me."

* * *

It's my fantasy. I'm finishing with my third student, a six-month-old colt, leading him around the paddock while teaching him voice and hand commands. Alice is watching and quietly giving me occasional suggestions. I could do this forever.

The big paint colt is smart and willing. In fifteen minutes, he's made good progress and I turn him loose in the large fenced field behind the barn. I watch him bound away like a puppy, get down, and roll on his back. I hear a tiny sound and realize Alice is beside me, leaning on the fence, watching him.

"You're good with the horses," she says. "Very patient."

"Thanks. Coming from you, it means a lot."

"You enjoy it?" she asks.

"When I played polo, the horses performed better for me than for the other guys. I understood what they were feeling. Tried to work with them."

"Volunteer anytime," she says, walking off.

I wonder whether she has any idea of what that means to me.

CHAPTER 25

BRUCE

IT'S A CRISP MORNING. Even at ten o'clock the hoodie feels good. No one knows my car and I'm somewhat disguised in a ball cap and sunglasses. Still, I frequently glance around, hoping I don't run into anyone who'd like to kill me. I need to talk with Lizzie soon to discuss how much I'm hated. It could have a big impact on my decision of where to build a life. Today though, I'm experiencing pure joy. Just to be free to go where I want. The simple pleasure of deciding whether I want to stop for coffee and a piece of pie is huge.

I need to take this slow. They give you a little counseling on adjusting, but as much as I try to deny it, I'm overwhelmed. I hadn't anticipated how many decisions you make in the real world. In prison, choices are so limited. Every minute or so I'm having to decide something. Should I get gas? Should I buy a real water bottle or keep getting plastic ones? Do I want to stop for a walk? Should I offer money to Sarah for food? Should I buy some? In my previous life, I never had to chip in for groceries.

I've just pulled into the parking lot at the big lodge in East Glacier but stay sitting in the car, continually replaying working with the horses this morning and remembering Alice's comment. When I first got compliments in the business office, I could hardly deal with them. I didn't grow up with encouragement. But coming from Alice, who I know has to work up to talking, it was incredibly special. How much can I volunteer? I want to drive back and do it again tonight. Animals are so forgiving. They don't know your life is a mess. They just want gentle treatment. I guess I do, too.

Eventually, I walk up the curving driveway leading to the Lodge's main entrance. The old lodge is majestic, with interior support pillars shaped out of old growth timber brought in from the Pacific Northwest on rail cars over a century ago. The inside columns are basically tree trunks, forty feet high and over three feet in diameter.

I read online that they harvested the trees in the winter before the sap began to run so they wouldn't swell and dislodge the bark left on the outside of the columns. Glacier was designated a National Park in 1910 and work began on the lodge in 1912 when the Great Northern Railroad funded it as a destination resort.

As I enter the front portico, I run straight into Willie Long, gasp, and take a step backwards.

It takes him several seconds to recognize me. I watch as his facial expression hardens.

"Hello, Willie," I manage.

A few seconds pass. "I got your...apology."

"I meant every word."

"Good," he mutters in a flat voice, "Good for you." He bulls his way through, almost colliding with me, as I hurriedly stepped out of his way. He continues determinedly out the door, without a backward glance.

I find a couch over by the huge stone fireplace and sit down to think it over. It hurts, I admit to myself, sighing repeatedly. No getting around it. I know from hearing Lizzie talk about Willie how loved and respected he is. He's a best friend and adopted brother to Win. I'd give anything to have even a neutral feeling from him. Of course not. I was almost responsible for killing Susan, the girl he loves. And I did it on purpose. No matter I regret what I did with every molecule in my body, nothing changes that.

If I stay in the area, this kind of thing will happen frequently. I'd be on my guard for years, if not forever. Should I put myself through it? Would some kind of atonement make things better for anyone? Is it fair to put people like Willie through having to encounter me? I didn't add happiness to his day.

After a while I'm calmer. I'll have to think more about this, but I push it aside for now and start looking around.

Muffled sounds echo across the sparsely filled central area as employees drape round tables with heavy white tablecloths and position place settings for a banquet. Only a small number of vacationers are milling around. The major road through the park is still blocked by snow and the summer tourist season won't officially start for two weeks.

Small shops in the lodge are being stocked. Peering through one window, I notice art displayed on walls behind the closed door. A hand-written sign dangles from a chain — *Gallery For Sale, Inquire Within*. I knock on the glass. An older woman peers around a corner.

* * *

Returning to the ranch, I have some things to consider. The idea of owning a small art-related business is increasingly appealing. The lodge gallery includes a well-lit alcove where I could paint if there were no customers. I could hide out, interacting mainly with tourists who don't know anything about me after stealthily slipping into the lodge. The sudden vision of me disguised in a fake mustache and droopy hat, looking exactly like Salvatore Dali, and skulking around the pillars, is so strong that I laugh out loud at myself. I'm suddenly in a great mood.

Hmm. I could have later store hours, which would allow me to spend time in the early mornings helping Alice with the horses. I'd have to find a tiny room or apartment not too far from the ranch. Anything would do. It would be a semblance of a real life while I try to figure myself out.

I have funds which could make this happen easily. I'd pay the very reasonable rent to the lodge for the space, and I could buy the business for $85,000 on contract. Even if I never sold a painting, I'd be fine. Who knows? I might even break even.

I need to seriously consider this. Constance Frisk, Connie, the current owner, informed me offers aren't exactly rolling in. She'll let me know whether there's any urgency.

Driving past the farmhouse, I pull up next to the barn. It has a welcoming feel — nickering sounds, warm interior with the sun on the roof, and the smell of hay, straw, and horses. I visit all my charges, scratching their ears and laughing as they nudge me with their heads, playing. Hugging one of the littlest fillies, I look up to see Alice who's been quietly watching me.

"Hi," I say. "Just enjoying the perks."

She smiles at me.

"Alice," I say. "Could I help you every morning while I'm here?"

"That would be nice," she replies, turns, and hustles away.

* * *

Several days later we're gathered for dinner and I've been mulling over my problem. It's Friday night and Lizzie and Win are headed out later for beers at the Dead Moose Tavern in East Glacier, meeting Willie and Susan, Tashi and Alec.

Willie has accepted Alec. They're not blood brothers, but Lizzie tells me they are relaxed enough to share beers and joke around. Alec tried to protect the girls as well as he could. Susan has completely forgiven him and so have Win and Lizzie. Even Ellie and Paul socialize with him, which is incredibly hard to believe. But it's been two and a half years, and I understand Alec has turned himself inside out making amends.

I on the other hand can't expect that, ever. It's what I need to talk about.

"I need to run something by you all," I say, as we finish our peach pie. "It's a difficult problem, and I need you to be completely honest, no pulled punches, okay?"

Everyone nods seriously.

"I'm trying to figure out what to do with my life, at least in the short run. This part of the country is heaven, but it's a big country." I'm trying to keep this light but fail miserably. "I ran into Willie at the Lodge. It was unpleasant, to put it mildly. He hates me — not that I blame him. And there are more people, Paul, Ellie, Susan, even Alec. I don't want them to dread meeting me — or be tempted to start something. Physical, I mean."

"Bruce..." Lizzie starts out, putting her hand on my arm.

"Let me get this out, okay? There's an art gallery in the Lodge for sale. If this *situation* wasn't going on, I'd buy it in a minute, run it, and paint there. And..." I glance at Alice. "And I'd love to help with the horses, but I don't know whether I should try to stay. I've upset everyone enough. I won't stay if sticking around would hurt people." I want to blather on, then force myself to stop. "So...? What do you think? For God's sake, be honest."

Everyone is silenced. It's one thing to come out here for a few days and another to live here. We all know it.

Finally, Win begins. "In all honesty, Bruce, you're right. It would cause problems. We're a close group who care about each other. I'd hate to think people would start taking sides over this." He takes Lizzie's hand across the table. "We've committed to be your friend, but at this point no one else has. Lizzie...?"

"We've talked this out before. If anyone had died or had horrible injuries, I'd say something different. Also, I hate it when people say, 'I've done my time, so everyone should get over it'. It's not that simple. But thank God, you have another chance." She smiles. "Someday, you need to talk to Paul about second chances, and, of course, Alec." She squares her shoulders. "I think you should try staying. If it becomes obviously painful for you or other people, you could leave."

I look over at Sarah.

"It shows how far you've come, Bruce, you've asked the question. But friendship and harmony are extremely important to me. I agree with Win and worry you could drive a wedge between friends." After a moment she continues with a frown. "Maybe no one's told you, but we've had criticism for just having you here temporarily. I had doubts beforehand, myself. But I have to say, I like you very much now. I want you to have a chance to be happy here."

I gather myself. "Alice."

"I want you to stay."

These are such good people. "I've been thinking about this all week. How does this sound? I'd like to try it for the summer. If by the first of September this is causing any sort of problem, I'll leave. I could move close enough, Great Falls or Helena, where I could come out and see you and not cause stress for anyone. That would be fine. But I'd like to try staying."

I clear my throat and press on. "Connie would accept a lease-option on the gallery for the summer and I could rent a little apartment or room close by. I'd be able to help with the horses in the mornings, and not spend other time here." I smile wryly. "I'd live far enough away so your friends could come over without worrying they'd stumble onto me."

Everyone defers to Win who was the most negative. He's pensive for a while, finally pushing himself back from the table. "Just as long as we don't push you in their faces, it could work. At least for a trial."

"Win, are you sure?"

"You should have your own place, though," he smiles at Lizzie. "I don't want to lose free labor."

I feel a flush of gratitude. "Anyone have any ideas where I might live near here? I wouldn't need much. Just a place to sleep and cook a little."

"I'll make a few phone calls," Sarah replies.

I'm back polishing saddles in the tack room and envisioning a simple life with the opportunity to try some serious painting. I can work with the horses. Alice's encouragement seems genuine. I've told everyone to think it over. I'm trying not to count on this. We'll talk tomorrow at breakfast. Win's going to sound out Willie and the rest at the Moose tonight. I sigh deeply for the hundredth time. If the consensus is that I should go, I will.

* * *

It's still early, but people don't sleep in on a ranch. Everyone stops talking as I come in.

"Well?" I ask.

"Well," Win begins, "it was very interesting. You think you can predict people, but they can surprise you. Let me start with Tashi and Alec. He told us specifics of what you had to deal with growing up. 'To give us perspective,' he said."

I hate even thinking about Father.

"I know something about psychological cruelty," Win continues. "Alec said you got the worst of it your entire life, even as a young child. Some details were difficult to listen to. He voted to give you a trial and so did Tashi. She and Willie battled it out over Alec and she wants you to have a similar chance. Susan was the one who surprised me. You did almost kill her."

I flinch. "Yes?"

"She said she doesn't want to talk to you, or hang out as she put it, but if she runs into you she'll be okay. I had to laugh. She said she's curious how you'll turn out in the end."

"Someday," Lizzie says, "I hope you get to know Susan. She's... unique."

"Also, Lizzie stuck up for you vigorously."

I smile at her. "And Willie?"

"He didn't disappoint. He's fighting hating you. Willie is a very special guy. He's our group conscience. If he thinks you're being unfair, or an ass, he'll let you know — even his best friends. You saw him during the blizzard. He never lost his cool and he had reasons to lose it. But this is Susan we're talking about. She's the only girl besides his sister he's ever loved. He lost it once before protecting Tashi. Beat a guy to a bloody pulp."

"What did he say, Win?" I persist.

"He wants you gone."

I'm saddened. I was encouraged for a few minutes. "I'll leave. He's right. I should."

"Wait," Lizzie adds. "It's not so simple. All the rest of us want you to have a chance here."

"And there are Paul, Ellie, Sam, and Cora to talk to," Win says. "Ellie will need to have a deciding vote eventually."

"And one more person," says Sarah. "Lizzie, you and Bruce should go in and have a talk with Vinnie."

Lizzie has been filling me in. I've known something about Vinnie — that she's Willie and Tashi's grandmother. Now I understand more. She's the decider. If she wants me out, I'm gone. Vinnie is going on 85 and is the tribal leader, although no one calls her that.

I have the feeling she'll see my core. If she believes I'm horrible and beyond redemption, it will be shattering. It sounds absurd, even to me, but it's what I believe.

Lizzie and I walk up the narrow concrete walkway leading to her little brown house, three blocks from the train station, two blocks from the post office, where Vinnie still volunteers part-time. She spends several hours in the morning sorting mail and catching up on the local news. She had to cut way back after a serious injury two years ago. Vinnie was standing on the side of the road, chatting, and was sideswiped by an out-of-control truck. Coincidentally, it happened the very same day I went to prison. We're connected by trauma in a way.

Lizzie knocks. Soon we hear a cheerful, "Come on in, you two."

I get a warm smile from sparkling blue eyes as I step warily into the tiny living room, but I know this elderly lady misses nothing. Even the room reflects a complex personality. White crocheted doilies protect the arms of ancient stuffed chairs. Native blankets are folded next to the fireplace with Blackfeet memorabilia crowding the mantle. Her exercise bike sits in front of a large modern TV, hanging on the wall.

"Sit right down," she says. "I made my famous oatmeal cookies. I've talked about switching to peanut butter, but it appears the world would come to an end."

I take a cookie to be polite, wondering whether I can choke it down with my nervous stomach. "Mrs. Long..." I begin as Lizzie gives her a hug. "Thank you for letting us come over."

"Call me Vinnie for pity's sake." She says with another warm smile. "Then I won't go looking around for my mother."

"This is embarrassing," she goes on. "You'd think I was Solomon going to divide up the baby. My phone's been ringing off the hook with opinions. I got the picture, though. You want to know whether you should clear out, so you don't scandalize people."

I gather my courage. "I don't want to hurt anybody, any more than I already have. I can start over somewhere else." I pause, trying to get the sentiment right. "But I have a few friends here now. They mean a lot to me. The only people I'm close to, I met in prison. Except for Bob, my lawyer, of course, and obviously my parents don't care." I realize I sound disjointed and force myself to stop. "But don't think I'm desperate." I add emphatically. "Now that I've figured out what's important, I'll be able to make friends. I... I don't need to stay here. I'd just like to. What do you think?" I stop this time when I run out of air.

"You do get right to the point, young man. I like that. Don't look so scared."

I take another deep breath and try to relax.

"Did you know Alice called me?"

"What?" Lizzie and I exclaim together.

"First time in my life I've talked to the girl on the phone, and I've known her since she was born, 33 years ago. I about fell off my chair."

I'm astonished. And heartened.

"Yes. She told me how good you are with her horses, and how hard you're trying to help out. She said she never knew anyone who went out of their way to tell the truth, even when it didn't benefit you. That impressed me. She said you even polish the tack until all hours to help out."

I shake my head with a half-smile. "I do it because it relaxes me."

"So, Lizzie girl. You haven't called. What do you think?"

"I'm biased. I sort of created this recruit. He's killing himself being grateful."

"He did almost kill your sister."

I wince.

"He... We were incredibly lucky. I could never have forgiven such a thing."

"And you want him to hang around, even though it will freak-out some people?"

I can see Lizzie begin to fidget. "Yes. Yes, I do."

Vinnie leans forward in her chair. "Why is this so important to you? Are you so sorry for him? What's really going on?"

I can see Lizzie thinking. "Well, I would like to see who Bruce could be if someone cared about him. From what I've learned, he's never had that. I've thought for a long time, even before all this, there could be someone special trapped inside, someone who could break free."

She stops, and they both look at me. I sit tensely, squinting my eyes, trying to keep myself in control, by holding my elbows into my sides as hard as I can.

"Bruce?" asks Vinnie.

"Bruce?" she asks again.

I look from one to the other. "Thank you, Lizzie," I murmur almost unintelligibly.

Vinnie is quiet for several minutes, thinking, as I take slow breaths. She leans forward again and looks me straight in the eye. "Do you think you can control your anger? What if something threatened you — so horribly you lashed out again?"

My hands are ice. "I've finally faced Father. He can't hurt me. He has nothing to take from me. He never had anything to give. I wish I'd learned that long ago. Now he can't touch me. I fight hating him." I smile wryly, then admit, "Sometimes I lose the fight."

"And your mother?"

Her sudden question causes a visceral reaction and much more pain. "I'm afraid I mean nothing to her." I murmur. "It's very hard to admit."

Vinnie and I look at each other solemnly. I have nothing else to say.

Some moments pass. Vinnie appears to be waiting.

I feel my blood turn cold. Lizzie also waits.

I begin haltingly. It's hard to expose myself so absolutely. "There is something else. I study people now." I pause, trying to say this precisely. "I believe there are three kinds of men. One kind would never do such a despicable thing. Never. Not under any circumstances. Another would do anything, anytime, given the proper opportunity and motivation. And... And the third could be persuaded to go either way. I've come to believe I am the third man. I'll have to guard against it my whole life."

There. I've bared my soul and await her verdict. The silence is profound.

A slow smile crosses her face. "I want him to stay, too, honey. We can always arrange an accident if he misbehaves."

I blink.

"Mostly kidding, young man. Lizzie, come give me a kiss."

I haven't said a word all the way back to the ranch. I finally notice the disintegrated cookie still wadded in my hand, roll down the truck window, and throw it away. I'm shaken completely. Lizzie believes in me, really cares about me. As does Vinnie.

As Lizzie and I are pulling up to the barn, Win comes walking around the corner and sees my ashen face.

"Well. You survived. What's the verdict?"

"She said I should stay."

"Good enough. Congratulations. You had me worried."

Lizzie is smiling at him. "Looks like we better find a place for Bruce to live."

No one had wanted to discuss it. Not until I met Vinnie. "I feel like I just ran a gauntlet."

"You did, man. Mom's got an idea. Come on in the house."

Sarah and Alice are working in the kitchen, making biscuits when I walk in, their hands covered in flour. They both look up as I smile weakly and nod.

"Good," says Sarah. "I can see by the look on your face it ended well."

"Now I need a place to stay. Win said you might have an idea."

"About three miles down the road toward Heart Butte, on the other side of the river, there's a Blackfeet friend of all of us. Her name is Sally Winslow and she's a good friend of Vinnie's. Alec stayed with her briefly several years ago. She's alone out there now. Her husband died six months ago. Her mother lived with them for a long time and her mother-in-law apartment has been sitting empty these past few years.

I look up expectantly.

"She'd like someone on the property. I told her the whole story. She said if Vinnie approved of you, it's good enough for her. And she could use the extra cash."

"Sounds perfect."

"We'll drive over tomorrow morning," she smiles. "Dinner's in an hour."

"I'll walk over to the barn and say hello to the horses."

* * *

I'm currently leaning my elbows over the top rail of the back paddock, watching two of the youngest babies playing, their moms grazing nearby. It's mid-May. The sun is high above the Rockies with warm breezes of summer just on the horizon. I'm going to be able to work with these beautiful animals in this beautiful place. I think back only a few days, remembering the gray walls of my cell and my hope for a better life. I grab a brush, go into the paddock, and start brushing one of the mares. She likes it, doesn't move away, and I lose myself in this mindless pleasure, eventually moving on to the second mare. After a half hour or so, I let myself out and see Alice coming with a grain bucket, stopping to dump some oats on the ground for each mare.

"Alice?"

She looks shyly at me.

"I wanted to say thank you for calling Vinnie. It was fine of you."

"You're a good man. I wanted to help." She touches my hand with hers, turns and walks quickly back toward the house.

After she disappears, I put my head down on my forearm resting on the top fence rail and start to cry, deep wracking sobs. It's several minutes before I can stop, finally taking a deep breath. I don't know how to deal with this level of kindness. Years ago, Ellie tried to love me, and it bounced off me as though I was a granite wall. I believed myself to be so unlovable, I was sure it was faked. No one on the planet could accuse Alice of being insincere. It would be impossible.

* * *

Sarah and Alice are accompanying me as I pull into a dirt driveway, leading toward a small square house set back three hundred feet from the main road. Sally's house is completely surrounded by hay fields, no shrubs or flowers, and adorned only by an immense glacial boulder, an erratic, left over from the last ice age. The house doesn't look like it's been painted since a world war. A tiny old lady appears on the porch wearing a big smile. She's about five feet tall, wrinkled and brown, and wearing a blue cotton housedress mostly covered by a big apron that falls halfway between her knees and her ankles.

"Hello," she says, "I'm Sally."

"Hello, Sally," I answer. "I hear you might rent me a room."

"It's a little house. My mother lived there. It's separated from the main house, but not by much."

We walk around back and see another smaller box-like structure, thirty feet away from the main house. Walking in the front door, I see a one-room space with a separate bathroom. The only unusual features are the countertops which are three feet high off the floor and very low cabinets.

"We built it for my mother," Sally explains, "and you think I'm short. She had to stand on a stool to even reach these low cupboards."

It's homey, though, with walls of knotty pine and a scuffed fir floor covered by braided rugs. Against the back wall rests a double bed covered with a patchwork quilt. A small kitchen alcove abuts the living area with an old Franklin stove providing heat. Two inviting, although aged, wine-colored, stuffed chairs sit in front of it. Surprisingly, it has a decent shower and a stacked washer-dryer in the larger-than-expected bathroom.

"Perfect," I say enthusiastically, "unless the price is more than my budget."

"How about $350 a month?" Sally asks.

"Sorry," I reply. "I can't pay less than $500."

"Really?" asks Sally.

"Yep. I'm firm," I say. We grin at each other.

"Hmm. Okay," she says, "but I'm throwing in a couple of dinners a week. We need to fatten you up some. Sarah, haven't you been feeding this boy?"

"I'm trying," Sarah says. "He eats like a grizzly bear with better table manners."

Everyone looks at me.

"Done," I say. "When can I move in? I have so much stuff it'll take five minutes."

"Tomorrow?" She says. "I want to dust."

"Don't dust, Sally. Here's two months deposit." I hand her $1000 in crisp $100 bills.

"I'm rich," she grins, deepening her smile wrinkles. "I don't think I ever had this much money in my hands in my entire life."

Making the final turn at the Sander's ranch entrance, we stop at the mailbox on the highway, greeting Win who's retrieving the mail. My grin answers his question.

"It was nice of you, Bruce, to pay her so much," Sarah puts in. "She's had a pretty hand-to-mouth life. Her husband tried hard, but never seemed to get ahead."

"I'll get it back with some meals. I'm not a very good cook. I lost a lot of weight in prison. The diet of canned corn and mystery meat was easy to put off. I haven't weighed this little since high school."

"It looks like a match," Win puts in. "Sally is known for her cooking. I bet she's driving into town this minute to spend some of that money on food. You're going to be a happy man." Win points down the road. "Yep. Here comes Sally."

Sure enough, heading toward us is an early 1970's Ford truck. A tiny lady's head just peers over the dashboard. She toots her horn and waves as she drives by.

"I'm going to go in to East Glacier tomorrow and see about the gallery," I say. "Alice, can I work with the horses in the mornings before I go in?"

"Yes," she says, then adds, "I could use the help mucking out stalls."

"I'd be delighted." I smile back.

* * *

It's our last night together at the ranch. Sarah went all out with a big pot roast. Three helpings later I can hardly breathe, asking to delay an apple betty for dessert, which I'm told is similar to apple crisp. I'm satiated, smug, and self-satisfied — the new owner of the Glacier Park Lodge Art Gallery. Connie agreed to stay a few days to orient me, then she's off to Milwaukee to spend the summer with her daughter and grandkids. Everything in the shop is on consignment. The entire inventory is displayed on the computer, plus artist's contact information, plus the financial database. This is going to be easy. I intend to talk to the individual artists, possibly soliciting new contributors down the line. I have to pinch myself, wondering occasionally whether I'll ever miss the old life — the tension and competition.

* * *

This past afternoon, after Connie gave me the keys and left, I allowed myself a few minutes to put my feet up on the desktop and survey my domain. At last. Something that is truly mine.

I considered any remaining problems on my drive home. Seemed the biggest would be not to smell like a horse when I get to work. I was sure I could negotiate a daily shower in exchange for cleaning out those stalls. I put on a country music station and laughed at my new music obsession, humming along with George Strait and Garth Brooks while puttering down the road. No need to hurry.

"You've had a busy few days." Lizzie says, interrupting my ongoing daydreaming at my farewell dinner. "It appears you're not a languisher."

"No. When I get an idea I usually act on it. I'm starting to get over my prison discharge paralysis. I see opportunities everywhere."

"You're going to be fascinating to watch this year," adds Win. "As I once told you, you're an interesting dude."

As they dig into hot apples and ice cream, I stand up to retrieve a sizable package wrapped in brown paper from my car, then hand it to Sarah.

"I want you all to know how much this has meant to me. This is a thank you."

She opens it and gasps. It's the oil painting I worked on evenings in prison and stopped locally to frame — a depiction of Two Medicine River from one of the pictures Lizzie sent me. The setting is late in the day, with the river a shimmering silver band, winding its way downward from the mountains of Glacier Park.

"Bruce. Did you paint this?"

I nod a little self-consciously.

"It's unbelievable," Sarah says, passing the large painting

awkwardly around the table. "I can see the brush strokes up close, but if you hold it away it transforms into a photograph. The shadows are perfect."

"When did your impulse to be an artist begin?" Lizzie asks.

"I always wanted to paint. Of course, Father quashed it, but now I can do what I want. I'm into oils now. And Win and Lizzie... You pick out a view from your new house or I'll paint whatever you'd like."

I get warm smiles in return. Maybe. Just maybe, I could belong here someday.

My life has settled into a pleasant rhythm. Get up at 6:30 and get over to the ranch by 7:30. Clean stalls for an hour or so then work training young horses with Alice until ten. Then a quick shower, dress for the Lodge, and open the gallery by eleven. It's open 'til six, after which I go home and either cook or eat with Sally. We've settled on her cooking Monday, Tuesday and Thursday with extra baked goods sent home with me. She's a grandmotherly figure. I have no memory of my own grandmother who allowed me this freedom. I wish I could thank her for the incredible gift.

I've been talking to Sally about reservation history, gaining insight into people I know and have heard of. I'm specifically pumping her about all the rescuers and associated friends. She's known Willie, Win and Lew Black River since they were born, and their parents back several generations. Sally isn't reticent about details. It's humbling insight. Win and Lew in particular have had serious, even paralyzing loss, and they've persevered.

After dinner I read or play my guitar, sometimes going over to watch TV with Sally. She likes N.C.I.S. and says she's in love with Tony. I fall in bed by eleven and can hardly wait to start over the next morning.

From talking to Alice, I've learned that Willie and several other friends have been working on the house. I've also learned Sam, Paul, Cora, and Ellie are coming out for Memorial Day weekend. I plan to hide out, promising Sally I'll paint her small house. You'd think she's died and gone to heaven. I told her to go in and pick out paint colors. She chose a medium yellow with dark green trim. I'm already scraping the outside.

I've sold two consignment pictures out of the gallery and find myself enjoying the summer tourists who are starting to materialize from all over the world. Adding to my contentment is the time spent with Alice as we work with the horses, sharing the pleasure of these beautiful animals.

There's something else — she's desirable. She's a strong woman in her own right but has grown up in a small world due to her shyness. Her family adores her. To cause her pain is unthinkable. She frequently goes out of her comfort zone to encourage and help me. I adore her, too.

I'm starting to have to fight off other feelings, attraction becoming the primary emotion. I've found myself burying that impulse with increasing frequency. I have no idea whether she has feelings for me or any other man. It's not something I can ask anyone, revealing too much about what I'm thinking. My life here and the support of the Sanders family is tenuous at best. I won't jeopardize that. All the same, I'm a man, and she's attractive in so many ways.

I wonder what it would be like to kiss her, nothing huge, just hold her gently and kiss her. But I won't. What if I frightened or disgusted her? It could end the happiness of working together, which I've come to realize is the high point of my life, so I'll enjoy her in my mind.

CHAPTER 26

ALEC

IT'S THE DAY BEFORE the start of the Memorial Day weekend. Win says Bruce is going to keep a low profile — basically hiding out until the holiday weekend is over. Understandable, considering Paul and Ellie are currently in the neighborhood. All this drama gives us something to talk about.

I've been a long time deciding whether I wanted to do this. I'm currently skulking in the shadows across the broad expanse of the lodge's main chamber, watching Bruce from afar. It's been over two and a half years since I last encountered my foster brother in Connecticut, and almost as long since he splattered my blood around a room in this very same hotel, then left to try to kill people who are now my friends.

Several times I've watched him come out of his shop, once walking across the lobby, passing close to me, carrying a large painting for a tourist. He was chatting away and looked relaxed and happy. Even with a haircut similar to his old one, he was almost unrecognizable. He was smiling. They stopped at the gift shop close to where I'm currently standing, while Bruce asked them to keep an eye on his gallery. He was teasing the lady's small daughter, making her giggle. Unbelievable. I've been hovering behind the column for fifteen minutes, trying to get this person in focus.

I've kept my hair significantly shorter over the last two years and, despite a brief glance, Bruce didn't recognize me either. I'm altered, too. I've been hearing smatterings of news about him, and my curiosity finally got the best of me. Stepping out of his shop with a closed sign on a chain, he looks up as I approach.

It takes him a moment to recover. "Come on in, Alec. Just let me lock up behind you."

"Nice place," I say, glancing around. "Unexpected, though."

"Yeah." I see him pause, probably trying to decide what the hell to say. "How are you?" he finally manages.

"Good. Better all the time. I'm with Tashi. It's everything."

"I've heard you're very happy."

"Yes. I've found some peace. A million miles from the maelstrom."

"Has Frederick discovered you're out here?"

"God, I hope not. Not as far as I know." The old distrust surfaces. "I assume you haven't shared that."

"It's wretched you have to ask. Never, in my life. I owe you that, and a lot more. Besides, I'm not entirely sure he wouldn't kill me first."

I nod gravely. "I never knew for sure whether he kept hitmen on the payroll, but it wouldn't surprise me. I worry he'll send someone out here in a raging vendetta. Are you aware his empire is dwindling? He's lost billions."

"I hadn't heard. I've been pretty much out of touch these last two years.' I smile. "It's suited me just fine."

"He must be a raging, drooling..." I pause. The man is his father.

"Interesting you follow him." Bruce shrugs. "Remembering his voice makes me physically ill. He was looking for you, after... After the blizzard. Before I went to prison. I informed him I had no news of you — that we hated each other. He didn't argue the point."

"No. I suppose not." I don't deny it was pretty much the truth. Not so far off even now. I can't make my voice warm up. Sitting down on his desktop, I look around the cluttered gallery, letting my eyes drift away to lower the intensity.

Bruce drags over a wooden chair and sits on it backwards, leaning toward me against its back. "Just so you know. I hate the man. My own fight is not to let that hatred further destroy my life."

When I don't respond, he continues. "Alec. I wrote you. I profoundly wish things could have been different. Win said you stuck up for me at the Dead Moose. That was beyond charitable."

I focus back on him. "Yeah, well, we're both survivors. I wish you'd bailed. You've had a lot of grief. I stopped by to tell you I can let our past go." I hesitate. "But it will be a cold day in hell before some people here forgive you."

"Do you feel accepted?"

"I'm still dealing with the long shadow. These are incomparable people. I don't feel completely one of them, but Tashi drew the line, especially with Willie. Paul can't entirely forgive me for what

I did to Ellie, no matter what I do to try to make it up. Your battle's going to be much harder. But you won't have a problem with me."

Despite my words, there's a wall between us. I don't want to let him in, to become a part of my group of friends. I don't owe him that. I don't want to absolve him, either.

After a moment, Bruce says, "I'm fortunate beyond words I have some support. Lizzie and Win and their whole family have been unbelievable. I... I probably should have left the area." He looks me intensely. "But someone held out a lifeline."

I smile wryly at him. "Yes, we both understand lifelines. You're privileged to have Vinnie on your side. Her opinion is worth its weight in gold. She even encouraged me to give you a second look."

He cringes slightly. "Did you ever have to go through the gauntlet with her? I dream about it and wake up sweating. I knew the consequences."

"Hell, yes. She can be a sweet barracuda. It was right after I got out of the hospital, after Paul... Did anyone tell you he almost killed me?"

"Lizzie and Win got into it a few weeks ago. The whole story is amazing, including Paul's temper. I've experienced it several times. I guess we're both lucky to be alive." He pauses. "Although I don't blame him."

"Strangely, in my case it helped. Everyone was so horrified by my near-death experience they started to forgive me."

"How do you feel about Willie and Paul? I don't think Willie would kill me outright, but if I run into Paul alone, I seriously hope to live through it."

"They're two of the best people I ever expect to know. But Paul has serious challenges — has fought personal battles on a scale of what we've gone through." He pauses, apparently deciding what he should say, then continues. "At one point he almost killed his brother, Sam."

"My God!

"Despite his past, he and Win are a lot alike if you can believe it." I shake my head, surprised I actually believe what I'm about to say. "Despite everything I've done, and Paul's temper, he's become my loyal friend."

Bruce hesitates, then begins haltingly. "I've needed to say this to your face. I feel profound shame that I hurt you. It was despicable.

There's no way to make something like that forgivable."

I feel a rush of my old hatred. "It was a gruesome blow, Bruce."

"It sickens me," he responds quietly.

I search his face in silence, trying to believe he means it — or is even capable of meaning it.

Finally, he mutters, "I wish I'd accepted your offer."

"I bet you do," I say lightly. "And I'll be ready next time. I didn't think an old man like you could still do the whip kick."

"There will never be another time, Alec," he says softly.

We study each other. The depth of his apparent pain surprises me.

"Well," I say, "I've gotta go. We'll run into each other from time to time. It won't be a problem. You should have a chance for something better."

Bruce holds out his hand. I hesitate, then nod, and grasp his. We shake hands solemnly before I walk off. When I turn quickly for one last glimpse, I catch him wiping his hand on his jeans and remember his clammy handshake.

I exhale deeply and also make my escape.

CHAPTER 27

BRUCE

SALLY VISITS EVERY HALF HOUR or so to see my progress. I started at the back of the house because it saves the best for last. It's good paint so I'll only need one coat and should finish the front side today, plus paint a few front window frames so she can see the effect of the trim.

As I move the ladder, Alice's truck pulls in the driveway.

"I stopped by to see how it's going," she says, "and brought Mom."

"Hi, honey," says Sally. "Isn't it beautiful? I'm going to feel like the Queen of Sheba in my new house."

I smooth a drip of yellow paint off a board with my brush. "Who knew a coat of paint would make such a big difference?"

"Perfect weather," Sarah says. "Everyone's at our place nailing down siding. Suddenly it looks like the kids may have a house someday." She continues on conspiratorially. "They're all going to Sam's for a cookout and on to the Moose afterwards. Why don't you come over for a little dinner? Alice and I miss you."

Alice smiles with what I interpret as passionate enthusiasm, then laugh at myself. Obviously delusional, but I allow myself to grin back encouragingly anyway. "When?" I ask Sarah.

"We'll call you when the coast is clear."

"Perfect.

Sarah and Alice made fried chicken, plus I've wallowed in mounds of mashed potatoes and gravy. I beg off a second piece of apple pie.

"It's a beautiful night," Sarah says.

"It's light 'til ten," Alice adds. "And you haven't ridden the eastern bluff trail yet."

"Maybe," I say. "I'll need help getting on. My stomach hurts."

"Mom, you want to come?"

"No," she smiles at Alice. "I'll watch the sunset from the porch.

You two go ahead. I'll tend to the dishes."

I walk to the barn to start saddling our horses. Alice will be riding her mare, Pearl, a flashy white Arabian-Quarter Horse cross. I start putting a saddle on Sarah's gelding, Arrowsmith, a big chestnut with four white socks.

As I lead them out of the barn, I stop in my tracks. Alice is wearing her hair free, a cascade falling far down her back, with a red and white Blackfeet beaded hair clip. I've never seen her hair out of a braid before. It's stunning.

She laughs at the look on my face, "I felt like going native. Are you coming or not?"

"Yeah," I say under my breath.

After walking the horses to loosen them up, we canter off down the bluff ridge, heading generally east. The light is golden, changing the land into a bright variegated carpet of vivid prairie shades. Masses of wildflowers cover the land in hundred-acre patchworks of color as our path winds its way through the grasslands, seeming to end where they touch the sky. As a new artist, the sensory input is almost overwhelming.

Alice enhances the view, dressed in simple jeans and a white peasant shirt with her black hair blowing long in the wind. We continue in a steady lope for miles in the evening sunshine as the sun edges closer to the ridgeline of the Rockies. At last she stops. We tie the horses in a small grove of trees and settle on a blanket, silently overlooking the river canyon.

"There's something about this country," I say finally. "I almost believe I hear sounds from the past, indistinct war cries and faint rifle shots off in the distance. It's eerie."

"I hear them all the time," she says. "Have you ever heard of the Marias Massacre?"

I shake my head.

"East of here in 1870, the US army massacred 170 Blackfeet, some say over 200 of our people, mostly women and children. Almost as many people as were killed in the Wounded Knee or Sand Creek massacres. They were all innocent people, not even the ones the army was looking for, but their blood was up. They killed them anyway." She sighs softly. "It ended the Blackfeet dominance in the Northern Great Plains. Our tribe is still trying to find its strength, almost a hundred and fifty years later. Our ancestors' past is part of who I am, Bruce... Who we all are."

Her story moves me deeply. I couldn't have imagined Alice would say so much, so eloquently. We're sitting close to each other. I long to put my arm around her. When I can bear it no longer, I slip my arm around her shoulders. She feels warm and accepting. I'm happy beyond belief she didn't pull away.

"I love to hear your voice," I manage.

She turns partway toward me, not disturbing my arm. "I can talk," she says quietly, "when I have something to say."

"And now I have something to ask. You know my shameful past. The abysmal thing I tried. You've never shown me anything except forgiveness and acceptance. Even from the first few days. Now I want to know. How can you allow me this chance?"

"Wait," she says, holding up hands. "I want to answer carefully."

Several minutes pass before she begins. "I don't know if you know about the boarding schools our children were forced to attend in the early 1900's. Tribal children were taken away against their will from their parents for years. They were beaten, many died and were buried in unmarked graves. Their culture and language were forbidden." She turns to look at me. "But the worst was the self-hatred and anger it generated. That anger and loss of dignity have transferred to modern times. Many tribal members are not able to forgive others and themselves for personal failure. Hatred is the result of those schools. "

"I don't see...?"

"Forgiveness of yourself and others is the only way forward. We have to leave hatred behind. Those who can forgive allow their best self to emerge. I've learned that. To see the good allows the best of others to emerge, too."

I can't say anything. I'm so moved and grateful, and deeply shaken. We sit for a long time in silence watching the river flow.

At the bluff edge, I see something. When I stand up to get it, I see that it's a large black and white feather. When I bring it back, she remarks, "It's a golden eagle feather, a good sign for your future."

I smile and give it to her. "Yours, too."

I slip my arm back around her shoulders. I'm fighting other feelings, other things I want to do. But at last, I let my arm drop, and we sit inches away from each other, looking off into space.

When we mount our horses and head home, I can just make out

the lights of the ranch house, visible in the gathering dusk, miles away to the west.

It's late and dark when we put the horses to bed. I've crossed into a new place with Alice. At the very least, she trusted me to talk about the tribal history. And she didn't pull away from me. I'm going to have to think about all that.

"Good night, Alice. It was a beautiful evening. Thank you."

She gives me an enigmatic smile, twirls the eagle feather in her fingers, and walks in her front door.

For the past several hours I've been tormented, besieged with doubt and longing. Jesus H. Christ. This is Alice I'm thinking about. Does she have any idea, any idea at all that I'm dying here? Sometime this evening, everything I've been denying exploded into focus.

I've been alone almost my whole life. I long to rest my head in her lap, have her look at me with those big hazel eyes, and accept me for what I'm trying to become. Is it possible I could put down the crushing burden of the monster I was? She gives me hope that I could.

I want other things, too. I can hardly create such a fantasy without feeling embarrassed. I wonder whether any man has ever seen her naked? Has she ever wanted a man to touch her? Does she want me? It seemed like she might. Is she a 33-year old virgin?

I know beyond a shadow of a doubt I want her. God help me.

* * *

Things are back to normal. Four more weeks have flown by. With the summer heat increasing, the rivers are filled with runoff from the mountains. I've seen Willie from a distance, going in or out of the Lodge, but he avoids me as I avoid him.

This weekend Paul will be done at McMinnville and Linfield College, probably for good. He'd gone back to teaching because one of the professors was on emergency leave, but will take two months off, starting this weekend, and begin full time with the EPA in the fall. He'll be out here with Ellie. She has a month off between jobs, so I'll have two more people to steer clear of.

Paul is coming for the summer to help Win with the house. From talking to Lizzie, I understand Win and Paul consider themselves brothers. I also understand I'm one of the few things they argue about.

It enrages Paul to even discuss me. I've wondered many times why he let me live that frigid night in the blizzard. It would have been so easy... Lizzie said he admitted to her once it was because there were witnesses, but she was never sure if he was kidding.

I'm working on several paintings and am displaying my own work. After all, it's my gallery. A lady from San Francisco bought one of my smaller paintings for $500. It hung in the gallery for less than a day. She was thrilled she got to meet the artist. It pays my Lodge rent for two weeks and I have a larger one in the works. Maybe I'll price it at $1,000. I thought about e-mailing a picture of it to Father, but he probably wouldn't be impressed enough to buy it.

Sally's paint job is finished. It pleases me no end that she's so delighted. She's had her girlfriends out to see it, including Vinnie. I joined them for iced tea and pizza. They all want me to come rent their houses next. Vinnie called me aside for congratulations. I'd like to paint Vinnie's house with gratitude for her goodwill. Maybe I will.

Things have returned to the status quo with Alice. I may have misjudged her. She seems content with friendship. Still, I can hardly wait until I get to the ranch in the mornings. It's probably safer. I have no idea how her family might react. Win might kill me, or Vinnie might arrange an accident.

Today is Friday and I was asked to close two hours early so they can test the alarm and sprinkler systems in the Lodge. I might go out and surprise Alice, see whether another trail ride is in the offing. Paul is due to show up tomorrow and I won't want to be around for a while.

Sarah's truck is gone. No one responds when I call out and Pearl's stall is empty, so Alice must be out riding somewhere.

I don't see her in any of the obvious places, and the trail is empty several miles to the east. It's hot enough for a swim, maybe she's at the natural pool. Around the first turnoff by the bell tree, I find Pearl, and tie Arrowsmith alongside her.

When I'm almost there, I realize I forgot to ring the bell, but before I can call her name, I see her through the foliage. She's lying on the flat rock above the pool, naked, with her head on her rolled-up jeans and her eyes closed. I'm paralyzed.

I'm also a living breathing human man. I inch my way closer. Her light tan skin still has beads of water on it, her hair is loose and damp, drying in the warm breeze, her breasts are full and round. I stand there several minutes watching her, then see her reach down to her side and raise her hand holding the eagle feather. She touches it to her lips and slowly moves it back and forth. Her lips twitch at the light touch. I ache with desire, but take a step back and then another, ultimately making it back to the bell tree, and stand there and stand there. At last, I ring the bell, turn, and walk slowly back toward the pool.

"Alice," I yell.

"Give me a minute," she yells back.

"Okay."

She's sitting up now with her jeans on and a damp white t-shirt. Her hair loose around her shoulders. I walk over, kneel by her side, and take her in my arms. She doesn't push me away. I tilt my head and touch her lips with mine. She melts into me. I feel her breasts pressed against me, her hands in my hair. "Alice," I sigh.

She finally turns, gazing into my eyes. "It took you long enough," she murmurs. "I thought I was going to have to get naked."

We've been at the pool for several hours. The day is starting to cool off, but not us. We're generating our own heat, touching each other. I don't know whether she's ever done this before, but she's a natural. I'm currently lying on my back with my shirt off while she strokes my chest, using her fingers in unique ways. I'm grinning so much it hurts.

It's been such a long time, several years and more, since I've felt anything like this — closeness with a woman I care about. Reaching up, I wrap my hands in her hair, pulling her down to me, teasing her, caressing her breasts under her t-shirt. She straddles me and we laugh together when I hear a twig snap. We turn together toward the sound.

"We found them," says a voice I'm not familiar with. It's full of anger and disgust. Paul with Win.

Alice pauses for a few seconds, then slowly swings her leg off me. Their faces are identical masks of stone as they turn and stalk off.

I'm trembling with anxiety. I've grown to deeply care about Win. I don't want him to despise me, more important, I desperately hope I haven't hurt Alice. She and I ride in silence back to the barn and put the horses away. She insists I leave. She'll deal with Win. It's almost dark as I watch her walk in the front door.

I wanted to go in with her, tell everyone it was my fault, that I'd never touch her again. But that seemed very wrong. It would embarrass her. Was it morally wrong to desire her, or express what I felt? Would it be wrong to care about, touch any reputable woman? Am I such a lost man? I'm waiting. Will I ever see Alice again, be able to help her with the horses? Will I have to leave? Someone will come to tell me.

Several hours later it's warm in the darkness with a dry wind blowing. I'm sitting on the granite boulder in Sally's front yard looking at the stars. I feel exactly like I used to feel, sitting helplessly, outside Father's study. Waiting for him to demolish my soul.

I decide I'll stay here, not moving, forever. But eventually I see headlights of a truck coming down the ridge of the mesa. It's a long way out, but I can hear it coming in the still night, a manual transmission. I hear the downshift. Sure enough, the truck turns in Sally's driveway. Win.

The truck door opens and closes. He walks over to my rock.

"Bruce," he says quietly.

"Did you bring a knife?" There's no humor in my voice. I remember once, long ago, he told me he would twist it in my gut for ten minutes if I ever came back up here.

He hunkers down on the rock next to me and we sit silently.

"I admit seeing you with Alice was a shock," he says eventually. "She's never even kissed anyone as far as I know."

I don't know how to answer that. Finally, "Do you want to kill me?"

"I'm into honesty," Win says. "It's probably good I didn't have a shotgun in my hands, but Alice would have killed me back."

"Is she okay?" I ask wretchedly.

"Is she okay! God! You should ask me whether I'm okay. She yelled at me for what seemed like hours. I've never heard her yell in her entire life. She must really like you."

"Really? She yelled?"

"Paul still's getting over it. He's seen only quiet, mousy Alice. Suddenly she's a raging, salivating tiger. Both of us had a major attitude adjustment." He shrugs. "I won't waste any more time protecting my helpless sister. She said something about using the bell next time or she'd shove it where the sun didn't shine."

"Wow," I say.

"Yeah," he responds.

"You're not going to banish me from the county? Threaten to cut off body parts? Twist a knife in my gut?"

"We already tried threats with you. Maybe we were bluffing."

"I don't think Paul was bluffing."

He smiles wryly at me in the starlight. "No. True enough."

"Win. Can I still come over? Have I ruined it with us?"

"Took me a bit, but we're good. You would have been proud of Alice. She told me she's never seriously cared about any guy in her life. *Picky* was the word she used. What did I want? Her to be lonely, loveless, to her grave? 'All those years when I was carousing around,' was the way she put it, did she throw tantrums at my exploits?" He sighs. "Like I said, she was mad."

"Wow," I say again. When I look over at him, he's shaking his head.

"Anyhow, I threw in the towel. She was right. Shit. I hope I never have girls. I'm beginning to think it would kill me."

"What about your mom and Lizzie?"

"They were cheering on Alice. Mom's turned the corner. You know how Lizzie feels."

"Thanks, Win."

"Oh, hell, you're welcome. You might not ask Paul to go bowling for a while, though."

He pats my knee, walks back to his truck, then pulls out on the empty road.

I'm still sitting on the rock. It must be three in the morning. Win left long ago and I'm trying to come to terms with all this. I guess dumbfounded is about right. Alice stuck up for me, cowering Win and Paul into submission. I keep smiling at the image. Maybe I do have a tiger by the tail.

Not only that, she was so passionate I felt like I was the one being seduced. I keep shaking my head in the dark. I probably should try to get some sleep, but now I'm thinking I can see her again in four hours or so. I keep sitting on the rock, hovering above myself, looking down on my *Thinker* statue.

* * *

As I pull up to the barn, she stops pitching hay to look at me. I walk up to her, take her in my arms, and tilt her mouth up to mine. She puts her hands behind my shoulders and pulls me to her. It's several minutes before I can come up for air.

"Jeez, Alice," I gasp with a big grin.

"Did Win apologize?" she asks, smoothing the hair out of my eyes.

"Sort of. Mostly we sat there adjusting to our new image of you."

"So...?" Do you like who I am?"

"I love who you are. I just can't friggin' believe it." I pause. "I've wanted to kiss you for weeks. I was afraid I'd scare you away."

"Not likely. Besides, you should have seen Win and Paul. I started having fun. I admit it. I got on a roll and they were so shocked, I kept going." She smiles to herself. "I may have to do it again."

"I'm going to try very hard not to make you mad," I declare. "On the other hand, passion is passion."

"You talk too much," she says, and kisses me again.

* * *

My life has improved exponentially. I'm like a crazed teenager with raging hormones. We haven't done it yet, but I'm planning a date night out in Great Falls — reservations at the best restaurant in town, room booked at the best hotel. It's great fun. I sent Alice two dozen yellow roses this afternoon. I text her often in addition to our morning meetings and she texts back — short provocative replies which make me laugh out loud, so at odds with my previous perception.

I'm the proud owner of a new suit. I used to have closets full back in Greenwich, but it didn't seem reasonable to fly back there, disable the alarm, sneak in and grab a handful, then try to get out without getting caught. The one I wore entering prison was several sizes too large, so I purchased one very dark, navy suit, tailored, with accessories. Alice is used to me in jeans and t-shirts. I should probably put a red carnation in my lapel buttonhole, so she can recognize me.

I'm fidgeting in anticipation as I knock on the door. Alice opens it. She has her thick hair piled high on her head, wearing a classic white chiffon dress which reminds me of Marilyn Monroe with her skirt flying up. It takes me a moment to say anything.

"You're the most beautiful women I ever saw," I say.

"You too," she says, then flushes as I laugh at her.

Lizzie, Win and Sarah are hovering in the background. We take pictures. I kick myself for not bringing an orchid corsage for humor's sake.

We've had our dinner by candlelight. We've had Champagne. We even danced a bit with Alice initially giggling. She'd never danced in her life, so I taught her a little. After walking back to our room arm-in-arm, I take off my suit coat and approach her.

"It seems like Win has gotten used to us." I say.

"His life depended on it."

"You continue to amaze me. Didn't you ever want anyone else? Before me?"

"They were children. I was waiting for you."

I put my arms around her back and find her zipper and slowly pull it down, then slip the dress off her arms and let it fall.

"I love watching you in jeans, riding a horse, but this is a new Alice — my sophisticated woman."

"That's the nice thing about movies — they give you ideas."

I start unbuttoning my shirt.

"Let me," she says.

I let her undress me. It's obvious I want her. I take her hand and lead her to the bed and slowly remove the rest of her clothes, teasing her, letting it build. My body seem so pale next to her beautiful darker skin as she strokes my chest.

Pulling her against me, I can feel her heart racing.

I lay her down on the bed and slide next to her, kissing her throat and moving downward, trying to go slow. It's her first time. I want her to want me so badly she can't stand it. I want her to plead with me to take her. My hand moves down her belly, massaging as I go. "Alice," I murmur, "I've wanted you for so long."

"Yes. Yes. Please. I want..."

"What do you want?" I whisper. "What exactly do you want?"

"I... I..."

Wait, I think to myself. Try to wait.

My hands move lower. She wraps her legs around me, pulling me to her, demanding. I can't hold it off any longer and give her what she wants. I'm lost in pleasing her.

CHAPTER 28

BRUCE

SHE NOW KNOWS WELL what she wanted. We made love three times. I'm in a glow of happiness after finally sleeping a little in the early dawn hours. Whatever else happens in my life, I'll have this. Father tried to dehumanize me, to eradicate human emotions. I know now he failed. I can still love. That I'm capable of giving and receiving love eclipses everything.

Never have I understood this level of caring desire. Had I known, I would have moved out of the darkness long before I did.

I look over at Alice asleep in my arms. I would do anything to protect her, to not have her hurt. For the first time, I understand fully what Willie and Paul have had to overcome to be in the same vicinity with me. It says everything about how much they care about Lizzie and Win and Alice to tolerate me here. I'm humbled by the thought.

I resolve to keep trying as hard as I can. It's all I can do. I reach over and touch Alice's cheek gently. Her eyes open. She smiles and reaches for me.

* * *

Carrying two plastic bags of groceries to my car, I glance casually around the parking lot. My life has returned to my earlier routine. The visiting friends who hate me have left, so I don't have to be so careful. I haven't seen either Ellie or Susan face to face. It will happen someday. Susan is still around so I expect to run into her. From talking to Lizzie, I know she's tough and not afraid of me, but the echo of this sordid mess goes on and on. I wonder for the thousandth time whether I should leave — not cause anyone any more pain. But now I have Alice. How can I?

Another one of my pictures sold for $1,200 plus three paintings on consignment and numerous smaller prints. I can't believe I'm making an independent living. I can let my grandmother's money sit and build. Sally cooks me wonderful dinners and so do Alice and Sarah. Alice and I ride the horses often and I've gone out with Win several times. I've ridden with excellent horsemen, but he's in a class by himself. Once he swings up on Cloud bareback, they become indistinguishable. Still, I can pretty much keep up with him. I've heard about the great race between Paul and Win several years go. They keep talking about a rematch, but it hasn't happened yet.

I've started getting mail delivered, a bank statement, an internet/ phone bill, even another letter from Walter. I feel like a middle-class American. When I get back to my apartment, there's a manila envelope waiting for me with Bob's law firm as a return address. Opening it, I find a smaller pale lavender envelope. It appears to be from my mother, so I sit on my steps in the late afternoon sun to open it.

Dearest Bruce,

I don't know where to start. I would have written you in prison, but I knew you couldn't do anything then and I thought it might cause you anguish. I should have left your father decades ago, taken you, but he would have found us. I had no independent funds to completely disappear and I was terrified. The intimidation, even to contact you now, has been unimaginable. With all you've gone through, can you now imagine his viciousness? He threatened you with bodily harm if I ever tried to leave him. I could never risk that.

I watched as he made your life hell and encouraged you and Alec to hate each other. I've failed you in so many ways. You are a grown man, and I understand from Bob that you and Alec are building new happy lives. It gives me hope to go on.

Could you, would you, help me get away from your father? I have no money or real friends. I do have this wonderful lawyer helping me now. He told me you've become close.

If you are willing to help me, let Bob Swanson know. Your father may try to kill me if he discovers my disloyalty.

I'm so sorry. I have always loved both you and Alec. I wish I had been stronger.

Your mother

I haven't talked to Alec since he appeared at the gallery, so I immediately call Win for his cell number. When I reach Alec, I quickly read him the letter. He's on his way over. As I wait, I try to come to terms with my conflicting emotions. I've had to deal with the pain of my mother not protecting me, not loving me, for so long, and now my life has taken such a positive turn. I can't turn my back on my own mother, but it's hard to care deeply — another of Father's gifts. I hear a truck turning in the driveway. Alec is here.

He reads the letter twice. "What do you think?" he asks. "Could it be anything but what it seems? Could it be a way for Frederick to find us?"

"He knows where I am. There was no reason to keep it a secret. I have nothing he wants. I left a forwarding address at the prison. My parole officer has it."

"You have a parole officer?"

"I do. We talk on the phone weekly, and he's in contact with local law enforcement." I smile. "I talk to Dave Miller regularly."

"Really? How has Dave been? With you, I mean."

"Professional. I only recently learned how intimately involved he is with everyone. But, Alec," I say, drawing him back by waving the letter, "what should we do about this?"

"Sorry," Alec says. "The obvious thing is to contact Bob Swanson. Do you have his number?"

I nod, pulling out my phone. It takes several minutes of holds and phone transfers before Bob comes on the line.

"Hello Bruce. You got the letter."

"Yes. What do you think? Is this on the level?"

"Your mother got my e-mail off the Internet and contacted me. She sounded frightened, but not desperate. She instructed me to read the letter before I forwarded it to you."

"What was your impression?"

"I believe it was what it seems. She wants to disappear but has no way to do it. I'm willing to help and have a way to communicate with her. Why don't you think about all this? Call back if you want to talk plans."

"Thanks Bob. I'll get back." I hang up.

"Between us we have plenty of money to help," Alec says. "I can get her a new identity."

"Yes, you've disappeared, but what if you're the real target?

You've got his money squirreled away. You've said his empire is dwindling. What if he wants it back or wants to harm you for bailing out? Or worse? You know how vindictive he is."

"But what if she's desperate and wants out?" Alec asks. "We can't leave her twisting in the wind — not if she's being truthful."

"I'm not willing to risk you. Even if my mother is sincere, we have to guarantee first you're protected."

He looks at me as if he's seeing me for the first time. "You surprise me."

I shake my head dismissively. "Let's get Bob back on the phone and tell him to keep your involvement under wraps."

I hit redial and he comes immediately on the line. I obliquely explain our fears. He understands instantly.

"As we've discussed before, your father uses wiretaps. The chance he's picking up our current conversations is remote, but it's possible." He pauses, clearing his throat. "I understand Alec has completely disappeared. You haven't any idea how to get hold of him."

Alec has been writing frantically and hands me a note.

"Give me a second, Bob. I need to consider something."

I come back on the line. "What if there were something valuable Father desperately wanted to get his hands on? Aside from underlying vindictiveness, what do you think he's capable of? The truth, Bob."

A pause. "We're talking about an amoral man who's had women beaten up, let alone what he did to you. And now that I'm aware of what he did to your mother, we'll need to be even more vigilant." I hear the outrage in his voice. "His empire is rotten and imploding. He's full of hate and capable of anything. He's willing to destroy anyone for spite, in a variety of ways — to hurt you by hurting anyone you love."

When I don't say anything he adds, "I've never encountered pure evil before."

I swallow hard. "How did you manage to break free?"

"I used everything I learned in law school, all my street smarts, trying to deflect, to refocus his evil eye away from me." He groans softly. "The alternative was to become evil, too. Sometime, when we have a long evening and a bottle of scotch, I'll detail it for you. I think... I hope I succeeded." He pauses. "I worry about my own family."

"Jeez, Bob," I say in an anguished voice. "What can we do? No one wants to abandon anyone, but I'm rebuilding a life out here. I can't have these people targeted. He's already ordered Tashi hurt. There are some things even you don't know about."

"Hmm. Okay. We need to keep his attention away from Montana. It means keeping your mother away, too. She's probably not a willing participant in any schemes, but I wouldn't want to bet my life on it." I hear expletives muttered. Then, "How about this idea? I'll let her know you'll help with money to get her situated in a new area. She can pick a place, not anywhere near you. We'll get her some papers to support a new identity and she can live quietly below the radar. A witness protection program if you will. When you want to visit her, you can show up unannounced."

I look at Alec, who's listened in to the conversation. He nods.

"Contact her," I say. "Explain I'm unwilling to risk my friends by having her locate out here. But if she can get away, I'll provide money and help set up a new identity."

I look at Alec who nods again.

"How much money do you think we need to get this going? And I want to pay you, as our lawyer, to facilitate this."

"Bruce," Bob responds, "this will be my pleasure. I did some things for your old man which could use a little redemption, too. This one's on me. I'll get in contact with her and get back. Twenty-five thousand or so would be adequate for the foreseeable future. Is that within your means?"

"Just a second," I say, as Alec scribbles another note. I see a thumbs-up drawing and the word 'Me'.

"Go ahead. Ask her to consider picking a nice sunny place I can visit in the winter."

"Okay. I'll let you know when we can pull this off. Send a cashier's check to the law firm now. When she's ready, I'll send you information to help set up her new identity by registered mail. I don't want to trust any other communication methods. Not these days."

After we hang up, I look at Alec. "That was extraordinarily nice."

"I feel extraordinarily nice. I'm beginning to believe it might be true."

If anyone understands, I do. We shake hands.

"Damn him to hell," Alec mutters.

I'm thinking about Alec. We've traveled a long harsh road together. We were two orphans in the truest sense. No matter what happens with Mother, it's hard to believe she and I will ever be close. On the other hand, I've had so many surprises these past two and a half years, anything is possible. It would be fascinating to sit down with her in a safe place and listen to what her world has been like.

I hope for one thing — that she's not a participant in any of Father's devious plans. I don't want Mother to know Alec is in Montana — not yet. It's sickening I don't know for sure on which side her loyalties lie. Words are cheap, something I need to remember in any communication with my mother. Alec and I will need to fabricate a story about where he might be, preferably Siberia or the moon or dead. Then we'll leak it."

There's nothing to do now but wait. I see Alice pull in the driveway. It's time I tell her about Mother.

Alice is the world's best listener. She sat quietly for two hours learning about my wretched family and my past. She didn't cry or get hysterical or furious, she just sat there and took it.

"So? What do you think?" I ask reluctantly. This is a lot to lay on anyone, especially in a new romance.

"You need to tell Win and Willie. Tashi is on your father's radar. Dave needs to be told. I'm not sure about Paul. If Ellie could be at risk, he'll go absolutely berserk."

Alice remains composed, and with all the other hotheads around here, she's a voice of reason. I'm cringing inwardly. Seems I'll have to deal with people who don't want to see my face or hear my voice. "I was hoping to keep a lid on all of this," I admit, "but you're right. If there's a possibility of anyone being hurt, it's not a choice."

I get a sad smile in response.

"Okay, let's call a meeting, but let me run this by Alec first. I don't want to make decisions without him. After all, Tashi's possibly most at risk. He might want to take her and run to Brazil."

I'm now on the phone with Alec, reiterating my discussion with Alice. Our conversation has included a lot of expletives. Bottom line, neither of us had fully accepted our friends could be targeted. "Pure evil," Bob's words.

"Do you agree we should meet with the people Alice suggested?"

"Give me a minute." Silence on the line. Then, "I don't think I can get Tashi to disappear, so yes. Let's try for tomorrow night. It's Friday. Everyone should be able to come."

"Should I...?"

"I'll call Willie and Dave. You can let Win know. Let him decide about Paul, but I don't think Win will allow him to be out of the loop."

"Do you want me to be there to present this?" I ask unwillingly. It goes unsaid this will be the first face-to-face with some people who hate me.

Another long pause. "It's necessary, Bruce. This is too important for me to speak for you."

"It keeps going on and on, doesn't it?" I don't have to explain what I mean.

"Maybe, someday, we can put this behind us," he mutters. "I hope to bloody hell we can."

* * *

It was decided the meeting should be held at Sarah's house. I look around for Vinnie and am surprised and disappointed she's not here. Did they want to keep this from her? And I would have felt shielded from hatred sitting next to her. Almost everyone else is here, though, including Paul who flew out at the last minute. He's not happy. He's livid in fact, and I don't blame him. Often, I find his hostile face glaring at me and have to look away. It's obvious he can barely tolerate breathing the same air.

Before the meeting, I had a talk with Susan, Willie standing guard. She'd requested it. It was the first time I'd seen her face since the courtroom when I apologized into her cold eyes. She's smaller than I remembered, so small that I had to look far down, making me feel even more wretched.

I put my hands in my jean's pockets. "Can you possibly try to forgive me?" I'd asked. "I know there's nothing I can say."

The question seemed to confuse her. She didn't answer.

I took a deep breath and tried again. "All I can do is to try to lead a good life, do positive things."

She still hadn't spoken.

"I'll never forget my actions that horrible day. I'm trying to make amends. Everything I can think of."

"Except leaving," she said coldly.

I looked down. "Yes, except that."

When I looked up, her eyes were a little more neutral. Willie tightened his arm around her shoulders.

"Keep trying, Bruce. Maybe you're telling the truth." She hesitated. "Forever is a long time to hate."

I'd been watching Willie. I had a feeling it wouldn't have taken much for him to crush me like a bug. Despite that, he was still trying. Why I wasn't sure. Then I thought again about Vinnie.

Paul and I are sitting as far from each other as possible on opposite sides of the room. Alec and I have just finished our summary of the situation. Tashi and Alice sit quietly at our respective sides. The letter has been read. We've explained our concerns for everyone, including our desire to proceed with setting up an alternate life for my mother far away from here. It's a lot to take in, especially for those who are hearing this for the first time. Willie had already been told the bare bones and is prepared to lead the discussion.

"Just how motivated is your father to do anybody harm?" Willie asks.

"That's the big question," I respond. "He could be maintaining a low profile, still trying to stay afloat, or he could be crazed with anger at his empire disintegrating. He could lash out at anyone who attracts his attention. I can't imagine remaining in the same house. Alec...?"

"My whole focus is for the people in this room. I can't imagine what he could do if it suited him. He's terrifying in the coldest way. Bruce and I don't know if leaving would help, especially since we don't know whom he might target."

"We should consider a preemptive strike," Paul mutters, with a clenched jaw.

"Could we get at him?" asks Willie.

I'm taken aback. The room goes dead silent. I understand Willie is usually restrained in his opinions. Maybe this explains why his grandmother wasn't invited.

We're hushed, waiting.

"I know," he says at last. "I'm usually the last one to discuss these sorts of options, but I have to look at Red Clearwater. Everyone knew he was a short fuse. He almost killed several of us as we put off dealing with him. I don't want to make the same mistake." He pauses. "But, if we do something...proactive, it's a terrible secret to keep. Look at us. There are sixteen or more people who'd have to keep a secret for a very long time. It would wear on us, even if the truth could be kept. We'd worry constantly about someone exposing the secret. It would erode the trust we share. I'm not eliminating the possibility, but first we need to try to find another way."

I'm overwhelmed on so many levels. The support these people provide each other is beyond belief. I grew up without either. As I glance at Alec, I see the same emotion mirrored in his eyes.

"How about if we set a trap for him and let him hang himself?"

I look at tiny Susan in surprise.

Willie turns to me. "You don't know Susan. When we need strategy, we look to her. Okay Kid," he smiles. "Give it a shot."

She smiles deviously. Apparently, she loves this kind of thing.

"Okay. How about if Alec and Bruce get his mother settled just like they planned? Once this happens, we leak to the asshole when they'll be there to see her. We don't let her know anything about it. We lure him to her apartment, which we've bugged, ask pointed questions about past crimes then record him incriminating himself. Then we have him arrested."

"Whoa," I think.

No one else seems surprised.

"It sounds very dangerous," Tashi argues. "I mean, what if he's out of his mind?"

Susan turns to Dave. "You're the expert. What do you think?"

Dave has been quiet so far, sitting unobtrusively in the background next to Paul. "Lots of problems," he admits. "First, what if he incriminates Alec and Bruce or does so after he's arrested? I suspect there are illegal things we know nothing about." He looks at us.

We look back steadily without comment.

"Second, what if he doesn't come alone? What if he comes to kill because he's so enraged she left him? Or more — probably sends an assassin. Or what if he wants something from you guys? Information? Money? And what if he's willing to do anything to get it? A trained thug can do crippling damage in a matter of seconds. Even to your mother." He hesitates and lowers his voice.

"Remember what Paul did."

Paul looks down at his hands. Alec walks across the room to put his hand on Paul's shoulder. It reminds me again that Alec's loyalty is to him, not to me.

"Seriously, guys. Keep thinking," Dave continues. "In the few seconds it took us to get to you, it could be all over."

That's sobering.

Significant time passes. Silence. People start shaking their heads.

Finally, when I can stand it no longer, I stand up. "This is going to be hanging over our heads forever. Does he want money or vengeance directed at Alec? Will he have my mother murdered when she betrays him? Alec can disappear, but she'll never be safe. He'll find her eventually. I can't ignore her. I want to go ahead with the original plan and get her resettled." It's hard to keep the despair out of my voice. "Should Alec and I leave indefinitely?"

"I guess you all know if Alec leaves I'm going, too," Tashi adds.

"We don't know who or even if there will be a target. We can't all leave," Lizzie emphasizes.

"She's right," agrees Susan. "At least we can keep the danger far away. Let's get her moved, Bruce."

All eyes shift back to me. "I need to go back there," I say, reluctantly. "The least I can do is try to find out where his anger is directed. See if Alec or Tashi are at risk. I'll approach him at home. Gauge his frame of mind. I can be timid and self-effacing, so I don't push his buttons. I've done it my entire life."

I look around the room, grimacing to myself. No one's thrown their body in front of me to stop me — I'm expendable. And it is MY father who's caused this disaster.

"Better than groping in the dark," Paul offers, staring coldly at me. "I suppose it could be dangerous," he mutters, "but I'm probably not the one to judge."

"You think?" Lizzie comments sharply.

"I should go, too," Alice adds quietly.

"Over my dead body," I burst out.

"Listen," Alice says, putting her hand softly on my arm.

Everyone does. No one ever hears Alice talk much.

"We make it a friendly call. I'm the new girlfriend. Bruce wanted to mend fences, apologize. We're in the area for an art show, meeting people who are waiting for us. Bruce does the talking. I'll be quiet, shy, and naïve. I'll flirt with him a little. He won't hurt Bruce if I'm there. If they think I'm a dumb Injin', it's all the better. I can distract him."

We all sit there stunned.

"I've been upstaged," says Susan.

We all look at Win.

"Shit, Alice. You let yourself out of your cage and look what happens."

She stares calmly back at him.

* * *

Greenwich, Connecticut. We're doing it. Initially, it seemed like insanity, but even I don't see Father going stark raving nuts and killing us, Godfather style, in his own home. Alec will be in the car around the corner with a recording device. He'll have a gun. We'll be bugged.

Alice is remarkably relaxed. Bad enough she'll be meeting my upper crust, condescending father, but it might be very dangerous. She seems mildly excited — you'd think she was going to a social event.

"Alice," I ask? "Aren't you even a little intimidated?"

"Why? As far as I know, neither of them is someone I need to impress. They have nothing I want."

Alec grabs her arm. "You're making too light of this. You've never met anyone like this guy. He's evil, a potential killer."

"I'll keep my eyes open," she looks soberly at him. "We'll tell them right away we have people waiting."

I know my face is rigid with tension. "Okay, let's do this and get it over with."

We're driven up to the front door in a cab. I ask the cabbie to wait — one more safety measure. I had called ahead, using a deferential tone, to set this up.

Pausing at the door, I stretch my neck to loosen up then ring the bell. One of our maids answers the door.

"Hello, Claudia," I say. "Good to see you again."

"Yes, sir," she replies uneasily. "Right this way please."

We're ushered into the smaller informal study on the front side of the house. Mother is sitting stiffly in a wingback chair. Father leans back from his desk as we walk in. Two extra chairs have been brought in, but we stand uncomfortably in the doorway.

"Well, Bruce," he says flatly. "It's been a while."

"Yes, a while," I say. "Two and a half years. Before the trial."

He studies me carefully. I revert automatically to having trouble with eye contact, our old dynamic.

"Come over here, Dora," he insists. "Say hello to Bruce and his friend."

Mother stands, gives me a small smile, then walks over to give me a brief kiss on my cheek. "I've missed you," she says. "You look remarkably well." Her voice sounds like she's commenting on the weather.

"Surprisingly," I begin, thinking about my rehearsed speech, "prison wasn't as grim as I expected. "Mostly boring, but I had a lot of time to think what I want out of life." That doesn't appear to thrill Father. "And I want you both to meet Alice Sanders. She's been a good...a steadying influence on me."

Mother reaches out to Alice, who's shyly smiling, shaking her hand softly before returning to her chair. Alice turns her gentle smile on father.

Father looks like he's sizing up a prize bull, actually squinting his eyes. "You're charming," he says, indicating we sit down. "Do you do something...? As an occupation?"

"Yes," she replies, still smiling warmly. "I train young horses."

"Do you now?" he says.

"Yes," she replies in a surprisingly steady voice. "Bruce is an excellent horseman. Do you ride?"

"Years ago. So did Dora. I met her at a horse event. She was into dressage way back then."

I watch him glance back and forth between my mother and Alice, who is now calmly sitting with her hands in her lap. The room is dead silent. When he finally speaks, it's with an unexpectedly subdued voice. "She was a beautiful 20 year old. I was entranced. You remind me, somehow."

Mother becomes rigid in her chair, which disturbs me.

"I was older of course, over thirty, but I remember the afternoon well. An early fall day with golden leaves. There's something hopeful about beautiful women and horses." He seems to snap back from the reverie. "Do you and Bruce share that passion?"

I've lowered myself uneasily into the second chair, listening to this conversation. There's something going on I don't understand.

Alice continues smiling gently, beginning a quiet summary of how I faked being a tenderfoot on Win's stallion. She's unexpectedly funny, providing personal details, including her desire to push my fanny up. The story gets genuine smiles out of Father. In addition to everything else happening, I'm shocked Alice is talking so much.

"That's fascinating," he says softly. "A new side of Bruce to consider." He looks at her reflectively for some time. "Don't let him crush you," he cautions seriously. "It would be such a shame. Women can let it happen."

"All right," Alice replies quietly.

He smiles at her in a way that can only be described as wistful. My mother looks like she's seen a ghost.

"By the way, what do you hear from Alec?" Father asks, pulling himself out of his reverie by focusing on me.

"Nothing," I say. "We weren't...close."

"No. I suppose not."

"I wrote him once from prison, using the only address I remembered, and never heard back. I tried contacting him through an old climbing buddy when I got out, but the guy said he hasn't heard from him in over two years. He thought he might have been killed, climbing in some remote area," I report deliberately. "If I ever hear anything, I'll let you know."

"He has something I want, and I'd like to talk to him." His voice becomes icy, humorless. "If you see him, tell him if he values his skin to give me a call."

He chuckles coldly, a singularly joyless sound. It chills me. That's the Father I remember. I feel a sudden impulse to grab Alice's hand and run, but he manages to bury the hostility. I sense the effort it takes for him to rein it in. It takes him several moments to manufacture lightness.

"And, how are you getting along money-wise? A change in lifestyle — private jets to steerage."

"I'm making a living painting and running a small art gallery. I've sold several of my own paintings."

"How wonderful," my mother says, leaning forward with spontaneous emotion before shrinking back into herself.

I pull out my iPhone to show her a copy of the larger painting of Two Medicine River. My newest technique is modern-impressionistic.

"It's lovely," she allows herself. "I would have never guessed."

"How's your world, Father?" I ask, then kick myself as his face changes. Any hint of warmth in the room disappears.

"Why do you ask?"

"I have...regrets."

Surprisingly, Father doesn't use the opportunity to twist a knife in my gut. "Why don't you ask Robert Swanson? He appears to follow my business dealings."

"I thought he left the firm. Are you still in touch?"

"Not precisely. But if you encounter him, you might let him know he would do well to mind his own business."

"Of course," I say, quickly coming to my feet. "Well, it was good to see your both. We need to go. As I said, we're meeting friends at an art show in the city."

"Bruce," Mother says quickly, "it meant a lot to see you."

I smile impassively at her.

"Sounds like you've built a decent life, Bruce," Father says. "Try not to jeopardize it."

"Goodbye," Alice says, also standing and taking a step toward the door. "It was nice to meet you both."

Mother smiles at her, but Father rises, moves rapidly around his desk, and reaches out for Alice's hand, holding it so long I begin sweating. It's all I can do not to knock his hand away. Finally, he lets her hand drop. I've been holding my breath.

"Depend on yourself," he says to her seriously. He turns and looks straight at me. "Horses can be dangerous."

* * *

"Damn," I mutter, as we get back in the Taxi. Alice and I stare at each other anxiously as we're driven to rejoin Alec.

"It was incredible," I say, getting back into his car. "He spoke maybe twenty sentences and managed to threaten everybody."

"I heard everything," Alec says. "What was your strongest impression?"

"That we need to get Mother out of there. Alice, what did you think?"

"A lot. First, he didn't think I was stupid. Too bad. And second, did you notice how scared your maid was?"

I shake my head.

"She was almost shaking. That was when I was most afraid. She expected something bad to happen. I'm glad to be out of there. Your father was so tightly wound. And the strange exchange we had. Do you know what he was getting at?"

"I've never seen him like that. Interested. Almost gracious. In addition, he seemed to be warning you, Alice."

"Maybe he thought you were like him, Bruce. Deep down. He was almost protective of me. He seemed to be blaming someone, possibly your mother, for being dominated by him and destroying the love he could have had for her. He's one sick bastard. There was fear in the room."

I agree silently, sensing my heart rate gradually return to normal.

Alice continues. "Your mother is not in league with him. She was terrified to say anything he wasn't orchestrating. Her hands were ice cold."

"One last thing I noticed," Alec says. "He usually threatens in private. Either he's nearly out of control or he doesn't give a shit anymore. Either way he didn't care whether Alice heard his threats."

"He wanted me to be frightened," I add. "That's what threats are. But scared I'd do what? I'm used to reading him and I didn't know."

"Crap," Alec admits. "Now I'm completely afraid of nothing specific and haven't a clue whether this helped or hurt."

* * *

We've assembled in Bob's law office in Chicago, believing we needed a face–to-face meeting on the way back to Montana. I've replayed the entire conversation. He wasn't surprised to be on Frederick's hit list.

"I dealt with this when I left the firm," Bob says. "I've protected myself in many ways, for any contingency. Violence would lead directly back to him personally." He pauses as he mulls it over. "My guess is you, Bruce, aren't his target. You're not rich enough and you're old news." He smiles wryly. "But I wouldn't go out of my way to push his buttons. Also, he appeared to be entranced by Alice."

"It's the last time he lays eyes on you," I say to her.

"That's fine with me." She says, showing rare unease.

"I don't want to know details, Alec," Bob adds, "but you need to be very careful. Cutting through the code, the most serious threat was against you. He thinks you owe him and wants money, contrition, or vengeance against you and any friends you might have."

Alec winces as I ask, "Is there any way we could get him indicted for crimes without implicating ourselves?"

Both Bob and Alec shake their heads.

"Then we're screwed," I mutter.

"Let's keep working on ideas and try to keep everyone safe. Sometimes opportunities open up," Bob offers. "I have news from your mother. She was frantic to get a private word to you, but never got an opportunity. She conceals her real feelings in front of your father. He *punishes* her physically for disloyalty. She said you seemed so happy with Alice it made her cry. She was delighted with your painting."

I struggle with the insight.

"And more. She wants to do this soon, immediately if possible. I'm working on it. Your money arrived, and we're set to go. She's chosen Flagstaff, Arizona. It's a nice college town with a more moderate climate than other Arizona cities." He takes a moment to smile and let this sink in. "She told me this is the most exciting thing to happen in her life since you were little boys. I've just opened a checking and savings account in her new name with a furnished apartment waiting for her. She won't take any electronic devices which could be traced. I needed to check with you before we pull the final plug."

Alec and I grin at each other. This is pretty exciting for us, too. "When's the earliest we can do this?"

"I've been talking to your mother on a disposable phone. She has lunch at a charitable foundation on Thursdays. She's prepared to go from there to the airport and disappear. All she'll take is her purse. We're planning on doing it this week." He pauses. "Well? What do you think?"

"Yes," I say.

Alec nods emphatically. "And what's her new name?"

"Sophia Russell. Charlie Russell is her favorite western painter. She wants to be a real western woman, known as Sophie, who wears nothing but jeans. I've enclosed all the details in this packet with copies of the new papers and ID."

"Sophie," I grin. "I've gotta see this. Quite a stretch from my coiffured, silk-dressed, society mother."

"Let's fly down right after she arrives in Flagstaff," Alec adds.

"All right. I'll set her free Thursday. I'll have a ticket waiting at the United Airlines ticket counter. I'll e-mail you with the flight number, but no other information in case it's hacked. I'll send five numbers and the flight number will be the middle three. I'll route her indirectly under several names, on several flights, to lose her."

Alec and I grin at each other.

"And one more thing, don't make any more visits to Connecticut. Frederick is trying to float a huge loan to keep his businesses solvent. The decision will be out any day. If he doesn't get it, he's probably ruined."

We nod glumly. I wish my mother was out of there.

* * *

Alec and I have tickets to fly to Arizona, Saturday morning, day after tomorrow. I check my watch. Mother should already be in the air. My phone vibrates.

"Hello, Bob. Is it going according to schedule?"

"Bruce. She never picked up the ticket."

My blood runs cold.

"And the word on the street is your father didn't get the loan."

"Now what?"

"I honestly don't know. I contacted the airline. They'll keep the tickets ready to be activated for the next available flight for a month. There are only two choices. Either we wait until next week or someone needs to go back there."

* * *

Our plane approaches Philadelphia International around nine PM. We attempted to hire a private plane until we figured out it would be quicker to jump on a commercial jet, which we made by seconds.

Another surprise. I'm beginning to think of Alec as extended family, not a brother, but on the same side, with a lot of shared history. I think he's stopped glaring at me behind my back.

I filled Alice in as she drove us to the airport. Mostly I talked, and she listened. Being a good listener is very underrated.

Alec and I discussed our lives during the long flight cross-country. It took him a long time to get his strength back after his altercation with Paul — six months or more. He feels normal now and can jog five miles at a fast pace. He doesn't know whether he could climb at world-class altitudes, but he said he could care less. He's doing climbing clinics in various cities in Montana and Washington State.

He no longer feels any animosity from Paul, whose guilt probably hastened their developing friendship. Ellie is mostly fine, but once in a while when they find themselves alone, he can feel her tensing up.

Despite that, he thinks they like each other a lot. He said he tries not to expose his scar to Ellie. Amazingly, they sometimes laugh about it. She may try some aversion therapy with the scar, similar to getting used to snakes. He's considering covering it up with plastic surgery if that doesn't work.

Ellie avoids me like the plague and is frightened of me, admitting to Lizzie she's resentful over our friendship. I don't know whether this can ever get better.

I'd give a lot if Willie and I could be friends. Paul, on the other hand, barely controls his fury. I dream about his knife digging into my neck. Alec has instructed me to stay clear.

CHAPTER 29

BRUCE

ALEC AND I RACE THROUGH the terminal getting frightened looks. We had no time to think about taking weapons, but I was able to arrange for a waiting rental car. It will be after 10:30 when we get to the house. We have no idea what we're going to find when we get there and don't dare risk a phone call.

Alec turns off the headlights, parking outside the premises, while I punch in the security code on the iron gate. Luckily it still works, swinging slowly open. Normally, the grounds are illuminated with area lighting, but tonight the property and huge residence are almost completely dark. The one exception is a dim light reflecting from Father's study on the first floor. In darkness, we make our way to the rear of the house. Approaching the back entrance, we find the servant's parking area deserted.

The rear door is wide open, slowly swaying in the light breeze. I lead the way through the darkened back halls, the only illumination coming from blinking security boxes that remain deactivated and scattered small electronic devices. I think to grab some nylon rope out of a utility drawer. We creep as silently as possible in the direction of the study.

As we approach it, I peer through the opening of the door left partially ajar. Mother is sitting in a chair across from Father's desk. Her eyes are closed, her face swollen with a dark bruise on her right chin. Through the opening, I can see only Father's lower arm with his fingers drumming on the desktop.

Suddenly he screams into his cellphone. "Damn you all. Circling the carcass. Vultures!" He slams down the phone on the desktop.

I see Mother jump at the sound. "Frederick, please."

"Shut up, Dora. Midnight. But if you bother me again..."

I see his fingers resume drumming on the desktop, then disappear to harshly punch a number on his cellphone. I can hear it ring and ring. No one answers.

The phone is slammed down again.

"Where the hell is everyone?" he growls. "All the loyal jesters..."

I back slowly away.

Alex and I huddle in the back hallway. "What do you think?" Alec whispers loudly. "Should we storm in and take her out? Does he have a gun?"

"He has one gun in his center desk drawer," I whisper. "Maybe others." I grab his arm. "Listen to me. When we go in, one of us needs to manhandle him out from behind the desk. We'll need to search him. We can tie him up, grab Mother, and split."

Now Alec grabs me by my shoulders. "We can't, Bruce. Think, Goddamn it! When he gets loose, he'll head for Montana. He'll hurt people. Our people."

"What are you suggesting?" I gasp. "We end him?"

"I don't want to be a murderer, even him. But can we risk Tashi and Alice and the rest?"

"I don't know. I don't know," I mutter.

"I'll do it," Alec says desperately. "He'll kill Tashi. He's already gone after her once. He'll be a rampaging freak. No one will be safe."

I put my hands on my head. "Let me think. Goddamn it." Thoughts flash through my head: images of my prison cell, the loss of color, the endless noise, Alice across a metal table in the visitors' area. No. I wouldn't, couldn't put her through it. No. No.

But there's no escape. He's trapped me — one final time.

"Alec. I'll do it — I've done time. He's my fucking father."

"Bruce, I..."

"We'll know everyone is safe. I'll confess. She's been beaten. It'll be self-defense to rescue Mother."

I start to shake. Maybe I can get off without too much time — years, though. Bob can manage the defense. Maybe someday it will be okay.

We stand together in the dark.

Alec puts his arms around me until my shaking ends.

There is nothing more to say. What I don't tell him is a big part of me wants to do this. I've hated him so hard and so long. We head back toward the study. I'll finally be the murderer he made me.

"I'm stronger," Alec says. "I'll tackle him. Hold him down. You look for a gun."

"I'll check the drawers and under the desk first. Then you search him. No mistakes on this."

He nods.

Just as we're ready to storm in the door, all hell breaks loose. Mother is screaming something. Heavy furniture is shoved noisily to one side.

I approach the office door just as Father flies around the desktop, grabbing Mother by the hair as we race in.

Alec explodes into the room, tackling him, forcing him with much difficulty face down on the floor, pulling his arms behind his back. All of Alec's body weight and strength keep him down.

Mother has stumbled clear, off to the side, falling on her knees.

He screams obscenities while I pull out drawers, flinging them away from me as I search. I find one gun, then a second one taped to a desk panel with duct tape.

"Stop the fucking noise," Alec screams, grabbing him by the hair and slamming his head hard against the floor.

"Get her out of here," I scream. My heart is racing.

I throw one of the guns down on the desktop, race over to Father with the other gun raised, and shove the muzzle into his back, kneeling on his body.

"Alec, first frisk him. Move. I don't want her to see this."

I turn back to Father, who's stopped struggling, and push the gun against his spine. "If you move a muscle, I'll pump the entire magazine into your back," I growl. Everyone in the room is gasping for air.

Leaning back, I let Alec have access. He kneels over, patting him down. Mother stumbles to her feet and walks unsteadily toward the desk.

"I hate your fucking soul," I hiss.

"He's clean," Alec says, standing up.

Just as Alec rises to get Mother out of the room, I hear a loud explosion next to me, then a second. A red river of blood appears from what remains of the back of Father's head, streaming onto the floor, forming a pool.

Mother holds the smoking gun. It slides onto the floor with a loud thud.

We freeze, motionless, speechless.

"I couldn't let you kill him," she says finally. "I didn't want you to be murderers, either one of you." She takes a moment to look directly at us both. "I've hidden from my responsibility all these years. I've let him torture you. I'll never make it up to you. But at least I could give you this."

We're completely stunned. Alec collapses, sliding to the floor. Father is dead. His fixed eyes appear to watch us. I close them and look at his hands. He still has hunks of Mother's hair in his fists. My first emotion to surface is deep frustration.

I wanted to be the one to do it.

Several minutes pass.

"What should we do now?" Alec asks, looking back and forth at both of us.

"I think I'll call Bob and then the police," Mother says, with unnatural calm.

I hope he's sitting down.

* * *

After consulting with Bob, we've decided to try to keep Alec out of it. He doesn't have any DNA or fingerprints on record anywhere. We take a quick look around. He wasn't near the blood spilled on the floor. He's not bleeding. We're just not going to mention him. Mother will say there have been many people, business associates, most unknown to her, coming and going in the past twenty-four hours as the empire collapsed.

Other than not disclosing Alec, we'll tell the truth. Mother sent me a letter. She was frightened for her life. I came back to try to get her away from Father. When I got here, I found he had attacked her, beaten her, and ripped hair out of her head. I fought him, struggling on the floor. She got to one of his guns, and then shot him to save me. It's the truth and will be our statement. Anything else will wait for Bob to get here. He's flying out early tomorrow from Chicago.

We begin to understand what she's been going through all these years. He'd beaten her recently to keep her in line, threatening our lives to control her. I'm anguished. I knew what he was like, what he was capable of. The one good thing is he's dead. I don't have to spend the rest of my life actively hating him — his only gift.

Mother is going to call the police. Alec will go back to Montana and lay low until we know how this will settle out. There's nothing else he can here do to help. I'll stay with Mother. My throat closes up. I want to see Alice. I want to go home. How long that will be?

Suddenly Mother gasps, then frantically screams, "Bruce? Alec? Listen. Oh, God, listen. The reason I started screaming... He was arranging for people to be targeted. No names were used, but it was Montana — people you love in Montana."

"When? Where?" Alec manages. "What exactly did he say?"

"He was muttering, 'I found the bastard at last. He'll pay. They'll all pay. Fly to Montana and earn your blood money.' That's when I started screaming. He threw the phone away and came at me."

"Get out there and warn everyone," I plead. "My God. He said, 'they'll pay'. Why in God's heaven did I bring Alice here? Have I made her a target?"

"He just found out where you were, Alec. He detests you. You got away with a lot of his money and changed sides."

"I'm on my way," he mutters, wincing. "I'll call everyone together. We'll try to come up with a plan."

The three of us look soberly at each other. The old man is dead. He's caused all our lives to be hell. Possibly someday, if we can get past this, we can have normal ordinary lives. We three slowly put our arms around each other. In spite of everything, I feel like I finally have a family.

"You keep the car," Alec says. "I'll disappear." And with that he's gone.

Mother dials 911.

We sit down to wait.

Less than a minute later, I hear footsteps racing down the long corridor leading from the back of the house. "Wait here," I whisper. "Don't move." I quickly grab the second gun and step into the hall. It's almost totally dark, but I can make out a stocky man, dressed in dark clothes, sliding to a halt thirty feet from me. A faint glimmer of a gun points at my chest. I raise mine.

We stand there for what seems an eternity. Neither of us speaks a word. My hand starts to shake.

Finally, a question in a deep calm voice. "Is he dead?"

"Yes."

I hear Mother's frantic cry. "Bruce? Bruce?" Then, "Are you alright?"

"Stay there," I yell and raise the gun higher. Ready.

The man takes a step backwards, still facing me. Then another. And another. He lowers his gun a bit. I do also. He turns and runs. The last sound I hear is the slamming of a door.

I tremble, leaning against the wall for a few seconds, panting.

"Mother," I yell finally. "It's okay. He ran away."

CHAPTER 30

ALEC

DRIVING DOWN THE TWO-TRACK at Win's, I easily identify the trucks and cars parked out front. Vinnie's pale-green 1972 Pontiac rests by the front porch. Willie needed her wisdom this time. I'd called him from the airport in Connecticut before I boarded the plane. I was afraid an assassin might be on his way, too, and Willie would need time to rally the troops.

Willie lost it. Willie never loses it. He used a lot of old Navy expletives I've never heard from him, or anyone else for that matter. He went on for several minutes. He had wanted to drive Tashi to the airport in Missoula.

Racing up the front steps, sober faces greet me as I blurt out, "We'll need a plan." Tashi runs to meet me, and as I put my arms around her, I whisper, "You are not to move a muscle alone." Willie greats me with a hardened stare.

It's taken almost a half hour to get through all the gruesome details. Everyone to a person was astonished at Bruce's offer to take my place as assassin, to get me off the hook. I believe they have real affection for me now, and to hear he was ready to go back to prison, possibly for life, challenged preconceptions. Paul seems troubled. He's been the most unforgiving. Sam also seems shaken.

Willie begins. "I've asked Tashi to leave with you, Alec. Most of us think it's the safest plan. But now that the bastard is dead, we don't know whether any pre-arranged contract is still in effect."

"Would Tashi have to leave for months?" I ask. "Years even? Will we ever know?" I start pacing. "I've been spinning this, all the way across the country. We don't know how capable this guy is, but we have to assume he's on the way. I have assets to get us out, a long way out, and the ability to make it happen. It's time for you to know. I have a law degree and expertise to establish new identities." I sigh deeply. "I let Bruce take the heat back there. I'm not proud of that. It's time to step up."

I look to Vinnie in desperation. "What should I do? I've caused so much trouble."

Everyone turns to her. "It's bad, Alec. No getting around it. But here's the situation. You're not a real family if you only enjoy the good times, then abandon each other when times are hard. That's what weak people do. We're not weak. We stick by each other. You're one of us now, as far as I'm concerned. And I'm not a wimp, Willie." She says, turning to her grandson, her voice rising. "You don't need to keep me out of the loop when you talk serious alternatives. Did you think I couldn't handle some things?"

I take a quick glance at Willie, who looks uncomfortable. Someone ratted on him.

She continues, "Someone said a while back we can't all run away. I agree. Fear, expecting the worst around every corner, is no way to live. That is just one woman's opinion, but I think we should all stay here and deal with what comes. Except..." She turns to look lovingly at Tashi. "Sweetheart, I think you should go."

I've been cowering and this old lady in her mid-eighties wants to fight back. Vinnie's courage has straightened our spines. I can guess what Tashi is going to say. She doesn't disappoint.

"Go Grandma. I'm staying. We'll stick it to the bastard."

Vinnie seems resigned. "You're my granddaughter, after all, and you got my general sentiment right."

"Willie?" I plead.

He turns to Tashi. "Would you go, just for a month or so? Please. For me."

Walking over, she kisses Willie's cheek. "No brother, I won't."

He looks back at me. "You see what I'm dealing with here."

"All right then," I say. "We're setting up a schedule to watch over you, Tashi. I'll take the ten PM to ten AM slot. Willie can coordinate the rest. And if you won't cooperate, I'm shipping you in a large animal crate to the Himalayas. I have friends over there. And I mean it." I glare at her.

She smiles back at me

* * *

Tashi and I are cozied up, a loaded gun under the bed. I'm handling the first shift. It's pleasant duty. It brings back old memories of watching her. Definitely more fun watching her naked. I'm twirling her hair around my fingers with a slight smile on my face.

"What are you thinking?" she asks.

"I'm amazed how long I lasted, watching you in the old days. Remember your lime-colored dress? I spent a good part of a San Diego college party wondering what you looked like without it."

She flips over onto me. "And now you know."

"I do, indeed."

"I love you, Alec."

I kiss her hard, almost in desperation. "You will try, sweetheart, won't you? Stick with Willie and me? We would both be desolate."

She looks at me, seriously. "I promise. I remember how I felt when I almost lost you."

We lie quietly for a time, then I say, "You would have been proud of Bruce. I didn't think he had backbone. For years we trembled in front of the devil incarnate."

"Changing point of view?"

"To know him is to know myself. We're on some strange, disjointed journey together." I shake my head sadly. "All the wasted years when we could have helped each other."

"Not wasted. They brought you to me."

CHAPTER 31

BRUCE

WITH BOB'S EXPERTISE, the legal situation has resolved itself to a point where we can go on with our lives — at least in the short run. I produced the letter Mother had written to show she was in fear for her life. In addition to current injuries, hospital records were found, documenting fractured ribs, fingers broken, a dislocated shoulder, even broken teeth. Frederick allowed her to get them repaired to keep up appearances. She was fortunate to have lived through it all.

With the time line documented, including the airline ticket to show I'd been in Philadelphia for less than an hour, it seemed highly unlikely his death had been pre-planned. Both of the guns were registered to Father. Only Mother's fingerprints were on the weapon. She had powder residue on her right hand. I had none. She had blood spatters strategically located on her right dress arm.

Servants came forward with testimony of observed physical cruelty in addition to frequent intimidation and threats. No one is discrediting Mother's testimony. There was no physical evidence to implicate me as the shooter or time to modify any evidence were that even possible. We really owe Bob. Alec and I are going to make this worth his while.

Mother and I are out on our own recognizance. We're not completely exonerated, but Bob has informed us the legal establishment believes justice was done. The household staff was terrified of him, having given depositions that they were afraid for Mother's life. After a long debriefing at the police station, they simply let us go without charges, under instructions to remain available through Bob.

Mother and I talked it over. She wants to follow through immediately with the move to Arizona. She has no close friends in Connecticut, and it will keep her out of the line of fire in Montana. She's dreamed of starting over for years and this is her chance. She won't have anyone local to help her, but she will have me, and Alec eventually, for support. He's in Montana guarding our friends.

I flew down with her to Flagstaff to help get her settled. It's beautiful here in early September, a sunny 72 degrees, dry and sparklingly clear. When we roll down the car windows, it smells of pine and sagebrush.

Mother's apartment is part of a four-plex near Northern Arizona University. We spent a nice afternoon buying a few things to make her apartment feel like home: red and brown couch pillows, a Navajo patterned woven bedspread, and sunflowers placed in a blue pottery vase. She's planning to take college classes and wants to start piano lessons. After all she's been through, she says every day is Christmas.

I'm taking her out to dinner for our last night, a nice Italian restaurant near the university. It's a Monday night and we arrive late for the dinner hour. The restaurant is almost deserted, so we're seated in the back with some privacy.

"Mom," I say hesitantly. "I need to get something off my chest. Dad told me often you were disgusted at how I turned out. I believed him. After all, I was disgusted with myself. I never pulled you aside to ask."

"Hold my hands, Bruce."

We hold hands across the tabletop. "We have to let this go. Let's talk a little about guilt tonight and then try our best to not think about it again. He told me the same crap — you hated me because I never stuck up for you. He said you were his to control, because you didn't have a real mother."

"I could go on and on," I groan. "All the miserable things he said about me and about you. Why couldn't we see he was the piece of shit the entire time? We're smart, both of us, and he almost destroyed us.

"I want you to tell me, Bruce. Tell me the one worst time when you missed a real mother," she murmurs, "then maybe I'll stop imagining all the times I let you down."

I sigh. "Okay. I'll tell you the worst and we'll trade. You tell me the worst time I let you down, too. Then we'll put this to rest and love each other."

Glasses of red wine arrive and we both take a quick sip. The waitress hesitates, wanting to ask something, but the intensity in our eyes seems to scare her, and she hurries away.

"You first," I say.

"You never let me down," she replies.

"No fair. If we're going to do this..."

"All right." She sighs. "Remember the night when he told you he wanted Ellie to leave the job or he'd have her threatened or worse. You were sitting outside your father's office. I was standing nearby. You saw me and turned away."

"Yes," I say quietly. "I remember."

"I went in after Alec came out. I knew what Frederick had done. He'd already told me what he was going to say to you. I came in and he laughed. 'See,' he said. 'He's going to let me do whatever I want to the girl. He doesn't know how to care about anyone. She's disposable.'"

"I screamed at him. Told him he'd turned you into a monster like him. He laughed again, and I left stifling tears. I wanted you to rescue both of us, Ellie and me, and you didn't."

My face is gray.

"All right," she says. "Your turn."

"I can't bear to hurt you."

"We need to do this," she insists. "Go on."

I sit there for several minutes and finally say, "The first night in prison...."

She nods.

"I thought I was going to die of hating myself. I was so lost and absolutely alone. I kept murmuring over and over, 'I want a mother. I want my mother.' I spent the whole night crying."

My eyes tear up and I blink, over and over.

"I love you, Bruce," she says, with more force than I have ever heard from her. "We're going to love each other so much we erase all this. I'm going to spend the rest of my life loving you. I already do. It makes me so happy. We're going to stand together in the sun."

I'm due to head back to Montana this afternoon. Mom wanted some time alone this morning. We'll go out for lunch and I'm off. I'm eager to get back. We're having a meeting at Win's tonight at eight.

I'm reading an online newspaper when I hear the door open. In walks a stranger. She has warm brown hair instead of the old platinum blonde and it's soft, wavy, and chin-length. She wears new slim leg jeans, a pale-yellow shirt, and looks fifteen years younger.

"My God," I say. "You look like a kid."

"I feel like a kid," Mother says, then giggles. "I threw out my dress in the store."

I look at her and get a lump in my throat. Maybe we really can start over.

I go over and wrap my arms around her. We've apologized to each other over and over about Father and we're done apologizing. He was a massive force. Neither of us was successful dealing with him.

"We're going to be happy," I tell her forcefully. "If for no other reason than to make him roll over in his grave."

"I'm so grateful to you both. Tell Alec again. It's so wonderful not to have to worry about money. I'm going to find a job and make some friends and try to support myself. I want to pay Alec back."

"Mom, it's nothing to Alec. Trust me. The money came from the old man anyway. Just lead your life and enjoy it."

"You go up there and protect those you love," she says. "Leave it to your father to spite us after his death. But if we resolve this, we can recover."

"I'll do my best."

"I want a painting of yours. It's all I want in this life — that and seeing you and Alec."

"It's all going to happen," I reply. "I'll call you when I get to Montana."

"Do you have any idea how wonderful it will be to have you call me when you get somewhere safely?"

I put my arm around her shoulders as we walk out the door.

CHAPTER 32

BRUCE

AS I WALK INTO THE TERMINAL in Great Falls, I see Alice standing with Win and Alec, smiling her gentle smile. "I'd decided I'd never let you see me behind bars," I murmur, pulling her to me. "I didn't know if I'd ever see you again." For a minute, we stand together in undisturbed silence. We have the two-hour drive back to talk.

"There's been nothing unusual," Win reports, finally. "We're not going places alone, especially the girls. It seems to us Tashi is probably the primary target, and Alec."

"Tashi doesn't like being careful but she's trying," Alec admits. "We don't even know whether the operative knows Frederick is dead. If he learned that, wouldn't he take the money and run? Why risk himself?"

"How's Willie?" I ask Win.

"Controlled rage. He's appointed himself Tashi's one-man bodyguard. He and Alec are taking turns staying with her around the clock. None of us know when this might come to a head."

I turn to him. "Alec? Are you okay?"

He shakes his head, his eyes darting around the immediate area. "How do you protect someone from a professional indefinitely? Tashi won't let herself be watched forever. What if we never know?"

There is no answer. In the gathering dusk, we scan the parking lot reflexively. It's uncharacteristically humid and overcast, with the same endless wind. The optimism I felt in Arizona is gone.

"What did you learn?" Alec asks once we're safely in the truck. "I know you must have talked about it. Why she didn't get away?"

"Everyone in the household was on edge. Several of the servants had heard rumors, shared them with Mom in hushed conversations. Everyone was waiting."

"Did they simply melt away?"

"Around 11:00, when she was getting ready to go to the

restaurant, Mother's housekeeper came to tell her everyone was leaving for good, pleaded with her to go with them. They were afraid he'd massacre anyone left."

"I guess they knew him better than we did."

"She said it was one of the worse mistakes of her life that she didn't go. She'd been cowed by him for so long, she couldn't manage to escape on the spur of the moment. She was afraid if she didn't keep to her routine he'd notice and drag her back. The servants piled out of the house, speeding away in a caravan."

I glance at Alec. His face is filled with horror and guilt.

"I know," I admit in a whisper. "She was all alone. One of Father's employees usually drove her, but he'd left with the rest. She hadn't thought of that. She didn't even know whether she could find car keys in the garage or if she could drive well enough to get away quickly. She pulled her few things together, but he caught her running to the garage with her largest purse." I pause for a shaky breath and glance at Alec. "He'd heard the gravel scattering from the cars and came to find her."

Alec groans. "Dear God."

"He manhandled her back into the house, hitting her several times. They'd been sitting there ever since. All those hours."

Alice's face reddens as I see angry tears flood her eyes.

"I'm glad she killed him for this reason," Win declares savagely. "She needed to do a powerful thing to get the abuse off her back — to stop being a victim. How could she put herself back together if one of you had done it and taken the heat?"

"I've thought of that too," Alec says softly.

I continue, "She believed he was going to kill her. His empire was gone, no one left whom he could control except her. She said his manic phone calls became noise to her after a while. She sat there hour after hour, thinking about missed opportunities."

"If only she'd been able to reach out to me," Alec mutters. "When you were in prison, I would have helped, but by then I had dropped out, too. Fear kept us all apart."

"I'm glad he's dead," Alice says ruthlessly. "I hope it doesn't haunt her."

"She said she was proud, if you can believe it. I did. She said she fought being extinguished. I understood that, too."

"I felt like he was trying to take me over," Alice agrees. "I can't describe it. The strongest person could have been bent to his will." She pauses. "Still, there was something very haunting in what he said. He knew, vaguely, he was alone. Absolutely alone.... That he was a hollow man."

"Look at Alec and me," I add. "It could have been us. Think of Mother as a 20-year-old. Her only regret was she didn't blow his head off years ago. Incredibly sad. She'd been in her own prison, blaming herself for our ruined lives. I told her we're not ruined. We're rebuilding a spectacular future out here."

"We can rebuild us, too," Alec states emphatically. "I've been tormented by your sacrifice, your willingness to go back to prison to protect me." His voice wavers. "Will you shake my hand?"

He reaches back over the front seat.

I lean forward and shake his hand heartily. "And stop feeling guilty. A big part of me wanted to kill him — for me, and for you, and for Mother."

He nods as I continue. "He walked her to the bathroom, and she had an opportunity to wash the blood off her face. She said she kept thinking of her empty seat on the plane. It gradually got dark. The phone calls became less frequent. He sat staring at her. 'I'll let you live till midnight, Dora," he said. "'Time to rethink your mistakes'."

"What if we hadn't been there, right there in the hall?"

"Wait 'til you see her," I say, "with her new hairdo and jeans and light in her eyes. We've given her back her life. I feel very, very good about that."

"One last hurdle," Win adds gravely.

We finally make it back to my little apartment. Alice and I are alone. She's become the center of my universe. It's only been four weeks since the pool. I take her into my arms and whisper into her hair, "I was so frightened I'd get sent away. That you'd give up on me."

"I've waited this long to find you," she says, stroking my arm. "I could wait a little longer if it came to that."

Alice breaks me and puts me back together after a lifetime of being broken and left to die. My hand winds into her hair, gently tilting her head to one side. I can feel the vibration of her sighs as I lift her in my arms and carry her to my bed. She lies still as I remove her clothes and start on mine.

Looking down at her, I murmur, "I'm going to go slow this time."

She beckons me to her. I lie above her on the bed, supporting myself so I tantalize her with my nearness. I have my way with her and she with me.

CHAPTER 33

BRUCE

IF WE COULD DO SOMETHING, anything, it would be better than waiting. Fighting carelessness, we review security again and again, looking over our shoulders, checking out tourist cars, people in restaurants, and in grocery store aisles. The tension is nearly unbearable.

Sam and Cora have been warned away. Why risk them? But Sam insisted, coming out alone for two weeks. He felt he had to help with surveillance, and planning to work on Win's house.

Ellie remains out of the area, working in the Dakotas. Paul flew out to see her last week and pleaded. Dave consults with a barrage of suggestions. Tribal law enforcement has been alerted. We have many more guns stashed nearby than I'm comfortable with, especially with the nightmare of Father's death fresh in my mind. A friend of Win's in DC, employed at the NSA, tried to track the guy by a number we found on Father's cell. It was a dead end.

Despite everything, we're making progress on Win's house. I'm somewhat accepted if I keep a low profile and do grunt work. It's hard for Willie to keep his aloofness. He occasionally smiles at me, catches himself, then rolls his eyes. After Alec told people about my offer to kill Father, it moved sentiment in my direction.

Except for Paul. I catch him glowering at me in unguarded moments. He never speaks to me. I worry he's going to find me alone somewhere and do God-knows-what. Violence to protect loved ones doesn't scare Paul. I wonder often whether I should leave, if that would help anything.

Tashi is living here at the ranch full time. Sander's land is isolated, with only one access road, so you can easily see anyone approaching over the grasslands. We patrol at night.

Everyone takes a turn at cooking. Alec prepares big batches of comfort food. Chili and taco soup are his specialties from old climbing expeditions.

The plumbing is completed, and they've started on wiring. One of Win's childhood friends is an electrician. The red, metal roof is finished, plus the stone chimney. Alice is surprising us with drywall skills. Seems she did the walls in the tack room in the barn and has a knack for it.

It's hard for Ellie not to visit during Lizzie's pregnancy, but Paul gets hysterical if she even brings it up. They talk on the phone.

* * *

It's been two weeks. Nothing. I'm back to my routine of cleaning stalls, puttering in the gallery, and working on Win's house on weekends. We all take turns patrolling, carrying rifles. Alec escorts Tashi everywhere and it wears on both of them. I willingly close the gallery anytime they require more help. My volunteering is progressively accepted. They need me. I feel less ostracized — until I catch Paul's eyes on me.

He's currently driving to Great Falls to pick up Sam. Everyone needed a break in routine. Willie went back to work part-time. It's high season and he can't put everything on others' shoulders indefinitely. He left yesterday to guide a tour to Sperry Glacier, one of the highest in the park, and a steep climb for the last fifteen hundred feet. Alec, Tashi and Susan left early this morning to meet him at the Sperry Chalet this afternoon. They'll all spend the night at the chalet, hike up to the glacier tomorrow, and return all the way down late Sunday afternoon.

I intend to spend the time with Alice — maybe a return trip to the pool. I want to see her skin with beads of water on it. I finally confessed the first encounter and how it ended my inner battle. The eagle feather definitely was a good omen.

The weather should be good through the weekend, although some low clouds are due in late Sunday afternoon. If hikers get into a whiteout, they can follow the trail down five hundred feet of elevation and pop out of it. No snow is forecasted, which is good — heavy snow would be no joke. Last August there was snow at the higher elevations, and in August 1992 portions of the park got eighteen inches. Backpackers had to be evacuated.

Mother called last night and had a chance to talk to Alec. She sounded so enthusiastic that we hardly recognized her voice, so different from the subdued one we've been used to all these years. She loves her piano lessons, taken from a struggling college student, and has made a new friend who just moved into her apartment. They walk for exercise together. She's working on getting a job and has found a mental-health counselor to help get her life in perspective. Not bad for three weeks.

Alec has talked to Paul about his hostility. Paul and Sam once had an estranged relationship which barely avoided tragedy. Paul admitted he's trying to let go of his hatred because it causes him intermittent rage and serious depression. So far, he's been unsuccessful.

It's Sunday afternoon around two. Alice and I are talking about starting a large pot of stew when Paul and Sam pull in the driveway. Crap! They were stopping in Great Falls to load up on groceries, beer and ice, but made it here unexpectedly early. I sigh deeply. There isn't the usual crowd of people to obscure my presence, so I put off dinner preparations, retreat, and hunker down in the back hall. Alice passes me in my hiding place and shakes her head. I know she thinks my hiding is a symptom of weakness, so I smile sheepishly. After slinking around for ten minutes, and feeling ridiculous, I attempt a call to the hikers.

The connection is weak, but I'm made to understand they're packing to start the trek down. It's still sunny there, but Alec mentions the clouds are starting to roll in at altitude. I check my watch. Even pushing hard, it will be seven or later until they make it here. No pressure to cook, so I slink out to the front deck, looking for Alice.

Surprisingly, Sam follows me out. "How's it going?" he asks.

"Better. Um, fine," I manage.

"Good," he replies. "House is coming right along."

"Yep," I say, beginning to sweat, but he moves away, giving me a weak smile. He ambles to the end of the long porch, turns, and continues to smile in my general direction.

I probably still disgust him, but his antagonism is becoming less obvious. I'm still trying to figure out his confusing friendliness, when he abruptly walks toward me with a serious expression.

"I should tell you...," he begins. "You need to know...."

We're interrupted by my cell ringing. It's Alec again.

"Hello up there. More news?"

"LISTEN! LISTEN TO ME!" He's screaming. "Go to my place and pick up my climbing gear — two duffels, a red one and a blue one. You know where the key is. Kick in the door if you have to."

"What?"

"Bring two men with you. Go directly to the Helipad at the clinic in Browning. A helicopter should be waiting. Bring coats. It's cold up here. Go."

"Alec? What?" I scream into the phone.

"I need those duffels and fog is rolling in. If the helicopter can't get them here, she'll die. Go. Go." The connection dies in a burst of static.

It takes several seconds. I grab Sam's arm. "Alec needs help. On the mountain."

I see him pause. Trusting me hasn't been a habit.

I try again. "For God's sake. He said someone could die."

Sam sprints into the house and emerges in seconds, hauling Paul by his arm. We take off running toward his car.

I share what little I know — not much, not even who *she* is. We speed to Alex and Tashi's apartment and race up the steps. The key is usually stashed under a front eave. No.

Paul makes one violent lunge at the door before Sam spies the key in a crack on the deck. It must have fallen.

We let ourselves in quickly and locate the two duffels.

Paul's been assigned to get any coats, hats, and gloves he can find.

We're out in two minutes and back in the car. It's three minutes to the clinic where we're amazed to find a warmed-up helicopter with blades circling on the pad.

"Come on. Come on." The pilot is frantically yelling, motioning to us with his arms. "In back," he screams to Sam and Paul.

We heave in the gear and coats and jump for it.

In seconds we're buckled in and airborne. I'm sitting in the co-pilot's seat. He gives me headphones with a mouthpiece, then motions to Sam and Paul to put their headsets on, too.

"Wiley Pratt," he says into his headset.

"Bruce Weingarten," I yell back.

"Don't need to yell."

When we settle into stable flight, I ask, "What do you know?"

"All I know is Dave Miller called. Pulled enough strings to get this police helicopter released from the pool. I was told not to shut down my engine. It takes ten minutes to stop rotating, cool down, and restart. He said you'd be there in less than that."

"Where are we going and why?"

"We're going up to Sperry Glacier. There's a girl deep down in one of the crevasses, wedged in."

I look up at the massing clouds, now seeming to condense magically out of clear air. "Can you get us there?"

"It's high for one of our glaciers, over eight thousand feet, but that's no problem. It's the cloud cover. I have to be able to see the ground to land or hover."

"They need these bags of gear. Can't we get close and drop them?"

"In a field of crevasses? If I can't see exactly where to lower them, I'm going to drop them in another hole. I need visibility. Get it?"

"Yes," I admit, getting really frightened now. "Do you know the name of the girl?"

He shakes his head no.

I turn to glance at Sam and Paul whose faces are frozen with anxiety. They've heard.

Enormous plumes of rolling clouds are suddenly building ahead. Wiley's face is etched with furrowed brow and clenched jaw muscles. There is no point in offering encouragement. If it's humanly possible to land, I believe he'll try. My stomach clenches so severely I wince. I need to see Tashi's and Susan's faces.

Almost immediately the ride gets rougher. We're buffeted constantly. Even though I'm used to helicopters, I feel sick, aware that we're surrounded by walls of rock. Often, I expect we'll crash, but Wiley manages to pull out of the dense whiteness at the last instant and get his bearings. We keep going. There are clouds all around us, but briefly we emerge in a pocket of clear air, climbing higher and higher. The pilot is muttering expletives under his breath, but he doesn't seem panicked. Finally, he points down to the toe of the glacier below us. He's going to try to follow it up to where the rescuers are waiting.

People are congregated off to the upper right side, waving their arms, when again we're enveloped in whiteness. I'm completely disoriented. I can't tell up from down, left from right. I only know

I'm not upside down because I'm not hanging in my shoulder straps. The pilot is looking at instruments and shaking his head.

"If I can't get us out of this soup we'll have to abort," he says. "It's just too dangerous."

I remember Alec's voice. "She'll be dead if I can't get my gear."

CHAPTER 34

ALEC

WE'VE ENJOYED A STRIKINGLY BEAUTIFUL, late summer afternoon, hiking near the head of Sperry Glacier on the west side of the park. The sapphire sky contrasts with aqua caverns, shimmering up from the glacial ice. Willie's clients are enjoying the last of the sun, stretched out, munching on energy bars, as white clouds billow not far above us. The sun disappears every few minutes, each time thrusting us into shade and simultaneously dropping the temperature fifteen degrees before reappearing. It's time to start down, but we linger contentedly few more minutes.

Willie hums happily to himself, tightening buckles on our gear for the decent, as we share a smile. Even Elliot, the eight-year-old monster on the trip, hasn't been able to dampen our spirits. Besides, Willie had informed me this kid will provide occupational training on how not to murder children who need murdering.

Willie almost refused to bring the family up here. His parents have been *disinterested* in controlling him the entire trip, happily turning the kid over to us to manage. Glaciers are very dangerous places. Local kids know never to venture onto one without adult supervision, cleats and a rope. Elliot's father assured us he would hold onto his son's hand every second. This kid listens to no one. His favorite activity has been to frighten away every bird, screaming and flapping his arms, then racing after it.

Willie has been patient and professional — except one final time, before we approached the glacier, when he took the kid aside and told him he'd cut his ears off if he ran away again. I watched as he took out his Swiss Army knife, opened a big blade, and showed it to Elliot. He's been better.

Susan and Tashi have been laughing together all day. Up here I've been able to put aside my other concerns. A breeze starts blowing in from the northwest, cooling the afternoon air. The few remaining sightseers head for the trail as Willie lines up packs to hand out to our clients. I head over to help him, scanning the area one last time for overlooked gear.

"Hey, Alec," I hear Tashi yell.

I turn and just manage to dodge an ice snowball thrown at my head. "Now you've done it," I yell back, picking up some snow and start molding it into a ball.

Suddenly, out of the corner of my eye, I see Elliot dart onto the glacier and immediately hear Willie's booming voice, "Elliot. Stop now."

I watch in dismay as the kid ignores him, running well out beyond the warning signs toward a gray jay perched on a block of ice. Elliot's father starts to yell. I'm furious he let loose of the kid, and horrified.

The bird takes off and flies to another perch farther out on the glacier. Running toward the bird, and just missing several open crevasses, Elliot suddenly disappears after falling into a snow-covered hole.

Everyone in the immediate area gasps in horror.

The kid's mother starts screaming while the father makes a sudden move to charge onto the glacier. Willie stops him, grabbing him from behind and holding him.

Almost immediately we hear a voice and the kid's head pops up out of the snow, looking terrified.

"Don't move," Tashi yells to him. "We'll get you." Before Willie can react, she starts moving gingerly toward Elliot across the ice -- thirty, forty feet.

The boy scrambles to his feet, pauses, then starts running directly toward her, arms outstretched, straight across the snowfield. He gets to within ten feet of Tashi when he trips, falls, and is buried up to his waist in snow.

Tashi can't help herself. Before I can scream a warning, she moves quickly, reaching out her arm to him.

He makes a sudden grab for her hand, pulling her forward on the slippery surface.

Even from this distance, I feel the rumbling collapse of ice and snow as they both disappear.

Someone screams. Willie runs over to Elliot's family. "Go over to the visitors' area and wait. No arguments. Do you friggin' hear me?"

"Yes, sir," the father agrees, taking his wife by the arm, pulling her off the ice.

"Willie," I yell. "Get the rope and axe."

I make my way cautiously to the hole and look down. The kid's hat is visible ten feet below me. No sign of Tashi. The crevasse curves away to the right, eliminating any sight of her.

"Tashi," I yell at the top of my lungs as the kid starts wailing.

"Tashi?" I yell again. I can't hear a response because of the kid bawling. It takes a lot not to scream at him. With all the control I can muster, I say forcefully, "Elliot. Be quiet. I need to hear the lady."

Amazingly, he shuts up.

I yell again, "Tashi, can you hear me?"

I can make out her voice, but it seems far away, "Alec? Alec, can you get me?"

I can barely make out her words.

"Yes, honey," I yell at the top of my lungs. "Don't worry. I'll get you. Willie's gone for a rope."

I hear one more word, weak and frightened. "Hurry."

At least she's alive. The wedged ice could have compressed her lungs suffocating her. Willie is moving carefully toward me, carrying the rope and an ice axe stored in the visitor's center for emergencies. We look at each other silently — *don't let this be too bad*.

"Can you see her?" Willie asks.

"No. But the kid's right here. Belay me."

He nods, starting to dig an anchor in the glacial ice for his boots to prevent slipping.

"Don't move a muscle. Sit quietly," I say to the terrified child.

I cut lengths of the rope to make prusik knots — tension knots with a loop for feet so you can ascend and descend a long rope. It's second nature, but I fumble in my anxiety.

I address Willie's unspoken question. "I don't know. I don't know. I'll go down and have a look."

He nods.

Big problems. No crampons, no jumars, no extra rope, damn it. Nothing I need. "Call Dave. Have him move hell and get a helicopter to the clinic now."

Willie nods, punching in Dave's number.

Praying for enough bars, I simultaneously try Bruce's number.

He answers.

Trying to speak rationally, I tell him what I need, ending the call with, "If the helicopter can't land, she'll die."

Now that I've said the words, it makes it real.

Willie's horror-stricken face reflects my own. He now knows the truth.

Quickly tying the rope around my waist, I throw the other end to Willie, who wraps it around himself.

With Willie belaying me, I cautiously move forward, lie on my stomach, and finally stretch to reach deep into the crevasse. I manage to grab the kid's hand, pulling so hard he flies out of the hole at me. I carefully move us both to a safe spot and untie the rope from my waist, putting it around the kid. "Take him off, Willie," I mutter. "Have them sit on him."

"Call Bart to come get them," he yells over his shoulder as he delivers Elliot to his frantic parents.

I quickly call one of Willie's apprentice packers to come up to guide the family down. "He'll run the whole way," I yell to Willie, who is now working his way carefully back.

Willie settles himself on the ice, bracing his feet into the ice holes, and again wraps the rope around himself.

God, I wish I had crampons. At least I have my heavy leather gloves. Securing my prusik knots in my pocket, I lower myself into the gloom, find myself hyperventilating, and take a few seconds to slow my breathing. It won't help Tashi if I fall apart down here. I move slowly down to a place about twenty feet above the curve where the space narrows so suddenly I can go no further. My body cuts off most of the light from above and I have to feel my way along. I have big shoulders. Willie is even bigger. Unless we can get a small experienced climber up here, I'm the only hope.

I try to wriggle sideways, but immediately see it's hopeless. I need all my gear. With enough time, I can chip away enough granite-like ice to the curve, so I possibly can get to her, but it will take hours. I'm close to despair. This is so bad, so terribly, terribly bad. I understand immediately I can lose her. I take a deep breath, steadying myself, then call down to her. "Tashi?"

"Alec?"

I can hear her fear. "Yes, Tashi. It's me."

Then I can hear her start sobbing. It breaks my heart. "How far are you? Can you see back up toward me?"

"No, I'm...I'm wedged...head down. I...I'm having trouble... breathing. Can you get me?"

I have to tell her some of the truth. "Not without more gear, honey. They're bringing it up on a helicopter. It should be here in ten minutes or so." I know it could take much longer. "Are you in pain?"

"No. Alec.... I love you. Help me, okay?"

"I will, honey. I have to go up to get more gear, and plan with Willie. Then I'll come right back down and stay with you until the gear gets here. You won't be alone. Okay?"

"Okay," she gasps.

I pull out my knots and in seconds I'm easily climbing back up the rope.

Willie makes eye contact as my head clears the rim. My face crumbles. His does also. We both know crying won't help her, but our eyes fill with tears. I do my best to control my agony. For Willie.

His cell rings. He swallows, putting it on speaker. "Yeah, Dave."

The sound of Dave's voice is reassuring. "They're on the way. ETA seventeen minutes if the weather cooperates. Wiley Pratt's the pilot. He'll get there if anyone on the planet can."

"Thank God it's Wiley," Willie manages. "I know he'll give everything."

"Anything else, Alec? Willie?" asks Dave.

"Pray," Willie answers.

He clicks off then turns to me. "Seventeen minutes." We automatically look at the clouds, which have turned ominously dark gray.

"I'm going down to be with her," I say. "It's all I can do until I get my stuff."

"Tell her I love her. Tell her for me."

"Of course, Willie."

I put the knots back in my pocket and descend again into the frozen world.

CHAPTER 35

BRUCE

MOTHER NATURE IS TORMENTING US. A window opens up and, again, I see people gathered near the glacier, frantically waving their arms. Once more a cloud blows over us, obstructing our view. "Please. Please. Please," I mutter.

At the last minute, we get a space of clear air. Wiley drops the helicopter like a stone on a crazy angle and all of a sudden, we're fifty feet above the glacier. He slowly drifts to a flat square of ice, big enough to get us safely off-loaded, while managing to hover the helicopter with the runners just skimming the surface.

"Grab the bags and jump for it," he yells. "Let me know whether I should leave the engine on. If there's someone to fly out."

We leap out and wave an all clear. He lifts off in the pocket of clear air, moving off to the side where there's a larger flat space to land near the tourist area. The engine is left on for now.

I can see Alec climbing out of a crevasse, several hundred feet away, as I work my way over to Willie.

His face is terrible, wild.

"Should he leave the engine on?" I yell. "Is there someone to take out?"

He shakes his head. No. I locate Susan. Tashi is nowhere to be seen.

Sam and Paul are already hauling the gear to Alec across the slippery ice. I carefully make my way back toward Wiley until I can see his eyes staring back at me. I make a slashing motion at my throat, the universal signal for cut it, cut the engine. Almost immediately the sound changes as the blade slows.

Susan approaches us as Willie assists Alec putting on climbing gear: textured gloves, body harness with carabineers, metal hooks and crampons. He moves to forcefully start chipping footholds in the ice with his ice axe several feet further back from the edge of the crevasse, finally clearing soft ice and snow from the lip.

"Susan," I plead, "what happened?"

We all huddle together to hear.

"One of Willie's group, a boy of eight, took off onto the ice. They'd been warned. This kid has been.... Willie didn't want him up here. His parents insisted."

I look around and see a family with a kid being restrained in a bear hug.

"There's new snow here. You can't see all the crevasses. The kid ran onto the glacier and fell in a hole. Tashi ran to get him. She fell through the snow and disappeared."

We're listening in horror as Susan continues, her voice trembling.

"One of Willie's employees is on his way up to lead the clients down. Willie won't leave.

"How did the kid get out?" Paul asks.

"He was only a few feet down on a ledge. Alec got him out easily. But the crevasse looks very deep. Alec couldn't see the bottom or Tashi. He went down as far as he could — about fifty feet." She bites her lip firmly to stop the trembling. "He couldn't chance getting stuck. Decided to wait."

It becomes evident. She could be dying.

"What has Alec been able to do?" I ask finally.

"He's been down there trying to talk to her. She's wedged in like a cork in a bottle." Susan says despairingly.

Alec is coiling ropes next to the edge. I carefully approach him and touch his shoulder.

"I'm going down for a better look," he says, his voice under firm control. "See how close I can hack my way to her."

"Can she talk?" I ask.

"A few words." He looks at me, fear breaking through. "Her voice was weak. She was breathless. I've got to get down there." He turns to Willie. "Can you belay me again? Or should I show one of the other guys?"

"Let me," Willie says. "At least it's something I can do."

We anchor Willie more securely on the ice with an ice screw. He settles himself on the ice on a foam pad with his feet in two deepened footholds cut in the ice. He wraps the rope around himself. "Go, Alec. I'm ready."

Alec drops over the lip. In addition to the one rope they used from the emergency cache, Alec has two good climbing ropes, each about two hundred feet long. He also had two extra pairs of crampons which Paul and I wear so we can carefully maneuver on the ice field. Sam and Susan stand a hundred feet back on the main trail.

Slowly Willie lets out a little rope, then a little more and more. We hear sounds of yelling deep in the crevasse. Then more sounds of ice being chipped and more yelling. Then we hear a call for slack rope, and Willie inches out another ten feet of line. More chipping.

"Two jerks on the line," Willie yells. He tries to pull up some of the rope but can't budge it. It's stuck.

"Ten seconds," we hear from the hole. "Then pull like hell."

Willie gives the rope a single sharp pull. He gets two sharp pulls in response. "Grab on," Willie says to Paul and me. "Now."

We strain as hard as we can. Suddenly the rope appears to clear, and we hear a voice.

"Okay. Okay. I can make it now." We hear sounds of crampons scraping on ice.

We wait for several minutes. A hand reaches up over the lip. Alec pulls himself up on the level ice and lies there, taking deep breaths.

One of Willie's young employees approaches us. He's double-timed it up from the base of the glacier, ready to take the clients down. He asks what more anyone can do to help.

Alec responds, "Put out a call through the mountaineering network for any very slender climber with balls who could run up here with headlamps."

It hits me. We're completely socked in. No more helicopters are coming, not with the cloud cover. Tomorrow will be too late. We're on our own. At least we have daylight. With daylight savings time, it will be light here until 8:00 or 8:30.

"Did you see her, talk to her?" Willie asks, his voice breaking.

"Yes, another few words. She's still so far down around the corner I couldn't see her. She doesn't know how far down she is beyond the curve. I could barely hear her. Her voice is weak."

"How bad?" Willie asks.

"She's already having trouble breathing. And she's very cold. It's killing me I can't help her, at least make her more comfortable." He puts his head down on his arms and groans.

I grab his upper arm. "What can I do? There has to be something."

Alec visibly gathers himself. "Here's the situation. I'm too big. My shoulders are too big. So are Willie's. The only way to get her out is to loop a rope around Tashi's two ankles — then we could pull to free her. If you can't get two arms or two legs together, you dislocate joints and get the person hopelessly stuck. Neither of us can get close to her. We're all too big."

"I could," says Susan. "I'm tiny. I could get close to wherever she fell."

"God love you, Susan," Alec says, "but you don't have the upper body strength. The ice has to be widened and smoothed for at least a twenty-foot section. There's no maneuvering room and it's glacial ice, as hard as stone. Even if you were down there you couldn't clear the ice in a week. And you'd have to be lowered upside down."

"Let me try," Willie says. "I could just blast through any ice. I can't just sit and let her die. Alec, please. Let me try."

"Willie, if I thought there was a chance in hell. But you're so big you couldn't get to within twenty feet of where I was working."

"It's got to be me," I say, calmly. "I've lost a lot of weight. I can compress my shoulders."

Everyone looks at me.

"It's our only chance," I plead. "For God's sake."

"He's right, Alec," Willie agrees. "Unless you can think of another way?"

"It's terrifying," Alec emphasizes. "You'd be upside down. Your breathing would be compressed."

"I don't care."

"There's almost no room to get leverage on the axe. I've been using a small metal hammer I use to pound in pitons. I was going to cut most the handle off one of the ice axes." He looks at me as if considering my past cowardly behavior. "The crevasses are constantly shifting. You could be wedged in like a cork in a bottle. You've never done anything like this. Are you still claustrophobic?"

"We're wasting time," I say, with all the conviction I can muster. I know this is my opportunity to redeem my past. I lie awake nights, remembering I'm a potential murderer — less than worthless. Maybe, finally, I can convince myself I deserve a life with good people.

But, damn it, I'm scared. When I first was in prison, even the confined cell made me feel like I was suffocating. I learned to deal with it. Maybe that will help me now. I look back and forth between Alec and Willie.

We have two long ropes, one to lower me upside down by my ankles, and another one to climb back up with jumars if I need to or, hopefully, attach to Tashi if I can get to her. Any rescue will depend on whether I can clear enough ice to get down there and get ropes around her ankles.

We force ourselves to take time with the climbing apparatus. I put on a climbing body harness, attaching what Alec thinks I'll use. We can't be lowering me up and down if we forget things.

Miraculously, Alec had a pulley in his duffel so Tashi or I can be pulled up. Without the pulley, which Alec doesn't usually have with him, this would probably be impossible.

After taking final deep breaths, I'm lowered into the crevasse. If I were experienced, I could start down with my head up, then maneuver upside down, but it would involve too many ropes and switches. All we need is for me to get tangled up down there. The best alternative is to lower me all the way upside down.

The mouth of the crevasse is wide, but it narrows almost immediately, and I become wedged in. I can wriggle forward, but just barely. I can see the exact spot Alec got stuck and stopped working. It's frighteningly tight. I'm fighting panic as the walls close in, trying to focus on what I have to do. I hate being upside down. The blood pounds in my head and I feel dizzy. Focus, I think, and start chipping.

Chip for a few minutes and rest. Chip for a few minutes and rest. I call down frequently to Tashi. "I'm coming. It's Bruce. Try to relax. I'm coming. I'm getting closer every minute."

She answers back, sometimes.

Every few minutes I hear a voice from above. "Okay down there?"

"Yes," I scream back. I'm supposed to give a hard jerk if I want to come up for a rest. The dizziness seems to be better and it's not too cold. I hate the closeness of the walls, pressing in on all sides. Sometimes I'm close to screaming and flailing, but I fight it down, over and over. At least twice I give in to despair, hanging silently upside down and feel tears pool in my eyes. It's a weird sensation having tears roll up over my forehead. With everything I've got, I take a deep breath and return to chipping. I'm Tashi's only chance in hell.

Maybe there's more fog overhead or it's getting late in the day, but the light dims even more as I inch deeper into the gloom. My body blocks more of the light from overhead. Tashi must be nearly unconscious or frightened beyond imagination. I try to keep talking to her, reassuring her. It helps me, too. I keep calling, "I'm another foot closer. I'm coming."

But I'm getting cold, deep down to my bones. Unexpectedly, I feel an overwhelming curtain of anguish settling over me like a shroud. It hits me — the cold, the despair. I'm back in the frozen car in the blizzard with people dying nearby in the cold. It's happening again: the supremacy of nature, my hopelessness, helplessness, and the horror of the situation. I let myself fall loose, dangling limply from the rope and twisting slowly in the icy world. The tears roll downward over my forehead.

I hear a faint voice from above. "Bruce? Bruce? Are you okay?"

Mustering my courage, I call encouragement to Tashi and start chipping. Three, five, ten feet. I'm well over halfway to the curve. Soon I should be able to see her. I'm within three feet from the edge, but I can't feel my fingers. In fact, I can't feel anything. My hands are numb. I see, rather than feel, myself drop the small axe, and it would have fallen all the way down to Tashi, except it's roped to my wrist through an eyelet on the end.

I've been down here a very long time. I'm guessing two hours, maybe much more. I yell to Tashi I need a short break to warm up, feeling horrible leaving her alone in the dark. I can hear soft whimpering. Giving the rope a quick jerk, I feel the pressure of the rope tighten around my legs and I'm slowly pulled upward. I try to fight my body shaking, then give up and let it do what it will.

They lay me on my back and support my shoulders, giving me some hot tea laced with honey. I finally expand my chest and take a full breath, filling my lungs, over and over, for the pleasure of breathing deeply. Willie has some chemical heating packs that they slide under my outer clothes, but I'm still shivering uncontrollably. It's been difficult to produce body heat with so little arc to use the axe.

At last, the shivering diminishes as I'm fed chunks of chocolate and more hot tea. "I've got to keep going," I insist, trying to sit up. "I'm close to the curve."

"Take a little more time," Alec implores. "If you go down too soon, we'll have to lift you right back up, or you'll pass out trying."

"Bruce," Willie murmurs, gripping my icy hand. "No matter how this all ends, I'll never forget it."

I nod shakily. Even my neck muscles are shivering.

"Bruce," Alec adds quietly. "You're making me very proud."

Wonderful words.

I down a last half-cup of hot tea. "Okay, I'm ready."

Upside down again and it's getting darker down in the hole. I wiggle back to my last position and call out to her, "Tashi, I had to warm up. I'm back. I'm coming. Tashi?"

No response.

"Tashi?" I scream.

Nothing.

I keep chipping and wriggling. I'm getting better at this. I can tell how wide a space I need to move onward. I'm getting more confident I can do this. But suddenly I slip, falling a foot downward and get really stuck. I lose it and start thrashing, flailing, hitting body parts against the sharp walls. Struggling is only making it worse. I'm wedged in tighter. Calming myself the best I can, I attempt to roll my shoulders to one side, then the other side to loosen them, but have less than an inch of room to move. I try dipping a shoulder to release it. My hand with the ice axe is caught at a bad angle, wedged in an ice pocket. It starts to hurt, badly.

I try to fight off the panic, lowering my other shoulder. Nothing. I scream. I scream again. I can't even jerk the rope for help. Both hands are caught away from the rope. I hear a faint voice from overhead, "Bruce? What's going on down there?"

It's Alec.

"I'm stuck," I yell with everything I've got. "Help me."

"Hold on," I hear.

The pull on the rope becomes fierce. My body stretches out longer and longer but doesn't give. I'm being pulled in two. My hand is being wedged so hard it feels like it's breaking.

"Stop!" I yell at the top of my lungs.

The pull stops.

"Hold on," I hear. "I'm coming down."

I hear scraping and Alec's voice gets louder. He's about fifteen feet above me. "We'll get you out. Don't worry. You're not in danger. We need to think this through."

The edge of panic backs off a bit.

"Okay. Okay. I'm okay."

"Try to calm down and take a few breaths."

I try.

"Listen," Alec says. "What one thing would help the most? Which shoulder or arm position?"

It takes several minutes to calm myself and really look. "If I could drop my right shoulder, I could release the ice axe." I pant. "Then I could tuck my arm to the side and you could pull me up a few feet."

"Okay. You're inexperienced in this. If you hyper-exhale, really push the air out, you'll gain several more inches. Trust me. Then do your best to get the axe out of the way. We'll wait to pull your body up out of the jam until we're sure the axe is repositioned. Okay?"

"Okay," I say. I'm hoping like hell he's not just saying this to calm me. I'm terrified.

"This is the way it's going to work. When I say 'go' I'll count ten seconds off. It'll take you that long to force the air out of your lungs. I'll give you ten more seconds to change the position of the axe the best you can and then we'll reevaluate. Okay?"

"Okay," I yell back.

"Ready?"

"Yes."

"Go."

I start exhaling, harder and harder, pushing the air out. I hear Alec counting. Seven. Eight. Nine. Ten. It works. I twist and pull and feel the axe move. I push one last time. The pain in my wrist is sharp, but I've moved it down. I've got the axe out of the way, but my arm is still in a bad position.

"Bruce?"

"It worked for the axe, but I need to do it again to get my arm repositioned."

"Take several deep breaths and I'll start counting."

"Got it."

Several seconds later I hear, "Go."

I blow out hard, as hard as I can. I have the extra room. I move my arm into my side. "Okay," I yell. "Pull. Now."

The horrible pull is back. I can feel my body stretch out. Just before I scream, I feel the glorious movement up. I'm free.

"It worked," I scream. I burst into tears. I know Alec can hear me, but I can't help it.

He gives me a minute. "Bruce? Should we pull you all the way up?"

I gasp several shaky breaths. "No. No. I'm close. I'm only a few feet from the curve."

A pause. I hear Alec's voice one more time. "You're my brother, man."

I swallow hard and start chipping. What I see in the next few minutes will mean life or death for Tashi. If there is too much glacial ice between us, I'll never be able to get her in time. Already I'm nearing the end of my endurance.

Inches to go. I peer around the edge. I can see her legs, fifteen or twenty feet below me.

"Tashi," I yell. "Can you move your feet? Let me know you hear me."

Nothing.

"Tashi. Try to move something. Pump your ankles."

Nothing.

I wriggle my body further and further toward her. It will be possible to get to her eventually, but I realize it will take another several hours of chipping to get close enough to attach ropes to her legs. I don't know whether we have much time, or any time at all. But I bet Susan could get there now. She's over fifty pounds smaller. I think a minute and want help deciding. I give the rope a sharp tug and am pulled upward.

CHAPTER 36

BRUCE

WHEN I'M BACK ON TOP, I begin to explain the situation, but before I can continue, Alec grabs me and hugs me so hard I can't breathe. I gasp for breath.

"Well done," he repeats, over and over. "Well done."

I take a second to look him in the eye and feel it.

As I explain, Susan begins to understand what I'm suggesting. I can tell she's scared. It's a long way into the gloom upside down, and very cold.

"I'll try," she says. "If I can't stand it, you can bring me back up, right? I'm scared of the closed-in walls."

"Yes, honey," Willie says. "Bruce can go back down, if it's too hard."

"I'm such a big bruiser it should feel like a bowling alley, to you, until the last few feet," I say.

"Willie, I've got to try."

We start transferring climbing gear to Susan. I start sipping hot tea and honey in case I have to go back down. Alec is trying to explain what she'll need to know without overwhelming her. I can see how difficult it is for him.

"Susan," I urge, "keep talking to us all the way down. It really helps."

She smiles grimly at me before we start lowering her down. She has one extra rope with a loop on the end and a slide, which will lock it in place around Tashi's ankles.

"I'm okay. I'm okay," Susan repeats, as she descends slowly into the frozen world.

We keep calling down. "You're doing great. Go slow. Good job."

Willie's jaw is clenched, trying to contain his anxiety. Both the women he loves are in the hole now. He can barely control the trembling in his voice, saying only a word or two when absolutely necessary. Before I remember I'm not a friend, I put my hand on his shoulder to encourage him. He turns to me and gives me a look of warmth despite tears in his eyes. Maybe he forgot, too.

It's almost dark now, but we have a Maglite to illuminate the crevasse. Thankfully, Wiley had one in the helicopter and it brightens the sheer walls a long way down through the ice. It must help Susan a lot. I would have hated to drop her into a black abyss.

We lower her slowly, but it's only four or five minutes until she's maneuvering herself around the curve. "I can see her," she yells up.

We let the rope out, inch by inch. Several more minutes pass. I know she has to be with Tashi now. I'm hoping she can get both feet. God knows what we'll do if she can't.

We wait and wait. Finally, there's a sharp pull on Susan's rope and we start to slowly pull her out, foot by foot. We see Susan's feet, her coat, and at last her head. Willie grabs her, settling her on his lap.

"I got the rope on both feet," she says. "I've got it pretty tight. It should hold. I couldn't rouse her, though."

We start pulling. She's stuck. We pull harder. Still stuck. We'll have to pull harder, even if we do great damage. It's her last chance. Third try and we feel sudden give in the line. Inch by inch we pull Tashi's body higher and higher. We pull slowly because she's unconscious. We don't want to scrape her face on the ice any harder than we have to.

Wiley runs over to start the helicopter. It's pitch-dark here and completely socked in, but he can fly straight up for a thousand feet or so, head southwest for a distance to get around Mt. Stimson, then swing east toward Great Falls. At that point he should be home free. He can descend beneath the clouds or use instruments for his heading.

Her body appears, arms hanging limply over her head. As Tashi is lifted out of the hole, we carefully lay her on a litter from the helicopter. She's breathing, but almost stiff from the cold. Alec starts breathing warm air into her. Wiley can take four people, including unconscious Tashi, so we quickly decide on Willie, Alec, and Susan. Before hurrying toward the helicopter, Willie turns toward me.

"Go," I insist. "Get her somewhere warm."

He nods and runs for the helicopter, but turns, looking back one last time as he waits his turn to get in. Willie watches out for everyone.

"We'll be fine," Sam yells. "Go on."

Willie waves as we start moving toward the trailhead. Immediately, we hear the sound of the helicopter revving up as it begins to lift almost straight up into the air, then move off to the southwest. Eventually, we hear it making the course correction far in the distance and head southeast. If you need help, the pulse of helicopter blades must be the most beautiful sound on earth.

Paul, Sam, and I plan to hike out. They've left some food and hot tea with us. I take a few steps, wobble, then stop to steady myself. I need time to pull myself together. I gave everything I had to give. My legs are trembling. We're not far from civilization and will use flashlights until they quit. We hope to make it to the trailhead in roughly two hours, depending on whether I can keep my legs under me.

We carefully make our way off the ice field and pause on some rocky ground to eat something. I'm with two people who really don't like me. In fact, both wanted me dead not so long ago. I no longer care. I did my best and it was very hard. I can't help sighing over and over, releasing tension.

We eat in silence for some time when Paul clears his throat. "I need to say something."

I look at him quizzically.

"Yeah, well.... I've been a long time coming around. I did almost cut your head off not too long ago."

I don't have a response to that.

"If Tashi makes it, we owe it to you. There's no getting around it. She's Willie's cherished sister. It would have destroyed his life. It may still, but you gave it your best. If there's any possibility of redemption, I figure you just did it. And if you saved Willie from a broken heart, I'll owe you forever."

I nod.

"Bruce," Sam adds, "if you'd died that night in the blizzard, it would have been my fault. I was amazed Paul didn't kill you. I.... I expected he would." I hear a heavy sigh. "I was as crazy as anyone that night. It's tormented me a lot since. We're the ones who've needed forgiveness. Paul and I had it out on the drive up from Great Falls. And now, if you'd died, Tashi wouldn't have had a chance. I'm sorry and I'm grateful. Incredibly grateful."

I'm quiet for a while, then mutter, "This is getting a little mushy."

They both choke down gasps of surprise.

Paul takes a deep breath. "There's more, Bruce."

"Yes?"

"Sam held my feet to the fire." He pauses. "I killed someone — my own mother. You probably know the story — my stupidity, subdued rage and hanging on to hatred. I thought I'd gotten over it. But look." He grimaces. "Everyone else has tried to give you another chance. I've been glowering at you, seething inside. If anyone should know what it is to be forgiven, look at me." He takes a deep breath. "What I'm trying to say is.... I'd be proud to have you as a friend."

He holds out his hand. I look at in wonder for a few moments, then grasp it.

I nod and we both look away, incredulous.

There is much to be thankful for this night.

CHAPTER 37

BRUCE

THE TRAIL IS WIDE AND OPEN. A half-moon backlights the thin cloud cover, and with the flashlight we make good time. After an hour, we turn off the flashlight and stop for water. I drink most of one bottle in one long swallow.

"Do you think there's news?" I ask.

Paul pulls out his cell and tries it. Willie answers immediately.

"Willie? How is she?"

Paul listens for a while and gives the phone to me. "He wants to talk to you," he says with a smile I can see in the moonlight.

"Bruce?"

"Yes. I'm here. Paul's smiling. I hope that means good news."

"Bruce. You saved her life. I'll never forget it. Never!"

I start smiling so hard my jaw hurts.

"It must have been horrible wedged in the hole. Alec keeps talking about it. He said he was in a similar situation once and it was appalling, like being upside down in a straightjacket. I don't know whether I could have held it together."

"I'm so glad. You know I have things to make up for. Is she really going to be okay?"

"Yes. Yes. The doctor is very encouraging. She has some frostbite, might lose a few toes, but they don't think so. She's awake and talking." His voice breaks then he steadies himself. "You were down in that freezing hell forever. I'm so grateful."

"I have the first happy life I've had, ever. I can never pay any of you back."

"Wait. Susan wants to talk to you."

She comes on the phone. "I was down there for ten minutes. You were freezing in that hole for hours. You're a hero."

"Is Alec okay?"

"He's in with Tashi. He keeps talking about you — his brother, he says. I'm so happy for you both. Get back quickly." She hangs up.

"His brother." Of all the nice things people are saying to me, it's the one which makes my throat close up.

"Has anyone called Alice and Win?" I ask.

"Go ahead," says Paul. "You might mention you're the man of the year."

"Enough," I say, holding up my hand. I punch in Alice's number. No answer.

I dial Win. Nothing. Odd. Win always picks up. He's on call for the fire department.

I dial Lizzie. It rings and rings.

"No one's answering," I mutter anxiously. "You don't think...?"

Paul gives me a frightened look, pulling out his own phone. He calls several people in quick succession, shaking his head. "I'm calling Willie," he says.

Willie answers. They talk for a minute.

"We all need to get to Win's," Paul says. "We'll meet them where the Heart Butte road crosses Two Medicine River. They'll get there somehow if Willie has to steal a car."

Mentally, I'm screaming. "Alice, No. No. Oh, God." I can't go back to the cold, lonely world without her. I need her. And Lizzie, my friend, my best friend. All I have now would not be possible if it weren't for her. She's very pregnant. Where are they? My heart stops beating for a few seconds.

We start double-timing it down the trail in the moonlight. I'm bargaining with the devil. We're an hour away from Willie's truck, which he left in the parking lot at the trailhead. I do my best to focus on where to plant my feet. I don't want anything to slow us down. I try not to think of possibilities. Then another thought surfaces. Maybe the rescue wasn't enough. Maybe only a life will even the scales.

* * *

Susan remains safely at the hospital in Great Falls with Tashi, who's now out of danger. Willie and Alec flag us down as we approach the southern shore of Two Medicine River.

Alec climbs in the back with Paul, while Sam and I scoot over to let Willie drive his own truck. We're grim as Willie pulls out onto the main road in a shower of gravel. It's after midnight as we climb the steep incline to the top of the mesa, immediately approaching the turnoff to the Sander's ranch. As we get close to the house, we see Win's truck parked off in the distance near the barn. It's dark, but easy to see in the moonlight. I hear a house door slam in the darkness as we approach. No one comes out to greet us as we pull up and park. Sarah's truck is parked nearby, and Lizzie's Subaru.

Anyone could see us coming in the moonlight, even without headlights, so we've left them on. Anyone in the house could have watched us for a half-mile down the dirt road so there's no element of surprise. We left the hunting rifle in the truck, but Willie has a handgun tucked in the back waistband of his jeans. We separate into two groups. Sam and Paul go around to the back, while Alec, Willie and I approach the front door.

Opening it, the first thing I see is Win immobilized with rounds of duct tape on one of the heavy dining room chairs. He has a gag in his mouth but doesn't seem seriously hurt. His hands are tied behind him.

All three women are sitting together on the couch, not tied up except plastic ties around their wrists in front of them. A muscular fiftyish man with a balding head of razor-cut hair sits on another chair close to Win. He wears jeans, showing muscular thighs, and a tight black t-shirt. The gun in his hand points in the rough direction of the floor. He doesn't seem particularly threatening. He looks... relaxed.

"Come in, gentlemen," he says loudly. "We've been waiting for you. And tell your friends in the back to join us." As he speaks, he moves the gun to a position touching the back of Win's head. "It would take a millisecond. Don't push me."

"Paul. Sam," Willie yells. "Get in here."

At his words, Sam and Paul move slowly in from the kitchen.

"Sit on the floor over there," the man says calmly, pointing toward the fireplace at the end of the couch. He throws us a handful of plastic ties. "Put them on each other, including around your ankles," he says evenly, "actually pushing the back of Win's head forward with the gun barrel. "Do it or I'll kill him."

We start doing what he says. I can see Willie hesitate, looking for any alternative.

"Sit down now," he says impassively to Willie. "I can plug a lot of people before you could get to me."

Willie's face crumbles and he sits down with the rest of us. He allows the plastic ties to be put on tightly, his gun now impotent in his back waistband. We're now helpless — the fit-looking man could kill us all in a matter of seconds, including the three women on the couch. I can see horror in Win's eyes above the gag.

"I wonder if you notified anyone." he asks rhetorically. "It will make some difference if I have to decide things quickly."

We stare at him. It's so quiet I can hear the ice cubes fall in the freezer into a bin.

"I'm guessing you didn't," he decides finally. "Things can get out of control fast — deadly fast. I'm guessing you considered that, too."

I look at the women on the couch, Alec, all of us, and my heart sinks.

"For the record," the man asks, as if inquiring about ball scores, "how's the young lady doing?"

"She'll make it," says Alec carefully.

"Do I look familiar, Alec?" he asks. "We've met before."

Alec's eyes widen. "You look different, but yes. You taught me to beat up a woman."

"Then you know I'm no fool," he says, looking around the room. "For simplicity's sake, think of me as Arturo."

"What are you going to do here?" I ask.

His eyes become cold. "There are several things at stake. I know the old man is dead. Would someone care to tell me how that came about?"

"What difference does it make to you?" I ask.

Now he openly glares at me. "The cruel bastard. What he did to his wife was beyond despicable. I had to intervene. Several times. Why didn't you *Gentlemen,"* he spits the word out, "get her out of there? Were you so fucking blind you didn't know she was a virtual prisoner all those years?"

He seems enraged, stands up suddenly, grabs my shirt front, and points the gun in my face.

I startle and shrink away from his hands, muttering, "I was.... I should have seen."

"Seen? Yes, you asshole. Yes, you should have seen. Answer me." He moves the gun barrel back and forth between Alec and me. "How did she finally get out of there?"

I shake my head to clear it. This is not the way I expected this to go.

"When she.... She asked for help," I stammer. "We pulled funds together, set up an alternative identity, and arranged for her to disappear."

He says nothing. His eyes are black coals. I'm certain if I say the wrong thing I'm a dead man.

I swallow and clear my throat. "We were right down to the wire. She didn't make a final contact. Alec and I flew back there to get her out."

"So, it was as I believed." He swings the gun toward Alec's face. "He was there, too."

"Yes, I was there," admits Alec. "If we hadn't been there, she'd be dead. He planned to kill her at midnight. He told her as much, tormenting her. It was the same night he found out he was ruined. He was raging mad, crazy."

"I know," the man growls. "I was there."

Ah. The running man.

"Who shot him?"

We sit paralyzed.

"One chance. Tell me the truth."

I look at Alec who nods at me.

"When we got to the house, Mother had been beaten. We saw her through the cracked study door and backed out in the hall to plan what to do. Her face was swollen, her lip cut. We.... I volunteered to end him."

Once again, an undecipherable look of hatred flashes across his face.

"He was my father. It was my duty." I hear gasps. This is the first time several people here have heard details. The room returns to dead silence.

Alec continues, "We heard screaming and couldn't wait. We burst into the study and overpowered him. Bruce yelled at me to get his mother out of the room, but I had to search him first for weapons. When we were both distracted, she grabbed one of the guns from the desk top." He sighs. "She shot him in the back of his head. Twice. She shot him to spare us."

"That's when Alec slipped away," I add. "Mother and I sat down to wait for the police."

"Everything you told authorities was correct, then?"

"She had new serious injuries, hair pulled out by the roots still in the bastard's hands. Her prints were on the gun. We waited hours at the police station while they examined hospital records." I realize my hands are balled in fists and stretch my fingers. "She had unreported, healed fractures, which showed up on x-ray." Eventually, they believed our story and let us go." I exhale deeply. "We had a life arranged for Mother in the Southwest. I flew down there with her." I study Arturo's black face. "She's doing well."

He glares back at me, then looks down at his gun.

"Did you come out here to kill people?" Willie asks directly.

"It's what I do." His voice is so matter-of-fact, it's chilling.

"Who?" I manage.

"The old man contracted me to kill Tashi," he pauses, "and one other person. Both were chosen to hurt the most people, but most of all Alec. Your father hated everyone, but Alec had betrayed him. Really amazing. I've never encountered such depravity."

"And then there was the extra money squirreled away — another betrayal." He grins sardonically before his face hardens."

"But you don't need to kill anyone," Alice argues. "He's dead."

Angelo takes a step toward her.

Even with my hands and feet tied, I manage to scramble to my feet, and lunge toward him.

He glares at me, shoving me harshly backwards, almost toppling me with a backhanded blow from the side of his gun. "Sit down, Bruce. I'm not going to hurt her."

We coldly stare at each other. Finally, slowly, I sit down.

He turns back to Alice. "No. You're right. I don't have to do anything the old man wants, not any more. He's made me a rich man over the years. And I know how to disappear."

"How would hurting Tashi help anything?" Alice tries again. "She almost died today. Isn't that enough?"

"I don't hurt defenseless women." He mutters. "Unlike several men in this room." His eyes bore into mine, then turn slowly to glare at Alec.

I feel the old nauseating guilt. I know Alec does, too. Water rises in my mouth and I have to spit it out.

"Who was the other target?" asks Willie.

"You guess," he says to all of us. "Whose death would hurt

everyone the most?"

I'm afraid to guess, to give this guy any ideas. We care about each other. I even think I might be included.

"Come on," Arturo taunts. "I'll give you a hint. This was your father's diabolical idea. What one person's death could hurt you all? Every one of you."

"You don't understand, do you?" Paul reacts, visibly trying to control his rage. "We're a family. Some of us came into this being damaged goods. This all started in guilt and anger and fear, and we've turned it into love. We're all indispensable. We won't guess."

Arturo stares at Paul for several long moments before responding. "My employer was vile. He was the devil incarnate. I'll give you a hint. His other target was older than three of you put together."

"Vinnie," we all gasp in horror.

"Yes," he snarls. "He wanted me to end a little old lady because you all love her. I guess you could say the old man turned my life around. I was afraid if I refused he'd find someone else to kill this grandmother. Does that ring a bell, Alec? At the end he was a whirling dervish, feverishly ordering murder. He'd completely gone over the edge. I overheard him on the phone as he came at your mother." His face becomes even blacker — his hatred exposed. "I heard her scream," he spits. "I heard her scream."

It takes several more moments before he's able to continue. "I was on the way back to kill him. I'd been planning it in some magnificent detail, but someone else did my work for me — apparently your mother. I'm glad you were willing to kill him, Bruce. Shows balls." He sneers, "Maybe I'll pardon you."

"Did you come to kill someone?" Alec asks.

He seems to explode out of his artificial calm. Scrambling over to Alec he grabs him by his shirt and growls, "I haven't decided. You know I can do it. I can execute anyone here and disappear. You heroes...." he laughs ruthlessly. "For all your preparations, you were a paper tiger. I climbed up the back bluff, not even a technical slope." He motions at Win. "Nothing like a stun gun to incapacitate a man. I waited until I could get one of you alone and poof, he was on the ground."

Arturo sighs, appearing to relax somewhat, then settles on the hearth next to Alec, his gun more or less pointed at his chest. "I cuffed him," he says, tipping his head toward Win, "and held the gun to his head. The ladies were so frightened I'd hurt him, they cooperated. That's the trouble with love. It incapacitates a person. Love can kill as well as hate."

"It came on slowly," he says, seeming to gain more control, as he resumes shifting the gun back and forth between Alec and me. "I didn't realize I cared about her until long after it started. Dora never knew I watched over her, and she never knew what I agreed to do to protect her." His face hardens again. "The devil and I fought for control. I never won, but I managed to control the damage. I even taught Alec how to hurt that beautiful girl without killing her. Apparently, he had a bit of decency to try to make up for it."

"It was to help her?" Alec gasps.

"My coaching kept you from doing deadly harm. Frederick never knew about the lesson. You should thank me, Alec. You can kill people with your fists." He looks around the room. "None of you get it, do you? I offered, pleaded with the monster, to let me do the beating. I knew what could happen. Alec could accidentally kill the girl. Old man Weingarten knew it, too. He was hoping Alec would kill her. Then he'd own Alec, forever. Or Alec would kill himself. I don't think the old man cared which."

I hear Alec cry out, pulling up his manacled hands to cover his eyes.

In addition, I hear a moan and my eyes turn to Paul. This is Ellie he's talking about.

Despondently, I decide. "I know who you want to kill and why," I say quietly. "You want to kill me because I abandoned my mother."

"You swine," he explodes, "And what did it ever get you — jail time and a mother with a broken heart." He thumps his chest. "I know. She talked to me about it — how much she loved you, how she felt tormented for letting it happen." His voice rising to a higher pitch, "What could she ever do? She was a small, loving woman who was broken by a cruel monster. All those years you stumbled along, drowning in your own misery, trying to make the old man choose you to lead his evil empire."

Suddenly, he stalks over, shoving the gun in Alec's face, almost in his mouth, denting in his cheek. His voice rises. "But you — you bastard! Those two years when Bruce was in prison...." He grabs Alec's hair with his other hand, tilting his head back. "I know. I know now." His voice rising to an even higher pitch. "I just learned about the physical abuse. She managed to hide it, even from me. All those emergency room visits while Bruce was in prison — you should have gotten her away." He's yelling now. "What the hell was wrong with you?"

Alec's face blanches in terror.

Tears well up in my eyes. For a little while today, I thought I might be okay — that I could put this behind me, deserve to try to make Alice happy. I hear a roar, the sound of the ground opening up beneath my feet, a shifting. I hear the gun being cocked. Alec closes his eyes.

"Stop," I scream. "Don't blame Alec. Blame me. I knew what he was capable of." I pause. "So did you, you fucking asshole! Blame yourself. You could have gotten her away."

Arturo moves the gun a fraction of an inch away from Alec's head. Then another inch. His face has become murderous. Returning to me, he presses the barrel of the gun against my temple. The gun is still cocked. One of the women has started to sob.

"Everything you say is true," I choke out. "But this isn't about me now." I plead, beseeching him. "If you do care about her, know that she loves me. Alec, too. We don't deserve it, but would you take away the joy she just found? If you care about her, you can't. You won't. Give her a chance to be loved — and give love."

Several minutes elapse in absolute silence except for my gasping.

"Where is she?" he finally asks.

"Flagstaff, Arizona," I choke. "She's taking classes and learning to play the piano. She made a friend."

"A friend?" he asks.

"A lady she takes walks with."

He's silent for another few moments. "You could be making this all up — this newfound honorable core." He almost spits the words. "Why don't we let her decide how nice you've been? I'll write out a few questions. Let her think you're calling to say hello. If I decide you're lying, we'll take a walk."

I turn to Alice. "Give me a second."

He gives me the briefest of nods.

"I love you," I say. "Always believe it."

Arturo cuts the ties on my ankles and indicates a chair, away from the others, by the front door. I walk carefully over and sit down. The gun is inches from my head.

"Your cell?"

"Left back pocket," I say.

After grabbing it, he begins to scroll down.

"It's under mother," I add. He looks at the contacts for a minute, then hands me the phone.

He hands me two questions after scribbling them on a piece of paper. "Put it on speaker," he orders.

I swallow, awkwardly grabbing the phone with my hands tied. I manage to let it ring, at the same time trying to calm the pounding of my heart.

"Hello, Bruce," she says. "It's so good to hear from you."

"Hi, Mother." I take a deep breath and try to sound normal. "Just called to say hello. What's happening in your life? How are the piano lessons?"

"Guess what? I'm playing Irish folk songs. They're so moving. Maybe I'll go to Ireland someday."

"A dream of yours?" I ask.

"Yes. I want to go to romantic out-of-the-way places."

"Any other specific countries?" I ask.

"Yes. First, I'd love to go back to Italy. It's so beautiful."

"I've been there several times and it is beautiful. You've been there before. Where in particular?"

"The area called The Cinque Terra. It's supposedly five small hillside villages on the west coast of Italy. I heard about them from a...a friend."

"I didn't know you had any friends from before."

"He wasn't actually a friend, but he was nice to me. He worked for your father. He'd often find me, and we'd talk a little. He was very kind. I fancied he sort of liked me." She pauses to chuckle to herself. "I sort of liked him, too. Anyway, he came from Italy, from the area I mentioned, and it sounded so lovely I wanted to see it. Maybe soon? When everything settles down?"

"How is your new friend — the one you walk with?"

"Wonderful. Her name is Juanita. She and I are going to have a girls' night out every other week and go see a romantic drama. Her husband likes movies with car chases and shoot-outs." She giggles again. The happy sound jars me, I've heard it so rarely. "When do you suppose I can come up?" she asks. "Has the *situation* resolved itself? I miss you both desperately, now that I've found you."

"I'll let you know. I have a feeling this will be over very soon. I miss you, too."

"Oh, one more thing. I'm growing out my hair and I'm going to take western riding lessons. I'm going to be a cowgirl."

"Mom, you sound so happy."

"I'm going to love it down here. And besides, I told you. All I want is to see you both. Tell Alec, won't you?"

"First thing. Bye, Sophie. I love you."

She giggles again and hangs up.

"Sophie?" Arturo asks as I disconnect.

"Sophia Russell. It's her new name. I'm trying to get used to it." I suddenly realize I never asked the two written questions from our captor.

He's standing still, looking out into space. He has the semblance of a real smile on his face, changing it completely. Finally, he turns and takes back the paper with the questions. "Never mind," he says in a gruff but somehow cheerful voice. Crumpling the list, he throws it in the dead fireplace. When he looks up, everyone is staring at him.

"I'm leaving. The truck will turn up with the keys under the seat. Consider the reign of King Weingarten over. I never want to think of him again." He walks over to Alec, slits his ankle ties, grabs him by his shirt, and hauls him to his feet. He's manhandled next to me, where we're positioned together in the open front doorway.

"You won't need to bother with me again on one condition," he says, his eyes penetrating ours. "Take good care of your mother. Let her know you love her. Make it up to her."

Alec and I step outside, watching him leave. He walks over to Win's truck like he owns it and climbs in. We continue to watch for a long time as he drives down the long dirt driveway, through the grasslands in the darkness, toward the main highway. We hardly notice our hands are still tied.

"What do you make of that?" Alec asks.

"He loves her," I answer quietly. "I recognize the symptoms."

As I walk back into the house, everyone is cutting off plastic ties and unwinding Win's duct tape. When my hands are free, I walk over to the fireplace and fish out the crumpled paper. On it are written two questions.

"Did you have anyone you considered a friend?"

"Do you need help?"

Shoving it in my pocket, I hurry to Win's side as they finish untying him.

"Jesus H. Christ," he groans, spitting out the gag. "I thought he was going to massacre as many of us as he could.

"What happened here, Win?" Willie asks.

"It came down just after we got the first news about Tashi. We were waiting to hear more, but I slipped out back to check on one of the horses with a sore leg. Boom. By the time I came to myself, I was helpless on the ground with my hands cuffed behind me. He told me if I didn't cooperate he'd end me and handle the women." He flinches. "I was horrified. I had to play for time. I didn't see what else I could do. He put the pistol into my back and walked me into the kitchen. I was looking for any opportunity, but nothing."

He looks at very pregnant Lizzie and has to stop for a moment.

Win continues, "We just sat there. No one pleaded or fell apart. I was proud. He settled down in the chair behind me, biding his time, hour after hour. He asked if anyone needed some water or to use the bathroom. He was aloof but polite. I desperately hoped you guys would realize there was big trouble and think of something." He takes a few seconds to stretch is tight shoulders. "But, as he said, I was dreading any kind of a fight."

"We couldn't afford people storming in with guns drawn," Willie explains. "He knew that, too. And he didn't come for a social call. You both dodged a bullet."

I notice Alec studying me with an undecipherable expression. "I was as good as dead," he says quietly, "but you made yourself his target, then managed to change his mind."

"I couldn't let him kill you," I say fervidly. "Not you. Not now." Then, stumbling awkwardly over to Alice on the couch, I collapse beside her. "It's been a big day. I'm done."

"Sorry, man," says Paul. "I'm going to tell everyone what you did today. We'll take a vote on whether you should be part of this family or not." He walks over to me, grabs my hand, and shakes it. "You're part of my family. I don't Goddamn care what anyone else thinks."

Everyone gapes at Paul.

I smile tiredly. "You were a tough nut. Glad you finally came around."

He puts his head back and laughs heartily. "Me, too, Bruce. And if I don't get something to eat soon, I'll die. Can we rustle up something?"

"I'm going to check on my frozen sister," Willie says, grabbing a jar of peanut butter, a knife, and a loaf of bread off the kitchen counter.

Alec, who's been pacing near the door, follows him out. "We'll call with a report," he yells, running for Willie's truck. Together they'll start the long drive down to Great Falls.

"Hold on for a few minutes, Paul," Win says. "Before you start your story, let me call Vinnie. If she can come out here, we should wait. She loves stories, and she needs to know about Tashi."

"It's 1:00 in the morning," Sarah reminds him.

"This sounds like a hell of a good story."

Sarah laughs. "Sure. Give her the choice.

It's amazing how good canned chili tastes when you've been freezing for hours and fighting off hysteria in an ice-hole. Paul, Sam, and I have been emptying out Sarah's pantry as fast as she can microwave it. We ate a loaf of bread and butter and many glasses of milk — comfort food.

I hear Vinnie's car pull in the driveway. Ah, I think. I hope she brought cookies.

Paul is a good storyteller, making me sound as if they should create an action figure in my image. I didn't mind. After all, my girl is hearing all this, and to tell the truth I'm pretty proud of myself. If I'd known what I was getting into, I don't know whether I would have had the courage to volunteer.

Sarah just brought me another coffee with a heavy slug of Baileys, a very heavy slug. I'm getting happier and happier. I have to fight grinning like an idiot with a plate of Vinnie's oatmeal cookies balanced on my chest. My head rests in Alice's lap as she feeds me cookie bits like a Roman emperor. Every few minutes, someone makes a comment about the next piece being poisoned and I laugh wildly — same old joke, over and over.

I'm drunk.

I don't remember being this happy with friends in my life.

Sam and Paul have also been drinking steadily and laughing inappropriately at anything remotely funny. The quality of Paul's story is deteriorating so everyone is laughing at that, too. He keeps saying, "You should have seen Bruce. He was Houdini," over and over.

Vinnie is sitting in her usual chair by the fireplace, smiling away.

"Okay, Vinnie," I say, somewhat slurring my words, "You haven't said anything, which is Goddamn unusual far as I can tell. So, spill." As I said, I've had a few.

She stands, walks over, and kisses me on the cheek. "Thank you for saving Tashi. It's the most wonderful thing. If anything had happened to her, it would have been the end of me."

I try with some difficulty to get to my feet and manage it after several attempts, finally putting my arms around her. "Thank you for my second chance. I've been outside in the cold for so long. I don't mean just today.

"And one more thing.... I've wanted to paint your house, but it would'a looked like sucking up."

I'm definitely drunk.

Win's phone rings. He listens for a minute and his smile keeps getting wider. He passes the phone to Vinnie who immediately starts crying. It's heartbreaking because it seems so out of character. She's the one who keeps others going. Sarah goes over and puts her arm around her.

After several minutes she says, "I love you, too, honey. I'll see you tomorrow."

Vinnie turns to us. "That was my darling granddaughter. It's hard to keep her down. Tashi's angry they wouldn't let her go home because she wants home-cooking. She's coming home to my house tomorrow to let me feed her."

She clears her throat. It's some moments before she can continue. "She said you kept calling down to her. She was terrified, in despair. She said she wanted to scream until she died." She pauses again. "But every few minutes she'd hear you saying, 'I'm closer. Hang on. I'm coming'. She believed you. And it gave her hope."

No one says a word, transfixed by the image before us.

"Vinnie," I begin. "Um.... There's one other little thing we need to tell you. Maybe you should sit down."

She gives me a questioning look, returns to her chair by the fire, and sits. "So? What?" she asks.

"Another thing made this day unusual." I launch into the story about Arturo, sobering up as I go. I don't stop talking for ten minutes.

"Vinnie," asks Win. "Are you okay?"

She's speechless.

"Vinnie?" asks Sarah again.

"Give me a minute. I'm old," she says.

We wait.

"You mean I was a target of a hit man?"

"Sort of," I say. "He pretended he was going to kill you so someone else wouldn't kill you first."

"Wow. It's sort of an honor for someone my age."

Vinnie looks at things in unusual ways.

"So, what are you going to do with the information a hit man is in love with your mother?"

"Huh?"

"You heard me. It's an interesting dilemma. What are you going to tell her?"

"I.... I don't know. I hadn't thought about it."

"You boys are a little slow on social issues."

"Maybe he'll never contact her?" I say.

"Sweetie, don't bet on it," she says, almost rubbing her hands in glee. "He came all the way out here to kill you because you weren't nice to her. I bet he's on his way to Arizona as we speak."

I wish Vinnie wasn't enjoying this so much.

"And you said she liked him and wanted to go to Italy. Arturo isn't exactly a WASP name, and when you think about it, neither is Sophia. Wow. This is material for a novel."

Most of us are looking at Vinnie with our mouths open.

"So?" she says. "Now what?"

"We really don't know he's killed anyone. We know nothing about him."

"Maybe in the long run you can find out something. Maybe you could hire a hit man to find him."

"Vinnie," we all groan.

"Okay. I got carried away. This probably isn't all that funny. But looking at this from the outside, I see a man who really loves this lady. She's obviously not in any danger from him and I suspect he wouldn't turn her into Bonnie for his Clyde. Not quickly, anyway. Goodness. And I thought my life couldn't get any more exciting."

"What should I tell her?"

"It's the big question. I really don't know. All kidding aside, you boys hardly know your mother. I'd try to get to know her before I made any quick decisions. We don't know whether she'd even take advice from you. She's been under that asshole's thumb for a long time. If I were her, I'd want to make my own choices."

"Well, the heat's off," I say. "Guess I'll invite Mom up for a visit."

"I haven't been up this late in thirty years," Vinnie says. "I think I'll go home and make a big batch of blueberry muffins. Everyone come over for brunch at eleven or so. Bring juice and four dozen eggs." She looks affectionately around the room. "I always said things got interesting when the Thomas brothers came to town, but Alec and Bruce have moved ahead of them. Thanks for calling me."

We hear her happily chuckling to herself on the way out the door.

* * *

Tashi, Alec, and Willie are minutes out and Vinnie is happily cooking a huge batch of scrambled eggs in the biggest cast-iron skillet I ever saw. I took a picture for Facebook of the pile of muffins. It looks like the Half Dome in Yosemite. Suddenly there are footsteps on the porch. In whirls Tashi followed by her grinning supporters. Running over to me, she throws her arms around me and starts to cry.

I bury my face in her hair, swallowing over and over. Alec and Susan have an idea what it was like down there, but Tashi and I really know. It was hell. We were both up against our own raging hysteria for hours in the dark, frightened nearly to death. I hold her for a long time. I was certain a hundred times she was dying. I'll never forget it. I'm sure it must be like being in mortal combat when you think you're going to die every minute for hours, but you survive and can hardly deal with it.

I see Willie's eyes. I can hardly look at them. They're so raw. Alec comes over and again puts his arm around my shoulders. I get goosebumps. We stood like this as nine-year-old boys, before Father....

CHAPTER 38

ALEC

A WEEK LATER BRUCE and I are driving to Great Falls to pick up Sophie who is arriving for an extended stay. She'll coincidentally experience the expanding annual reunion of this intertwined family of friends.

I catch myself trying to define this woman. We had a progressively distant relationship over the years, but now I'm told she loved us all along but was silenced by fear and violence. When I have trouble believing it, I remember the gunshot going off next to Bruce's head. I know one thing for sure — she was the only mother I had since the dismal day I was left alone with a raving drunken lunatic. I experienced only those few moments of closeness before I fled the murder scene in Connecticut.

Bruce has driven silently, lost in his own thoughts.

"Bruce?" I say finally.

"Hmm?"

"This is nice, isn't it?"

"Us, you mean?"

"Who would have ever thought?" I smile incredulously to myself. "Who started this?

Bruce turns to look seriously at me. "Lizzie. Obviously. But I always come back to you. If you hadn't pulled the plug on Father, you could have been killing people by now. If I'd gotten his engineered vice-presidency, I'd have been suicidal under Frederick's thumb for all of my days. We would have hated each other and hated ourselves."

I exhale forcefully. "I think about that a lot."

"Then of course there was Paul, rescuing Ellie at the rest area — a random decision which changed all our lives. What if he'd stopped at the next one?"

"Jesus!"

"Yeah," Bruce grimaces. "Paul and I despised each other from our first encounter in Browning."

"Why, do you think?"

"I was a caricature. He was real. He and Ellie had chemistry. And he was...crazy." He smiles. "Crazier, back then. If we'd been alone, it could have escalated right there to a death fight. We were both on the edge. Sobering thought."

"Who would have won, Bruce?"

"I've had personal experience with Paul's strength when he's been enraged, several times. But I'd had karate training. It would have been vicious. Looks like I'll never find out. Thank God."

"No. You're good. I never thought you'd get over that hurdle." I glance at him, quizzically. "I'm still not used to liking you. It catches me up, sometimes."

Bruce looks over at me with a look of frigid rage, maintaining it long enough, I have to gasp a breath.

Suddenly, he grins, laughing at me.

I pull back with a shudder. "Could you change your hair or something? I want to forget the pin-striped devil from hell."

"Fine. Pick a look."

"I always fancied you in a Mohawk."

"Wrong tribe."

"Hmm? God, you were a prick, though."

He looks at me pensively. "It was so close, Alec. Do you still wonder if we're trash underneath?"

"I don't worry about you, Bruce. Not since you offered to kill the old man for me. I'll never forget it. I should have argued. I should have talked you out of it. You were a felon, for God's sake. They could have put you away for the rest of your life. I stood there."

"I never thought it was for you to do. Never."

"All the same, I haven't been willing to do something for you, or anyone else that would cause me such personal pain. Plus, what you did turning Angelo away from me. Be proud, Bruce. I am." I turn and see him smiling to himself.

"I guess I am proud."

"You're allowed."

We drive in silence for some time.

"I'd like Sophie to find some real happiness," I say.

"Maybe there'll be a man in her life soon," he says, giving me a bemused smile. "Preferably, one who doesn't kill people for an occupation."

"Nothing would surprise me anymore," I mutter.

"I like thinking about her as Mom, rather than Mother," Bruce says, smiling broadly. "Expect a change."

* * *

When she walks off the plane with a whimsical grin, I gasp. She could have walked by me unrecognized with wavy brown hair, wearing a white tank top, cotton plaid shirt, and Nikes. She looks forty. I give her an astonished hug. "I can't believe it. This cannot be the same person."

Openly staring, Bruce adds, "Mom, you're gorgeous. Are you fighting off men?"

"Yes. I love it. I may let some of them win."

Spontaneously, we laugh together. A first. I can't remember hearing her truly laugh in my life. "I'm not calling you Mom. Can I buy you a drink?"

She smiles ambiguously. "Frederick didn't acquire me to be a future business partner."

We shake our heads. Lots to consider.

Bruce is driving the return trip with his mother sitting next to him. We have the two-hour trip to Sander's ranch, with scenery rivaling calendar pictures the entire way.

I pull out a cardboard chart, folded in the middle, which can stand independently. "I made you a diagram of our friends," I say, handing it forward over the back of her seat. "It includes labeled connections between people. I almost included pictures. It will take months for you to hear all the stories, but we're all interconnected." I hand it to her.

"I'm glad to get something back from your excellent Stanford education." She adds seriously, then laughs.

I'm not sure of her humor. It never came out before.

Bruce pulls in to a cafe in Choteau before we finish the drive to the ranch. There are things we need to talk about.

"Sophie," I say, stumbling over her name as we sit down. "I need to apologize for all those years of not understanding, not helping. It was appalling."

She bites her lip. "Our lives were all terrible, Alec. Quicksand and fog."

"But now I want to know. Why didn't you get out?"

"Why didn't both of you?" she asks back.

We all consider that.

She looks at her hands. "He almost destroyed you both. He made you hate me."

"I never hated you," Bruce admits forcefully. "It was myself I hated. And Alec for being a rival."

"Which was worse. Don't you see? I'll never forgive him for that."

"We have to," I argue. "All of us do. We can't let hatred poison us."

"Alec?" Sophie asks again. "Why didn't you leave? How did he keep you twisting in the wind? After law school, you could have left."

"Initially, he didn't seem cruel. For years he perpetuated the illusion of family and loyalty. It started with the damn rings. He was a master at exploiting my Achilles heel. I was alone. He provided a mirage, put his arm around my shoulders occasionally, smiled conspiratorially at me, if you can believe it. He must have gritted his teeth."

Bruce looks away as I continue. "He did it once in front of you. You'd done something to displease him and you stormed out of the room. You probably don't remember."

"Oh, I remember," he mutters, turning back. "I remember every single thing. He never touched me except to grab my arm and squeeze. Another punishment. Another failure. It was his master stroke — one more type of pain."

I nod in agreement. "Part of his brilliance was to appear reasonable — to keep me hooked. I remember when I finally understood — the night I first tried to refuse him. I had shared my own dream, my plans of going off on my own after I graduated. It was my third year in law school." I smile wryly. "I can feel my stomach turn after all this time. His mask snapped off so violently it almost made a sound. He threatened to ruin any chance of a law career — sabotage any independent effort. 'I owed him — big time,' he said. I stayed."

Sophie puts her hand on mine. "The counseling helps. It can't be this easy to be happy. I keep waiting for flashbacks." She lowers her voice. "Strange. I never have nightmares of shooting him. Never."

We sit silently.

Bruce turns to his mother and asks, “Did you ever love him?”

“I thought I did, at first. I was so young, barely 21. I never questioned his control at the start. As I began to assert myself, it came out. He wouldn’t allow me to have my own life. Controlled my friends, even my thoughts. Eventually, I knew he was afraid, too. He guessed I’d escape if I could.” She grimaces. “Perceptive, really.”

“How did he get control, early on?” Bruce asks.

She smiles. “I got pregnant.”

“Did he even want...?”

She takes his hand across the table. “That was when I still thought I loved him. Less than a year after I married him. Yes. He wanted you, Bruce — a son. He was eager, even excited. I’ve been thinking about it recently. The day you were born was the happiest day of my life. He came into the hospital room and I put you in his arms for the first time. He had the strangest reaction. He looked terrified and said, ‘There’s something wrong with me, Dora.’”

We sit silently thinking of the consequences.

“We could have banded together,” I say. “Talked, helped each other, protected each other. All those years.”

“I want to get this all out in the open,” she says. “I didn’t want to go into the whole thing until we were together. He didn’t start physical violence until the last few years, about the time everything got crazy with your vice-presidency. He’d rant about how important it was for supremacy, absolute control. It was the ever-receding horizon he could never reach.” Her eyes show anger, another emotion I’ve never seen in her before. “I suggested he get help, that he was destroying anything worth having. But he started hitting me instead. Disloyalty.”

Bruce and I sit in stunned silence.

“He was in complete control when he did it,” she goes on. “You want to know how immoral he was? He wouldn’t let me take pain medicine. Said he wanted it to hurt.” Her eyes narrow. “I hated him. I don’t have one regret.”

“He was hurting you when Bruce was in prison and I didn’t help. You had no one. If only I’d given you a contact number.” Putting my hands around the back of my neck in anguish, I groan. “I’m so terribly sorry.”

"Stop, Alec. Stop. I didn't tell you to make you feel bad. I should have left. I had a little money hidden away. It wasn't like I was locked up. But I waited, hoping I could hold it together until Bruce got released. Frederick screened all my mail, including e-mail. I procrastinated. I could have found you, but I felt so guilty." She pauses, apparently deciding whether to go on. "Then he broke bones in my hands as a threat."

"Didn't anyone notice?"

"I told people it was arthritis flaring up. I finally hinted to *someone* I'd been physically hurt. Amazingly, it stopped. Until that last night."

Arturo. He must have interfered. "Someone?" I ask.

"An employee." She flashes an amused smile. "The one I told you about. He'd frequently find an isolated place to ask how I was. He'd hold my hand. That's how he finally found out. I almost trusted him with the whole truth, but I worried if I were wrong your father would find out."

"What was his name?" Bruce asks with a quick glance back at me.

"Arturo. He went by Arthur White, but I called him Arturo. He seemed pleased. He told me stories about growing up in Italy." She smiles wistfully. "I'm starting to dream about my future. I'd like to sit in the warm sun, barefoot, eating olives and crusty bread and drink red wine."

That's a conversation stopper.

As we return to the car, I ask, "Are you going to keep it, your name I mean? You could be Dora, again."

"No. I like Sophie. It's a new world out there. I don't want anything reminding me of my old life. You boys are so different. Even you don't remind me."

A few moments later, she asks, "Tell me about your girlfriends. I'm so pleased you each have someone to care about. How absolutely wonderful."

"I'll start," I say. "Here's the board."

Bruce rolls his eyes at me as I lean over the back seat and position it on her lap.

"I was stalking Tashi for Frederick," I say, pointing to her name connected by several colored lines to other names. He wanted her hurt as a warning, but I was working against him. I fell in love with her while I was trying to protect her. Her mother is a full-blooded Blackfeet and her dad is white. She's breathtakingly beautiful and wild and very brave, and...."

"He's biased. She's ugly as a dog," Bruce interrupts, laughing as I glower at him — my most vicious glower. Not nearly in his league.

"But Bruce can say anything he wants," I put in. "He saved her life a week ago."

"What?"

"We have a lot of stories — several months' worth. She's also Willie's sister. Show her on the chart, Alec."

I reach over the seat, pointing at Willie's name.

"And your lady, Bruce? I've wished every day since your visit I could have gotten to know her. She was so fearless."

"The chart. Okay. I admit it. The damn thing was a good idea."

"About time you admitted how brilliant I am." Alec laughs. "Last time was twenty years ago."

"That was the last time."

I hit the back of his seat hard with my fist.

"Anyway," Bruce goes on, grinning. "Alice is Win's sister. Win is a best friend of Willie's from childhood who, if you recall, is Tashi's brother. Damn. This is hopeless."

He tries a new approach. "She trains young horses. Remember?"

"She trains him, too," I put in. "He gets up two hours early every morning to shovel manure with her. And then thanks her for it."

"An hour knee deep in manure with Alice is better than a lifetime...."

"He keeps trying to convince me of its virtues," I interrupt, "but I told him I read Tom Sawyer."

"Do you boys realize how different you are?" she interrupts. "You're talking a blue streak, laughing, and kidding each other."

"I learned to laugh in prison," Bruce admits, then changes the subject. "I'm hoping you'll be here for Lizzie's baby. He's due September thirteenth."

"She means a lot to you, doesn't she?"

"Lizzie had every reason to hate me. She gave me encouragement when my life was the darkest."

I look from Bruce to Sophie. I'm sitting in the back seat, so I can gaze at either one for long periods without their knowing. The concept of family overpowers me. Maybe I could count on these people. Maybe we could care about each other deeply. I've never investigated my biological family and I've never wanted to. They are nothing to me. But as I look at these two people, struggling to find a firm relationship and a new life, I'm overcome with emotion. Sophie feels sort of like my mother. Bruce feels like my brother.

We drive in silence for a while, me enjoying the comfortable feeling. I drift back in time to the distant past, trying to remember my own mother. Now I begin to wonder whether she also has a story to tell, an explanation of why she left me alone that dark night which might make some sense, lessen my feeling of abandonment. Maybe someday I'll try to track her down if she's still alive. Curiosity if nothing else.

CHAPTER 39

BRUCE

WIN AND LIZZIE'S NEW HOUSE is what Win always envisioned — a classic saltbox shape, painted tan, with a red metal roof and huge porch, extending the entire length of the house, dramatically overlooking the river. It's a perfect place for Sam or Bruce to play their guitars in the evenings, overlooking the sun setting behind the Rockies. It's also a place for endings and new beginnings.

People are dropping by to meet Mother. With the help of the chart which sits propped by the foot of her chair, she's getting most of them in some kind of order. She and Alice have become good friends. They go riding together. It's been interesting getting her impressions of the friends who are becoming so important to me. She likes them all, but some are special.

She adores Win. It's irritating, but he does affect women — everyone from babies to — there's no limit. He took her out with Lizzie for a rerun of his macho Indian warrior demo, took off most of his clothes and rode around bareback screaming war whoops. She says she's not sleeping well after that. Crap. This is my mother, for God's sake.

Willie is another person she loves, but so do we all. I'm humbled seeing affection when he looks at me. There's nothing like eternal gratitude to encourage our friendship.

And she absolutely adores Tashi. She says she reminds her of herself before all the delight in life was knocked out of her.

This emerging, enthusiastic individual has almost nothing in common with the quiet shadow we used to know. It shows how much damage a powerful, controlling personality can do. There's no changing such a person. It's best to get away, as far and as fast as you can.

We spend evenings on Win and Lizzie's new porch. Alec and my housewarming gift consisted of six heavy wooden chairs on which to sit and enjoy the view. They're in constant use by the stream of visitors talking with Mom and waiting with Lizzie. She looks like a beautiful lady with her feet propped up, holding a big pumpkin.

Ellie just got here, together with her mom and dad. They'll be here until after the baby is born. It's not comfortable around them but not hostile. Manageable.

Just as I back out of the kitchen screen door with an armload of ice bags, Ellie approaches me. "Will you walk with me?"

I nod self-consciously, putting the ice in the washtub.

We start walking east along the crest of the bluff, passing Paul who gives me a smile and a thumbs-up. Ellie sees, but says nothing. I wait for her to begin.

"I never thought I'd see Paul smile at you in my life," she says. "I would have bet a lot."

Even with my new accepted status, I'm anxious being alone with Ellie. I stand much farther away from her than I might someone else. Neither of us says anything.

"Do you feel safe with me?" I finally ask.

"Depends," she says. "I'm reasonably confident you won't try to push me off the cliff."

"Oh, Ellie," I say.

"Of course, I've heard what you did for Tashi. It was a wonderful thing."

"I was terrified."

"You didn't give up." She says, but her voice remains impersonal.

"Does it make up a little? Before?"

She stops and turns to me. We're still standing six feet from each other. "It does to everyone else. Even my parents are trying. Mom always liked you. You used to try to be nice to her." She pauses. "She even told me she's impressed with how far you've come."

I sigh and close my eyes. "And you?"

"I want it to," she says with intensity. "I want to let it all go. But it was such a betrayal."

"And I hit you, Ellie."

"Yes."

"Seriously. Are you afraid of me?"

I see her glance backward toward the ranch. "Yes. It's hard to be out here alone with you."

My eyes fill. "I've seen you walk away, avoid me. I wish I could somehow erase those terrible memories."

"You're still on edge. Constantly. But you cover it up fairly well."

"I'm a flawed person, Ellie. I admitted it to Vinnie not so long ago. I can never let my guard down."

She studies me, apparently surprised.

I continue. "I've been hoping what I was privileged to do for Tashi would help. I wish it was you I'd saved."

"Are you saying you feel shame?"

"You doubt it?" I say in desperation. "Are you saying you believe I'm such a lost soul, I can't feel crushing guilt?"

"Then tell me. I need to know."

"You're aware what made me who I was. I had no reason to keep walking down such a dismal path, but it was all I knew. You tried to help me, but that person was an empty shell."

"Do you deserve love now?"

I feel the blood drain from my face. Such a horrifying question. It's several moments before I can form an answer. "I was in the crevasse trying to prove it to myself. I would have fought anyone taking the chance away — to convince myself I deserved to exist."

"I never knew you at all," she admits quietly. "Lizzie knew you better than I did. We've talked about it. She's risked our relationship to stick up for you. She saw something real in you. I never looked."

"Lizzie saved my life."

"If I could believe you were deeply sorry...."

"Sorry?" I say, shaking my head despairingly. "I awakened from a years-long hellish nightmare, finding myself a would-be murderer in a frozen blizzard. I tried to get back to you in your crumpled car. I had no coat. I was beaten back in seconds, flattened onto the ice by the wind." I visualize the scene and shudder. "I managed to crawl the two hundred feet back to my car. I beat my head on the steering wheel in agony, picturing your porcelain face, frozen hard. Because of me. Because of me."

She says nothing.

"If I could have given my life, I would have in a second. I pleaded, prayed to a God I hardly believed in, to trade my life for yours that horrible day." I study her skeptical face. "In the courtroom there was nothing I could say to make you believe me. But inside I was joyful you were both alive. Everyone's thoughts were apparent. I was hated and despised, but I was so grateful. I'm still grateful, every minute of every day. Every time I see you."

She stands there looking at me. Not believing but not disbelieving, either.

"You seem devoted to Alice."

"She knows me, all my horrible past, and she can look at me with love. It's a miracle. I love her. And Lizzie who gave me a chance. If you can believe nothing else, believe I can feel it. And if you can believe that, maybe you can believe my horror and shame for hurting you and Susan."

I search her face. The coldness in her eyes drains away. She sighs deeply. "I'm glad for you, Bruce. I'm glad for myself. I believe I can let the hatred go."

Another miracle.

We turn and walk back to people who love us.

The night is warm, so we sit out and watch the stars come out. We've lined the new fire pit with river rocks and have a good fire going. I've been sitting contentedly, sipping a cold beer, and listening to Sam strum his guitar when Lizzie stands up with some difficulty, turns to Win and says, "I think I'll have a baby. Are you coming?"

Ten of us trooped into the clinic in Browning, but the night lengthened. One by one, since things were going slowly, most of us left and went home to bed. I wanted to stay, but some things are family things. I was so excited that I didn't get any sleep, and around 4:30 when I couldn't stand it, I drove back to the Browning clinic.

I found Mr. O'Connell sitting alone in the waiting room, but he looked up when I came in. "Won't be long now," he says, with a friendly smile so I know we're at some ease with each other. Both mothers are in with Lizzie and Alice comes out frequently with updates. We sit in companionable silence, but after a half hour or so Sean clears his throat.

He turns to me. "Bruce, you've been on a hard journey."

I nod.

"As you can imagine, I've talked to many of our friends, trying to get a handle on you."

It's hard to make eye contact so I look down — my old habit.

"I'd been able to partially forgive you, even understand you on an intellectual level, but you know who moved me completely in your corner."

I look up at him.

"Paul hadn't ever opened up about his past problems. He told me of his struggles with Sam, his counseling, and his temper — the possibility of being a danger to Ellie. He said if anyone understands second chances it's him." He pauses. "It took a lot for him to tell me all that. He didn't have to, you know."

"Paul told you? Risked telling you everything?"

"If Paul values you so much. If he can believe in you wholeheartedly, then so can I." He reaches over and puts his hand on my shoulder.

People start arriving. Among the first are Paul and Ellie.

Soon after, Win comes through a door with someone in his arms. We look down and see a red, squinty–eyed, tiny guy with a shock of black hair.

"I stole him, just for a minute," he says.

We five adults admire the most beautiful baby in the world.

Win hands the baby to Paul. "Meet another Paul," he says. "Paul Sean Sanders."

"Really?" Paul says. "Really, Win?"

"What do you think, Godfather?"

It takes him a minute. "It's mighty fine," he says.

Family and friends have gathered for the extended Labor Day weekend. Nearly constant cooking commences with empty dishes exchanged for mounded ones placed on long wooden tables set out on the grass under large tan umbrellas. Lizzie has been mostly caring for Paulie, taking naps with him, and bringing him out for short visits. He's the only baby, but Dave and Linda have brought five-year-old Abbie, who's been informed she has a new cousin, so she thinks she owns him. Thousands of pictures have been taken, probably tens of thousands.

We're spending this last evening enjoying the perfect September weather — clear and warm with light breezes that follow the Two Medicine River valley eastward. Over thirty people sit on lawn chairs and on blankets, spilling over from the porch area onto the thick grass.

I'm currently standing on the deck with Alice, talking to Paul and Alec, when Mother rises and links arms companionably with Sarah as they walk together to join us. "I'd like to say something to you boys," she begins. "This is the happiest ending to...." She pauses, not needing to say it. "I'm eternally thankful for this glorious place, and especially for our new friends."

Sarah adds warmly, "Come back soon, at least for the Christmas holidays. The guestroom is open for you."

"Ordinarily, I would love to, but I have something already planned for this year. I haven't even told the boys." She smiles ambiguously at me. "I'm finally packing my suitcase."

I shake my head questioningly at her.

"You remember," she responds, laughing. "I'm finally escaping.... To Italy, the Cinque Terra region, with an old friend."

It takes me a second to realize who the old friend might be. As I'm absorbing this exceptional news, Lizzie and Win walk over to join us with Paulie in Win's arms. Win seems uncharacteristically a little unsteady.

"How do you feel about all this, Dad?" Paul asks, seriously.

Win gives us all a look of incredulousness, then manages, "Exhausted."

After we laugh at his and Lizzie's droopy eyes, he takes a minute to answer seriously. "I've been doing a lot of thinking," he says. "I want Paulie to value the important things in this world. I want to show him its beauty and teach him to act with nobility."

"And he is beautiful," Paul says.

Win smiles at Paul. "He is that."

I feel Lizzie's hand on my shoulder. "Dad said you waited with him."

I cover her hand with mine.

Win steps over to me and says, "Bruce, can you hold this kid while I throw a little wood on the fire?"

I'm stunned at the offer. I brace myself and hold out my awkward arms as Win transfers his son to me.

I swallow hard. "Thank you."

He grins and walks away.

Everyone is smiling at me.

The End

Made in USA - North Chelmsford, MA
1345027_9781949872750
12.06.2022 1715